CHICAGO STORIES

DOVER THRIFT EDITIONS

Edited by
James Daley

DOVER PUBLICATIONS, INC.
MINEOLA, NEW YORK

DOVER THRIFT EDITIONS

GENERAL EDITOR: MARY CAROLYN WALDREP
EDITOR OF THIS VOLUME: ALISON DAURIO

Bibliographical Note

Chicago Stories, first published by Dover Publications, Inc., in 2016, contains a new selection of works made by James Daley, who also provided the Editor's Note on pages iii–iv.

Library of Congress Cataloging-in-Publication Data

Chicago stories / edited by James Daley.
    pages cm.—(Dover thrift editions)
  ISBN-13: 978-0-486-80285-5
  ISBN-10: 0-486-80285-X
    I. Daley, James, 1979– editor.
PS572.C5C46 2016
810.8'03277311—dc23

2015030863

Manufactured in the United States by LSC Communications
80285X02   2017
www.doverpublications.com

Editor's Note

While the stories in this collection were certainly chosen for their representation of Chicago as a physical setting, it was equally important that they exemplify some of the character of this great American city. For a city that inspires stories such as these—where fortunes are won and lost, ambitions realized and shattered, prejudices succumbed to and overcome—I think there could not be a more fitting description of its character than that offered by Nelson Algren, who wrote the following in his iconic 1951 essay, *Chicago: City on the Make:*

> *It's the place built out of Man's ceaseless failure to overcome himself. Out of Man's endless war against himself we build our successes as well as our failures. Making it the city of all cities most like Man himself—loneliest creation of all this very old poor earth.*

Although the subjects and styles of these stories may vary, in each one we find characters whose internal conflicts both reflect and react to the conflicts of the city; characters whose lives are defined by their ability and inability to overcome their own weaknesses and prevail against the overwhelming forces of a city as boundless and challenging as Chicago.

In the very first story of this collection, George Ade's *The Judge's Son*, we find characters struggling against the power of their own success and failures. In this brief character sketch, two men sit in the lobby of a flophouse, lamenting about how each has been cast aside by a city that loved them before their luck turned sour. They find solace in their shared suffering, until one of them gets word that he has just been left a large inheritance, and quickly finds the other man not worthy of his time.

Similarly, many stories in this collection share in common the theme of an optimist's confrontation with the realities of the "big city." In Susan Glaspell's *From A to Z* we find an idealistic young woman who moves to Chicago with dreams of a glamorous publishing job on Michigan Avenue, only to wind up editing dictionaries on Dearborn Street. In *The Extra Major* by Will Cuppy, we find a naïve young freshman at the University of Chicago laboring to make sense of his position at the bottom of the collegiate totem pole.

While it often seems that the young idealists' fates are sealed before they reach the city limits, other stories illustrate how even the hardened and the well-connected are humbled by the windy city. *Reform in the First*, Brand Whitlock's short piece about Chicago politics, describes how a wealthy member of the upper class is defeated in his governmental ambitions by the South Side political machine. On the other side of the spectrum, Nelson Algren, in his timeless story, *A Bottle of Milk for Mother*, tells the tale of a poor Polish hoodlum who gets cornered for a murder by the machinations of a police department that pays little attention to matters of truth or justice in its pursuit of a conviction.

One of the most common ways we see characters at war with themselves is through their many attempts to overcome the limitations of their class. In Maugham's *The Fall of Edward Barnard*, we find the story of a wealthy young man who leaves Chicago after losing his inheritance, only to find happiness in a simple life that his relations back home will never understand. Meanwhile, in William John Pickard's *A Spider Phaeton,* a poor young reporter is so overjoyed at being invited to a fancy Lake Forest party that he makes a fool of himself in an attempt to trick his hosts about his lack of social standing.

Finally, in perhaps the most poignant examples of a city struggling to overcome its own failures, we have three stories that offer unique and personal portraits of Chicago's long history of racial conflict. Richard Wright's *The Man Who Went to Chicago* tells the story of a black man confronting white society as he moves from one terrible job to the next. On the other side of that same coin is Saul Bellow's *Looking for Mr. Green*, which follows an educated white man who takes a job delivering relief checks during the Great Depression, only to find mistrust and suspicion while trying to make a delivery in a mostly-black neighborhood. Then there is Stuart Dybek's haunting story, *Chopin in Winter*, which explores the intimate relationships of a Polish family as it struggles to come to terms with a daughter who has become pregnant with a mixed race child.

It is the aim of this anthology that, through these stories, readers will discover a sense of Chicago that goes beyond a mere sense of place; that by reading about the heartache, struggles, trials, and triumphs of the characters within these pages, one might discover something of the heart of this great city, and why it continues to inspire some of our nation's finest literature.

James Daley
Editor

ACKNOWLEDGMENTS

Algren, Nelson. "A Bottle of Milk for Mother" from *The Neon Wilderness: Stories*. Copyright © 1941 by Nelson Algren. Reprinted with the permission of The Permissions Company, Inc., on behalf of Seven Stories Press; www.sevenstories.com.

Bellow, Saul. "Looking for Mr. Green" from *Mosby's Memoirs and Other Stories*. Copyright © 1951; renewed © 1979 by Saul Bellow. Used by permission of Viking Books, an imprint of Penguin Publishing Group, a division of Penguin Random House LLC.

Dybek, Stuart. "Chopin in Winter" from *The Coast of Chicago*. Copyright © 1990 by Stuart Dybek. Reprinted by permission of Farrar, Straus and Giroux, LLC.

Wright, Richard. "The Man Who Went to Chicago" from *Eight Men*. Copyright © 1940, 1961 by Richard Wright; renewed © 1989 by Ellen Wright. Reprinted by permission of HarperCollins Publishers.

Contents

Contents

THE JUDGE'S SON (1906)

George Ade

TWO MEN SAT by one of the narrow south windows of the Freedom Hotel. They were tipped back in their straight wooden chairs and their feet rested against the scarred sill of the window.

One of the men was tall, with a tan-coloured moustache and a goatee. He wore a black slouch hat, which was pulled forward over one eye so that it gave him a suggestion of rural bravado. The other man was younger, hollow-cheeked, and with hair and beard of dead blackness. His light-coloured stiff hat seemed preposterously out of season, for a slow but steady sift of snow was coming down.

Both men wore clothes of careful cut, but the shape had gone from the garments. The elbows were shiny, the vest buttons were not uniform and the fronts were sadly spotted.

In the room with the two men were some fifty other men, marked by adversity, most of them holding with weakened pride to some chattel of better days.

As many as could find places at the windows sat and looked with fascinated idleness at the rushing money-makers outside. Others put their backs to the dim light and read from scraps of newspapers. There was a smothering odour of pipe-smoke, which floated in vague ribbons above the clustering heads. Sometimes—but not often—the murmur of conversation was broken by laughter.

It is a good thing the Freedom Hotel calls itself a hotel, otherwise it would be a lodging-house. These men in the bare "office" were being sheltered at a weekly rate of $1.50, and each had a cubby-hole for a home—a mere shell of wood open at the top. The upper floors of the Freedom Hotel were subdivided into these tiny pens. Here the tired and discouraged men came crawling every night. From these boxes the frowsy and unrested men emerged every morning.

1

The wreckage on an ocean beach washes together as if by choice and the wrecks of a city mobilise of their own free will. The man who is down must find some one with whom he can rail at the undeserving prosperous.

The Freedom Hotel sheltered a community of equals, all worsted in the fight, some living on the crumbs of a happier period, some abjectly depending on the charity of friends and relatives, and some struggling along on small and unreliable pay.

There was a 400-page novel in every life there, but the condensed stories of the two men at the window must suffice for the present.

The older, the one with the slouch hat—son of wealthy merchant in Indiana town—inherited money—married—learned to gamble—took up with Board of Trade—wife died—more reckless gambling—moved to Chicago—went broke—Freedom Hotel.

The younger, with black hair and beard—son of a judge in Western city—reared with great care by mother—sent to college—learned to drink—repeatedly forgiven by father through the intercession of the mother—mother died—father cast son from home—son in Chicago, employed in a collection agency—went on a drunk—Freedom Hotel.

The victim of gambling did most of the talking.

"They can't always keep me down, now, you can bet on that," he said, nervously combing his goatee with thumb and finger. "I wish I could have had about ten thousand last week. I'd have shown some of these fellows."

"If I had ten thousand I wouldn't chance a cent of it," said the other, his eyes twitching.

"Well, I'll beat the game yet, you see if I don't. I've got three or four fellows in this town to get even with—fellows that I spent my money on when I had it; fellows that could come to me and get fifty or a hundred just for the askin' of it, and there ain't one of 'em to-day that'd turn over his finger to help me—not one of 'em. That's what you get when you're down, young man. If you want to find out who your friends are, just wait till you go broke."

"I know all about it," said the other. With a shaky hand he took the last cigarette from a package.

"I was thinkin' when I turned in to my bunk last night, 'Well, this is a devil of a place for a man that had a room at the Palmer House, when it was the talk of the whole country.' That was when

I used to drive my own trotter and hire a man to take care of him. When I'd come to Chicago, the hotel clerks used to jump over the counter to shake hands with me. If I wanted a steak, I went to Billy Boyle's for it. If I was over on Clark Street and wanted a game, I could get a private roll. It was 'Phil' here and 'Phil' there, and nothin' too good for me. Do you think I could go to any one o' them to-day and get a dollar? A dollar! Not a cent—not a red cent. That's what you get when you're in hard luck."

"You can't tell me anything about it," said the other, in a restrained voice, for his lungs were filled with cigarette-smoke, which he was breathing slowly through his nostrils. "Didn't I go to college with fellows that live right here in this town, and don't they pass me on the street every day or two without recognising me? Why, when I think that I came of a family that—ah, well, it's all right. Money talks here in Chicago, and if you haven't got money you're little better than a tramp."

"Well, I'll have it again and I'll make some of these fellows sorry they ever threw me down. I'll make 'em sweat. If I don't—" and he ran into profanity.

"Here's a telegram for you," said some one at his elbow.

It was the "clerk" of the Freedom—a short man with an indented nose, who went about in his shirtsleeves.

"For me?" asked the speculator, in surprise.

"That's what it says here—Philip Sanderson. It come over from 136."

"That's right."

"I signed for it."

He tore open the envelope and read the message. It seemed that he gazed at it for a full minute without speaking or moving. Then he arose and hurried away. The judge's son rubbed his eyes and felt vainly for another cigarette.

"Your partner's gone," said the clerk that evening.

"Who—Sanderson?" asked the judge's son.

"Yes, this afternoon. He didn't have much packin' to do. What do you think? An old aunt of his died down in Indiana and he told me he'd come in for about five thousand."

"Well, I'll swear," said the judge's son, "and he didn't leave any word?"

"Nope."

A week later the judge's son was walking in State Street.

The cold north wind was blowing.

His summer derby had to be held in place. The other hand was deep in his trousers' pocket.

His old sack-coat was tightly buttoned and the collar was turned up. The judge's son seemed to be limping in each foot, but it was not a limp. It was the slouch of utter dejection.

He was within thirty feet of the main entrance to the Palmer House when he saw a man come out.

The judge's son had to take a second look, to be sure of his own senses. Instead of the old and crumpled slouch there was a new broad-brimmed felt hat of much shapeliness. The winter overcoat was heavy chinchilla, with a velvet collar. Sanderson was smoking a long cigar. He had been shaved recently. His shoes were brightly polished. As he stood back in the sheltered doorway he worked his left hand into a blood-red glove.

The judge's son stood some fifteen feet away and hesitated. Then he slunk to the shelter of a column and spoke to his partner.

"Well, Sanderson, they seem to be coming pretty easy for you."

Sanderson looked at the speaker, squinting through the smoke.

He said nothing. His hand being well into the glove, he fastened the clasp at the wrist with a springy snap. With a satisfied lick he turned his cigar once over in his mouth. A flake of ash had fallen on the chinchilla coat. He brushed it off. Then he pushed through the swinging doors and went back into the hotel.

REFORM IN THE FIRST (1910)

Brand Whitlock

THE SENATORIAL CONVENTION in the First District was to convene at ten o'clock, in a dingy little hall in lower Clark Street, lighted by windows so long unwashed that they looked like ground glass. From the chandeliers, black and sticky with dead flies, shreds of tissue paper fluttered, relics of some boisterous fête an Italian society had given there long ago. The floor was damp in arabesque wrought by a sprinkling-can, for the janitor had sprayed water there to lay the dust he was too indifferent to remove. Perhaps a hundred chairs were set in amphitheatrical order, and before them stood a kitchen table, on which was a white water pitcher, flanked by a glass, thickened by various sedimentary deposits within.

In the saloon below, at nine o'clock, scores of delegates were already shuffling in the sawdust that covered the floor, holding huge schooners of beer in their hairy fists, gorging grossly at the free lunch table, with bologna, rank onions and rye bread. The foam of the beer clung to their mustaches, which, after each sip, they sucked between their lips. Most of them managed, at the same time they were eating and drinking, by a dexterous sleight-of-hand, to smoke cheap domestic cigars, and a cloud of white smoke rolled along the low ceiling. Each new arrival was greeted with some obscene but endearing epithet, and the room rang with laughter and profanity. A keg of beer had been provided by one of Conway's managers, and the bartender, wiping his hands on a dirty towel, was rid, so long as the keg lasted, of the responsibility of keeping account of drinks, and of ringing up the change on the cash register. At eleven o'clock the keg was empty, the free lunch table abandoned to the flies, and the delegates scuffled up the dingy stairs to the hall. Half an hour later the chairman of the senatorial district committee pounded the kitchen table with a leg of a broken chair, and shouted:

"The convention will be in order."

This declaration made no impression upon the babel of voices, the laughter, the profanity, the noise of shuffling feet and scraping chairs. The delegates were scrambling to their places, seating themselves by wards. Reporters flung themselves into seats at a second table and gazed about the room, noting who were there. The political men of the morning papers did not trouble themselves to take seats. They loafed among the politicians in a way superior to the reporters for the afternoon papers, as if they were politicians themselves, making history instead of recording it.

Meanwhile the noise did not abate, and the committeeman was growing red in the face. The morning was warm, and the room, already cloudy with tobacco smoke, was filling with a noisome human odor. The atmosphere was feculent. Delegates removed their coats, hanging them over the backs of their chairs. Finally the chairman of the committee, growing impatient, split the table with his club and yelled:

"Damn it all, boys, come to order!"

And then, eager to resign such a difficult command, he hastened to announce:

"The committee has named Honorable John P. Muldoon to act as temp'ry chairman."

He handed the chair leg to John P. Muldoon, who, stroking back his curly hair from his brow, began to beat the table impartially.

All this while Underwood stood against the wall, looking on. The question that had been agitating him for weeks was about to be decided, but now that the ordeal was actually upon him, the consciousness beat numbly against his brain, so that the whole scene lacked reality, almost interest. He was dazed. He was about to take his baptism of political fire, and he trembled like a white novitiate.

Underwood belonged to one of the oldest families of Chicago—the name had been known there before the fire. His father, who had lately taken him into his law firm, continued to cling in his conservatism to an old stone house in Michigan Avenue long after his neighbors had abandoned their mansions to uncertain boarders, and either retreated farther south or advanced to the North Side. John Underwood had come out of Harvard with a young lawyer's ambition in politics, an ambition that had the United States senate merely as a beginning of its home stretch, and when the year rolled around in which state senators were to be elected in the odd numbered districts he decided that it was time to begin.

The newspapers had scented the sensation that lurked in the candidature of a young man like Underwood in a district like the First, and because he was rich, because he wore good clothes, because he went into what is called society, promptly dubbed him a reformer, and thus weighted he had set out upon his race for the nomination. He liked to see his name in the newspapers, liked to think of himself as a reformer, though he was embarrassed in this attitude by the fascinating figure of the political boss he had hoped to become—a well-dressed, gentlemanly boss, of course, who, while at home in those saloons where he permitted the convivial familiarity of the boys, nevertheless took his luncheons at his club. He fell into a way of speaking of the First as "my district," spoke of it, in fact, as if he, instead of Malachi Nolan and "Cinch" Conway, owned it, and when certain ward politicians in the first days of the campaign called upon him, Underwood was pleased to lend them money, just as he was pleased to comply with the requests of certain others who organized the John W. Underwood First Ward Campaign Club, and sent a committee to inform him that they were assembled in the club rooms ready to transact business, and beer only four dollars a keg. He winked confidentially at himself in the mirror that night as he gave a final touch to his white cravat and surveyed his fine young form arrayed in evening clothes for the reform banquet at the Palmer House. His speech was *The Tendencies of Modern Politics*. The newspapers said it was a very brilliant speech, breathing lofty political sentiments that were bound to make John W. Underwood votes. Also, the Reform Club indorsed his candidature.

As Underwood leaned against the greasy wall of the little hall on lower Clark Street this morning, the whole campaign flashed before him, just as the events of a lifetime are said in books to flash before the mind of a drowning man. He recalled every vivid detail of the call Baldwin had made upon him, how he entered his private office without troubling the pale, pimpled office boy to announce him, how he lifted from his carefully parted hair his straw hat with its youthful band of blue, and laughed out, "John, my boy, how are you? Hot, isn't it?" He could see Baldwin as he sat in the solid oak chair that stood intimately beside his roll-top desk, fanning his ruddy face with the hat, which had impressed a broad red band on his forehead. Underwood had been glad enough to close *Cooley on Taxation* and revolve his chair to face Baldwin, just as if he had been a client, for Baldwin was the most important politician who had ever called upon him professionally.

Underwood remembered clearly how Baldwin's excellent teeth glistened when he smiled, how he lighted a Turkish cigarette and, tilting up his chin, blew a long, airy stream of blue smoke through the thick hairs of his mustache. He could even remember how carefully Baldwin sheltered the flame of the match for Underwood's cigarette, in that curious spirit of economy men always practice with regard to matches, much as if there were only one match left in the whole world. And then he could recall almost word for word their conversation. Baldwin had frankly told him that Conway had him handicapped, because he had the city hall with him and controlled the Fifth Ward. Simmons, Baldwin had said, didn't cut much ice; he had some labor leaders with him, and would get a bunch of delegates from his own ward, but that was about all. In fact, said Baldwin, concluding his judicial summing up, Conway could win out, hands down, if it were not for his recent quarrel with Malachi Nolan. Underwood remembered that during all this frankness he had reflectively drawn rude little geometrical figures on an envelope and had been somehow afraid to look up at Baldwin, for the noted lobbyist had sat there transfixing him with an eye that could read the mind of a man when it was impinged on politics—that is, practical politics—as easily as it could a poker hand across a table stacked with blue chips.

He knew Baldwin had come with some practical proposition, and when the lobbyist suggested that he was too respectable, and would run better in some residence district, that the boys looked upon him as a reformer, and that the silk stockings were not practical enough to help him, Underwood had felt that at last it was coming. It was simple enough. Baldwin had been talking that very morning about Underwood's candidature to Mr. Weed of the Metropolitan Motor System, and to Mr. Peabody, president of the Gas Company, and they had been very much interested. They had an anxiety to see good men nominated that year, for they had large business interests that were more or less affected by legislation, and had feared they would have to settle on Conway. Conway had experience in legislative matters, and had been friendly enough in the city council, yet they felt they could hardly trust him—he was

such a grafter, and in such things, Baldwin blandly assured Underwood, they had to depend upon a man's honor alone, and so they
had sent Baldwin to suggest that Underwood meet them at luncheon, and talk matters over. Baldwin, with his love of ease and
luxury, had preferred a dinner over at the Cardinal's in the evening, but Mr. Peabody had something on hand with the trustees of
his church and couldn't meet them then. Baldwin had taken out
his watch at this point, with the air of a man who suddenly remem-
bers some important engagement—the details all came back with a
fidelity that was painful—and stood awaiting Underwood's reply,
with the open watch ticking impatiently in his palm.

Of course, Underwood had understood—and he wished ardently
to be nominated and elected. He could see himself swinging idly in
a big chair behind a walnut desk in the senate chamber, just as an
actor sees himself, with an artist's ecstatic, half-frightened gasp, in
some new part he is about to study. The position would give him
much importance, he would be riding back and forth between
Chicago and Springfield on a pass, it would be so pleasant to be
addressed as senator, to be consulted, to head delegations in state
conventions and cast the solid vote for any one he pleased; besides,
it would be a good training for Washington, he could practise in
oratory and parliamentary law just as he practised on friendless paupers over in the criminal court when his father influenced some
judge to appoint him to defend an indigent prisoner. It meant only
one little word, he could be wary of promises. His heart had
expanded, he had turned half around in his chair to face Baldwin,
when suddenly the reformer within him rose to object, pointed to
his ideals, rehearsed the speech on *The Tendencies of Modern Politics*,
recalled all the good words the independent papers had spoken of
him, urged the beauty of great sacrifices for principle. At the idea
of self-sacrifice, Underwood had felt a melting self-pity, he admired
himself in this new rôle of a self-sacrificing reformer. And so he
flung the cigarette out of the window, watched it whirl down to
the melting tar of the roofs below and said firmly:

"I have an engagement this morning, Mr. Baldwin. I'm sorry,
but I guess I can't come."

Once more Underwood saw the pleasantness leave Baldwin's
face, saw him fleck a flake of ash from the white waistcoat he wore
with his summer suit of blue, and snapping the lid of his watch shut,
he once more heard him say in a final and reproachful tone:

"Well, all right; sorry, my boy."

Underwood wondered that morning in the noisy convention hall, whether, if he had the decision to make over again, he would decline such influence. It had been the cause of much doubt and some regret at the time. The boss within him had protested—surely it was a political mistake—and the boss was louder than the reformer, and more plausible. He came forward with a brilliant scheme. He recalled Baldwin's reference to the rivalry between Nolan and Conway. Underwood remembered that when he suggested the possibility of Nolan's running for the nomination himself, Baldwin had shaken his head—there wasn't enough in it, he said. Nolan could do very much better in the council, where he was. Besides, Mr. Weed and Mr. Peabody disliked him.

Underwood thought out his scheme that afternoon, while hunting in the digest for cases in point to be cited in a case his father was preparing for the appellate court. The work of looking up cases in point, while its results are impressive and seem to smell of the lamp, had in reality grown quite automatic to Underwood, and as he loafed over digests and reports and jotted down his notes, he elaborated the scheme, just what he would say and do, how he would appear, and so forth. And so, when he entered Malachi Nolan's place in Dearborn Street, early that evening, he was fully prepared. The details of this incident came back just as the details of Baldwin's visit had done—the empty saloon, the alderman himself leaning over his bar, his white apron rolled into a big girth about his middle, the cigar in the round hole at the corner of his mouth gone out, denoting that it was time for him to go down the alley to Billy Boyle's and get his porterhouse and baked potato.

Underwood watched Malachi Nolan mix his Martini cocktail, splash it picturesquely into a sparkling glass and bejewel it with a Maraschino cherry, then gravely take a cigar for himself and stow it away in his ample waistcoat. Then, as Nolan mopped the bar with professional sweep of his white-sleeved, muscular arm, Underwood unfolded his brilliant scheme, skirting carefully the acute suspicions of an old politician. But Nolan mopped, blinking inscrutably, at last putting the damp cloth away in some mysterious place under the counter. The fat Maltese cat, waiting until the moisture on the bar had evaporated, stretched herself again beside the silver urn that held the crackers and the little cubes of cheese. Still Nolan blinked in silence, like a hostile jury with its mind made up, until at last, in desperation, Underwood blurted out his proposition. Nolan blinked some more, then, half opening his blue Irish eyes, grunted:

"Well, I like your gall."

Underwood's spirits fell, yet he was not disappointed. It was, after all, just what he had expected. It served him right for his presumption, if nothing more—though the subdued reformer within had hinted at other reasons. He hung his head, twirling his empty glass disconsolately. He did not see the light that twinkled in the blue eyes, he had not then known how very ready Nolan was to form any combination that would beat Conway and Baldwin, especially with a reformer like himself who had money to spend on his ambitions. He had not discerned how badly the man whom the newspapers always cartooned with the First Ward sticking out of his vest pocket, needed a reformer in his business, as the saying is. Hence his glad surprise when Nolan wiped his big hand on his apron like a washerwoman and held it out, saying:

"But I'm wit' ye."

Then the campaign, under Nolan's management, in the most wonderful legislative district—a cosmopolitan district, bristling with sociological problems, a district that has fewer homes and more saloons, more commerce and more sloth, more millionaires and more paupers, and while it confines within its boundaries the sky-scrapers, clubs, theaters and hundred churches of a metropolis, still boasts a police station with more arrests on its blotter than any other in the world. Night after night, with Nolan's two candidates for the house, he spent in saloons where a candidate must treat and distribute his cards that the boys may size him up; lodging houses and barrel houses in lower Clark Street, where sweating negroes and frowsy whites drank five-cent whisky with him; blazing saloons along the levee, where even the poor, painted girls at the tables lifted their glasses when he ordered the drinks for the house; crap games and policy shops in lower Clark Street, the Syrian, Arabic, Chinese and Italian quarters down by the squalid Bad Lands, and at last a happier evening along the Archey Road. Underwood had three weeks of this, and as he stood in the convention hall that morning, unwashed, unshaven, his linen soiled, his shoes muddy, his own friends would not have known him, though he cared little enough for this now—they had all forgotten to go to the primaries the day before, and those for whom he had sent carriages had been

too busy, or too respectable, to respond. The taste of bad beer and
the scorch of cheap cigars still smacked in his mouth—indeed, he
did not get them entirely out until he came back from Mt. Clemens
two weeks after the nomination.

But they were balloting for permanent chairman now. It would
be a test vote; it would disclose his own strength and the strength
of Conway. He looked over the red faces before him. He saw
Conway himself moving among the delegates, snarling, cursing,
quarreling with the friends of years; he saw Conway's candidate for
the house, McGlone, over in the Second Ward delegation, his coat
off, a handkerchief about his fat neck, a fuming cigar between his
chubby fingers, turning on his heavy haunches to revile some man
who was numbered with Nolan's crowd; he saw in the First Ward
delegation, Malachi Nolan, clean-shaven, in black coat and cravat,
his iron gray hair cropped short, calm alone of all the others. He
would have looked the priest more than the saloon-keeper, had he
smoked his cigar differently. Now and then he solemnly raised his
hand, with almost the benediction of a father, to still the clamor of
his delegation, which, with its twenty-one votes, was safe at all
events for Underwood.

Muldoon was Conway's man—they would try to make the temporary organization permanent. D'Ormand was Underwood's candidate. And Muldoon won. Underwood had lost the first round.

The candidates for senator were to be placed in nomination first.
Underwood stood in the crowded doorway and heard Conway's
name presented. Then, in the cheering, with his heart in his sanded
throat, he heard the chairman say:

"Are there any other nominations?"

There was a momentary stillness, and then he heard a thick,
strong-voice:

"Misther Chairman!"

"The gentleman from the First Ward."

"Misther Chairman," the thick, strong voice said, "I roise to
place in nomynation the name of wan—"

It was the voice of Malachi Nolan, and Underwood suddenly
remembered that Nolan was to place his name before the convention. He listened an instant, but could not endure it long. He could
not endure that men should see him in the hour when his name
was being thus laid naked to the world. Reporters were writing it
down, perhaps the crowd would laugh or whistle or hiss. Besides,

candidates do not remain in the convention hall; they await the committee of notification in some near-by saloon. He squeezed through the mass of men who stood on tiptoes, stretching their necks to see and hear the old leader of the First Ward, and fled.

The first ballot was taken—Conway, 31; Underwood, 30; Simmons, the dark horse, 8; necessary to a choice, 35. The vote was unchanged for twenty-six ballots, till the afternoon had worn away, and the trucks had jolted off the cobblestones of Clark Street, till the lights were flaring and hot tamale men, gamblers, beggars, street walkers, all the denizens of darkness were shifting along the sidewalks, till the policemen had been changed on their beats, and Pinkerton night watchmen were trying the doors of stores, till Chinamen shuffled forth, and Jewesses and Italian women emerged for their evening breath of air, bringing swart and grimy children to play upon the heated flags. The hall was lighted, just as if some Italian festival were to be held there. The reporters' places at the table were taken by the men who did politics for the morning papers, themselves reduced at last to the necessity of taking notes. They brought reports of the results in other senatorial conventions held about town that day—it seemed to be assured that John Skelley had carried the country towns, Lemont, Riverside, Evanston, and so on. In certain west side districts this man had won, in certain north side districts that man had been successful. It looked as if the old gang was going to break back into the legislature.

And so the interest in this one remaining convention deepened, the strain tightened, the crowd thickened. The delegates, tired and sullen, shed their waistcoats, tore off their moist and dirty collars and settled down to an angry fight. The amphitheatrical arrangement of the chairs had long been broken. The ward delegations now formed circles about their leaders. The damp arabesques wrought by the janitor's superficial sprinkling-can had long since been superseded by arabesques of tobacco juice. The floor was littered with scraps of paper, the spent ballots with which the stubborn contest had been waged. The First Ward delegation was in a solid ring, and in the center of it sat Malachi Nolan, his elbows on his knees, tearing old ballots into tiny specks of paper and strewing them on the floor, but keeping all the while a surveying eye on the Fifth Ward delegation, now divided into two groups, one of which surrounded Howe, the other huddling about Grogan, the lawyer, who, with disheveled hair, a handkerchief about his neck, stood glaring angrily at Nolan, his eyes shadowed by heavy circles telling of weariness and the strain.

Now and then the leaders made desperate attempts to trade, harrying Simmons, offering him everything for his seven votes. Simmons himself, in his turn, tried to induce each faction to swing its strength to him.

But the situation remained unchanged.

Once Nolan sent for Underwood and whispered to him. He thought he knew one or two Conway men who could be got very cheaply, but the boy shook his head—the reformer within him demurred —and yet he smiled sardonically at the reformer thinking of the primaries and the convention itself.

Then Malachi Nolan caught the chairman's shifty eye and moved an adjournment until morning. But even as he spoke, Grogan scowled at Muldoon, shook his head at his followers, and the room rang with their hoarse shouts:

"No! no! no!"

Heartened by this confession of weakness on Nolan's part, they kept on yelling lustily:

"No! no! no!"

They even laughed, and Muldoon smote the table, to declare the motion lost.

On the forty-seventh ballot, one of the Simmons votes went over to Conway, and there was a faint cheer. On the forty-eighth, one of the Simmons votes went to Underwood, and parity was restored. On the forty-ninth, Underwood gained another of Simmons' votes—Nolan, it seemed, had promised to get him on the janitor's pay-roll in the state house—and the vote was tied. This ballot stood:

	First Ward	Second Ward	Fifth Ward	Total
Conway......	—	10	22	32
Underwood...	21	4	7	32
Simmons......	—	5	—	5

The Simmons men were holding out, waiting to throw their strength to the winner. When the sixty-seventh ballot had been taken, Muldoon, squinting in the miserable light, at the secretary's figures, hit the table with the chair leg and said:

"On this ballot Conway receives 32, Underwood 32, Simmons 5. There being no choice, you will prepare your ballots for another vote."

Just then one of the Conway men from the Second Ward left his place, and touched one of Nolan's fellows in the First Ward delegation—Donahue—on the shoulder. Donahue started. The man whispered in his ear, and returned to his delegation, keeping his eye on Donahue. Underwood looked on breathlessly. Nolan, revolving slowly, held his hat for every vote—last of all for Dona-hue's. The man dropped his folded ballot into the hat and hung his head. Nolan calmly picked the ballot out of the hat and gave it back to Donahue, who looked up in affected surprise.

"What's the trouble, Malachi?" he said as innocently as he could. He was not much of an actor.

"This won't do," Nolan said, giving the ballot back to the man.

"It's all right, Malachi, honest to God it is!" protested Donahue.

"Thin I'll just put this wan in for ye, heh?" said Nolan, drawing another ballot from the pocket of his huge waistcoat and poising it above the hat.

The crowd had pressed around the First Ward delegation. The convention had risen to its feet, craning red necks, and out of the mass, Grogan cried:

"Aw, here, Malachi Nolan, none o' that now!"

Nolan turned his rugged face toward him and said simply:

"Who's runnin' this dillygation, you or me?"

"Well—none o' your bulldozing—we won't stand it!" replied Grogan angrily, his blue eyes blazing.

"You get to hell out o' this." And so saying, Nolan dropped the ballot into the hat and turned to face the chair.

"Have you all voted?" inquired Muldoon.

"First Ward!" the secretary called.

Nolan squared his shoulders, not having looked in his hat or counted the ballots there, and said slowly and impressively:

"On behalf av the solid dillygation av the First Ward, I cast twenty-wan votes for John W. Underwood."

"Misther Chairman! Misther Chairman!" cried Grogan, waving his hand in the air, "I challenge that vote! I challenge that vote!"

"The gentleman from the Fifth Ward challenges the vote—"

"Misther Chairman," said Nolan, standing with one heavy foot on his chair and leveling a forefinger at Muldoon, "a point of order!

The gintleman from the Fifth Ward has no right to challenge the vote av the First Ward—he's not a mimber of the dillygation!"

"Let the First Ward be polled," calmly ruled Muldoon. Nolan took his foot from his chair and stepped to Donahue's side. Every man in the First Ward delegation, as his name was called from the credentials, cried "Underwood!" As the secretary neared the name of Donahue, Nolan laid his hand heavily on the fellow's shoulder.

"Donahue!" called the secretary.

The fellow squirmed under Nolan's hand.

"Donahue!"

"Don't let him bluff you!" cried some one from the Fifth Ward.

"Vote as you damn please, Jimmie!"

"T'row the boots into 'im, Donnie!"

"Soak him one!"

"Take your hands off him, Bull Nolan!"

So they bawled and Donahue wriggled. But the hand of Nolan, like the hand of Douglas, was his own, and gripped fast. Grogan, his face red, his eyes on fire, leaped from his place in his delegation, and started across the chairs for Nolan. The big saloon-keeper gave him a look out of his little eye. His left shoulder dipped, his left fist tightened. Grogan halted.

"Vote, Jimmie, me lad," said Nolan, in a soft voice.

"Underwood!" said Donahue, in a whisper. His weak, pinched, hungry face turned appealingly toward Grogan. His blear eyes were filmy with disappointment.

"He votes for John W. Underwood, Misther Chairman," said Nolan complacently. The vote was unchanged. The chairman ordered another ballot.

And then, all at once, as if a breath from a sanded desert had been blown into the room, Underwood was sensible of a change in the atmosphere. The air was perhaps no hotter than it had been for hours at the close of that stifling day, no bluer with tobacco smoke, no heavier with the smell borne in from Clark Street on hot night winds that had started cool and fresh from the lake four blocks away, a smell compounded of many smells, the smell ascending from foul and dark cellars beneath the sidewalk, the smell of stale beer, the ammoniac smell of filthy pavements, mingled with the feculence of unclean bodies that had sweated for hours in the vitiated air of that low-ceilinged, crowded room. It had a strange moral density that oppressed him, that oppressed all, even the politicians, for they ceased from cursing and from speech, and now sat sullen, silent, suspiciously eying their companions. It was an atmosphere charged with some ominous foreboding, some awful fear. Underwood had never felt that atmosphere before, yet, with a gasp that came not as an effect of the heat, he recognized its meaning.

A hush fell. Muldoon, his black, curly locks shining with perspiration, was leaning on his improvised gavel, his keen eye, the Irish eye that so readily seizes such situations, darting into every face before him.

And suddenly came that for which they were waiting. A man entered the hall and strode straight across the floor into the Fifth Ward delegation, into the group where the Underwood men were clustered about their leader. He wore evening clothes, his black dinner-coat and white shirt bosom striking a vivid note in the scene. He walked briskly, but his mind was so intent upon his pose that it was not until he had removed his cigarette from his lips and had observed Underwood, that his white teeth showed beneath his reddish mustache in the well-known smile of George R. Baldwin. He elbowed his way into the very midst of the Underwood men from the Fifth Ward, and leading one of them aside, talked with him an instant, and then returned him, as it were, to his place in the delegation. Then he brought forth another, whispered to him for an earnest moment, and sent him back, with a smile and a slap on the shoulder. The third delegate detained him longer, and once, as he argued with him, the slightest shade of displeasure crossed Baldwin's face, but in an instant the smile replaced it, and he talked—convincingly, it seemed. Before Baldwin returned this man to his delegation, he shook hands with him.

The secretary was calling the wards, and Nolan had announced the result in his delegation. The Fifth Ward was a long while in preparing its ballots. There was trouble of some sort there, among the Underwood men. Nolan was urging, expostulating, cursing, commanding. The air was tense. It seemed to Underwood that it must inevitably be shattered by some moral cataclysm in the soul of man. Grogan's brow was knit, as he waited, hat in hand. The delegates voted. Feverishly, with trembling fingers, Grogan opened and counted the bits of paper. Then he sprang to his feet, with a wild, glad light in his face.

"Mister Chairman!" he cried, "the Fifth Ward casts twenty-five votes for Conway and four for Underwood!"

The three bolters in the Fifth Ward delegation sat with defiance in their faces, but they could not sustain the expression, even by huddling close together. They broke for the door, wriggling their way through masses of men, who made their passage uncertain, almost perilous. A billow of applause broke from the Conway men, and submerged the convention. Delegates all over the hall were on their feet, clamoring for recognition, but Malachi Nolan's voice boomed heavily above all other voices. His fist was in the air above all other fists.

"Misther Chairman!" he yelled, "I challenge that vote!"

"Misther Chairman!" yelled Grogan, "a point of order! The gentleman isn't a member of the Fifth Ward delegation and can not challenge its vote!"

"The point of order is well taken," promptly ruled the chair. "The gentleman from the First Ward is out of order—he will take his seat."

Men were screaming, brandishing fists, waving hats, coats, anything, scraping chairs, pounding the floor with them. There were heavy, brutal oaths, and, here and there, the smack of a fist on a face. In the tumult, the five Simmons votes went to Conway. Muldoon was beating the table with his club and crying:

"Order! order! order!"

"To hell with order!" bawled some one from the First Ward delegation.

"On this ballot," Muldoon was calling, "there were sixty-nine votes cast; necessary to a choice, thirty-five. James P. Conway has received forty votes; John W. Underwood, twenty-nine, and George W. Simmons"—he paused, as if to decipher the vote— "none. James R. Conway, having received the necessary number of votes, is therefore declared the nominee of this convention."

Underwood was stunned. He staggered through the horrible uproar toward the door. He longed for the air outside, even the heavy air of lower Clark street, where the people surged along under the wild, dazzling lights, in two opposite, ever-passing processions. His head reeled. He lost the sense of things, the voices about him seemed far away and vague, he felt himself detached, as it were, from all that had gone before. But as he pressed his way through the crowd that blocked the entrance, and plunged toward the stairs, he saw Baldwin, mopping the red band on his white brow. Baldwin recognized him, and said, with his everlasting smile:

"Sorry, my boy—next time!"

THE EXTRA MAJOR (1910)

Will J. Cuppy

I

THE QUARTERLY ANNOUNCEMENTS are exceedingly useful. They are good to wrap sandwiches and things in, and to fan with in class; also, they enable the sophomores to tell whether the "snaps" come at convenient periods. Some freshmen read them through to the last footnote—no one else ever does—under the impression that they may take their choice of the courses, or perhaps in the belief that the big white folders are the veritable catalogues of their own accomplishments four years later. Both conceptions are interesting.

But the freshmen need no warning against dangerous mental exertion. Only a few of them—those with abnormally developed foreheads—injure their health in that way. The rest are busy scurrying about the campus for the valuable something or other they think they are going to find. The something or other usually finds them; often on the first day, and occasionally when it seems almost too late. You may call it College Spirit, or merely an Idea. It is not in the Announcements.

Phil Jennings, who used to insist upon making observations like these, modestly admitted that he had evolved them out of the adventures of his freshman year. When he threatened to go into details, his friends would groan cheerfully and tell him that the same old things happened to about a thousand others. But that, as Phil would solemnly remark, was precisely the point.

Philip Howard Jennings, Jr., had no special convictions on the significance of the collegiate experience when he came to Chicago.

He just hoped he would get a great deal out of the University, as his father had advised. This was rather fortunate, since opinionated freshmen are both unhappy and annoying; they suffer more or less when their notions sicken and die, and they worry the sophomores, who do not learn to smile at all human frailties until farther along in the year.

Philip Howard Jennings, Jr., was eighteen years of age and fairly good-looking, and he was usually hungry. He had a good head, which contained a healthy freshman brain.

The boy began by registering for three majors—a major, he learned, was the unit of work, and he would get nine each year. In the dean's office, he conferred with the small freshman next in line about the advisability of taking one or two Sociology courses, while the fellow in front was trying the official soul with original suggestions concerning his schedule. The small freshman, who winked confidentially and bobbed his head at each whispered communication, said he knew which were the "snap" classes. A fellow out under the clock had told him. But Phil asked no questions when he was instructed to take English 1, German 1 and History 1; therefore the dean smiled kindly upon him—about fifty other freshmen were waiting to be ministered to. The dean shook hands quite cordially when he noticed the name at the top of the registration slip, and said he knew Phil Jennings and was glad to meet his son. That made up for the Sociology courses. Many a freshman would have liked to know Dean Jackson and shake hands with him that way.

When Phil had paid his tuition, he felt that at last he was a part of the University. And he liked the feeling. He liked the great, gray, English Gothic buildings, with their steep, red roofs and their plain, strong outlines, and he liked what he saw through the windows. Most of all, he liked the looks of the fellows all about him. He liked everything and everybody on the campus, with the single exception of Freddy Ball, whom he detested. As Freddy was his roommate, he could not ignore the obtrusive fact that he existed.

A singularly painful dispensation of Providence had condemned Phil and Freddy to unpleasant companionship. It was their misfortune to be cousins, and both were heartily ashamed of it. Their mothers, the most loving of sisters, would have been terribly shocked had they known of the unnatural animosity harbored by their sons. For that reason alone the boys had refrained from damaging each other's faces, and always exchanged Christmas and birthday gifts, accompanied by excessive written expressions of regard, which were meant to be withering.

A little girl with irresistible pigtails and an entrancing giggle had started the trouble. This charming young person moved away and was forgotten, but the cousinly warfare continued. Freddy told his friends that he could stand Phil Jennings if he were not such a tin saint on top of his meanness, and Phil thought he might be able to endure Freddy if he weren't such a loud-mouthed little insect. And now Mrs. Jennings and Mrs. Ball had conceived the uncanny plan of making college chums of their sons, explaining with simple foresight that the boys could not possibly become lonesome under such an arrangement. They had taken the trouble to insure the joint occupancy of the very room where the sweet communion was to thrive.

Phil was not the kind that turns the other cheek, but he imagined, as he drank in all the new mysteries of that first morning, that even Freddy might improve in the inspiring surroundings. He felt that he would even be willing to forgive him a few things. After a hasty luncheon at the Commons, where he wondered about the portraits, and at the size of the crowd, he found Freddy in the room in Hitchcock, tacking pictures into the wall, against the combined regulations of the Department of Buildings and Grounds and the Head of the House.

"I'm certainly glad I came, Fred," he began, out of the fulness of his heart. "Just see those buildings. And the dean—Dean Jackson—knows father. I remember now that father said— "

"For Heaven's sake, cut out your father for a minute," sputtered Freddy, who was quite warm and excited because the wall kept chipping off and because he had nearly swallowed a tack a moment before. "Try to forget that you're related to your father. Your father's in Kansas and you're here. You—"

Freddy stopped suddenly and said "Damn!" very incisively, when the hammer slipped and struck his chubby forefinger. Phil scorned to reply or even to laugh at the accident, but dragged his trunk to the center of the floor and set to work.

It took an hour to decorate the room. When it was finished, John came in with some linen and said, "You all's freshmans, ain't yo'?" and then departed with a knowing smile on his black face. For the decorations were distinctive; a senior could have drawn conclusions even more comprehensive than the janitor's. Freddy had chosen the wall opposite the door with an eye to the possibilities of the broad mantelpiece, which he had embellished with a collection of miscel-laneous objects, including a copper chafing-dish, a pottery tobacco-jar, a nickel alarm-clock, a small cloisonné vase, a glaring red poster of the Evil One surrounded by a group of sophisticated young women, and a print of the "Mona Lisa." Above this exhibition he hung a tennis net trimmed with an armful of souvenir dance pro-grams. Along the molding he strung a line of actresses' photographs, clipped from a theatrical magazine. He filled the vacant spaces with cartoons that had been reproduced in the annual of the academy he had attended the year before.

Phil gave the place of honor in the center of his wall to the framed photographs of his father and mother. The high school graduating class, each proud member sternly displaying the self-consciousness characteristic of this pinnacle of educational achievement, occupied an important position directly under Mr. and Mrs. Jennings. The picture of a girls' club and a dozen sepia prints of familiar masterpieces, done in passe-partout by Mrs. Jennings, completed the impression. Freddy sniffed at the result when he had finished a pleased survey of his own riotous handi-work, and asked his cousin if he did not fear he had overdone the thing. Then he followed John downstairs. He had not improved.

A freshman needs a long time to empty his trunk, if he is an orderly person and wants to find nooks and corners for the disposal of the bushels of perfectly useless things he has brought with him. If not, he pitches the heap of left-overs into his closet—Freddy's closet already contained a heterogeneous mass. Phil had just discovered a top shelf for his superfluous shoes and hats when the postman brought him a letter from his father, with a note from his mother enclosed. He read them both without smiling. There was nothing to smile about.

"It is strange that this offer should have come so soon after you left," his father's letter concluded. "I forgot to say that Halderman's secretary rushed down to the station to see you, but missed the train. As you had decided some time ago to take up this work if you could get it, I wished to notify you at once. Of course, you know I am not thinking of the financial side of it, but I believe it would do you more good than college. You know the opportuni-ties with Halderman are very exceptional. It's a capital beginning for a young man. However, you are to decide for yourself."

His mother's note was quite unlike her ordinarily calm and gentle letters. It concerned Freddy. Freddy's mother had been weeping about her boy ever since he left. She had confessed, hysterically, that he was not what he seemed to be—in fact, he was inclined to be wild and reckless. He smoked cigarettes and said strange things in his sleep. He had come home one night in a very queer condition. His mother feared it was beer.

"Phil, dear," Mrs. Jennings wrote, "do something to stop him before it is too late. We know your influence over him. Be with him as much as possible. Remember, Phil, it will be worth while."

Phil seriously doubted this last assertion, and also the necessity for missionary work. But anyhow, he decided, he would observe Freddy more closely, and if he had been going it too fast, he might do something about it.

His father's letter had sent unhappy thrills over his freshman being. It was not pleasant to get that kind of advice on his first day at college, even though he knew his father would not insist upon his accepting the offer from Halderman. Phil threw the letters into the drawer of his study-table. Just now he wanted to explore the campus.

He wanted to get the lay of the wide network of cement walks and find out for himself where his classes would be held. He could remember easily enough on which floors of Cobb his courses would come, but he had no idea what the rooms would look like. And he had been told that there were a lot of museums in which you could stroll around for hours without beginning to exhaust their mysteries. Those queer stone benches by the walks had looked interesting, too.

As he was very innocent, he did not know that it is contrary to the rules of sociability for a good-looking freshman to wander alone about the campus on opening day. He was just sauntering slowly away from Hitchcock when three youths, approaching arm in arm, hailed him.

"You are Jennings, aren't you?" asked one of them, whom Phil recognized as the fellow that had come into the registration room in the morning, apparently searching for some one. He seemed so sure of his man that he did not wait for Phil's answer.

"I heard you were here—heard it from Dean Jackson," he explained; "and I looked up your room number. No, thanks, we can't go up," as Phil turned and was about to invite them in. "My name is Taylor, and I want you to meet Wallace and Norton here. Hope we're not keeping you from an engagement."

"No, I was not going any place in particular. Glad you came," Phil answered.

"Certainly, we're not detaining you," agreed the one introduced as Wallace, gravely smoothing his red hair. "We're just holding you up. You can't get away when you're surrounded on three sides, like an archipelago, can you?"

"An archipelago is not surrounded on three sides, Red," said Norton, the stocky, earnest-faced fellow. "That's an isthmus or a plateau or something."

"Some day the 'profs' are going to get on to those fellows," laughed Taylor. "They ought to take a tonic for their minds, if they have any such organs."

"The mind is not an organ, Albert. Is it, Jennings?" appealed the red-headed one.

Phil admitted his ignorance of the point in question. He thought it strange that he should be discussing geographical and physiological problems with three young men that he had never seen until a moment before.

"Can you dine with us at the Rho house this evening, Jennings?" asked Taylor. "I hope you can."

"I'll drop in at your room and pick you up," Wallace volunteered.

"Thanks, I'll come, and I'll find it all right myself," Phil said. "Don't bother to call for me."

Taylor wrote the address of the Rho house on a card, and the three fellows shook hands with Phil and rushed into Snell Hall.

Halfway to Cobb, Phil met Freddy, skipping joyously along toward the room with a stubby-bodied, red-cheeked little fellow, who seemed to be telling a remarkable experience of some sort. Freddy was slapping him on the back and screaming appreciation.

"Phil, shake hands with Mr. Blythe. Blythe, this is Jennings, my cousin," Freddy said as they came up, in the courteous tone he always employed when he felt superior. "You've heard me speak of Tommy Blythe that I prepped with? Well, this is Blythe."

This proud identification of the stubby boy seemed to please him quite as thoroughly as it did Freddy. He chuckled delightedly and admitted that he was indeed the very fellow, but he hoped Ball had not told all there was to tell. He frowned darkly and shook his head at the mere recollection of these awful deeds. Evidently he regarded himself as a dangerous man. But his eyes were so round and blue, and his other features so fair and guileless that Phil was not much affected by his efforts to create the illusion of horrid debauchery, even when he lighted a long, gold-tipped cigarette and puffed at it savagely. The gorgeousness of Tommy's raiment, too, was merely youthful; a real desperado would have wept at the buckles on the shoes and the cut of the trousers. Phil noticed a small button in the left lapel of his coat. Freddy was making signs for him just to look at it.

"Tommy wants us to go over to the Phi Tau house to dinner tonight," Freddy announced, accenting the Greek letters broadly. "Tommy is a Phi Tau pledge. I accepted for you, of course. I'll see you at the room at six o' clock."

"The Rhos—too bad, too bad," lamented Tommy, when Phil told him of his previous appointment. "Because you'd have had a good time at our house. I'm afraid the Rhos are slow." It was fortunate for Tommy Blythe that his Phi Tau seniors did not hear this; they might have disciplined him.

"Well, come to lunch tomorrow then, Jennings," he added affably. "All right, Jennings. See you tomorrow, Jennings."

Phil looked back over his shoulder and saw the two of them skipping along past Snell and punching each other's ribs in the joy of their reunion. He was glad Freddy had found a mate; later he was not certain about that. He walked on, stopping occasionally to take in the sweep of the campus and the different views of the buildings. When he reached Cobb, he thought he would see how it felt to sit on the attractive stone bench in front of the entrance. Several fellows were lounging on it, chatting familiarly. Phil sat down on the edge, next the walk. No one had told him that he must not do this.

The nearest fellow, who had been watching the freshman, slouched forward.

"I beg a thousand pardons, young man, but I can't recall your face, though I may have heard the name," he said. "Let me see. Smith, perhaps?"

The stranger was very insolent, Phil thought, but he gave his last name.

"Oh, it's Jennings, is it?" the tall one ejaculated. "He says his name is Jennings," he announced to the others. "Willy Jennings, I suppose? No? Philip—how careless."

He turned again and loudly informed the rest of the group that they were mistaken if they imagined the freshman's name was

Willy, because it was Philly—Philly Jennings or Jenny Phillips, as they preferred.

"Didn't the people in your town ever hear of the 'C' Bench, Philly?" the fellow sadly inquired. "No? Well, the people on the 'C' Bench never heard of your town, either, so there you are."

Phil flashed. He could feel a hot streak across the back of his neck. He resented the attack, but he knew it was because he was a freshman, and he thought he should not be "fresh." The other fellows had not laughed. They looked rather bored and they told the bully about it.

"Dry up, you Blacky!" and "Oh, how funny," and "Sass him back, freshman," they called, and then resumed their conversation as if nothing had happened. One of them, who had started to leave, came up and said, "Freshmen are not allowed to sit on this bench, that's all." And when Phil slid off the seat and started away, the fellow caught up with him.

"Blacky was funny three times today, but it gets tiresome," he said. "The 'C' Bench is for upper-classmen, but there's no sense in Blacky's method of enforcing the rule. By the way, my name's Harding. I suppose you're kind of lonesome. Are you?"

"A little bit," Phil admitted. Everybody seemed to know that he was a freshman.

"I'll tell you, come over to my fraternity house to dinner and get acquainted," Harding suggested, as if that clever idea had just struck him with much force. He seemed disappointed when he learned of the Rho date, but said they might as well stroll over anyway, for "a pipeful" before dinner. The freshman agreed. He began to wonder slightly at the repeated offers of hospitality, and the extreme pleasure everybody seemed to have in his company. You see, he hadn't prepped with Freddy, who had belonged to a fraternity at the academy and consequently knew all about college life. But he had heard of a thing called rushing, and he knew he was experiencing it when he had been in the Zeta Mu house about a minute.

The Zeta Mus were obviously on their best behavior. They treated the freshman with such marked deference, and hung so eagerly upon his few words that anybody would have known it. Each man wrung his hand and said, in the same fervent tone of voice, that he was delighted to see him. Four or five fellows who had been tousling one another's hair in the next room, ran upstairs and combed themselves and ran down again. They also were delighted.

Somebody asked Phil if he had registered yet, and as the freshman seemed to appear interested in that subject and said that he
should have to study the next day, the Zeta Mus suddenly began an
animated discussion of the latest entrance requirements. The Zeta
Mus believed in this system. Shortly before, they had been debating
the relative merits of two brands of imported beer with a freshman
who lived in Chicago and was very wise.

A pale, bespectacled young man, named Sober Rawlstone,
immediately attached himself to Phil, led him into a corner on the
pretext of showing him the house, and began to talk earnestly. Phil
had been mentally ticketed and assigned to Class B in the Zeta Mu
rushing list. Class B always received Rawlstone's instant
attention.

"You know, Jennings," he said, "it is a pretty tough proposition
to get started in college—started right, I mean. Of course, study and
all that is a hardship sometimes, isn't it?"

Rawlstone wished to be perfectly sure that he was addressing a
youthful grind before he proceeded. Phil replied that he should not
exactly call it a hardship. He feared he might hurt the pale fellow's
feelings if he answered in another way.

"I remember my own case as a freshman," Rawlstone went on,
now certain of his ground. "I came here to study, and I had a
mighty hard time doing it at first. It was this fraternity and that
fraternity until I had just about enough time left to go to classes.
There are many distractions in college life, Jennings, and one has to
settle down quickly if one means to go after good grades."

So far, Rawlstone's remarks were true.

"And marks, my boy, are what count," he continued, lowering
his voice. "I happened to join this fraternity, and I'll never regret
it, because it gave an impetus to my work. I never could have got
through in some of the crowds here. Every fraternity has its own
specialty, you see, and ours is study, my boy—study. Some of the
crowds go in for athletics and some for the speed limit, but I think
you must have noticed how interested all our fellows are in their
classes. Now, that's all, but if you need any advice, come to me,
Jennings—come to me."

Phil thanked Rawlstone, who said, "Not at all—not at all," and
he was glad when it was time to leave for the Rho house; happier
still when the last of the Zeta Mus had wrung his hand and assured
him of the rapture his visit had afforded them.

Phil hoped the Rhos would not make him feel quite so uncomfortable as the Zeta Mus. He was quickly reassured. He almost forgot that he was a freshman before dinner had fairly begun.

Norton and Wallace and Taylor pounced upon him at once, demanding his version of "that archipelago story." Wallace said that Al and Norry had been accusing him of some fool remark about the thing, and that they had looked it up in the dictionary and therefore felt safe in " joshing" him. Al and Norry held that he had described an archipelago as a large body of fish partly submerged by the Gulf Stream. Whatever it was, Red was certain that Al and Norry had said it. He remembered distinctly that they had said it together in a very loud tone.

The dispute was renewed in the dining room when the deep-throated gong had sounded, and Phil lost every trace of embarrassment in trying to answer impartially, which was so impossible that it was amusing. Landon, who seemed to be older than the rest, advised him to withhold judgment in view of the serious nature of the accusations, and threatened them all with contempt of court if they objected to his ruling. Then Landon and Norton told stories, and when the dinner was finished and the fellows had drifted into the big living rooms, the other freshman guests as well as Phil seemed to be enjoying themselves hugely. Nobody seemed in the least impressed by the importance of the occasion.

Norry Norton sat with Phil on the front room window-seat for a time and talked about the generally excellent spirit of the incoming freshmen, and then he pointed out the pictures of the Rhos of former years and of the University athletic teams, which almost covered the walls of the three adjoining rooms. Phil noticed Norry in some of the football pictures, and asked him what position he played. He learned that Norry was only a sub. back and "very rotten," but that Ted Larned, the fellow singing a comic song over by the piano, was left tackle and a holy terror in an open field and could defeat an ordinary team alone, almost. Many other Rhos were in the track, baseball and football pictures, and in other groups, which were honor societies.

Ted Larned finished his comic song and announced that he had decided to entertain with his last and greatest effort, which would be worthy of tumultuous applause. It turned out to be a familiar college tune, and Phil and the other freshmen clapped their hands, though no one else did. The next was even better. All the fellows jumped up and crowded around the piano when the one they called Squib struck the opening chords, and they all sang, strong and loud, especially on the chorus. It was a song about Chicago. One of Norry's arms was around Phil's shoulders and his other one was around the shoulders of the fellow on the other side. They sang some more then, and when they stopped, they mauled each other about, and seemed livelier than ever.

There was a Rho bull-terrier, spotless white, but for a red spot on one side, where, Al Taylor said, the Phi Tau bulldog had been foolish enough to leave a tooth-mark. Bill had up and taught the Phi Tau pup what he should have known before. Bill permitted himself to be swung by the tail, trundled by the hind legs, and rolled downstairs. The freshmen considered him a wonder, and insisted upon a constant repetition of his limited program of tricks until he finally lost his manners and snapped at the strangely presumptuous little boys, who then turned their attention to the stunts and the buzz of talk.

Phil could not make up his mind just what the Rhos stood for. Rawlstone had said that each crowd specialized in something; but here, surely, were all sorts of fellows. Some seemed serious, and some rather irresponsible, and sometimes they seemed neither or both. Landon, now, must be quite important. Norton and Taylor had been asking him about certain problems of their own, and he had set them right at once. A moment later he had danced a jig with Red Wallace and engaged in a hot-hand competition with Grant and Hawkins, two of the Rho pledges. It was the same with the others. Phil thought these fellows were about the finest he had ever seen.

Stringer, one of the freshmen—the one that had sat beside him in the dean's office—supplied a great quantity of unrelated information regarding the Rho men. He told Phil, in the confidential stage whisper he had employed in pointing out the possibilities of the senior courses, that he had been "pumping" one of the other freshmen and had learned a lot. That big fellow Landon was called Bugs for short, and the very blond fellow was Pop Walters. The one playing the banjo was in the Dramatic Club, and about everything else there was. The skinny chap leaning against the wall was a wonder in the half-mile and the champion prep. runner of the state; he was only a freshman, but he could tear off a half in no time at all, and he had never been pushed. Morris, the one at the piano, was in the Blackfriars, and he made a "queen" of a girl—couldn't tell the difference.

"They're pretty fine fellows, I can tell you, aren't they!" Stringer whispered. "Don't you think it's great?"

"Yes, it is," said Phil, softly. He believed exactly as Stringer did. It *was* great. He thought about it all the way to his room, while Norry was walking home with him. He promised to come again—half a dozen times—and he would have made it even more if Norton had insisted.

Phil imagined he had learned a good deal that first day. When he saw that Freddy had not returned to the room, he got out his new writing paper and started to compose some home letters. He would tell his father that he had decided not to accept Halderman's offer. That would be easy enough. He would simply say that he liked college far too well to leave it now, impressing the fact that he was certain of getting a great deal out of it. That assurance might please his father—he had so carefully emphasized the necessity of securing full value at the University.

First, he intended to calm his mother's fears about Freddy. His aunt was just frightened by the silly stuff she had read about college life. Phil was fairly certain that his cousin's dissipations had not reached an alarming stage, despite the frequent hints of his dark deeds.

A noise in the hall disturbed him as he was beginning the letter to his mother. The door opened and Freddy came in, followed by Tommy Blythe. Both stood blinking at the light for a moment: Freddy, very pale of face and watery of eye, leaning listlessly against the wall; Tommy bracing his stubby body against a dirty piece of iron piping.

"Hello, fellows," Phil greeted them.

"Good evening, Jennings. How do you like my cane, eh?" said Tommy Blythe, bringing the section of heavy piping to the floor with a mighty and uncertain thump, perilously near Phil's toes.

"Good evening, Jennings. How do you like his cane, huh?" echoed Freddy.

"I could brain a man with that," observed Tommy, with another whack of his new toy that sent him sprawling to the floor.

"He could brain a man, he could brain a man," repeated Freddy in a very stupid tone, as he slid down beside Tommy. Both were smiling feebly.

"I thought, Freddy," mumbled Tommy, dwelling upon each word with grotesque gravity—"I really and truly understood that you were more of a tank."

He seemed dreadfully hurt over it. Phil thought he was going to weep.

"I said, Frederick, you old stiff, you," Tommy went on, with an attempt at a wink in Phil's direction—"I repeat that I was laboring under the delusion that your capacity was larger than seems to be the case."

Freddy did not hear this, because he was asleep. His head was in Tommy's lap. But Tommy did not notice it, and kept turning from side to side in a bewildered effort to find him.

"I hope you will not mind Freddy, Jennings," he said. "I think he has gone to bed without saying good night."

Tommy finally crawled to his feet, allowing Freddy's head to thump against the floor, and sat down in the Morris chair. He solemnly raised his right leg as high as he could, held it aloft with one hand while he unbuckled his shoe and threw it against the wall, and lowered the member to the floor. This accomplished, he repeated the process with the other leg.

"Now, I think I shall retire, if you will pardon the liberty of doing so," he said. "I feel quite sleepy, you know."

Phil might have enjoyed this spectacle at some other time. At this particular time, he did not. He got up and guided Tommy into Freddy's sleeping apartment. He dragged Freddy into the same room, took off his coat and trousers—there was a Phi Tau pledge-button in the coat lapel—and piled him into the narrow cot with Tommy, who was already asleep with his yellow head angelically resting on one of Mrs. Ball's drawn-work pillows.

Then he returned to the study-table and tore up the letter he had begun. He stood for a while looking out at the shining arc-lights dotting the campus. For the first time he saw them flicker and turn black.

II

Phil Jennings was merely an average freshman. He was not overinclined toward the virtuous—which is much the same thing; and he had a fair sense of proportion. He did not blubber about Freddy Ball's first exhibition of wickedness, chiefly because he was disgusted. The next morning, when he had thought it over, he wrote his mother that he would be responsible. He really believed Freddy would not do it again, but in this he cruelly misjudged his cousin. That night Freddy was carried upstairs by a cabman. The following two nights he did not return at all, but arrived later with a patch over one eye and a silly walk. This seemed to indicate his intention to do the thing properly.

Late in the week Phil sat down and took stock of the situation, which he imagined he saw quite clearly. He had given his word that he would shelter and protect a young idiot who happened to be his cousin and who was trying hard to go to the devil. It was to be one of those crazy missionary stunts. He laughed a little grimly at the remembrance of Freddy's marked indisposition that morning.

Then there were the fraternities. Since Freddy had jumped at the Phi Tau bid because Tommy Blythe had told him to, it looked as if he should have to give up the Rhos—and that meant Norry Norton and Al Taylor and Red Wallace. Roberts, the Phi Tau junior, had told him that it would seem strange if he went with any other crowd than his cousin's. Evidently Roberts had not noticed that he and Freddy were not exactly chummy.

Phil had seen a dozen fraternities. He had almost been made to feel that he was important. He had met so many fellows that he could not begin to remember their names. Most of them were fine, especially the Rhos. The Zeta Mus had given a dance, at which a girl had related how studious and serious the Zeta Mus were. The same young woman, having consumed large quantities of Phi Tau macaroons and lemon-ice at a similar function given by that organization, had dropped broad hints concerning the surpassing opportunities for a good time within the Phi Tau circle. The girl had a poor memory for faces.

The Rhos treated him as one of themselves, and he felt he would rather join them than do anything else he knew. He politely declined the bids of Zeta Mu and of several other crowds. He told Roberts, the Phi Tau junior, that he could not possibly decide for two weeks, and that he could not accept any rushing invitations in the meantime. He told Norry Norton the same thing—and that hurt. He thought it was a queer coincidence when he received a letter informing him that Halderman must have his final answer on the very day he had set for his fraternity decision. But he did not know until afterward just how queer it was.

The boy began to feel that something was wrong with his head. He could not figure out just why he was so confused about Freddy and the Phi Taus and the Rhos and the University. He spent one whole morning sitting on a bench in front of the German Building in Jackson Park, gazing into the cloud-banks far out in the lake. He did not go to the first football games, which proved that something *was* wrong.

The next week he stayed in his room as much as he could. He hurried to and from his classes and cut chapel because he didn't want to see people. The rushing fell off, and he thought the Rhos were cool because they let him alone, when they were only giving him time. He saw Al Taylor and the bunch swing past Hitchcock on their way to one of the games, and then he was certain they didn't care. And when he heard the Phi Taus coming upstairs, he dropped out of the north window and ran for a Fifty-fifth Street car. The Phi Taus could not understand it; neither could Phil.

After this he tried to concentrate his attention on English 1 and to persuade himself that Freddy was improving. His English themes on college life were such curious mixtures of misinformation and youthful pessimism that the instructor confined his written criticism to a large interrogation-point and a sympathetic inquiry about the condition of his stomach. So the faculty were just like the rest!

Little Stringer slapped him on the back one day and asked him much the same thing, only he said "gizzard" instead of stomach.

"I haven't seen you in the devil of a time," said Stringer. "You see I've gone Zeta Mu. Isn't it strange how fellows will get separated?" And Phil was mightily grateful for the little fellow's friendship. That happened the day before he was to see the Phi Taus and the Rhos.

An inspiration came to him next morning in German class—an inspiration that was not strictly according to the freshman code. It is quite correct for freshmen to exchange advice and counsel on certain topics; on the best interlinear translation of Livy or the various methods of prolonging a recitation until the bell rings. These things must be learned, of course. It is not, however, considered conventional to wrestle with a fellow-freshman's ideas on temperance and cuts, and such things. These are a fellow's own business. So far, Phil had observed the proprieties. In fact, it had not occurred to him that he might gain time by discussing Freddy's status with that young man himself. Phil was nervous that morning, and in a slightly uncharitable state of mind toward his cousin, who had used vividly picturesque language about being awakened at eight o'clock. He shifted about in his seat so much that he annoyed the fellow in the next chair, who was trying to copy down every word of the instructor's remarks concerning the *umlaut*.

Freddy, arrayed in his fuzzy red dressing-gown, with his feet on the table, his hands back of his head and a cigarette in his month, was taking his ease in the Morris chair when Phil entered. Phil removed his coat, put on his fuzzy blue dressing-gown, and sat down on the other side of the table. Both of them looked very young and good.

"Have you been to your classes, Freddy?" asked Phil. He meant to feel around, and he fully intended to be decent about it.

"No, Philly." Freddy's tones were sweet and low and his facial expression absolutely seraphic. Mrs. Ball might have beamed her motherly pride, if it had not been for the cigarette.

"You should have gone to History. We had a quiz," Phil said, in a louder tone. He did not care for Freddy's angelic fits.

"Did we?" Freddy stretched his legs luxuriously and emitted a yawn.

"Yes, we did," and Phil's voice rose; "but I don't suppose it makes any difference to you. You've cut everything for the last week and a half."

"Well, what of it?" demanded Freddy, sitting up suddenly. "Whose affair is that?"

"Oh, it's not mine," Phil returned. "It's yours partly, and partly it's not. I simply wondered how you felt about it, for reasons of my own."

Freddy arose in wrath. "What do you mean by that, you tin saint?" he exclaimed. "What reasons?"

"Shut up, Fred. Shut up and sit down. I'll tell you now what I was leading up to, and then you can go ahead and make a little fool of yourself if you want to."

Phil had not been leading up to anything, as a matter of fact. He simply was too excited to stop and the words kept coming. Freddy, surprised at first by his quiet cousin's show of temper, stared in a sort of astonished disbelief at this uncomplimentary broadside, and obediently seated himself.

"I'll tell you," Phil went on. "I'll tell you, you little fool. You've set out to be an imitation bad man—you and that crazy little sport of a Blythe. You've been trying to live up to the reputation you think you've got, I suppose. And all the time I've been drooling around the campus like a damned sissy, waiting for you to quit it. I thought you might stop, you always get so sick after your baby drunks."

This high and mighty attitude was not just like Phil Jennings. Freddy continued to stare.

"I might have known you wouldn't have the sense to stop." Phil stood up and walked over to Freddy's chair. "That shows what a fool I've made of myself. Now go on out and sport around again. I'm through with it. I'm through with college. I'm through with you, you pink-and-white little idiot."

Freddy arose once more, and his fuzzy red dressing-gown rubbed against Phil's blue one. "Pink-and-white idiot" was too much!

"Take that back, you—you sneaking preacher," he roared.

Phil did not take it back. There was but one thing to do. They started at once. Phil's left arm guarded off the blow that Freddy aimed at his face, and the two grappled. There wasn't any science in it—just outraged youth on both sides. The hand-embroidered dressing-gowns tripped the warriors, and they fell heavily, struggling and scuffling halfway across the room. They rolled and kicked and punched and mopped the floor with each other. Once Freddy had Phil on his back and all but vanquished, but he wriggled loose. Then Phil pinned Freddy prone for an instant while he got his breath.

One of Freddy's windmill sweeps of arm caught the tobacco-jar on the mantelpiece, and it crashed to the hearth with the chafing-dish and the "Mona Lisa." Only the tall, leering devil and the sophisticated young women were left, mute spectators of the combat. From across the room, Mr. and Mrs. Jennings and the graduating class looked down serenely.

It was not very edifying. There was blood where Freddy's fist had collided with Phil's nose, and there was a rapidly swelling, bluish protuberance above Freddy's left eye, where the study-table had interfered. Finally, in a flying, whirling rush from Freddy's bedroom, where the battle had swung for a moment, the tail of the fuzzy red dressing-gown caught on a sharp metal corner and held its owner fast, tugging in impotent rage a yard from the prostrate Phil, who had tumbled headlong on the slippery floor. There came a tap at the door. The warriors still glared. Roberts, the Phi Tau junior, walked into the room.

It took Phil just two minutes to wash his face and leave. He was quivering all over. He walked away from the campus as fast as he could and out into Washington Park. He must have gone for miles, doubling in his tracks along the graveled paths, for his legs were tired when he looked up and saw the gigantic red brick chimney of the power house rising near. He stopped at the corner drug store on his way back, and bought some stationery and a book of stamps. He circled past Hitchcock and ran up to the fourth floor of Cobb and began to write. When he had finished the letter and put it in his pocket, he did not feel so much relieved as he had supposed he would. This may have been because he had done without luncheon.

He had a disagreeable feeling that he was deserting. But, surely, he reflected, he had good cause to leave the place. What had the big, cold, gray University done for him? Had he received full value? And what had come of his fine ideas about saving Freddy Ball? Whose fault was it? Most of all he tried to believe that he had kept faith on that score. He had failed to fit into college and he couldn't stay. The boy with the healthy freshman brain gazed at the weird mathematical diagrams on the blackboard and thought these foggy thoughts until the dusk crept in at the windows. It really was foolish of him to miss luncheon.

The lights were beginning to twinkle from every part of the campus when he came out of the door of Cobb. Some one shouted his name. It was Roberts, the Phi Tau.

"What made you dig away so suddenly, Jennings?" he called. "I wasn't going to choke you. I was after that lively young relative of yours."

"Freddy? Did you choke him?"

"I certainly did. Rammed a bunch of official communications down his throat. And now I'm going to tell you about it because I think you ought to hear. You see, I know what the rough house was about." Roberts seemed to think it was funny. "You needn't look incredulous," he laughed, "but Freddy has been seeing things. He's been very abject—said some sentimental things about his family. He's taken the pledge, has Freddy. Incidently, Tommy Blythe has followed suit. He's perfectly harmless now, and he doesn't care who knows it.

"I was calling in a semi-official capacity this morning when I interrupted the bout," continued Roberts, "I had a little present for Freddy in the shape of some light yellow envelopes. I didn't like to see them sticking in the junior rack, so I lifted them. Down in everything, of course, including Gym. and Public Spouting. It was an awful shock, especially the letter from the dean. Deany dropped a gentle hint about ordering the hearse to stop for Freddy. Said he and Freddy didn't seem to be getting on together. He was scared stiff—Freddy, not the dean. Tommy came up a little later with a duplicate set of correspondence, and then it was mostly remorse on both sides.

"I never attended such a soul-baring clinic. You see, they are afraid their mothers will hear about it. They told me everything, because they think I've been an awful sport myself. There was nothing very terrible—just too many steins, but they believe they have gone the pace."

"You think this sudden conversion will last, Roberts?" Phil asked doubtfully.

"Last? It's got to last or it's good-by to those children, and they know it. You see, Jennings, it works automatically. Those yellow envelopes exercise a restraining influence that's positively delightful. Better than a million preachments. You can't stay here without grubbing a little bit. It's a case of buck up or get out."

They had stopped at the broad intersection of the walks beside Kent Laboratory.

"And it's not only the University that disciplines naughty freshmen," Roberts added. "The Phi Tau fraternity thinks it has something to do with that. We don't need any floaters of that kind. Oh, don't worry about Freddy. He's trapped for a while, and when he gets straight with the 'U,' maybe he can go and commit his crimes quietly and circumspectly, without bothering other people. He'll be able to take care of himself then. And now, Jennings, I want to ask you how you feel on the fraternity question."

The meaning of Roberts' news had been soaking into Phil gradually,

"And now about yourself, Jennings."

Phil knew what was coming. The Phi Tau extended the bid in a few earnest words. When he had finished, he said:

"Well, is it all right, Jennings?"

Phil had no need to figure out an answer. He knew how he felt. He wished Norry Norton instead of Roberts had asked that question. And then he realized with a start that even that could make no difference—now.

"I can't accept, Roberts," he began. "I—"

Over by the Reynolds Club a sharp whistle sounded, high and musical and clear—the call of the Rhos. It was answered by another and then another somewhere in the dark.

"I can't, Roberts," he repeated simply. "That's all I can tell you. I can't do it, but I want to thank you for what you've done and—and it was mighty fine of you."

Roberts was genuinely grieved. He did not repeat his invitation, because there was something in the freshman's voice that he knew was final. Also, he had heard that whistle, and he was looking straight into the boy's eyes when it sounded. They shook hands. Phil was standing alone in the shadow when the Rhos bumped into him. There were three of them—the same three he had met the first day at college. His freshman heart labored strangely under the letter in his pocket.

"Phil Jennings, where have you been!" Norton demanded.

"Been looking under the sidewalks for you," said Al Taylor.

"And up the trees," added Wallace.

Norton and Taylor put their arms in Phil's and dragged him along with them across the campus.

"You're going to dinner with us," sang Red, dancing along in front of him. "And then to the mass meeting. Big doings."

And now, for some reason, the City Gray seemed different—much different. It was beautiful, Phil thought; more beautiful than he could have believed, and certainly not cold, nor heartless. Even the breeze that blew in his eyes was intimate and friendly. Lights were shining from many windows now; from Cobb and Haskell and Walker and Law, and from the Women's Quadrangles beyond the stretch of Sleepy Hollow and the sunken tennis courts. It was good to look at these things, and it was good to feel the tug of arms locked in his and to hear the soft, low snatches of the Chicago songs the fellows were humming. Phil's throat tightened a little. He did not know why.

He learned a few things about his University during dinner hour, when he sat again at the upper-class table. Landon had been carrying on a spirited discussion of college topics with a fellow named Destyn, who was visiting him. There had been various comparisons, and Destyn was not convinced. So they introduced the question at dinner.

"But, good Lord, Landon, you haven't the traditions," Destyn insisted.

"I know, Destyn, I know all that," returned Landon. "Your argument is beautifully familiar. It's like greeting an old friend. Even the freshmen are acquainted with it."

"I suppose you have a fine rebuttal cooked up, too," Destyn smiled. "Now crush me with it."

"No, that's not the way we do it," said Landon. "We haven't any stock rebuttals. We don't try to impress our antiquity upon people, Destyn. It's true, we *are* young—the college part of us. I suppose that's what you mean." He spoke slowly and musingly. The others were listening.

"No, Destyn, we haven't, strictly speaking, all of the customs that were handed to you when you entered college. Some of our fathers went to the Old University, but even they didn't leave us much in that line. I think they had a rather hard time getting that sort of poetry out of Chicago as it was then—the city's waking up to lots of things now. And still, my father comes out here on Alumni Day and speaks his piece and gets about a thousand years younger.

"You see, some of us have helped to make what we call our traditions—that's putting it rather loosely, perhaps. Why, I saw the very stones of Hitchcock piled together only a short time before I came to college—when I was in prep. school. There wasn't any Mandel Hall then, or even a Mitchell Tower, or Hutchinson, or a Reynolds Club. There wasn't any 'C' Bench. I saw that made, and I saw the Law building go up. I planted some of the ivy you admired today.

"We haven't had time to lay back and think of the past—of our past, I mean. We've been building all the time. There's something in creating these things, you know—yes, there's something in making them, Destyn."

One of the other seniors took up the argument. An old grad. spoke rather heavily of the "development of the Chicago personality," and one of the freshmen, who was dying to hear his own voice again, piped in something about the Three-Quarters Club. Destyn was not impressed by all this, of course, because he had not intended to be. But to Phil it was new and strange and fine. Even the football parley that followed seemed less important.

"What are the prospects for tomorrow's game?" the grad. asked, and that started it.

"Really, I hate to say," Red spoke up. "It seems so brutal. We will annihilate the poor things, of course."

Red's view of the case was slightly overdrawn, the others thought. The "poor things" were Chicago's strongest rivals, and it was a matter of general concern that the game had been scheduled for an earlier date than usual. Three or four fellows protested against Red's statement.

"The Old Man doesn't seem to think so," remarked Taylor. "I'm sure he'd feel more cheerful if he knew the real facts."

Red fixed a discouraged glance upon Al. "You're going to see a different team tomorrow," he declared. "And after it's over, you will have an opportunity to drag in your favorite poetry about Dicky Lee."

"What's in the air?" "What about Dicky Lee?" demanded the Rhos. Everybody wanted to hear the news about the great half-back.

"A new formation with Lee all over the field, that's all. The best we ever had, and it's going to make history. It's a pity we have to spring it tomorrow, but it's got to come out. It's simply the last word in the Old Man's football language."

Only the football squad and a few favored ones knew of the play. Red had coaxed the news from Ted Larned on the solemn understanding that he would "keep his mouth shut for once." Larned and Norton never told the secrets of the team.

"The yell-fest is going to be in Kent tonight—early. Better move," Red suggested, and the fellows hurried for their wraps.

Phil was eager to see this man Lee. It might be his last chance! The fellows were all talking about him as they walked across the campus.

Phil asked Taylor if he thought Lee could really win the game with the new play.

"Dicky Lee and the Old Man together can do about anything," Taylor told him. "As sure as we're walking into Kent, Dicky Lee will win, if what Red says is true. And, Phil, I want you to stick with me after the mass meeting. I want to talk to you. Norry and I were going to see you before dinner, but he had to rush over to meet the team, you know."

They pushed through the crowd that filled the wide stairway inside the doors of Kent Theater, and found standing room behind the last row of seats, high up against the rear wall of the sloping auditorium. The band was playing—no other music is like it. Fellows were sitting in the middle aisle and leaning against the side walls. One part of the hall was occupied by the girls. Phil could look down over their nodding heads to the stage, where four fellows with megaphones were holding an excited conference. One of them had just rushed in with half a dozen others, who had mixed into the mob. The crowd cheered for them just because it wanted to yell.

In less than a minute a confused murmur was running through the hall, and the tone of it was ominous. "Don't you believe it!" "Dicky Lee?" "Yes, Dicky Lee." Phil wondered what Lee had done now.

"What is it, Miles?" Red asked the boy in front of him.

"Lee is hurt, they say. Ankle smashed."

"Did you hear that, Al?" Red asked in a frightened whisper. "Did you hear that? Dicky Lee's ankle's broken."

Others were asking the same thing in the same scared voice. Kent became almost quiet.

"The team!" shouted one of the cheer-leaders.

Everybody stood up. A big fellow stepped through the stage entrance into the light, and the noise broke. The sharp, staccato battle cry of Chicago rang out again and again. It was repeated with "the team" on the end, fast and strong, while the big fellow and his followers stalked to their seats. The cheer-leaders waved their megaphones wildly. And the crowd was watching the entrance. Everybody strained necks and pushed and jumped while they yelled, trying to catch the first glimpse of Dicky Lee. Ten of the regulars and a small group of subs. had come through the dark hole. Maybe Dicky would come last, with the Old Man. There was a second or two of suspense, and the Old Man walked in, at the back of his football children—alone.

"Where is he?" the thousand whispered to themselves and their neighbors.

At that particular instant Dicky Lee the Great was cursing his stars in his room, where he had been carried after that soul-sickening snap in the last minute of practice.

Phil heard Red and Al exchange excited exclamations:

"That means Norry."

"He'll play Norry."

It was the first thing the crowd thought of. The eyes of the thousand were fixed on Norry Norton. Norry Norton, sub. right half! The cheering continued, but it had to be worked up by the leaders. At a sign from one of these, the noise stopped. A young fellow— Phil recognized him as an instructor—stepped out and faced the crowd.

"You want to know what has happened, and the boys want me to tell you," he said. "You may know already. Lee is out of it. He fractured his ankle on the field this evening after the rest of the men had left the field. He can't play tomorrow, but we'll have eleven men on Marshall Field, and we'll all be back of them. Just one more word. Norton will play right half. It's pretty sudden and it's a hard job, but if you know Norton—"

"Who is Norton?" somebody yelled, and the thousand greeted him wildly and stamped their feet on the floor as Norry was pushed into the center of the stage.

"I can't play like Dicky Lee," Norry began. "I can't play like the other fellows. But—"

Norry's voice was husky and his lips twitched. The crowd rose to him. The freshmen, who scarcely knew who he was, almost yelled their heads off, because the others were going mad about him. Norry stood there for a moment while the storm of crashing sound came down to him. He turned slowly then and found his seat. But the thousand had not finished. They forgot to save their throats for the game. They forgot everything but the boy sitting there beside the Old Man. They gave Norry Norton his due.

"Norry's worked three years for that team," Al Taylor shouted in Phil's ear. "Three long years he's worked like a Turk and sat on the side-lines, and he didn't expect any glory."

Phil didn't hear what the next speaker said. "Three long years he's worked like a Turk!" Al's phrase rang in his head. Three long years without any glory! Three long years subbing for Dicky Lee. Three years working for the "U." It went to his heart like a challenge. It was what he had waited for. And because a freshman is a noise-producing animal, he vented his feelings in a shout that was drowned in the roar of a great, cumulative volume of sound. They were yelling for the Old Man now, and he was looking up at them with a quiet smile on his face—a smile that was as young and happy as Norry's, for strangely enough, the Old Man was not old at all.

Probably you know the rest of the things Phil saw and heard. He has not forgotten them. He never will.

When it was over, he clambered down from his high place and joined in the stumbling rush for the doors. He was grasping the shoulders of a little fellow in front, who was very good at worming his way through tiny holes. Some shoving freshmen plumped him fair into the arms of a fellow in the hall, where the mob was breaking. The fellow was laughing and so was Phil. They both said "Wow!" at the impact, and looked up. Phil Jennings and Freddy Ball were laughing in each other's faces. They kept on laughing.

When they had found Al Taylor and Roberts, the Phi Tau, and Tommy Blythe, the repentant, the five of them strolled out of Kent, as far as the crossing of the walks. Al and Phil went on together.

"And now we'll talk it over," Taylor said. "We can't see Norry tonight."

He stopped to drop an envelope into the letter-box by Cobb. Phil's hand went suddenly to his inside pocket. He drew out a forgotten letter, stamped and addressed, and looked at it in the glow of the campus lights. Al held open the slot of the green box, invitingly.

"No, Al," said the freshman. "I'm going to keep it—as a curiosity."

Sometimes, when freshmen were present, the fellows would let Phil tell about the mass meeting that woke him up. One of the freshmen was always sure to pipe, "Did Norton win the game?" Then everybody would grin, because Norry's run is part of history.

FROM A TO Z (1912)

Susan Glaspell

THUS HAD ANOTHER ideal tumbled to the rubbish heap! She seemed to be breathing the dust which the newly fallen had stirred up among its longer dead fellows. Certainly she was breathing the dust from somewhere.

During her senior year at the university, when people would ask: "And what are you going to do when you leave school, Miss Willard? " she would respond with anything that came to hand, secretly hugging to her mind that idea of getting a position in a publishing house. Her conception of her publishing house was finished about the same time as her class-day gown. She was to have a roll-top desk — probably of mahogany — and a big chair which whirled round like that in the office of the under-graduate dean. She was to have a little office all by herself, opening on a bigger office — the little one marked "Private." There were to be beautiful rugs — the general effect not unlike the library at the University Club — books and pictures and cultivated gentlemen who spoke often of Greek tragedies and the Renaissance. She was a little uncertain as to her duties, but had a general idea about getting down between nine and ten, reading the morning paper, cutting the latest magazine, and then "writing something."

Commencement was now four months past, and one of her professors had indeed secured for her a position in a Chicago "publishing house." This was her first morning and she was standing at the window looking down into Dearborn Street while the man who was to have her in charge was fixing a place for her to sit.

That the publishing house should be on Dearborn Street had been her first blow, for she had long located her publishing house on that beautiful stretch of Michigan Avenue which overlooked the lake. But the real insult was that this publishing house, instead of having a building, or at least a floor, all to itself, simply had a place penned off in a bleak, dirty building such as one who had done work in sociological research instinctively associated with a box factory. And the thing which fairly trailed her visions in the dust was that the partition penning them off did not extend to the ceiling, and the adjoining room being occupied by a patent medicine company, she was face to face with glaring endorsements of Dr. Bunting's Famous Kidney and Bladder Cure. Taken all in all there seemed little chance for Greek tragedies or the Renaissance.

The man who was "running things" — she buried her phraseology with her dreams — wore a skull cap, and his moustache dragged down below his chin. Just at present he was engaged in noisily pulling a most unliterary pine table from a dark corner to a place near the window. That accomplished, an ostentatious hunt ensued, resulting in the triumphant flourish of a feather duster. Several knocks at the table, and the dust of many months — perhaps likewise of many dreams — ascended to a resting place on the endorsement of Dr. Bunting's Kidney and Bladder Cure. He next produced a short, straight-backed chair which she recognised as brother to the one which used to stand behind their kitchen stove. He gave it a shake, thus delicately indicating that she was receiving special favours in this matter of an able-bodied chair, and then announced with brisk satisfaction: "So! Now we are ready to begin." She murmured a "Thank you," seated herself and her buried hopes in this chair which did not whirl round, and leaned her arms upon a table which did not even dream in mahogany.

In the *other* publishing house, one pushed buttons and uniformed menials appeared — noiselessly, quickly and deferentially. At this moment a boy with sandy hair brushed straight back in a manner either statesmanlike or clownlike — things were too involved to know which — shuffled in with an armful of yellow paper which he flopped down on the pine table. After a minute he returned with a warbled "Take Me Back to New York Town" and a paste-pot. And upon his third appearance he was practising gymnastics with a huge pair of shears, which he finally presented, grinningly.

There was a long pause, broken only by the sonorous voice of Dr. Bunting upbraiding someone for not having billed out that stuff to Apple Grove, and then the sandy-haired boy appeared bearing a large dictionary, followed by the man in the skull cap behind a dictionary of equal unwieldiness. These were set down on either side of the yellow paper, and he who was filling the position of cultivated gentleman pulled up a chair, briskly.

"Has Professor Lee explained to you the nature of our work?" he wanted to know.

"No," she replied, half grimly, a little humourously, and not far from tearfully, "he didn't — explain."

"Then it is my pleasure to inform you," he began, blinking at her importantly, "that we are engaged here in the making of a dictionary."

" A *dic* —?" but she swallowed the gasp in the laugh coming up to meet it, and of their union was born a saving cough.

"Quite an overpowering thought, is it not?" he agreed pleasantly. "Now you see you have before you the two dictionaries you will use most, and over in that case you will find other references. The main thing" — his voice sank to an impressive whisper — "is *not* to infringe the copyright. The publisher was in yesterday and made a little talk to the force, and he said that any one who handed in a piece of copy infringing the copyright simply employed that means of writing his own resignation. Neat way of putting it, was it not?"

"Yes, *wasn't* it — neat?" she agreed, wildly.

She was conscious of a man's having stepped in behind her and taken a seat at the table next hers. She heard him opening his dictionaries and getting out his paper. Then the man in the skull cap had risen and was saying genially: "Well, here is a piece of old Webster, your first 'take' — no copyright on this, you see, but you must modernise and expand. Don't miss any of the good words in either of these dictionaries. Here you have dictionaries, copy-paper, paste, and Professor Lee assures me you have brains — all the necessary ingredients for successful lexicography. We are to have some rules printed to-morrow, and in the meantime I trust I've made myself clear. The main thing" — he bent down and spoke it solemnly — "is *not* to infringe the copyright." With a cheerful nod he was gone, and she heard him saying to the man at the next table: "Mr. Clifford, I shall have to ask you to be more careful about getting in promptly at eight."

She removed the cover from her paste-pot and dabbled a little on a piece of paper. Then she tried the unwieldy shears on another piece of paper. She then opened one of her dictionaries and read studiously for fifteen minutes. That accomplished, she opened the other dictionary and purused it for twelve minutes. Then she took the column of "old Webster," which had been handed her pasted on a piece of yellow paper, and set about attempting to commit it to memory. She looked up to be met with the statement that Mrs. Marjory Van Luce De Vane, after spending years under the so-called best surgeons of the country, had been cured in six weeks by Dr. Bunting's Famous Kidney and Bladder Cure. She pushed the dictionaries petulantly from her, and leaning her very red cheek upon her hand, her hazel eyes blurred with tears of perplexity and resentment, her mouth drawn in pathetic little lines of uncertainty, looked over at the sprawling warehouse on the opposite side of Dearborn Street. She was just considering the direct manner of writing one's resignation — not knowing how to infringe the copyright — when a voice said: "I beg pardon, but I wonder if I can help you any?"

She had never heard a voice like that before. Or, *had* she heard it? — and where? She looked at him, a long, startled gaze. Something made her think of the voice the prince used to have in long-ago dreams. She looked into a face that was dark and thin and — different. Two very dark eyes were looking at her kindly, and a mouth which was a baffling combination of things to be loved and things to be deplored was twitching a little, as though it would like to join the eyes in a smile, if it dared.

Because he saw both how funny and how hard it was, she liked him. It would have been quite different had he seen either one without the other.

"You can tell me how *not* to infringe the copyright," she laughed. "I'm not sure that I know what a copyright is."

He laughed — a laugh which belonged with his voice. "Mr. Littletree isn't as lucid as he thinks he is. I've been here a week or so, and picked up a few things you might like to know."

He pulled his chair closer to her table then and gave her a lesson in the making of copy. Edna Willard was never one-half so attractive as when absorbed in a thing which someone was showing her how to do. Her hazel eyes would widen and glisten with the joy of comprehending; her cheeks would flush a deeper pink with the coming of new light, her mouth would part in a child-like way it had forgotten to outgrow, her head would nod gleefully in token that she understood, and she had a way of pulling at her wavy hair and making it more wavy than it had been before. The man at the next table was a long time in explaining the making of a dictionary. He spoke in low tones, often looking at the figure of the man in the skull cap, who was sitting with his back to them, looking over copy. Once she cried, excitedly: "Oh — I *see!*" and he warned, "S — h!" explaining, "Let him think you got it all from him. It will give you a better stand-in." She nodded, appreciatively, and felt very well acquainted with this kind man whose voice made her think of something — called to something — she did not just know what.

After that she became so absorbed in lexicography that when the men began putting away their things it was hard to realise that the morning had gone. It was a new and difficult game, the evasion of the copyright furnishing the stimulus of a hazard.

The man at the next table had been watching her with an amused admiration. Her child-like absorption, the way every emotion from perplexity to satisfaction expressed itself in the poise of her head and the pucker of her face, took him back over years emotionally barren to the time when he too had those easily stirred enthusiasms of youth. For the man at the next table was far from young now. His mouth had never quite parted with boyishness, but there was more white than black in his hair, and the lines about his mouth told that time, as well as forces more aging than time, had laid heavy hand upon him. But when he looked at the girl and told her with a smile that it was time to stop work, it was a smile and a voice to defy the most tell-tale face in all the world.

During her luncheon, as she watched the strange people coming and going, she did much wondering. She wondered why it was that so many of the men at the dictionary place were very old men; she wondered if it would be a good dictionary — one that would be used in the schools; she wondered if Dr. Bunting had made a great deal of money, and most of all she wondered about the man at the next table whose voice was like — like a dream which she did not know that she had dreamed.

When she had returned to the straggling old building, had stumbled down the narrow, dark hall and opened the door of the big bleak room, she saw that the man at the next table was the only one who had returned from luncheon. Something in his profile made her stand there very still. He had not heard her come in, and he was looking straight ahead, eyes half closed, mouth set — no unsurrendered boyishness there now. Wholly unconsciously she took an impulsive step forward. But she stopped, for she saw, and felt without really understanding, that it was not just the moment's pain, but the revealed pain of years. Just then he began to cough, and it seemed the cough, too, was more than of the moment. And then he turned and saw her, and smiled, and the smile changed all.

As the afternoon wore on the man stopped working and turning a little in his chair sat there covertly watching the girl. She was just typically girl. It was written that she had spent her days in the happy ways of healthful girlhood. He supposed that a great many young fellows had fallen in love with her — nice, clean young fellows, the kind she would naturally meet. And then his eyes closed for a minute and he put up his hand and brushed back his hair; there was weariness, weariness weary of itself, in the gesture. He looked about the room and scanned the faces of the men, most of them older than he, many of them men whose histories were well known to him. They were the usual hangers on about newspaper offices; men who, for one reason or other — age, dissipation, antiquated methods — had been pitched over, men for whom such work as this came as a godsend. They were the men of yesterday — men whom the world had rushed past. She was the only one there, this girl who would probably sit here beside him for many months, with whom the future had anything to do. Youth! — Goodness! — Joy! — Hope! — strange things to bring to a place like this. And as if their alienism disturbed him, he moved restlessly, almost resentfully, bit his lips nervously, moistened them, and began putting away his things.

As the girl was starting home along Dearborn Street a few minutes later, she chanced to look in a window. She saw that it was a saloon, but before she could turn away she saw a man with a white face — white with the peculiar whiteness of a dark face, standing before the bar drinking from a small glass. She stood still, arrested by a look such as she had never seen before: a panting human soul sobbingly fluttering down into something from which it had spent all its force in trying to rise. When she recalled herself and passed on, a mist which she could neither account for nor banish was dimming the clear hazel of her eyes.

The next day was a hard one at the dictionary place. She told herself it was because the novelty of it was wearing away, because her fingers ached, because it tired her back to sit in that horrid chair. She did not admit of any connection between her flagging interest and the fact that the place at the next table was vacant.

The following day he was still absent. She assumed that it was nervousness occasioned by her queer surroundings made her look around whenever she heard a step behind her. Where was he? Where had that look carried him? If he were in trouble, was there no one to help him?

The third day she did an unpremeditated thing. The man in the skull cap had been showing her something about the copy. As he was leaving, she asked: "Is the man who sits at the next table coming back?"

"Oh yes," he replied grimly, "he'll be back."

"Because," she went on, "if he wasn't, I thought I would take his shears. These hurt my fingers."

He made the exchange for her — and after that things went better.

He did return late the next morning. After he had taken his place he looked over at her and smiled. He looked sick and shaken — as if something that knew no mercy had taken hold of him and wrung body and soul.

"You have been ill?" she asked, with timid solicitude.

"Oh no," he replied, rather shortly.

He was quiet all that day, but the next day they talked about the work, laughed together over funny definitions they found. She felt that he could tell many interesting things about himself, if he cared to.

As the days went on he did tell some of those things — out of the way places where he had worked, queer people whom he had known. It seemed that words came to him as gifts, came freely, happily, pleased, perhaps, to be borne by so sympathetic a voice. And there was another thing about him. He seemed always to know just what she was trying to say; he never missed the unexpressed. That made it easy to say things to him; there seemed a certain at-homeness between his thought and hers. She accounted for her interest in him by telling herself she had never known any one like that before. Now Harold, the boy whom she knew best out at the university, why one had to *say* things to Harold to make him understand! And Harold never left one wondering — wondering what he had meant by that smile, what he had been going to say when he started to say something and stopped, wondering what it was about his face that one could not understand. Harold never could claim as his the hour after he had left her, and was one ever close to anyone with whom one did not spend some of the hours of absence? She began to see that hours spent together when apart were the most intimate hours of all.

And as Harold did not make one wonder, so he did not make one worry. Never in all her life had there been a lump in her throat when she thought of Harold. There was often a lump in her throat when the man at the next table was coughing.

One day, she had been there about two months, she said something to him about it. It was hard; it seemed forcing one's way into a room that had never been opened to one — there were several doors he kept closed.

"Mr. Clifford," she turned to him impetuously as they were putting away their things that night, "will you mind if I say something to you?"

He was covering his paste-pot. He looked up at her strangely. The closed door seemed to open a little way. "I can't conceive of 'minding' anything you might say to me, Miss Noah," — he had called her Miss Noah ever since she, by mistake, had one day called him Mr. Webster.

"You see," she hurried on, very timid, now that the door had opened a little, "you have been so good to me. Because you have been so good to me it seems that I have some right to — to —"

His head was resting upon his hand, and he leaned a little closer as though listening for something he wanted to hear.

"I had a cousin who had a cough like yours," — brave now that she could not go back — "and he went down to New Mexico and stayed for a year, and when he came back — when he came back he was as well as any of us. It seems so foolish not to" — her voice broke, now that it had so valiantly carried it — "not to —"

He looked at her, and that was all. But she was never wholly the same again after that look. It enveloped her being in a something which left her richer — different. It was a look to light the dark place between two human souls. It seemed for the moment that words would follow it, but as if feeling their helplessness — perhaps needlessness — they sank back unuttered, and at the last he got up, abruptly, and walked away.

One night, while waiting for the elevator, she heard two of the men talking about him. When she went out on the street it was with head high, cheeks hot. For nothing is so hard to hear as that which one has half known, and evaded. One never denies so hotly as in denying to one's self what one fears is true, and one never resents so bitterly as in resenting that which one cannot say one has the right to resent.

That night she lay in her bed with wide open eyes, going over and over the things they had said. "*Cure?*" — one of them had scoffed, after telling how brilliant he had been before he "went to pieces" — "why all the cures on earth couldn't help him! He can go just so far, and then he can no more stop himself — oh, about as much as an ant could stop a prairie fire!"

She finally turned over on her pillow and sobbed; and she wondered why — wondered, yet knew.

But it resulted in the flowering of her tenderness for him. Interest mounted to defiance. It ended in blind, passionate desire to "make it up" to him. And again he was so different from Harold; Harold did not impress himself upon one by upsetting all one's preconceived ideas.

She felt now that she understood better — understood the closed doors. He was — she could think of no better word than sensitive.

And that is why, several mornings later, she very courageously — for it did take courage — threw this little note over on his desk — they had formed a habit of writing notes to each other, sometimes about the words, sometimes about other things.

"IN-VI-TA-TION, *n.* That which Miss Noah extends to Mr. Webster for Friday evening, December second, at the house where she lives — hasn't she already told him where that is? It is the wish of Miss Noah to present Mr. Webster to various other Miss Noahs, all of whom are desirous of making his acquaintance."

She was absurdly nervous at luncheon that day, and kept telling herself with severity not to act like a high-school girl. He was late in returning that noon, and though there seemed a new something in his voice when he asked if he hadn't better sharpen her pencils, he said nothing about her new definition of invitation. It was almost five o'clock when he threw this over on her desk:

"AP-PRE-CI-A-TION, *n.* That sentiment inspired in Mr. Webster by the kind invitation of Miss Noah for Friday evening.

"RE-GRET, *n.* That which Mr. Webster experiences because, for reasons into which he cannot go in detail, it is impossible for him to accept Miss Noah's invitation.

"RE-SENT-MENT, *n.* That which is inspired in Mr. Webster by the insinuation that there are other Miss Noahs in the world."

Then below he had written: "Three hours later. Miss Noah, the world is queer. Some day you may find out — though I hope you never will — that it is frequently the things we most want to do that we must leave undone. Miss Noah, won't you go on bringing me as much of yourself as you can to Dearborn Street, and try not to think much about my not being able to know the Miss Noah of Hyde Park? And little Miss Noah — I thank you. There aren't words enough in this old book of ours to tell you how much — or why."

That night he hurried away with never a joke about how many words she had written that day. She did not look up as he stood there putting on his coat.

It was spring now, and the dictionary staff had begun on W.

They had written of Joy, of Hope and Life and Love, and many other things. Life seemed pressing just behind some of those definitions, pressing the harder, perhaps, because it could not break through the surface.

For it did not break through; it flooded just beneath.

How did she know that he cared for her? She could not possibly have told. Perhaps the nearest to actual proof she could bring was that he always saw that her overshoes were put in a warm place. And when one came down to facts, the putting of a girl's rubbers near the radiator did not necessarily mean love.

Perhaps then it was because there was no proof of it that she was most sure. For some of the most sure things in the world are things which cannot be proved.

It was only that they worked together and were friends; that they laughed together over funny definitions they found, that he was kind to her, and that they seemed remarkably close together.

That is as far as facts can take it.

And just there — it begins.

For the force which rushes beneath the facts of life, caring nothing for conditions, not asking what one desires or what one thinks best, caring as little about a past as about a future — save its own future—the force which can laugh at man's institutions and batter over in one sweep what he likes to call his wisdom, was sweeping them on. And because it could get no other recognition it forced its way into the moments when he asked her for an eraser, when she wanted to know how to spell a word. He could not so much as ask her if she needed more copy-paper without seeming to be lavishing upon her all the love of all the ages.

And so the winter had worn on, and there was really nothing whatever to tell about it.

She was quiet this morning, and kept her head bent low over her work. For she had estimated the number of pages there were between W and Z. Soon they would be at Z;— and then? Then? Shyly she turned and looked at him; he too was bent over his work. When she came in she had said something about its being spring, and that there must be wild flowers in the woods. Since then he had not looked up.

Suddenly it came to her — tenderly, hotly, fearfully yet bravely, that it was she who must meet Z. She looked at him again, covertly. And she felt that she understood. It was the lines in his face made it clearest. Years, and things blacker, less easily surmounted than years — oh yes, that too she faced fearlessly — were piled in between. She knew now that it was she — not he — who could push them aside.

It was all very unmaidenly, of course; but maidenly is a word love and life and desire may crowd from the page.

Perhaps she would not have thrown it after all — the little note she had written — had it not been that when she went over for more copy-paper she stood for a minute looking out the window. Even on Dearborn Street the seductiveness of spring was in the air. Spring, and all that spring meant, filled her.

Because, way beyond the voice of Dr. Bunting she heard the songs of far-away birds, and because beneath the rumble of a printing press she could get the babble of a brook, because Z was near and life was strong, the woman vanquished the girl, and she threw this over to his desk:

"CHAFING-DISH, *n*. That out of which Miss Noah asks Mr. Webster to eat his Sunday night lunch tomorrow. All the other Miss Noahs are going to be away, and if Mr. Webster does not come, Miss Noah will be all alone. Miss Noah does not like to be lonely."

She ate no lunch that day; she only drank a cup of coffee and walked around.

He did not come back that afternoon. It passed from one to two, from two to three, and then very slowly from three to four, and still he had not come.

He too was walking about. He had walked down to the lake and was standing there looking out across it.

Why not? — he was saying to himself — fiercely, doggedly. Over and over again — Well, *why not?*

A hundred nights, alone in his room, he had gone over it. Had not life used him hard enough to give him a little now? — longing had pleaded. And now there was a new voice — more prevailing voice — the voice of *her* happiness. His face softened to an almost maternal tenderness as he listened to that voice.

Too worn to fight any longer, he gave himself up to it, and sat there dreaming. They were dreams of joy rushing in after lonely years, dreams of stepping into the sunlight after long days in fog and cold, dreams of a woman before a fireplace — her arms about him, her cheer and her tenderness, her comradeship and her passion — all his to take! Ah, dreams which even thoughts must not touch — so wonderful and sacred they were.

A long time he sat there, dreaming dreams and seeing visions. The force that rules the race was telling him that the one crime was the denial of happiness — his happiness, her happiness; and when at last his fight seemed but a puerile fight against forces worlds mightier than he, he rose, and as one who sees a great light, started back toward Dearborn Street.

On the way he began to cough. The coughing was violent, and he stepped into a doorway to gain breath. And after he had gone in there he realised that it was the building of Chicago's greatest newspaper.

He had been city editor of that paper once. Facts, the things he knew about himself, talked to him then. There was no answer.

It left him weak and dizzy and crazy for a drink. He walked on slowly, unsteadily, his white face set. For he had vowed that if it took the last nerve in his body there should be no more of that until after they had finished with Z. He knew himself too well to vow more. He was not even sure of that.

He did not turn in where he wanted to go; but resistance took the last bit of force that was in him. He was trembling like a sick man when he stepped into the elevator.

She was just leaving. She was in the little cloak room putting on her things. She was all alone in there.

He stepped in. He pushed the door shut, and stood there leaning against it, looking at her, saying nothing.

"Oh — you are ill?" she gasped, and laid a frightened hand upon him.

The touch crazed him. All resistance gone, he swept her into his arms; he held her fiercely, and between sobs kissed her again and again. He could not let her go. He frightened her. He hurt her. And he did not care — he did not know.

Then he held her off and looked at her. And as he looked into her eyes, passion melted to tenderness. It was she now — not he; love — not hunger. Holding her face in his two hands, looking at her as if getting something to take away, his white lips murmured words too inarticulate for her to hear. And then again he put his arms around her — all differently. Reverently, sobbingly, he kissed her hair. And then he was gone.

He did not come out that Sunday afternoon, but Harold dropped in instead, and talked of some athletic affairs over at the university. She wondered why she did not go crazy in listening to him, and yet she could answer intelligently. It was queer — what one *could* do.

They had come at last to Z. There would be no more work upon the dictionary after that day. And it was raining — raining as in Chicago alone it knows how to rain.

They wrote no notes to each other now. It had been different since that day. They made small effort to cover their raw souls with the mantle of commonplace words.

Both of them had tried to stay away that last day. But both were in their usual places.

The day wore on eventlessly. Those men with whom she had worked, the men of yesterday, who had been kind to her, came up at various times for little farewell chats. The man in the skull cap told her that she had done excellent work. She was surprised at the ease with which she could make decent reply, thinking again that it was queer — what one could do.

He was moving. She saw him lay some sheets of yellow paper on the desk in front. He had finished with his "take." There would not be another to give him. He would go now.

He came back to his desk. She could hear him putting away his things. And then for a long time there was no sound. She knew that he was just sitting there in his chair.

Then she heard him get up. She heard him push his chair up to the table, and then for a minute he stood there. She wanted to turn toward him; she wanted to say something — do something. But she had no power.

She saw him lay an envelope upon her desk. She heard him walking away. She knew, numbly, that his footsteps were not steady. She knew that he had stopped; she was sure that he was looking back. But still she had no power.

And then she heard him go.

Even then she went on with her work; she finished her "take" and laid down her pencil. It was finished now — and he had gone. Finished? — *Gone?* She was tearing open the envelope of the letter.

This was what she read:

"Little dictionary sprite, sunshine vender, and girl to be loved, if I were a free man I would say to you — Come, little one, and let us learn of love. Let us learn of it, not as one learns from dictionaries, but let us learn from the morning glow and the evening shades. But Miss Noah, maker of dictionaries and creeper into hearts, the bound must not call to the free. They might fittingly have used my name as one of the synonyms under that word Failure, but I trust not under Coward.

"And now, you funny little Miss Noah from the University of Chicago, don't I know that your heart is blazing forth the assurance that you don't *care* for any of those things — the world, people, common sense — that you want just love? They made a grand failure of you out at your university; they taught you philosophy and they taught you Greek, and they've left you just as much the woman as women were five thousand years ago. Oh, I know all about you — you little girl whose hair tried so hard to be red. Your soul touched mine as we sat there writing words — words — words, the very words in which men try to tell things, and can't — and I know all about what you would do. But you shall not do it. Dear little copy maker, would a man standing out on the end of a slippery plank have any right to cry to someone on the shore — 'Come out here on this plank with me?' If he loved the someone on the shore, would he not say instead — 'Don't get on this plank?' Me get off the plank — come with you to the shore — you are saying? But you see, dear, you only know slippery planks as viewed from the shore — God grant you may never know them any other way!

"It was you, was it not, who wrote our definition of happiness? Yes, I remember the day you did it. You were so interested; your cheeks grew so very red, and you pulled and pulled at your wavy hair. You said it was such an important definition. And so it is, Miss Noah, quite the most important of all. And on the page of life, Miss Noah, may happiness be written large and unblurred for you. It is because I cannot help you write it that I turn away. I want at least to leave the page unspoiled.

"I carry a picture of you. I shall carry it always. You are sitting before a fireplace, and I think of that fireplace as symbolising the warmth and care and tenderness and the safety that will surround you. And sometimes as you sit there let a thought of me come for just a minute, Miss Noah — not long enough nor deep enough to bring you any pain. But only think — I brought him happiness after he believed all happiness had gone. He was so grateful for that light which came after he thought the darkness had settled down. It will light his way to the end.

"We've come to Z, and it's good-bye. There is one thing I can give you without hurting you, — the hope, the prayer, that life may be very, very good to you."

The sheets of paper fell from her hands. She sat staring out into Dearborn Street. She began to see. After all, he had not understood her. Perhaps men never understood women; certainly he had not understood her. What he did not know was that she was willing to *pay* for her happiness — *pay* — pay any price that might be exacted. And anyway — she had no choice. Strange that he could not see that! Strange that he could not see the irony and cruelty of bidding her good-bye and then telling her to be happy!

It simplified itself to such an extent that she grew very calm. It would be easy to find him, easy to make him see — for it was so very simple — and then....

She turned in her copy. She said good-bye quietly, naturally, rode down in the lumbering old elevator and started out into the now drenching rain toward the elevated trains which would take her to the West Side; it was so fortunate that she had heard him telling one day where he lived.

When she reached the station she saw that more people were coming down the stairs than were going up. They were saying things about the trains, but she did not heed them. But at the top of the stairs a man in uniform said: "Blockade, Miss. You'll have to take the surface cars."

She was sorry, for it would delay her, and there was not a minute to lose. She was dismayed, upon reaching the surface cars, to find she could not get near them; the rain, the blockade on the "L," had caused a great crowd to congregate there. She waited a long time, getting more and more wet, but it was impossible to get near the cars. She thought of a cab, but could see none, they too having all been pressed into service.

She determined, desperately, to start and walk. Soon she would surely get either a cab or a car. And so she started, staunchly, though she was wet through now, and trembling with cold and nervousness.

As she hurried through the driving rain she faced things fearlessly. Oh yes, she understood — everything. But if he were not well — should he not have her with him? If he had that thing to fight, did he not need her help? What did men think women were like? Did he think she was one to sit down and reason out what would be advantageous? Better a little while with him on a slippery plank than forever safe and desolate upon the shore!

She never questioned her going; were not life and love too great to be lost through that which could be so easily put right?

The buildings were reeling, the streets moving up and down — that awful rain, she thought, was making her dizzy. Labouriously she walked on — more slowly, less steadily, a pain in her side, that awful reeling in her head.

Carriages returning to the city were passing her, but she had not strength to call to them, and it seemed if she walked to the curbing she would fall. She was not thinking so clearly now. The thing which took all of her force was the lifting of her feet and the putting them down in the right place. Her throat seemed to be closing up — and her side — and her head....

Someone had her by the arm. Then someone was speaking her name; speaking it in surprise — consternation — alarm.

It was Harold.

It was all vague then. She knew that she was in a carriage, and that Harold was talking to her kindly. "You're taking me there?" she murmured.

"Yes — yes, Edna, everything's all right," he replied soothingly.

"Everything's all right," she repeated, in a whisper, and leaned her head back against the cushions.

They stopped after a while, and Harold was standing at the open door of the cab with something steaming hot which he told her to drink. "You need it," he said decisively, and thinking it would help her to tell it, she drank it down.

The world was a little more defined after that, and she saw things which puzzled her. "Why, it looks like the city," she whispered, her throat too sore now to speak aloud.

"Why sure," he replied banteringly; "don't you know we have to go through the city to get out to the South Side?"

"Oh, but you see," she cried, holding her throat, "but you see, it's the *other* way!"

"Not to-night," he insisted; "the place for you to-night is home. I'm taking you where you belong."

She reached over wildly, trying to open the door, but he held her back; she began to cry, and he talked to her, gently but unbendingly. "But you don't *understand!*" she whispered, passionately. "I've *got* to go!"

"Not to-night," he said again, and something in the way he said it made her finally huddle back in the corner of the carriage.

Block after block, mile after mile, they rode on in silence. She felt overpowered. And with submission she knew that it was Z. For the whole city was piled in between. Great buildings were in between, and thousands of men running to and fro on the streets; man, and all man had builded up, were in between. And then Harold — Harold who had always seemed to count for so little, had come and taken her away.

Dully, wretchedly — knowing that her heart would ache far worse to-morrow than it did to-night — she wondered about things. Did things like rain and street-cars and wet feet and a sore throat determine life? Was it that way with other people, too? Did other people have barriers — whole cities full of them — piled in between? And then did the Harolds come and take them where they said they belonged? Were there not *some* people strong enough to go where they wanted to go?

THE BOUNTY JUMPER (1915)

Mary Synon

". . . While faith, that in the mire was fain to wallow,
   Returns at last to find
The cold fanes desolate, the niches hollow,
   The windows dim and blind,

"And strown with ruins around, the shattered relic
   Of unregardful youth,
Where shapes of beauty once, with tongues angelic,
   Whispered the runes of Truth."
            —From "The Burden of Lost Souls."

ON THE DAY before Isador Framberg's body was brought back to Chicago from Vera Cruz, James Thorold's appointment as ambassador to Forsland was confirmed by the Senate of the United States. Living, Isador Framberg might never have wedged into the affairs of nations and the destinies of James Thorold. Marines in the navy do not intrigue with chances of knee-breeches at the Court of St. Jerome. More than miles lie between Forquier Street and the Lake Shore Drive. Dead, Isador Framberg became, as dead men sometimes become, the archangel of a nation, standing with flaming sword at the gateway to James Thorold's paradise.

For ten years the Forsland embassy had been the goal of James Thorold's ambition. A man past seventy, head of a great importing establishment, he had shown interest in public affairs only within the decade, although his very build, tall, erect, commanding, and his manner, suavely courteous and untouched by futile haste, seemed to have equipped him with a natural bent for public life. Marrying late in life, he seemed to have found his bent more tardily than did other men. But he had invested wealth, influence, and wisdom in the future of men who, come to power, were paying him with this grant of his desire. The news, coming to him unofficially but authoritatively from Washington, set him to cabling his wife and daughter in Paris and telegraphing his son whose steamer was just docking in New York. The boy's answer, delayed in transit and announcing that he was already on his way to Chicago, came with the morning newspapers and hurried his father through their contents in order that he might be on time to meet Peter at the station.

The newspapers, chronicling Thorold's appointment briefly, were heavy with harbingering of the funeral procession of the boy who had fallen a fortnight before in the American navy's attack upon Vera Cruz. The relative values that editors placed upon the marine's death and his own honoring nettled Thorold. Ambassadors to the Court of St. Jerome were not chosen from Chicago every day, he reasoned, finding Isador Framberg already the fly in the amber of his contentment. To change the current of his thought he read over Peter's telegram, smiling at the exuberant message of joy in which the boy had vaunted the family glory. The yellow slip drove home to James Thorold the realization of how largely Peter's young enthusiasm was responsible for the whetting of his father's desire to take part in public affairs. For Peter's praise James Thorold would have moved mountains; and Peter's praise had a way of following the man on horseback. Thorold's eager anticipation of the boy's pride in him sped his course through rosy mists of hope as his motor-car threaded the bright drive and through the crowded Parkway toward the Rush Street bridge.

A cloud drifted across the sky of his serenity, however, as a blockade of traffic delayed his car in front of the old Adams homestead, rising among lilacs that flooded half a city square with fragrance. The old house, famous beyond its own day for Judge Adams's friendship with Abraham Lincoln and the history-making sessions that the little group of Illinois idealists had held within its walls, loomed gray above the flowering shrubs, a saddening reminder of days that James Thorold must have known; but Thorold, glimpsing the place, turned away from it in a movement so swift as to betoken some resentment and gave heed instead to the long line of motors rolling smoothly toward the city's heart.

Over the bridge and through the packed streets of the down-town district Thorold, shaken from his revery of power and Peter, watched the film that Chicago unrolled for the boulevard pilgrims. The boats in the river, the long switch-tracks of the rail-roads, the tall grain-elevators, the low warehouses from which drifted alluring odors of spices linked for James Thorold the older city of his youth with the newer one of his age as the street linked one division of the city's geography with another. They were the means by which Chicago had risen from the sand-flats of the fifties to the Michigan Avenue of the present, that wide street of the high skyline that fronted the world as it faced the Great Lakes, squarely, solidly, openly. They were the means, too, by which James Thor-old had augmented his fortune until it had acquired the power to send him to Forsland. To him, however, they represented not lad-ders to prosperity but a social condition of a passing generation, the Chicago of the seventies, a city distinctively American in popula-tion and in ideals, a youthful city of a single standard of endeavor, a pleasant place that had been swallowed by the Chicago of the present, that many-tentacled monster of heterogeneous races, that affected him, as it did so many of the older residents, with an over-whelming sensation of revolt against its sprawling lack of cohesion. Even the material advantages that had accrued to him from the growth of the city could not reconcile James Thorold to the fact that the elements of the city's growth came from the races of men whom he held in contempt. What mattered it, he reasoned, that Chicago waxed huge when her grossness came from the unassimi-lated, indigestible mass of Latins and Greeks, Poles and Russians, Czechs, Bulgars, Jews, who filled the streets, the factories, and the schools?

The prejudice, always strong within him, rose higher as he found his machine blocked again, this time by the crowd that stood across Jackson Boulevard at La Salle Street. Even after the peremptory order of a mounted police officer had cleared the way for him James Thorold frowned on the lines of men and women pressed back against the curbstones. The thought that they were waiting the coming of the body of that boy who had died in Mexico added to his annoyance the realization that he would have to fight his way through another crowd at the station if he wished to reach the train-shed where Peter's train would come. The struggle was spared him, however, by the recognition of a newspaper reporter who took it for granted that the ambassador to Forsland had come to meet the funeral cortège of the marine and who led him through a labyrinthine passage that brought him past the gates and under the glass dome of the train-shed.

Left alone, Thorold paced the platform a little apart from the group of men who had evidently been delegated to represent the city. Some of them he knew. Others of them, men of Isador Framberg's people and of the ten tribes of Israel, he did not care to know. He turned away from them to watch the people beyond the gates. Thousands of faces, typical of every nation of Europe and some of the lands of Asia, fair Norsemen and Teutons, olive-skinned Italians and men and women of the swarthier peoples of Palestine, Poles, Finns, Lithuanians, Russians, Bulgars, Bohemians, units of that mass which had welded in the city of the Great Lakes of America, looked out from behind the iron fence. The tensity written on their faces, eager yet awed, brought back to James Thorold another time when men and women had stood within a Chicago railway terminal waiting for a funeral cortège, the time when Illinois waited in sorrow to take Abraham Lincoln, dead, to her heart. The memory of that other day of dirges linked itself suddenly in the mind of James Thorold with the picture of the lilacs blooming in the yard of the Adams homestead on the Parkway, that old house where Abraham Lincoln had been wont to come; and the fusing recollections spun the ambassador to Forsland upon his heel and sent him far down the platform, where he stood, gloomily apart, until the limited, rolling in from the end of the yards, brought him hastening to its side.

Peter Thorold was the first to alight.

A boy of sixteen, fair-haired, blue-eyed, ruddy-cheeked, springing from the platform of the Pullman into his father's arms, he brought with him the atmosphere of high adventure. In height, in poise of shoulders, in bearing, in a certain trick of lifting his chin, he was a replica of the dignified man who welcomed him with deep emotion; but a difference — of dream rather than of dogma — in the quality of their temperaments accolade the boy. It was not only that his voice thrilled with the higher enthusiasms of youth. It held besides an inflexibility of tone that James Thorold's lacked. Its timbre told that Peter Thorold's spirit had been tempered in a furnace fierier than the one which had given forth the older man's. The voice rang out now in excited pleasure as the boy gripped his father's shoulders. "Oh, but it's good to see you again, dad," he cried. "You're a great old boy, and I'm proud of you, sir. Think of it!" he almost shouted. "Ambassador to Forsland! Say, but that's bully!" He slipped his arm around his father's shoulder, while James Thorold watched him with eyes that shone with joy. "What do you call an ambassador?" he demanded laughingly.

"Fortunately," the older man said, "there is no title accompanying the office."

"Well, I should think not," the boy exclaimed. "Oh, dad, isn't it the greatest thing in the world that you're to represent the United States of America?"

James Thorold smiled. "No doubt," he said dryly. His gaze passed his son to glimpse the crowd at the gate, frantic now with excitement, all looking forward toward some point on the platform just beyond where the man and boy were standing. "These United States of America have grown past my thought of them," he added. The boy caught up the idea eagerly. "Haven't they, though?" he demanded. "And isn't it wonderful to think that it's all the same old America, 'the land of the free and the home of the brave?' Gee, but it's good to be back in it again. I came up into New York alongside the battleship that brought our boys home from Mexico," he went on, "and, oh, say, dad, you should have seen that harbor! I've seen a lot of things for a fellow," he pursued with a touch of boyish boastfulness, "but I never saw anything in all my life like that port yesterday. People, and people, and people, waiting, and flags at half-mast, and a band off somewhere playing a funeral march, and that battleship with the dead sailors — the fellows who died for our country at Vera Cruz, you know — creeping up to the dock. Oh, it was — well, I cried!" He made confession proudly, then hastened into less personal narrative.

"One of them came from Chicago here," he said. "He was only nineteen years old, and he was one of the first on the beach after the order to cross to the customhouse. He lived over on Forquier Street, one of the men was telling me — there are six of them, the guard of honor for him, on the train — and his name was Isador Framberg. He was born in Russia, too, in Kiev, the place of the massacres, you remember. See, dad, here comes the guard!"

Peter Thorold swung his father around until he faced six uniformed men who fell into step as they went forward toward the baggage-car. "It's too bad, isn't it," the boy continued, "that any of the boys had to die down in that greaser town? But, if they did, I'm proud that we proved up that Chicago had a hero to send. Aren't you, dad?" James Thorold did not answer. Peter's hands closed over his arm. "It reminds me," he said, lowering his voice as they came closer to the place where the marines stood beside the iron carrier that awaited the casket of Isador Framberg's body, "of something the tutor at Westbury taught us in Greek last year, something in a funeral oration that a fellow in Athens made on the men who died in the Peloponnesian War. 'Such was the end of these men,'" he quoted slowly, pausing now and then for a word while his father looked wonderingly upon his rapt fervor, "'and they were worthy of Athens. The living need not desire to have a more heroic spirit. I would have you fix your eyes upon the great-ness of Athens, until you become filled with the love of her; and, when you are impressed by the spectacle of her glory, reflect that this empire has been acquired by men who knew their duty and who had the courage to do it, who in the hour of conflict had the fear of dishonor always present to them.'" With the solemnity of the chant the young voice went on while the flag-covered casket was lifted from car to bier. "'For the whole earth is the sepulchre of famous men; not only are they commemorated by columns and inscriptions in their own country, but in foreign lands there dwells also an unwritten memorial of them, graven not in stone but in the hearts of men. Make them your examples, and, esteeming courage to be freedom and freedom to be happiness, do not weigh too nicely the perils of war.'"

He pulled off his cap, tucking it under his arm and dragging his father with him to follow the men who had fallen in behind the marines as they moved forward toward the gates and the silent crowd beyond. Almost unwillingly James Thorold doffed his hat. The words of Peter's unexpected declamation of Pericles's oration resounded in his ears. "Once before," he said to the boy, "I heard that speech. Judge Adams said it one night to Abraham Lincoln."

"Father!" Peter's eyes flashed back from the cortege to meet James Thorold's. "I never knew that you knew Abraham Lincoln." His tone betokened an impression of having been cheated of some joy the older man had been hoarding. But James Thorold's voice held no joy. "Yes," he said. "I knew him."

The gates, sliding back, opened the way for the officers who led the procession with which Isador Framberg came back to the city of his adoption. The crowd yawned to give space to the guard of honor, walking erectly beside the flag-draped coffin, to the mourners, men and women alien as if they had come from Kiev but yesterday, to the little group of men, public officials and rabbis, who trailed in their wake, and to James Thorold and Peter, reverently following. Then it closed in upon the cortège, urging it silently down the broad stairways and out into the street where other crowds fell in with the strange procession. Surging away after the shabby hearse, drawn by its listless horses and attended by the marines, the crowd left the Thorolds, father and son, on the pavement beside the station. "Don't you want to go?" There was a wistfulness in Peter's voice that told his father that the boy had sensed some lack of responsiveness in him. "He's going to lie in state to-day at the city hall. Don't you think we should go, dad?" Not Peter's query but Peter's eyes won his father's answer. "After a while," he promised. "Then let's find a breakfast," the boy laughed. "I spent my last dollar sending you that telegram."

All the way over to his father's club on Michigan Avenue, and all through the breakfast that he ordered with lusty young appetite, Peter kept up a running fire of reminiscence of his European adventures. That the fire held grapeshot for his father when he talked of the latter's worthiness for the ambassadorship to Forsland he could not guess; but he found that he was pouring salt in a wound when he went back to comment upon Isador Framberg's death. "Why make so much of a boy who happened to be at Vera Cruz?" the older man said at last, nettled that even his son found greater occasion for commendation in the circumstance of the Forquier Street hero than in his father's selection to the most important diplomatic post in the gift of the government. Peter's brows rose swiftly at his father's annoyance. He opened his lips for argument, then swiftly changed his intention. "Tell me about Judge Adams, dad," he said, bungling over his desire to change the topic, "the fellow who knew his Pericles."

"It's too long a story," James Thorold said. He watched Peter closely in the fashion of an advocate studying the characteristics of a judge. The boy's idealism, his vivid young patriotism, his eager championship of those elements of the new America that his father contemned, had fired his personality with a glaze that left James Thorold's smoothly diplomatic fingers wandering over its surface, unable to hold it within his grasp. He had a story to tell

Peter — some time — a story of Judge Adams, of the house among the lilacs, of days of war, of Abraham Lincoln; but the time for its telling must wait upon circumstance that would make Peter Thorold more ready to understand weakness and failure than he now seemed. Consciously James Thorold took a change of venue from Peter Thorold of the visions to Peter Thorold of the inevitable disillusions. But to the former he made concession. "Shall we go to the city hall now?" he asked as they rose from the table.

The city hall, a massive white granite pile covering half of the square east of La Salle Street and north of Washington and meeting its twin of the county building to form a solid mass of masonry, flaunted black drapings over the doorways through which James Thorold and his son entered. Through a wide corridor of bronze and marble they found their way, passing a few stragglers from the great crowd that had filled the lower floors of the huge structures when Isador Framberg's body had been brought from its hearse and carried to the centre of the aisles, the place where the intersecting thoroughfares met. Under a great bronze lamp stood the catafalque, covered with the Stars and Stripes and guarded by the men of the fleet.

Peter Thorold, pressing forward, took his place, his cap thrust under his arm, at the foot of the bier, giving his tribute of silence to the boy who had died for his country. But James Thorold went aside to stand beside an elevator-shaft. Had his son watched him as he was watching Peter, he would have seen the swift emotions that took their way across his father's face. He would have seen the older man's look dilate with the strained horror of one who gazed back through the dimming years to see a ghost. He would have seen sorrow, and grief, and a great remorse rising to James Thorold's eyes. He might even have seen the shadow of another bier cast upon the retina of his father's sight. He might have seen through his father's watching the memory of another man who had once lain on the very spot where Isador Framberg was lying, a man who had died for his country after he had lived to set his country among the free nations of the earth. But Peter Thorold saw only the boy who had gone from a Forquier Street tenement to the Mexican sands that he might prove by his dying that, with Irish, and Germans, and French, he too, the lad who had been born in Kiev of the massacres, was an American.

With the surge of strange emotions flooding his heart, Peter Thorold crossed to where his father stood apart. The tide of his thought overflowed the shore of prose and landed his expression high on a cliff of poetry. No chance, but the urging of his own exalted mood, brought from him the last lines of Moody's "Ode in Time of Hesitation":

"Then on your guiltier head
Shall our intolerable self-disdain
Wreak suddenly its anger and its pain;
For manifest in that disastrous light
We shall discern the right
And do it, tardily. — O ye who lead,
     Take heed!
Blindness we may forgive, but baseness we will smite."

But to the older man, seeing as he stood the picture of that other catafalque to which he had crept one night in the lilac time of a year nearly a half century agone, the words flung anathema. He leaned back against the bronze grating of the shaft with a sudden look of age that brought Peter's protective arm to his shoulder. Then, with Peter following, he went out to the sun-bright street.

Like a man in a daze he dismissed his car, crossing pavements under Peter's guiding until he came to the building where the fortunes of the great Thorold mercantile business were administered. Through the outer room, where clerks looked up in surprise at the appearance which their chief presented on the morning when they had learned of the Forsland embassy, he led Peter until they came to the room where he had reigned for twenty years. It was a room that had always mirrored James Thorold to his son. Tall bookcases, stiff, old-fashioned, held long rows of legal works, books on history, essays on ethical topics, and bound volumes of periodicals. Except for its maps, it was a lawyer's room, although James Thorold never claimed either legal ability or legal standing. Peter seldom entered it without interest in its possibilities of entertainment, but to-day his father's strange and sudden preoccupation of manner ingulfed all the boy's thought. "What is it, dad?" he asked, a tightening fear screwing down upon his brain as he noted the change that had come over the mask that James Thorold's face held to the world.

James Thorold made him no answer. He was standing at the wide walnut table, turning over and over in his hands the letters which his secretary had left for his perusal. Finally, he opened one of them, the bulkiest. He scanned it for a moment, then flung it upon the floor. Then he began to pace the room till in his striding he struck his foot against the paper he had cast aside. He picked it up, tossing it toward Peter. The boy turned from his strained watching of his father's face to read the letter. It was the official notification of the Senate's confirmation of the President's appointment of James Thorold as ambassador to the Court of St. Jerome.

"Why, father!" Incredulity heightened the boyishness in Peter's tone. James Thorold wheeled around until he faced him. "Peter," he said huskily, "there's something you'll have to know before I go to Forsland — if ever I go to Forsland. You'll have to decide." The boy shrank from the ominous cadence of the words. "Why, I can't judge for you, dad," he said awkwardly. "Our children are always our ultimate judges," James Thorold said.

"I have sometimes wondered," he went on, speaking to himself rather than to the puzzled boy, "how the disciples who met Christ but who did not go his way with him to the end felt when they heard he had died. I knew a great man once, Peter. I went his way for a little while, then I took my own. I saw them bring him, dead, over the way they have brought that boy to-day. I came down to the court-house that night, and there, just where that boy lies, Peter, I made a promise that I have not kept."

Again he resumed his pacing, speaking as he went, sometimes in low tones, sometimes with tensity of voice, always as if urged by some force that was driving him from silence. The boy, leaning forward at the edge of the chair, watched his father through the first part of the story. Before the end came he turned away.

"You remember," James Thorold began, his voice pleading patience, "that I've told you I came to Chicago from Ohio before the war? I was older than you then, Peter, but I was something of a hero-worshipper, too. Judge Adams was my hero in those troublous times of the fifties. I knew him only by sight for a long time, watching him go in and out of the big white house where he lived. After a time I came to know him. I was clerking in a coffee-importing house during the day and studying law at night. Judge Adams took me into his office. He took me among his friends. Abraham Lincoln was one of them.

"I remember the night I met Lincoln. Judge Adams had talked of him often. He had been talking of him that day. 'Greatness,' he had said, 'is the holding of a great dream, not for yourself, but for others. Abraham Lincoln has the dream. He has heard the voice, and seen the vision, and he is climbing up to Sinai. You must meet him, James.' That night I met him in the old white house.

"We were in the front parlor of the old house," James Thorold continued, resetting the scene until his only listener knew that it was more real to him than the room through which he paced, "when some one said, 'Mr. Lincoln.' I looked up to see a tall, awkward man standing in the arched doorway. Other men have said that they had to know Lincoln a long time to feel his greatness. My shame is the greater that I felt his greatness on the instant when I met his eyes.

"There was talk of war that night. Lincoln did not join in it, I remember, although I do not recall what he said. But when he rose to go I went with him. We walked down the street past dooryards where lilacs were blooming, keeping together till we crossed the river. There our ways parted. I told him a little of what Judge Adams had said of him. He laughed at the praise, waving it away from himself. 'It's a good thought, though,' he said, 'a great dream for others. But we need more than the dreaming, my friend. When the time comes, will you be ready?'

"I held out my hand to him in pledge.

"My way home that night took me past the armory where the Zouaves, the boys whom Ellsworth trained, were drilling. You remember Ellsworth's story, Peter? He was the first officer to die in the war." The boy nodded solemnly, and the man went on. "With Abraham Lincoln's voice ringing in my ears I enlisted.

"Years afterward, when Abraham Lincoln was President, war came. I'd seen Lincoln often in the years between." James Thorold stopped his restless pacing and stood at the end of the table away from Peter, leaning over it slightly, as he seemed to keep up his story with difficulty. "He came often to Judge Adams's house. There were evenings when the three of us sat in the parlor with the dusk drifting in from the lake, and spoke of the future of the nation. Judge Adams thought war inevitable. Abraham Lincoln thought it could be averted. They both dreaded it. I was young, and I hoped for it. 'What'll you do, Jim, if war should come?' they asked me once. 'I'd go as a private,' I told them.

"If the war had come then I should have gone with the first regiment out. But when the call sounded Ellsworth had gone to New York and the Zouaves had merged with another regiment. I didn't go with them in the beginning because I told myself that I wanted to be with the first troop that went from Illinois to the front. I didn't join until after Lincoln had sent out his call for volunteers.

"You see," he explained to the silent boy, "I had left Judge Adams's office and struck out for myself. Chicago was showing me golden opportunities. Before me, if I stayed, stretched a wide road of success."

"And you didn't go?" Peter interrupted his father for the first time. "I thought —" His voice broke.

"I went," James Thorold said. "The regiment, the Nineteenth, was at the border when Lincoln gave the call. There was a bounty being offered to join it. I would have gone anyhow, but I thought that I might just as well take the money. I was giving up so much to go, I reasoned. And so I took the bounty. The provost marshal gave me the money in the office right across the square from the old court-house. I put it in the bank before I started south.

"I left Chicago that night with a great thrill. I was going to fight for a great cause, for Abraham Lincoln's great dream, for the country my father had died for in Mexico, that my grandfather had fought for at Lundy's Lane. I think," he said, "that if I might have gone right down to the fighting, I'd have stood the test. But when I came to Tennessee the regiment had gone stale. We waited, and waited. Every day I lost a little interest. Every day the routine dragged a little harder. I had time to see what opportunities I had left back here in Chicago. I wasn't afraid of the fighting. But the sheer hatred of what I came to call the uselessness of war gnawed at my soul. I kept thinking of the ways in which I might shape my destiny if only I were free. I kept thinking of the thousand roads to wealth, to personal success, that Chicago held for me. One night I took my chance. I slipped past the lines."

"Father!" The boy's voice throbbed with pain. His eyes dilated with horror at the realization of the older man's admission, fixed their gaze accusingly on James Thorold. "You weren't a — a deserter?" He breathed the word fearfully.

"I was a bounty-jumper."

"Oh!" Peter Thorold's shoulders drooped as if under the force of a vital blow. Vaguely as he knew the term, the boy knew only too well the burden of disgrace that it carried. Once, in school, he had heard an old tutor apply it to some character of history whom he had especially despised. Again, in a home where he had visited, he had heard another old man use the phrase in contempt for some local personage who had attempted to seek public office. Bounty-jumper! Its province expressed to the lad's mind a layer of the inferno beneath the one reserved for the Benedict Arnolds and the Aaron Burrs. Vainly he bugled to his own troops of self-control; but they, too, were deserters in the calamity. He flung his arms across the table, surrendering to his sobs.

Almost impassively James Thorold watched him, as if he himself had gone so far back into his thought of the past that he could not bridge the gap to Peter now. With some thought of crossing the chasm he took up his tale of dishonor. Punctuated by the boy's sobs it went on.

"I came back to Chicago and drew the money from the bank. I knew I couldn't go back to the practise of law. I changed my name to Thorold and started in business as an army contractor. I made money. The money that's made us rich, the money that's sending me to Forsland" — a bitterness not in his voice before edged his mention of the embassy — "came from that bounty that the provost marshal gave me."

He turned his back upon the sobbing boy, walking over to the window and staring outward upon the April brightness of the noonday ere he spoke again. "You know of the Nineteenth's record? They were at Nashville, and they were at Chattanooga after my colonel came back, dead. I went out of Chicago when his body was brought in. Then Turchin took command of the brigade. The Nineteenth went into the big fights. They were at Chickamauga. Benton fell there. He'd been in Judge Adams's office with me. After I'd come back he'd joined the regiment. The day the news of Chickamauga came I met Judge Adams on Washington Street. He knew me. He looked at me as Peter might have looked at Judas."

Slowly Peter Thorold raised his head from his arms, staring at the man beside the window. James Thorold met his look with sombre sorrow. "Don't think I've had no punishment," he said. "Remember that I loved Judge Adams. And I loved Abraham Lincoln."

"Oh, no, no!" The boy's choked utterance came in protest. "If you'd really cared for them you wouldn't have failed them."

"I have prayed," his father said, "that you may never know the grief of having failed the men you have loved. There's no heavier woe, Peter." Again his gaze went from the boy, from the room, from the present. "I did not see Abraham Lincoln again until he was dead," he said. "They brought him back and set his bier in the old court-house. The night he lay there I went in past the guards and looked long upon the face of him who had been my friend. I saw the sadness and the sorrow, the greatness and the glory, that life and death had sculptured there. He had dreamed and he had done. When the time had come he had been ready. I knelt beside his coffin; and I promised God and Abraham Lincoln that I would, before I died, make atonement for the faith I had broken."

Peter's sobbing had died down to husky flutterings of breath, but he kept his face averted from the man at the other side of the table. "I meant to make some sort of reparation," James Thorold explained, listlessness falling like twilight on his mood as if the sun had gone down on his power, "but I was always so busy, so busy. And there seemed no real occasion for sacrifice. I never sought public office or public honors till I thought you wanted me to have them, Peter." He turned directly to the boy, but the boy did not move. "I was so glad of Forsland — yesterday. Through all these years I have told myself that, after all, I had done no great wrong. But sometimes, when the bands were playing and the flags were flying, I knew that I had turned away from the Grail after I had looked upon it. I knew it to-day when I stood beside that boy's coffin. I had said that times change. I know now that only the time changes. The spirit does not die, but it's a stream that goes underground to come up, a clear spring, in unexpected places. My father died in Mexico. I failed my country. And Isador Framberg dies at Vera Cruz."

"For our country," the boy said bitterly.

"And his own," his father added. "For him, for his people, for all these who walk in darkness Abraham Lincoln died. The gleam of his torch shone far down their lands. His message brought them here. They have known him even as I, who walked with him in life, did not know him until to-day. And they are paying him. That dead boy is their offering to him, their message that they are the Americans."

Into Peter Thorold's eyes, as he looked upon his father, leaped a flash of blue fire. Searchingly he stared into the face of the older man as Galahad might have gazed upon a sorrowing Percival. "You're going to give up Forsland?" he breathed, touching the paper on the table. "I gave up Forsland," James Thorold said, "when I saw you at Isador Framberg's side. I knew that I was not worthy to represent your America — and his." He held out his hands to Peter longingly. The boy's strong one closed over them. Peter Thorold, sighting the mansion of his father's soul, saw that the other man had passed the portals of confession into an empire of expiation mightier than the Court of St. Jerome.

BREAKING INTO FAST COMPANY (1915)

Zane Grey

THEY MAY SAY baseball is the same in the minor leagues that it is in the big leagues, but any old ball player or manager knows better. Where the difference comes in, however, is in the greater excellence and unity of the major players, a speed, a daring, a finish that can be acquired only in competition with one another.

I thought of this when I led my party into Morrisey's private box in the grand stand of the Chicago American League grounds. We had come to see the Rube's break into fast company. My great pitcher, Whittaker Hurtle, the Rube, as we called him, had won the Eastern League Pennant for me that season, and Morrisey, the Chicago magnate, had bought him. Milly, my affianced, was with me, looking as happy as she was pretty, and she was chaperoned by her mother, Mrs. Nelson.

With me, also, were two veterans of my team, McCall and Spears, who lived in Chicago, and who would have traveled a few miles to see the Rube pitch. And the other member of my party was Mrs. Hurtle, the Rube's wife, as saucy and as sparkling-eyed as when she had been Nan Brown. Today she wore a new tailor-made gown, new bonnet, new gloves—she said she had decorated herself in a manner befitting the wife of a major league pitcher.

Morrisey's box was very comfortable, and, as I was pleased to note, so situated that we had a fine view of the field and stands, and yet were comparatively secluded. The bleachers were filling. Some of the Chicago players were on the field tossing and batting balls; the Rube, however, had not yet appeared.

A moment later a metallic sound was heard on the stairs leading up into the box. I knew it for baseball spiked shoes clanking on the wood.

The Rube, looking enormous in his uniform, stalked into the box, knocking over two chairs as he entered. He carried a fielder's glove in one huge freckled hand, and a big black bat in the other.

Nan, with much dignity and a very manifest pride, introduced him to Mrs. Nelson.

There was a little chatting, and then, upon the arrival of Manager Morrisey, we men retired to the back of the box to talk baseball.

Chicago was in fourth place in the league race, and had a fighting chance to beat Detroit out for the third position. Philadelphia was scheduled for that day, and Philadelphia had a great team. It was leading the race, and almost beyond all question would land the flag. In truth, only one more victory was needed to clinch the pennant. The team had three games to play in Chicago and it was to wind up the season with three in Washington. Six games to play and only one imperatively important to win! But baseball is uncertain, and until the Philadelphians won that game they would be a band of fiends.

"Well, Whit, this is where you break in," I said. "Now, tip us straight. You've had more than a week's rest. How's that arm?"

"Grand, Con, grand!" replied the Rube with his frank smile. "I was a little anxious till I warmed up. But say! I've got more up my sleeve today than I ever had."

"That'll do for me," said Morrisey, rubbing his hands. "I'll spring something on these swelled Quakers today. Now, Connelly, give Hurtle one of your old talks—the last one—and then I'll ring the gong."

I added some words of encouragement, not forgetting my old ruse to incite the Rube by rousing his temper. And then, as the gong rang and the Rube was departing, Nan stepped forward for her say. There was a little white under the tan on her cheek, and her eyes had a darkling flash.

"Whit, it's a magnificent sight—that beautiful green field and the stands. What a crowd of fans! Why, I never saw a real baseball crowd before. There are twenty thousand here. And there's a difference in the feeling. It's sharper—new to me. It's big league baseball. Not a soul in that crowd ever heard of you, but, I believe, tomorrow the whole baseball world will have heard of you. Mr. Morrisey knows. I saw it in his face. Captain Spears knows. Connie knows. I know."

Then she lifted her face and, pulling him down within reach, she kissed him. Nan took her husband's work in dead earnest; she gloried in it, and perhaps she had as much to do with making him a great pitcher as any of us.

The Rube left the box, and I found a seat between Nan and Milly. The field was a splendid sight. Those bleachers made me glow with managerial satisfaction. On the field both teams pranced and danced and bounced around in practice.

In spite of the absolutely last degree of egotism manifested by the Philadelphia players, I could not but admire such a splendid body of men.

"So these are the champions of last season and of this season, too," commented Milly. "I don't wonder. How swiftly and cleanly they play! They appear not to exert themselves, yet they always get the ball in perfect time. It all reminds me of—of the rhythm of music. And that champion batter and runner—that Lane in center—isn't he just beautiful? He walks and runs like a blue-ribbon winner at the horse show. I tell you one thing, Connie, these Quakers are on dress parade."

"Oh, these Quakers hate themselves, I don't think!" retorted Nan. Being a rabid girl-fan it was, of course, impossible for Nan to speak baseball convictions or gossip without characteristic baseball slang. "Stuck on themselves! I never saw the like in my life. That fellow Lane is so swelled that he can't get down off his toes. But he's a wonder, I must admit that. They're a bunch of stars. Easy, fast, trained—they're machines, and I'll bet they're Indians to fight. I can see it sticking out all over them. This will certainly be some game with Whit handing up that jump ball of his to this gang of champs. But, Connie, I'll go you Whit beats them."

I laughed and refused to gamble.

The gong rang; the crowd seemed to hum and rustle softly to quiet attention; Umpire McClung called the names of the batteries; then the familiar "Play!"

There was the usual applause from the grand stand and welcome cheers from the bleachers. The Rube was the last player to go out. Morrisey was a manager who always played to the stands, and no doubt he held the Rube back for effect. If so, he ought to have been gratified. That moment reminded me of my own team and audience upon the occasion of the Rube's debut. It was the same—only here it happened in the big league, before a championship team and twenty thousand fans.

The roar that went up from the bleachers might well have scared an unseasoned pitcher out of his wits. And the Quakers lined up before their bench and gazed at this newcomer who had the nerve to walk out there to the box. Cogswell stood on the coaching line, looked at the Rube and then held up both arms and turned toward the Chicago bench as if to ask Morrisey: "Where did you get that?"

Nan, quick as a flash to catch a point, leaned over the box-rail and looked at the champions with fire in her eye. "Oh, you just wait! wait!" she bit out between her teeth.

Certain it was that there was no one who knew the Rube as well as I; and I knew beyond the shadow of a doubt that the hour before me would see brightening of a great star pitcher on the big league horizon. It was bound to be a full hour for me. I had much reason to be grateful to Whit Hurtle. He had pulled my team out of a rut and won me the pennant, and the five thousand dollars I got for his release bought the little cottage on the hill for Milly and me. Then there was my pride in having developed him. And all that I needed to calm me, settle me down into assurance and keen criticism of the game, was to see the Rube pitch a few balls with his old incomparable speed and control.

Berne, first batter for the Quakers, walked up to the plate. He was another Billy Hamilton, built like a wedge. I saw him laugh at the long pitcher.

Whit swayed back, coiled and uncoiled. Something thin, white, glancing, shot at Berne. He ducked, escaping the ball by a smaller margin than appeared good for his confidence. He spoke low to the Rube, and what he said was probably not flavored with the milk of friendly sweetness.

"Wild! What'd you look for?" called out Cogswell scornfully. "He's from the woods!"

The Rube swung his enormously long arm, took an enormous stride toward third base, and pitched again. It was one of his queer deliveries. The ball cut the plate.

"Ho! Ho!" yelled the Quakers.

The Rube's next one was his out curve. It broke toward the corner of the plate and would have been a strike had not Berne popped it up.

Callopy, the second hitter, faced the Rube, and he, too, after the manner of ball players, made some remark meant only for the Rube's ears. Callopy was a famous waiter. He drove more pitchers mad with his implacable patience than any hitter in the league, The first one of the Rube's he waited on crossed the in-corner; the second crossed the out-corner and the third was Rube's wide, slow, tantalizing "stitch-ball," as we call it, for the reason that it came so slow a batter could count the stitches. I believe Callopy waited on that curve, decided to hit it, changed his mind and waited some more, and finally the ball maddened him and he had to poke at it, the result being a weak grounder.

Then the graceful, powerful Lane, champion batter, champion base runner, stepped to the plate. How a baseball crowd, any crowd, anywhere, loves the champion batter! The ovation Lane received made me wonder, with this impressive reception in a hostile camp, what could be the manner of it on his home field? Any boy ball-player from the lots seeing Lane knock the dirt out of his spikes and step into position would have known he was a 400 hitter.

I was curious to see what the Rube would pitch Lane. It must have been a new and significant moment for Hurtle. Some pitchers actually wilt when facing a hitter of Lane's reputation. But he, on his baseball side, was peculiarly unemotional. Undoubtedly he could get furious, but that only increased his effectiveness. To my amazement the Rube pitched Lane a little easy ball, not in any sense like his floater or stitch-ball, but just a little toss that any youngster might have tossed. Of all possible balls, Lane was not expecting such as that, and he let it go. If the nerve of it amazed me, what did it not do to Lane? I saw his face go fiery red. The grand stand murmured; let out one short yelp of pleasure; the Quaker players chaffed Lane.

The pitch was a strike. I was gripping my chair now, and for the next pitch I prophesied the Rube's wonderful jump ball, which he had not yet used. He swung long, and at the end of his swing seemed to jerk tensely. I scarcely saw the ball. It had marvelous speed. Lane did not offer to hit it, and it was a strike. He looked at the Rube, then at Cogswell. That veteran appeared amused. The bleachers, happy and surprised to be able to yell at Lane, yelled heartily.

Again I took it upon myself to interpret the Rube's pitching mind. He had another ball that he had not used, a drop, an unhittable drop. I thought he would use that next. He did, and though

Lane reached it with the bat, the hit was a feeble one. He had been fooled and the side was out.

Poole, the best of the Quakers' pitching staff, walked out to the slab. He was a left-hander, and Chicago, having so many players who batted left-handed, always found a southpaw a hard nut to crack. Cogswell, field manager and captain of the Quakers, kicked up the dust around first base and yelled to his men: "Git in the game!"

Staats hit Poole's speed ball into deep short and was out; Mitchell flew out to Berne; Rand grounded to second.

While the teams again changed sides the fans cheered, and then indulged in the first stretch of the game. I calculated that they would be stretching their necks presently, trying to keep track of the Rube's work. Nan leaned on the railing absorbed in her own hope and faith. Milly chattered about this and that, people in the boxes, and the chances of the game.

My own interest, while it did not wholly preclude the fortunes of the Chicago players at the bat, was mostly concerned with the Rube's fortunes in the field.

In the Rube's half inning he retired Bannister and Blandy on feeble infield grounders, and worked Cogswell into hitting a wide curve high in the air.

Poole meant to win for the Quakers if his good arm and cunning did not fail him, and his pitching was masterly. McCloskey fanned, Hutchinson fouled out, Brewster got a short safe fly just out of reach, and Hoffner hit to second, forcing Brewster.

With Dugan up for the Quakers in the third inning, Cogswell and Bannister, from the coaching lines, began to talk to the Rube. My ears, keen from long practice, caught some of the remarks in spite of the noisy bleachers.

"Say, busher, you've lasted longer'n we expected, but you don't know it!"

"Gol darn you city ball tossers! Now you jest let me alone!"

"We're comin' through the rye!"

"My top-heavy rustic friend, you'll need an airship presently, when you go up!"

All the badinage was good-natured, which was sure proof that the Quakers had not arrived at anything like real appreciation of the Rube. They were accustomed to observe the trying out of many youngsters, of whom ninety-nine out of a hundred failed to make good.

Dugan chopped at three strikes and slammed his bat down. Hucker hit a slow fly to Hoffer. Three men out on five pitched balls! Cogswell, old war horse that he was, stood a full moment and watched the Rube as he walked in to the bench. An idea had penetrated Cogswell's brain, and I would have given something to know what it was. Cogswell was a great baseball general, and though he had a preference for matured ball-players he could, when pressed, see the quality in a youngster. He picked up his mitt and took his position at first with a gruff word to his players.

Rand for Chicago opened with a hit, and the bleachers, ready to strike fire, began to cheer and stamp. When McCloskey, in an attempt to sacrifice, beat out his bunt the crowd roared. Rand, being slow on his feet, had not attempted to make third on the play. Hutchinson sacrificed, neatly advancing the runners. Then the bleachers played the long rolling drum of clattering feet with shrill whistling accompaniment. Brewster batted a wicked ground ball to Blandy. He dove into the dust, came up with the ball, and feinting to throw home he wheeled and shot the ball to Cogswell, who in turn shot it to the plate to head Rand. Runner and ball got there apparently together, but Umpire McClung's decision went against Rand. It was fine, fast work, but how the bleachers stormed at McClung!

"Rob-b-ber!"

Again the Head of the Quakers' formidable list was up. I knew from the way that Cogswell paced the coaching box that the word had gone out to look the Rube over seriously. There were possibilities even in rubes.

Berne carefully stepped into the batter's box, as if he wanted to be certain to the breadth of a hair how close he was to the plate. He was there this time to watch the Rube pitch, to work him out, to see what was what. He crouched low, and it would have been extremely hard to guess what he was up to. His great play, however, was his ability to dump the ball and beat out the throw to first. It developed presently, that this was now his intention and that the Rube knew it and pitched him the one ball which is almost impossible to bunt—a high incurve, over the inside corner. There was no mistaking the Rube's magnificent control. True as a plumb line he shot up the ball—once, twice, and Berne fouled both—two strikes. Grudgingly he waited on the next, but it, too, was over the corner, and Berne went out on strikes. The great crowd did not, of course, grasp the finesse of the play, but Berne had struck out—that was enough for them.

Callopy, the famous spiker, who had put many a player out of the game for weeks at a time, strode into the batter's place, and he, too, was not at the moment making any funny remarks. The Rube delivered a ball that all but hit Callopy fair on the head. It was the second narrow escape for him, and the roar he let out showed how he resented being threatened with a little of his own medicine. As might have been expected, and very likely as the Rube intended, Callopy hit the next ball, a sweeping curve, up over the infield.

I was trying to see all the intricate details of the motive and action on the field, and it was not easy to watch several players at once. But while Berne and Callopy were having their troubles with the Rube, I kept the tail of my eye on Cogswell. He was prowling up and down the third-base line.

He was missing no signs, no indications, no probabilities, no possibilities. But he was in doubt. Like a hawk he was watching the Rube, and, as well, the crafty batters. The inning might not tell the truth as to the Rube's luck, though it would test his control. The Rube's speed and curves, without any head work, would have made him a pitcher of no mean ability, but was this remarkable placing of balls just accident? That was the question.

When Berne walked to the bench I distinctly heard him say: "Come out of it, you dubs. I say you can't work him or wait him. He's peggin' 'em out of a gun!"

Several of the Quakers were standing out from the bench, all intent on the Rube. He had stirred them up. First it was humor; then ridicule, curiosity, suspicion, doubt. And I knew it would grow to wonder and certainty, then fierce attack from both tongues and bats, and lastly—for ball players are generous—unstinted admiration.

Somehow, not only the first climaxes of a game but the decisions, the convictions, the reputations of pitchers and fielders evolve around the great hitter. Plain it was that the vast throng of spectators, eager to believe in a new find, wild to welcome a new star, yet loath to trust to their own impulsive judgments, held themselves in check until once more the great Lane had faced the Rube.

The field grew tolerably quiet just then. The Rube did not exert himself. The critical stage had no concern for him. He pitched Lane a high curve, over the plate, but in close, a ball meant to be hit and a ball hard to hit safely. Lane knew that as well as any hitter in the world, so he let two of the curves go by—two strikes. Again the Rube relentlessly gave him the same ball; and Lane, hitting viciously, spitefully, because he did not want to hit that kind of a ball, sent up a fly that Rand easily captured.

"Oh, I don't know! Pretty fair, I guess!" yelled a tenor-voiced fan; and he struck the keynote. And the bleachers rose to their feet and gave the Rube the rousing cheer of the brotherhood of fans.

Hoffer walked to first on a base on balls. Sweeney advanced him. The Rube sent up a giant fly to Callopy. Then Staats hit safely, scoring the first run of the game. Hoffer crossed the plate amid vociferous applause. Mitchell ended the inning with a fly to Blandy.

What a change had come over the spirit of that Quaker aggregation! It was something to make a man thrill with admiration and, if he happened to favor Chicago, to fire all his fighting blood. The players poured upon the Rube a continuous stream of scathing abuse. They would have made a raging devil of a mild-mannered clergyman. Some of them were skilled in caustic wit, most of them were possessed of forked tongues; and Cogswell, he of a thousand baseball battles, had a genius for inflaming anyone he tormented. This was mostly beyond the ken of the audience, and behind the back of the umpire, but it was perfectly plain to me. The Quakers were trying to rattle the Rube, a trick of the game as fair for one side as for the other. I sat there tight in my seat, grimly glorying in the way the Rube refused to be disturbed. But the lion in him was rampant. Fortunately, it was his strange gift to pitch better the angrier he got; and the more the Quakers flayed him, the more he let himself out to their crushing humiliation.

The innings swiftly passed to the eighth with Chicago failing to score again, with Philadelphia failing to score at all. One scratch hit and a single, gifts to the weak end of the batting list, were all the lank pitcher allowed them. Long since the bleachers had crowned the Rube. He was theirs and they were his; and their voices had the peculiar strangled hoarseness due to over-exertion. The grand stand, slower to understand and approve, arrived later; but it got there about the seventh, and ladies' gloves and men's hats were sacrificed.

In the eighth the Quakers reluctantly yielded their meed of praise, showing it by a cessation of their savage wordy attacks on the Rube. It was a kind of sullen respect, wrung from the bosom of great foes.

Then the ninth inning was at hand. As the sides changed I remembered to look at the feminine group in our box. Milly was in a most beautiful glow of happiness and excitement. Nan sat rigid, leaning over the rail, her face white and drawn, and she kept saying in a low voice: "Will it never end? Will it never end?" Mrs. Nelson stared wearily.

It was the Quakers' last stand. They faced it as a team that had won many a game in the ninth with two men out. Dugan could do nothing with the Rube's unhittable drop, for a drop curve was his weakness, and he struck out. Hucker hit to Hoffer, who fumbled, making the first error of the game. Poole dumped the ball, as evidently the Rube desired, for he handed up a straight one, but the bunt rolled teasingly and the Rube, being big and tall, failed to field it in time.

Suddenly the whole field grew quiet. For the first time Cogswell's coaching was clearly heard.

"One out! Take a lead! Take a lead! Go through this time. Go through!"

Could it be possible, I wondered, that after such a wonderful exhibition of pitching the Rube would lose out in the ninth?

There were two Quakers on base, one out, and two of the best hitters in the league on deck, with a chance of Lane getting up.

"Oh! Oh! Oh!" moaned Nan.

I put my hand on hers. "Don't quit, Nan. You'll never forgive yourself if you quit. Take it from me, Whit will pull out of this hole!"

What a hole that was for the Rube on the day of his break into fast company! I measured it by his remarkable deliberation. He took a long time to get ready to pitch to Berne, and when he let drive it was as if he had been trifling all before in that game. I could think of no way to figure it except that when the ball left him there was scarcely any appreciable interval of time before it cracked in Sweeney's mitt. It was the Rube's drop, which I believed unhittable. Berne let it go by, shaking his head as McClung called it a strike. Another followed, which Berne chopped at vainly. Then with the same upheaval of his giant frame, the same flinging of long arms and lunging forward, the Rube delivered a third drop. And Berne failed to hit it.

The voiceless bleachers stamped on the benches and the grand stand likewise thundered.

Callopy showed his craft by stepping back and lining Rube's high pitch to left. Hoffer leaped across and plunged down, getting his gloved hand in front of the ball. The hit was safe, but Hoffer's valiant effort saved a tie score.

Lane up! Three men on bases! Two out!

Not improbably there were many thousand spectators of that thrilling moment who pitied the Rube for the fate which placed Lane at the bat then. But I was not one of them. Nevertheless my throat was clogged, my mouth dry, and my ears full of bells. I could have done something terrible to Hurtle for his deliberation, yet I knew he was proving himself what I had always tried to train him to be.

Then he swung, stepped out, and threw his body with the ball. This was his rarely used pitch, his last resort, his fast rise ball that jumped up a little at the plate. Lane struck under it. How significant on the instant to see old Cogswell's hands go up! Again the Rube pitched, and this time Lane watched the ball go by. Two strikes!

That whole audience leaped to its feet, whispering, yelling, screaming, roaring, bawling.

The Rube received the ball from Sweeney and quick as lightning he sped it plateward. The great Lane struck out! The game was over—Chicago, 1; Philadelphia, 0.

In that whirling moment when the crowd went mad and Milly was hugging me, and Nan pounding holes in my hat, I had a queer sort of blankness, a section of time when my sensations were deadlocked.

"Oh! Connie, look!" cried Nan. I saw Lane and Cogswell warmly shaking hands with the Rube. Then the hungry clamoring fans tumbled upon the field and swarmed about the players.

Whereupon Nan kissed me and Milly, and then kissed Mrs. Nelson. In that radiant moment Nan was all sweetness.

"It is the Rube's break into fast company," she said.

THE GAY OLD DOG (1917)

Edna Ferber

THOSE OF YOU who have dwelt — or even lingered — in Chicago, Illinois (this is not a humorous story), are familiar with the region known as the Loop. For those others of you to whom Chicago is a transfer point between New York and San Francisco there is presented this brief explanation:

The Loop is a clamorous, smoke-infested district embraced by the iron arms of the elevated tracks. In a city boasting fewer millions, it would be known familiarly as downtown. From Congress to Lake Street, from Wabash almost to the river, those thunderous tracks make a complete circle, or loop. Within it lie the retail shops, the commercial hotels, the theaters, the restaurants. It is the Fifth Avenue (diluted) and the Broadway (deleted) of Chicago. And he who frequents it by night in search of amusement and cheer is known, vulgarly, as a loop-hound.

Jo Hertz was a loop-hound. On the occasion of those sparse first nights granted the metropolis of the Middle West he was always present, third row, aisle, left. When a new loop cafe was opened, Jo's table always commanded an unobstructed view of anything worth viewing. On entering he was wont to say, "Hello, Gus," with careless cordiality to the head-waiter, the while his eye roved expertly from table to table as he removed his gloves. He ordered things under glass, so that his table, at midnight or thereabouts, resembled a hot-bed that favors the bell system. The waiters fought for him. He was the kind of man who mixes his own salad dressing. He liked to call for a bowl, some cracked ice, lemon, garlic, paprika, salt, pepper, vinegar and oil, and make a rite of it. People at near-by tables would lay down their knives and forks to watch, fascinated. The secret of it seemed to lie in using all the oil in sight and calling for more.

That was Jo — a plump and lonely bachelor of fifty. A plethoric, roving-eyed and kindly man, clutching vainly at the garments of a youth that had long slipped past him. Jo Hertz, in one of those pinch-waist belted suits and a trench coat and a little green hat, walking up Michigan Avenue of a bright winter's afternoon, trying to take the curb with a jaunty youthfulness against which every one of his fat-encased muscles rebelled, was a sight for mirth or pity, depending on one's vision.

The gay-dog business was a late phase in the life of Jo Hertz. He had been a quite different sort of canine. The staid and harassed brother of three unwed and selfish sisters is an under dog. The tale of how Jo Hertz came to be a loop-hound should not be compressed within the limits of a short story. It should be told as are the photoplays, with frequent throw-backs and many cut-ins. To condense twenty-three years of a man's life into some five or six thousand words requires a verbal economy amounting to parsimony.

At twenty-seven Jo had been the dutiful, hard-working son (in the wholesale harness business) of a widowed and gummidging mother, who called him Joey. If you had looked close you would have seen that now and then a double wrinkle would appear between Jo's eyes — a wrinkle that had no business there at twenty-seven. Then Jo's mother died, leaving him handicapped by a death-bed promise, the three sisters and a three-story-and-basement house on Calumet Avenue. Jo's wrinkle became a fixture.

Death-bed promises should be broken as lightly as they are seriously made. The dead have no right to lay their clammy fingers upon the living.

"Joey," she had said, in her high, thin voice, "take care of the girls."

"I will, ma," Jo had choked.

"Joey," and the voice was weaker, "promise me you won't marry till the girls are all provided for." Then as Jo had hesitated, appalled: "Joey, it's my dying wish. Promise!"

"I promise, ma," he had said.

Whereupon his mother had died, comfortably, leaving him with a completely ruined life.

They were not bad-looking girls, and they had a certain style, too. That is, Stell and Eva had. Carrie, the middle one, taught school over on the West Side. In those days it took her almost two hours each way. She said the kind of costume she required should have been corrugated steel. But all three knew what was being worn, and they wore it — or fairly faithful copies of it. Eva, the housekeeping sister, had a needle knack. She could skim the State Street windows and come away with a mental photograph of every separate tuck, hem, yoke, and ribbon. Heads of departments showed her the things they kept in drawers, and she went home and reproduced them with the aid of a two-dollar-a-day seamstress. Stell, the youngest, was the beauty. They called her Babe. She wasn't really a beauty, but some one had once told her that she looked like Janice Meredith (it was when that work of fiction was at the height of its popularity). For years afterward, whenever she went to parties, she affected a single, fat curl over her right shoulder, with a rose stuck through it.

Twenty-three years ago one's sisters did not strain at the household leash, nor crave a career. Carrie taught school, and hated it. Eva kept house expertly and complainingly. Babe's profession was being the family beauty, and it took all her spare time. Eva always let her sleep until ten.

This was Jo's household, and he was the nominal head of it. But it was an empty title. The three women dominated his life. They weren't consciously selfish. If you had called them cruel they would have put you down as mad. When you are the lone brother of three sisters, it means that you must constantly be calling for, escorting, or dropping one of them somewhere. Most men of Jo's age were standing before their mirror of a Saturday night, whistling blithely and abstractedly while they discarded a blue polka-dot for a maroon tie, whipped off the maroon for a shot-silk, and at the last moment decided against the shot-silk in favor of a plain black-and-white, because she had once said she preferred quiet ties. Jo, when he should have been preening his feathers for conquest, was saying:

"Well, my God, I *am* hurrying! Give a man time, can't you? I just got home. You girls have been laying around the house all day. No wonder you're ready."

He took a certain pride in seeing his sisters well dressed, at a time when he should have been reveling in fancy waistcoats and brilliant-hued socks, according to the style of that day, and the inalienable right of any unwed male under thirty, in any day. On those rare occasions when his business necessitated an out-of-town

trip, he would spend half a day floundering about the shops select-
ing handkerchiefs, or stockings, or feathers, or fans, or gloves for
the girls. They always turned out to be the wrong kind, judging by
their reception.

From Carrie, "What in the world do I want of a fan!"

"I thought you didn't have one," Jo would say.

"I haven't. I never go to dances."

Jo would pass a futile hand over the top of his head, as was his
way when disturbed. "I just thought you'd like one. I thought
every girl liked a fan. Just," feebly, "just to — to have."

"Oh, for pity's sake!"

And from Eva or Babe, " I've *got* silk stockings, Jo." Or, "You
brought me handkerchiefs the last time."

There was something selfish in his giving, as there always is in
any gift freely and joyfully made. They never suspected the exquisite pleasure it gave him to select these things; these fine, soft, silken
things. There were many things about this slow-going, amiable
brother of theirs that they never suspected. If you had told them he
was a dreamer of dreams, for example, they would have been
amused. Sometimes, dead-tired by nine o'clock, after a hard day
downtown, he would doze over the evening paper. At intervals he
would wake, red-eyed, to a snatch of conversation such as, "Yes,
but if you get a blue you can wear it anywhere. It's dressy, and at
the same time it's quiet, too." Eva, the expert, wrestling with Carrie over the problem of the new spring dress. They never guessed
that the commonplace man in the frayed old smoking-jacket had
banished them all from the room long ago; had banished himself,
for that matter. In his place was a tall, debonair, and rather danger-
ously handsome man to whom six o'clock spelled evening clothes.
The kind of a man who can lean up against a mantel, or propose a
toast, or give an order to a man-servant, or whisper a gallant speech
in a lady's ear with equal ease. The shabby old house on Calumet
Avenue was transformed into a brocaded and chandeliered rendez-
vous for the brilliance of the city. Beauty was there, and wit. But
none so beautiful and witty as She. Mrs.— er — Jo Hertz. There
was wine, of course; but no vulgar display. There was music; the
soft sheen of satin; laughter. And he the gracious, tactful host, king
of his own domain —

"Jo, for heaven's sake, if you're going to snore go to bed!"

"Why — did I fall asleep?"

"You haven't been doing anything else all evening. A person would think you were fifty instead of thirty."

And Jo Hertz was again just the dull, gray, common-place brother of three well-meaning sisters.

Babe used to say petulantly, "Jo, why don't you ever bring home any of your men friends? A girl might as well not have any brother, all the good you do."

Jo, conscience-stricken, did his best to make amends. But a man who has been petticoat-ridden for years loses the knack, somehow, of comradeship with men. He acquires, too, a knowledge of women, and a distaste for them, equaled only, perhaps, by that of an elevator-starter in a department store.

Which brings us to one Sunday in May. Jo came home from a late Sunday afternoon walk to find company for supper. Carrie often had in one of her schoolteacher friends, or Babe one of her frivolous intimates, or even Eva a staid guest of the old-girl type. There was always a Sunday night supper of potato salad, and cold meat, and coffee, and perhaps a fresh cake. Jo rather enjoyed it, being a hospitable soul. But he regarded the guests with the undazzled eyes of a man to whom they were just so many petticoats, timid of the night streets and requiring escort home. If you had suggested to him that some of his sisters' popularity was due to his own presence, or if you had hinted that the more kittenish of these visitors were palpably making eyes at him, he would have stared in amazement and unbelief.

This Sunday night it turned out to be one of Carrie's friends.

"Emily," said Carrie, "this is my brother, Jo."

Jo had learned what to expect in Carrie's friends. Drab-looking women in the late thirties, whose facial lines all slanted downward.

"Happy to meet you," said Jo, and looked down at a different sort altogether. A most surprisingly different sort, for one of Carrie's friends. This Emily person was very small, and fluffy, and blue-eyed, and sort of — well, crinkly looking. You know. The corners of her mouth when she smiled, and her eyes when she looked up at you, and her hair, which was brown, but had the miraculous effect, somehow, of being golden.

Jo shook hands with her. Her hand was incredibly small, and soft, so that you were afraid of crushing it, until you discovered she had a firm little grip all her own. It surprised and amused you, that grip, as does a baby's unexpected clutch on your patronizing fore-finger. As Jo felt it in his own big clasp, the strangest thing happened to him. Something inside Jo Hertz stopped working for a moment, then lurched sickeningly, then thumped like mad. It was his heart. He stood staring down at her, and she up at him, until the others laughed. Then their hands fell apart, lingeringly.

"Are you a school-teacher, Emily?" he said.

"Kindergarten. It's my first year. And don't call me Emily, please."

"Why not? It's your name. I think it's the prettiest name in the world." Which he hadn't meant to say at all. In fact, he was perfectly aghast to find himself saying it. But he meant it.

At supper he passed her things, and stared, until everybody laughed again, and Eva said acidly, "Why don't you feed her?"

It wasn't that Emily had an air of helplessness. She just made you feel you wanted her to be helpless, so that you could help her.

Jo took her home, and from that Sunday night he began to strain at the leash. He took his sisters out, dutifully, but he would suggest, with a carelessness that deceived no one, "Don't you want one of your girl friends to come along? That little What's-her-name — Emily, or something. So long's I've got three of you, I might as well have a full squad."

For a long time he didn't know what was the matter with him. He only knew he was miserable, and yet happy. Sometimes his heart seemed to ache with an actual physical ache. He realized that he wanted to do things for Emily. He wanted to buy things for Emily — useless, pretty, expensive things that he couldn't afford. He wanted to buy everything that Emily needed, and everything that Emily desired. He wanted to marry Emily. That was it. He discovered that one day, with a shock, in the midst of a transaction in the harness business. He stared at the man with whom he was dealing until that startled person grew uncomfortable.

"What's the matter, Hertz?"

"Matter?"

"You look as if you'd seen a ghost or found a gold mine. I don't know which."

"Gold mine," said Jo. And then, "No. Ghost."

For he remembered that high, thin voice, and his promise. And the harness business was slithering downhill with dreadful rapidity, as the automobile business began its amazing climb. Jo tried to stop it. But he was not that kind of business man. It never occurred to him to jump out of the down-going vehicle and catch the up-going one. He stayed on, vainly applying brakes that refused to work.

"You know, Emily, I couldn't support two households now. Not the way things are. But if you'll wait. If you'll only wait. The girls might — that is, Babe and Carrie —"

She was a sensible little thing, Emily. "Of course I'll wait. But we mustn't just sit back and let the years go by. We've got to help."

She went about it as if she were already a little matchmaking matron. She corraled all the men she had ever known and introduced them to Babe, Carrie, and Eva separately, in pairs, and en masse. She arranged parties at which Babe could display the curl. She got up picnics. She stayed home while Jo took the three about. When she was present she tried to look as plain and obscure as possible, so that the sisters should show up to advantage. She schemed, and planned, and contrived, and hoped; and smiled into Jo's despairing eyes.

And three years went by. Three precious years. Carrie still taught school, and hated it. Eva kept house, more and more complainingly as prices advanced and allowance retreated. Stell was still Babe, the family beauty; but even she knew that the time was past for curls. Emily's hair, somehow, lost its glint and began to look just plain brown. Her crinkliness began to iron out.

"Now, look here!" Jo argued, desperately, one night. "We could be happy, anyway. There's plenty of room at the house. Lots of people begin that way. Of course, I couldn't give you all I'd like to at first. But maybe, after a while —"

No dreams of salons, and brocade, and velvet-footed servitors, and satin damask now. Just two rooms, all their own, all alone, and Emily to work for. That was his dream. But it seemed less possible than that other absurd one had been.

You know that Emily was as practical a little thing as she looked fluffy. She knew women. Especially did she know Eva, and Carrie, and Babe. She tried to imagine herself taking the household affairs and the housekeeping pocketbook out of Eva's expert hands. Eva had once displayed to her a sheaf of aigrettes she had bought with what she saved out of the housekeeping money. So then she tried to picture herself allowing the reins of Jo's house to remain in Eva's hands. And everything feminine and normal in her rebelled. Emily knew she'd want to put away her own freshly laundered linen, and smooth it, and pat it. She was that kind of woman. She knew she'd want to do her own delightful haggling with butcher and vegetable peddler. She knew she'd want to muss Jo's hair, and sit on his knee, and even quarrel with him, if necessary, without the awareness of three ever-present pairs of maiden eyes and ears.

"No! No! We'd only be miserable. I know. Even if they didn't object. And they would, Jo. Wouldn't they?"

His silence was miserable assent. Then, "But you do love me, don't you, Emily?"

"I do, Jo. I love you — and love you — and love you. But, Jo, I — can't."

"I know it, dear. I knew it all the time, really. I just thought, maybe, somehow —"

The two sat staring for a moment into space, their hands clasped. Then they both shut their eyes, with a little shudder, as though what they saw was terrible to look upon. Emily's hand, the tiny hand that was so unexpectedly firm, tightened its hold on his, and his crushed the absurd fingers until she winced with pain.

That was the beginning of the end, and they knew it.

Emily wasn't the kind of girl who would be left to pine. There are too many Jo's in the world whose hearts are prone to lurch and then thump at the feel of a soft, fluttering, incredibly small hand in their grip. One year later Emily was married to a young man whose father owned a large, pie-shaped slice of the prosperous state of Michigan.

That being safely accomplished, there was something grimly humorous in the trend taken by affairs in the old house on Calumet. For Eva married. Of all people, Eva! Married well, too, though he was a great deal older than she. She went off in a hat she had copied from a French model at Fields's, and a suit she had contrived with a home dressmaker, aided by pressing on the part of the little tailor in the basement over on Thirty-first Street. It was the last of that, though. The next time they saw her, she had on a hat that even she would have despaired of copying, and a suit that sort of melted into your gaze. She moved to the North Side (trust Eva for that), and Babe assumed the management of the household on Calumet Avenue. It was rather a pinched little household now, for the harness business shrank and shrank.

"I don't see how you can expect me to keep house decently on this!" Babe would say contemptuously. Babe's nose, always a little inclined to sharpness, had whittled down to a point of late. "If you knew what Ben gives Eva."

"It's the best I can do, Sis. Business is something rotten."

"Ben says if you had the least bit of —" Ben was Eva's husband, and quotable, as are all successful men.

"I don't care what Ben says," shouted Jo, goaded into rage. "I'm sick of your everlasting Ben. Go and get a Ben of your own, why don't you, if you're so stuck on the way he does things."

And Babe did. She made a last desperate drive, aided by Eva, and she captured a rather surprised young man in the brokerage way, who had made up his mind not to marry for years and years. Eva wanted to give her her wedding things, but at that Jo broke into sudden rebellion.

"No, sir! No Ben is going to buy my sister's wedding clothes, understand? I guess I'm not broke — yet. I'll furnish the money for her things, and there'll be enough of them, too."

Babe had as useless a trousseau, and as filled with extravagant pink-and-blue and lacy and frilly things as any daughter of doting parents. Jo seemed to find a grim pleasure in providing them. But it left him pretty well pinched. After Babe's marriage (she insisted that they call her Estelle now) Jo sold the house on Calumet. He and Carrie took one of those little flats that were springing up, seemingly over night, all through Chicago's South Side.

There was nothing domestic about Carrie. She had given up teaching two years before, and had gone into Social Service work on the West Side. She had what is known as a legal mind, hard, clear, orderly, and she made a great success of it. Her dream was to live at the Settlement House and give all her time to the work. Upon the little household she bestowed a certain amount of grim, capable attention. It was the same kind of attention she would have given a piece of machinery whose oiling and running had been entrusted to her care. She hated it, and didn't hesitate to say so.

Jo took to prowling about department store basements, and household goods sections. He was always sending home a bargain in a ham, or a sack of potatoes, or fifty pounds of sugar, or a window clamp, or a new kind of paring knife. He was forever doing odd little jobs that the janitor should have done. It was the domestic in him claiming its own.

Then, one night, Carrie came home with a dull glow in her leathery cheeks, and her eyes alight with resolve. They had what she called a plain talk.

"Listen, Jo. They've offered me the job of first assistant resident worker. And I'm going to take it. Take it! I know fifty other girls who'd give their ears for it. I go in next month."

They were at dinner. Jo looked up from his plate, dully. Then he glanced around the little dining-room, with its ugly tan walls and its heavy dark furniture (the Calumet Street pieces fitted cumbersomely into the five-room flat).

"Away? Away from here, you mean — to live?"

Carrie laid down her fork. "Well, really, Jo! After all that explanation."

"But to go over there to live! Why, that neighborhood's full of dirt, and disease, and crime, and the Lord knows what all. I can't let you do that, Carrie."

Carrie's chin came up. She laughed a short little laugh. "Let me! That's eighteenth-century talk, Jo. My life's my own to live. I'm going."

And she went. Jo stayed on in the apartment until the lease was up. Then he sold what furniture he could, stored or gave away the rest, and took a room on Michigan Avenue in one of the old stone mansions whose decayed splendor was being put to such purpose.

Jo Hertz was his own master. Free to marry. Free to come and go. And he found he didn't even think of marrying. He didn't even want to come or go, particularly. A rather frumpy old bachelor, with thinning hair and a thickening neck. Much has been written about the unwed, middle-aged woman; her fussiness, her primness, her angularity of mind and body. In the male that same fussiness develops, and a certain primness, too. But he grows flabby where she grows lean.

Every Thursday evening he took dinner at Eva's, and on Sunday noon at Stell's. He tucked his napkin under his chin and openly enjoyed the home-made soup and the well-cooked meats. After dinner he tried to talk business with Eva's husband, or Stell's. His business talks were the old-fashioned kind, beginning:

"Well, now, looka here. Take, f'rinstance your raw hides and leathers."

But Ben and George didn't want to take f'rinstance your raw hides and leathers. They wanted, when they took anything at all, to take golf, or politics, or stocks. They were the modern type of business man who prefers to leave his work out of his play. Business, with them, was a profession — a finely graded and balanced thing, differing from Jo's clumsy, downhill style as completely as does the method of a great criminal detective differ from that of a village constable. They would listen, restively, and say, "Uh-uh," at intervals, and at the first chance they would sort of fade out of the room, with a meaning glance at their wives. Eva had two children now. Girls. They treated Uncle Jo with good-natured tolerance. Stell had no children. Uncle Jo degenerated, by almost imperceptible degrees, from the position of honored guest, who is served with white meat, to that of one who is content with a leg and one of those obscure and bony sections which, after much turning with a bewildered and investigating knife and fork, leave one baffled and unsatisfied.

Eva and Stell got together and decided that Jo ought to marry.

"It isn't natural," Eva told him. "I never saw a man who took so little interest in women."

"Me!" protested Jo, almost shyly. "Women!"

"Yes. Of course. You act like a frightened school boy."

So they had in for dinner certain friends and acquaintances of fitting age. They spoke of them as "splendid girls." Between thirty-six and forty. They talked awfully well, in a firm, clear way, about civics, and classes, and politics, and economics, and boards. They rather terrified Jo. He didn't understand much that they talked about, and he felt humbly inferior, and yet a little resentful, as if something had passed him by. He escorted them home, dutifully, though they told him not to bother, and they evidently meant it. They seemed capable, not only of going home quite unattended, but of delivering a pointed lecture to any highwayman or brawler who might molest them.

The following Thursday Eva would say, "How did you like her, Jo?"

"Like who?" Jo would spar feebly.

"Miss Matthews."

"Who's she?"

"Now, don't be funny, Jo. You know very well I mean the girl who was here for dinner. The one who talked so well on the emigration question."

"Oh, her! Why, I liked her, all right. Seems to be a smart woman."

"Smart! She's a perfectly splendid girl."

"Sure," Jo would agree cheerfully.

"But didn't you like her?"

"I can't say I did, Eve. And I can't say I didn't. She made me think a lot of a teacher I had in the fifth reader. Name of Himes. As I recall her, she must have been a fine woman. But I never thought of her as a woman at all. She was just Teacher."

"You make me tired," snapped Eva impatiently. "A man of your age. You don't expect to marry a girl, do you? A child!"

"I don't expect to marry anybody," Jo had answered.

And that was the truth, lonely though he often was.

The following year Eva moved to Winnetka. Any one who got the meaning of the Loop knows the significance of a move to a north shore suburb, and a house. Eva's daughter, Ethel, was growing up, and her mother had an eye on society.

That did away with Jo's Thursday dinner. Then Stell's husband bought a car. They went out into the country every Sunday. Stell said it was getting so that maids objected to Sunday dinners, anyway. Besides, they were unhealthy, old-fashioned things. They always meant to ask Jo to come along, but by the time their friends were placed, and the lunch, and the boxes, and sweaters, and George's camera, and everything, there seemed to be no room for a man of Jo's bulk. So that eliminated the Sunday dinners.

"Just drop in any time during the week," Stell said, " for dinner. Except Wednesday — that's our bridge night — and Saturday. And, of course, Thursday. Cook is out that night. Don't wait for me to 'phone."

And so Jo drifted into that sad-eyed, dyspeptic family made up of those you see dining in second-rate restaurants, their paper propped up against the bowl of oyster crackers, munching solemnly and with indifference to the stare of the passer-by surveying them through the brazen plate-glass window.

And then came the War. The war that spelled death and destruction to millions. The war that brought a fortune to Jo Hertz, and transformed him, over night, from a baggy-kneed old bachelor whose business was a failure to a prosperous manufacturer whose only trouble was the shortage in hides for the making of his product — leather! The armies of Europe called for it. Harnesses! More harnesses! Straps! Millions of straps! More! More!

The musty old harness business over on Lake Street was magically changed from a dust-covered, dead-alive concern to an orderly hive that hummed and glittered with success. Orders poured in. Jo Hertz had inside information on the War. He knew about troops and horses. He talked with French and English and Italian buyers — noblemen, many of them — commissioned by their countries to get American-made supplies. And now, when he said to Ben or George, "Take f'rinstance your raw hides and leathers," they listened with respectful attention.

And then began the gay dog business in the life of Jo Hertz. He developed into a loop-hound, ever keen on the scent of fresh pleasure. That side of Jo Hertz which had been repressed and crushed and ignored began to bloom, unhealthily. At first he spent money on his rather contemptuous nieces. He sent them gorgeous fans, and watch bracelets, and velvet bags. He took two expensive rooms at a downtown hotel, and there was something more tear-compelling than grotesque about the way he gloated over the luxury of a separate ice-water tap in the bathroom. He explained it.

"Just turn it on. Ice-water! Any hour of the day or night."

He bought a car. Naturally. A glittering affair; in color a bright blue, with pale-blue leather straps and a great deal of gold fittings and wire wheels. Eva said it was the kind of a thing a soubrette would use, rather than an elderly business man. You saw him driving about in it, red-faced and rather awkward at the wheel. You saw him, too, in the Pompeiian room at the Congress Hotel of a Saturday afternoon when doubtful and roving-eyed matrons in kolinsky capes are wont to congregate to sip pale amber drinks. Actors grew to recognize the semi-bald head and the shining, round, good-natured face looming out at them from the dim well of the parquet, and sometimes, in a musical show, they directed a quip at him, and he liked it. He could pick out the critics as they came down the aisle, and even had a nodding acquaintance with two of them.

"Kelly, of the *Herald*," he would say carelessly. "Bean, of the *Trib*. They're all afraid of him."

So he frolicked, ponderously. In New York he might have been called a Man About Town.

And he was lonesome. He was very lonesome. So he searched about in his mind and brought from the dim past the memory of the luxuriously furnished establishment of which he used to dream in the evenings when he dozed over his paper in the old house on Calumet. So he rented an apartment, many-roomed and expensive, with a man-servant in charge, and furnished it in styles and periods ranging through all the Louis. The living room was mostly rose color. It was like an unhealthy and bloated boudoir. And yet there was nothing sybaritic or uncleanly in the sight of this paunchy, middle-aged man sinking into the rosy-cushioned luxury of his ridiculous home. It was a frank and naive indulgence of long-starved senses, and there was in it a great resemblance to the rolling-eyed ecstasy of a school-boy smacking his lips over an all-day sucker.

The War went on, and on, and on. And the money continued to roll in — a flood of it. Then, one afternoon, Eva, in town on shopping bent, entered a small, exclusive, and expensive shop on Michigan Avenue. Exclusive, that is, in price. Eva's weakness, you may remember, was hats. She was seeking a hat now. She described what she sought with a languid conciseness, and stood looking about her after the saleswoman had vanished in quest of it. The room was becomingly rose-illumined and somewhat dim, so that some minutes had passed before she realized that a man seated on a raspberry brocade settee not five feet away — a man with a walking stick, and yellow gloves, and tan spats, and a check suit — was her brother Jo. From him Eva's wild-eyed glance leaped to the woman who was trying on hats before one of the many long mirrors. She was seated, and a saleswoman was exclaiming discreetly at her elbow.

Eva turned sharply and encountered her own saleswoman returning, hat-laden. "Not to-day," she gasped. "I'm feeling ill. Suddenly." And almost ran from the room.

That evening she told Stell, relating her news in that telephone pidgin-English devised by every family of married sisters as protection against the neighbors and Central. Translated, it ran thus:

"He looked straight at me. My dear, I thought I'd die! But at least he had sense enough not to speak. She was one of those limp, willowy creatures with the greediest eyes that she tried to keep softened to a baby stare, and couldn't, she was so crazy to get her hands on those hats. I saw it all in one awful minute. You know the way I do. I suppose some people would call her pretty. I don't. And her color! Well! And the most expensive-looking hats. Aigrettes, and paradise, and feathers. Not one of them under seventy-five. Isn't it disgusting! At his age! Suppose Ethel had been with me!"

The next time it was Stell who saw them. In a restaurant. She said it spoiled her evening. And the third time it was Ethel. She was one of the guests at a theater party given by Nicky Overton II. You know. The North Shore Overtons. Lake Forest. They came in late, and occupied the entire third row at the opening performance of "Believe Me!" And Ethel was Nicky's partner. She was glowing like a rose. When the lights went up after the first act Ethel saw that her uncle Jo was seated just ahead of her with what she afterward described as a Blonde. Then her uncle had turned around, and seeing her, had been surprised into a smile that spread genially all over his plump arid rubicund face. Then he had turned to face forward again, quickly.

"Who's the old bird?" Nicky had asked. Ethel had pretended not to hear, so he had asked again.

"My uncle," Ethel answered, and flushed all over her delicate face, and down to her throat. Nicky had looked at the Blonde, and his eyebrows had gone up ever so slightly.

It spoiled Ethel's evening. More than that, as she told her mother of it later, weeping, she declared it had spoiled her life.

Ethel talked it over with her husband in that intimate, kimonoed hour that precedes bedtime. She gesticulated heatedly with her hair brush.

"It's disgusting, that's what it is. Perfectly disgusting. There's no fool like an old fool. Imagine! A creature like that. At his time of life."

There exists a strange and loyal kinship among men. "Well, I don't know," Ben said now, and even grinned a little. "I suppose a boy's got to sow his wild oats some time."

"Don't be any more vulgar than you can help," Eva retorted. "And I think you know, as well as I, what it means to have that Overton boy interested in Ethel."

"If he's interested in her," Ben blundered, "I guess the fact that Ethel's uncle went to the theater with some one who wasn't Ethel's aunt won't cause a shudder to run up and down his frail young frame, will it?"

"All right," Eva had retorted. "If you're not man enough to stop it, I'll have to, that's all. I'm going up there with Stell this week."

They did not notify Jo of their coming. Eva telephoned his apartment when she knew he would be out, and asked his man if he expected his master home to dinner that evening. The man had said yes. Eva arranged to meet Stell in town. They would drive to Jo's apartment together, and wait for him there.

When she reached the city Eva found turmoil there. The first of the American troops to be sent to France were leaving. Michigan

Boulevard was a billowing, surging mass: Flags, pennants, bands, crowds. All the elements that make for demonstration. And over the whole — quiet. No holiday crowd, this. A solid, determined mass of people waiting patient hours to see the khaki-clads go by. Three years of indefatigable reading had brought them to a clear knowledge of what these boys were going to.

"Isn't it dreadful!" Stell gasped.

"Nicky Overton's only nineteen, thank goodness."

Their car was caught in the jam. When they moved at all it was by inches. When at last they reached Jo's apartment they were flushed, nervous, apprehensive. But he had not yet come in. So they waited.

No, they were not staying to dinner with their brother, they told the relieved houseman. Jo's home has already been described to you. Stell and Eva, sunk in rose-colored cushions, viewed it with disgust, and some mirth. They rather avoided each other's eyes.

"Carrie ought to be here," Eva said. They both smiled at the thought of the austere Carrie in the midst of those rosy cushions, and hangings, and lamps. Stell rose and began to walk about, restlessly. She picked up a vase and laid it down; straightened a picture. Eva got up, too, and wandered into the hall. She stood there a moment, listening. Then she turned and passed into Jo's bedroom. And there you knew Jo for what he was.

This room was as bare as the other had been ornate. It was Jo, the clean-minded and simple-hearted, in revolt against the cloying luxury with which he had surrounded himself. The bedroom, of all rooms in any house, reflects the personality of its occupant. True, the actual furniture was paneled, cupid-surmounted, and ridiculous. It had been the fruit of Jo's first orgy of the senses. But now it stood out in that stark little room with an air as incongruous and ashamed as that of a pink tarleton danseuse who finds herself in a monk's cell. None of those wall-pictures with which bachelor bedrooms are reputed to be hung. No satin slippers. No scented notes. Two plain-backed military brushes on the chiffonier (and he so nearly hairless!). A little orderly stack of books on the table near the bed. Eva fingered their titles and gave a little gasp. One of them was on gardening. "Well, of all things!" exclaimed Stell. A book on the War, by an Englishman. A detective story of the lurid type that lulls us to sleep. His shoes ranged in a careful row in the closet, with shoe-trees in every one of them. There was something speaking about them. They looked so human. Eva shut the door on them, quickly. Some bottles on the dresser. A jar of pomade. An ointment such as a man uses who is growing bald and is panic-stricken too late. An insurance calendar on the wall. Some rhubarb-and-soda mixture on the shelf in the bathroom, and a little box of pepsin tablets.

"Eats all kinds of things at all hours of the night," Eva said, and wandered out into the rose-colored front room again with the air of one who is chagrined at her failure to find what she has sought. Stell followed her, furtively.

"Where do you suppose he can be?" she demanded. "It's —" she glanced at her wrist, "why, it's after six!"

And then there was a little click. The two women sat up, tense. The door opened. Jo came in. He blinked a little. The two women in the rosy room stood up.

"Why —Eve! Why, Babe! Well! Why didn't you let me know?"

"We were just about to leave. We thought you weren't coming home."

Jo came in, slowly. "I was in the jam on Michigan, watching the boys go by." He sat down, heavily. The light from the window fell on him. And you saw that his eyes were red.

And you'll have to learn why. He had found himself one of the thousands in the jam on Michigan Avenue, as he said. He had a place near the curb, where his big frame shut off the view of the unfortunates behind him. He waited with the placid interest of one who has subscribed to all the funds and societies to which a prosperous, middle-aged business man is called upon to subscribe in war time. Then, just as he was about to leave, impatient at the delay, the crowd had cried, with a queer dramatic, exultant note in its voice, "Here they come! Here come the boys!"

Just at that moment two little, futile, frenzied fists began to beat a mad tattoo on Jo Hertz's broad back. Jo tried to turn in the crowd, all indignant resentment. "Say, looka here!"

The little fists kept up their frantic beating and pushing. And a voice — a choked, high little voice — cried, "Let me by! I can't see! You man, you! You big fat man! My boy's going by — to war — and I can't see! Let me by!"

Jo scrooged around, still keeping his place. He looked down. And upturned to him in agonized appeal was the face of little Emily. They stared at each other for what seemed a long, long time. It was really only the fraction of a second. Then Jo put one great arm firmly around Emily's waist and swung her around in front of him. His great bulk protected her. Emily was clinging to his hand. She was breathing rapidly, as if she had been running. Her eyes were straining up the street.

"Why, Emily, how in the world! —"

"I ran away. Fred didn't want me to come. He said it would excite me too much."

"Fred?"

"My husband. He made me promise to say good-by to Jo at home."

"Jo?"

"Jo's my boy. And he's going to war. So I ran away. I had to see him. I had to see him go."

She was dry-eyed. Her gaze was straining up the street.

"Why, sure," said Jo. "Of course you want to see him." And then the crowd gave a great roar. There came over Jo a feeling of weakness. He was trembling. The boys went marching by.

"There he is," Emily shrilled, above the din. "There he is! There he is! There he —" And waved a futile little hand. It wasn't so much a wave as a clutching. A clutching after something beyond her reach.

"Which one? Which one, Emily?"

"The handsome one. The handsome one. There!" Her voice quavered and died.

Jo put a steady hand on her shoulder. "Point him out," he commanded. "Show me." And the next instant. "Never mind. I see him."

Somehow, miraculously, he had picked him from among the hundreds. Had picked him as surely as his own father might have. It was Emily's boy. He was marching by, rather stiffly. He was nineteen, and fun-loving, and he had a girl, and he didn't particularly want to go to France and — to go to France. But more than he had hated going, he had hated not to go. So he marched by, looking straight ahead, his jaw set so that his chin stuck out just a little. Emily's boy.

Jo looked at him, and his face flushed purple. His eyes, the hard-boiled eyes of a loop-hound, took on the look of a sad old man. And suddenly he was no longer Jo, the sport; old J. Hertz, the gay dog. He was Jo Hertz, thirty, in love with life, in love with Emily, and with the stinging blood of young manhood coursing through his veins.

Another minute and the boy had passed on up the broad street — the fine, flag-bedecked street — just one of a hundred service-hats bobbing in rhythmic motion like sandy waves lapping a shore and flowing on.

Then he disappeared altogether.

Emily was clinging to Jo. She was mumbling something over and over. "I can't. I can't. Don't ask me to. I can't let him go. Like that. I can't."

Jo said a queer thing.

"Why, Emily! We wouldn't have him stay home, would we? We wouldn't want him to do anything different, would we? Not our boy. I'm glad he volunteered. I'm proud of him. So are you, glad."

Little by little he quieted her. He took her to the car that was waiting, a worried chauffeur in charge. They said good-by, awkwardly. Emily's face was a red, swollen mass.

So it was that when Jo entered his own hallway half an hour later he blinked, dazedly, and when the light from the window fell on him you saw that his eyes were red.

Eva was not one to beat about the bush. She sat forward in her chair, clutching her bag rather nervously.

"Now, look here, Jo. Stell and I are here for a reason. We're here to tell you that this thing's got to stop."

"Thing? Stop?"

"You know very well what I mean. You saw me at the milliner's that day. And night before last, Ethel. We're all disgusted. If you must go about with people like that, please have some sense of decency."

Something gathering in Jo's face should have warned her. But he was slumped down in his chair in such a huddle, and he looked so old and fat that she did not heed it. She went on. "You've got us to consider. Your sisters. And your nieces. Not to speak of your own —"

But he got to his feet then, shaking, and at what she saw in his face even Eva faltered and stopped. It wasn't at all the face of a fat, middle-aged sport. It was a face Jovian, terrible.

"You!" he began, low-voiced, ominous. "You!" He raised a great fist high. "You two murderers! You didn't consider me, twenty years ago. You come to me with talk like that. Where's my boy! You killed him, you two, twenty years ago. And now he belongs to somebody else. Where's my son that should have gone marching by to-day?" He flung his arms out in a great gesture of longing. The red veins stood out on his forehead. "Where's my son! Answer me that, you two selfish, miserable women. Where's my son!" Then, as they huddled together, frightened, wild-eyed. "Out of my house! Out of my house! Before I hurt you!"

They fled, terrified. The door banged behind them.

Jo stood, shaking, in the center of the room. Then he reached for a chair, gropingly, and sat down. He passed one moist, flabby hand over his forehead and it came away wet. The telephone rang. He sat still. It sounded far away and unimportant, like something forgotten. I think he did not even hear it with his conscious ear. But it rang and rang insistently. Jo liked to answer his telephone when at home.

"Hello!" He knew instantly the voice at the other end.

"That you, Jo?" it said.

"Yes."

"How's my boy?"

"I'm — all right."

"Listen, Jo. The crowd's coming over to-night. I've fixed up a little poker game for you. Just eight of us."

"I can't come to-night, Gert."

"Can't! Why not?"

"I'm not feeling so good."

"You just said you were all right."

"I *am* all right. Just kind of tired."

The voice took on a cooing note. "Is my Joey tired? Then he shall be all comfy on the sofa, and he doesn't need to play if he don't want to. No, sir."

Jo stood staring at the black mouth-piece of the telephone. He was seeing a procession go marching by. Boys, hundreds of boys, in khaki.

"Hello! Hello!" the voice took on an anxious note. "Are you there?"

"Yes," wearily.

"Jo, there's something the matter. You're sick. I'm coming right over."

"No!"

"Why not ? You sound as if you'd been sleeping. Look here —"

"Leave me alone!" cried Jo, suddenly, and the receiver clacked onto the hook. "Leave me alone. Leave me alone." Long after the connection had been broken.

He stood staring at the instrument with unseeing eyes. Then he turned and walked into the front room. All the light had gone out of it. Dusk had come on. All the light had gone out of everything. The zest had gone out of life. The game was over — the game he had been playing against loneliness and disappointment. And he was just a tired old man. A lonely, tired old man in a ridiculous, rose-colored room that had grown, all of a sudden, drab.

THE FALL OF EDWARD
BARNARD (1921)

W. Somerset Maugham

BATEMAN HUNTER SLEPT badly. For a fortnight on the boat that
brought him from Tahiti to San Francisco he had been thinking of
the story he had to tell, and for three days on the train he had
repeated to himself the words in which he meant to tell it. But in a
few hours now he would be in Chicago, and doubts assailed him.
His conscience, always very sensitive, was not at ease. He was uncertain that he had done all that was possible, it was on his honour to
do much more than the possible, and the thought was disturbing
that, in a matter which so nearly touched his own interest, he had
allowed his interest to prevail over his quixotry. Self-sacrifice
appealed so keenly to his imagination that the inability to exercise it
gave him a sense of disillusion. He was like the philanthropist who
with altruistic motives builds model dwellings for the poor and finds
that he has made a lucrative investment. He cannot prevent the
satisfaction he feels in the ten per cent which rewards the bread he
had cast upon the waters, but he has an awkward feeling that it
detracts somewhat from the savour of his virtue. Bateman Hunter
knew that his heart was pure, but he was not quite sure how stead-
fastly, when he told her his story, he would endure the scrutiny of
Isabel Longstaffe's cool grey eyes. They were far-seeing and wise.
She measured the standards of others by her own meticulous
uprightness and there could be no greater censure than the cold
silence with which she expressed her disapproval of a conduct that
did not satisfy her exacting code. There was no appeal from her
judgment, for, having made up her mind, she never changed it. But
Bateman would not have had her different. He loved not only the

beauty of her person, slim and straight, with the proud carriage of her head, but still more the beauty of her soul. With her truthfulness, her rigid sense of honour, her fearless outlook, she seemed to him to collect in herself all that was most admirable in his country-women. But he saw in her something more than the perfect type of the American girl, he felt that her exquisiteness was peculiar in a way to her environment, and he was assured that no city in the world could have produced her but Chicago. A pang seized him when he remembered that he must deal so bitter a blow to her pride, and anger flamed up in his heart when he thought of Edward Barnard.

But at last the train steamed in to Chicago and he exulted when he saw the long streets of grey houses. He could hardly bear his impatience at the thought of State and Wabash with their crowded pavements, their hustling traffic, and their noise. He was at home. And he was glad that he had been born in the most important city in the United States. San Francisco was provincial, New York was effete; the future of America lay in the development of its economic possibilities, and Chicago, by its position and by the energy of its citizens, was destined to become the real capital of the country.

"I guess I shall live long enough to see it the biggest city in the world," Bateman said to himself as he stepped down to the platform.

His father had come to meet him, and after a hearty handshake, the pair of them, tall, slender, and well-made, with the same fine, ascetic features and thin lips, walked out of the station. Mr Hunter's automobile was waiting for them and they got in. Mr Hunter caught his son's proud and happy glance as he looked at the street.

"Glad to be back, son?" he asked.

"I should just think I was," said Bateman.

His eyes devoured the restless scene.

"I guess there's a bit more traffic here than in your South Sea island," laughed Mr Hunter. "Did you like it there?"

"Give me Chicago, dad," answered Bateman.

"You haven't brought Edward Barnard back with you."

"No."

"How was he?"

Bateman was silent for a moment, and his handsome, sensitive face darkened.

"I'd sooner not speak about him, dad," he said at last.

"That's all right, my son. I guess your mother will be a happy woman to-day."

They passed out of the crowded streets in the Loop and drove along the lake till they came to the imposing house, an exact copy of a chateau on the Loire, which Mr Hunter had built himself some years before. As soon as Bateman was alone in his room he asked for a number on the telephone. His heart leaped when he heard the voice that answered him.

"Good-morning, Isabel," he said gaily.

"Good-morning, Bateman,"

"How did you recognise my voice?".

"It is not so long since I heard it last. Besides, I was expecting you."

"When may I see you?"

"Unless you have anything better to do perhaps you'll dine with us to-night."

"You know very well that I couldn't possibly have anything better to do."

"I suppose that you're full of news?"

He thought he detected in her voice a note of apprehension.

"Yes," he answered.

"Well, you must tell me to-night. Good-bye."

She rang off. It was characteristic of her that she should be able to wait so many unnecessary hours to know what so immensely concerned her. To Bateman there was an admirable fortitude in her restraint.

At dinner, at which beside himself and Isabel no one was present but her father and mother, he watched her guide the conversation into the channels of an urbane small-talk, and it occurred to him that in just such a manner would a marquise under the shadow of the guillotine toy with the affairs of a day that would know no morrow. Her delicate features, the aristocratic shortness of her upper lip, and her wealth of fair hair suggested the marquise again, and it must have been obvious, even if it were not notorious, that in her veins flowed the best blood in Chicago. The dining-room was a fitting frame to her fragile beauty, for Isabel had caused the house, a replica of a palace on the Grand Canal at Venice, to be furnished by an English expert in the style of Louis XV; and the graceful decoration linked with the name of that amorous monarch enhanced her loveliness and at the same time acquired from it a more profound significance. For Isabel's mind was richly stored, and her conversation, however light, was never flippant. She spoke now of the *Musicale* to which she and her mother had been in the afternoon, of the lectures which an English poet was giving at the Auditorium, of the political situation, and of the Old Master which her father had recently bought for fifty thousand dollars in New York. It comforted Bateman to hear her. He felt that he was once more in the civilised world, at the centre of culture and distinction; and certain voices, troubling and yet against his will refusing to still their clamour, were at last silent in his heart.

"Gee, but it's good to be back in Chicago," he said.

At last dinner was over, and when they went out of the dining-room Isabel said to her mother:

"I'm going to take Bateman along to my den. We have various things to talk about."

"Very well, my dear," said Mrs Longstaffe. "You'll find your father and me in the Madame du Barry room when you're through."

Isabel led the young man upstairs and showed him into the room of which he had so many charming memories. Though he knew it so well he could not repress the exclamation of delight which it always wrung from him. She looked round with a smile.

"I think it's a success," she said. "The main thing is that it's right. There's not even an ashtray that isn't of the period."

"I suppose that's what makes it so wonderful. Like all you do it's so superlatively right."

They sat down in front of a log fire and Isabel looked at him with calm grave eyes.

"Now what have you to say to me?" she asked.

"I hardly know how to begin."

"Is Edward Barnard coming back?"

"No."

There was a long silence before Bateman spoke again, and with each of them it was filled with many thoughts. It was a difficult story he had to tell, for there were things in it which were so offensive to her sensitive ears that he could not bear to tell them, and yet in justice to her, no less than in justice to himself, he must tell her the whole truth.

It had all begun long ago when he and Edward Barnard, still at college, had met Isabel Longstaffe at the tea-party given to introduce her to society. They had both known her when she was a child and they long-legged boys, but for two years she had been in Europe to finish her education and it was with a surprised delight that they renewed acquaintance with the lovely girl who returned. Both of them fell desperately in love with her, but Bateman saw quickly that she had eyes only for Edward, and, devoted to his friend, he resigned himself to the rôle of confidant. He passed bitter moments, but he could not deny that Edward was worthy of his good fortune, and, anxious that nothing should impair the friendship he so greatly valued, he took care never by a hint to disclose his own feelings. In six months the young couple were engaged. But they were very young and Isabel's father decided that they should not marry at least till Edward graduated. They had to wait a year. Bateman remembered the winter at the end of which Isabel and Edward were to be married, a winter of dances and theatre-parties and of informal gaieties at which he, the constant third, was always present. He loved her no less because she would shortly be his friend's wife; her smile, a gay word she flung him, the confidence of her affection, never ceased to delight him; and he congratulated himself, somewhat complacently, because he did not envy them their happiness. Then an accident happened. A great bank failed, there was a panic on the exchange, and Edward Barnard's father found himself a ruined man. He came home one night, told his wife that he was penniless, and after dinner, going into his study, shot himself.

A week later, Edward Barnard, with a tired, white face, went to Isabel and asked her to release him. Her only answer was to throw her arms round his neck and burst into tears.

"Don't make it harder for me, sweet," he said.

"Do you think I can let you go now? I love you."

"How can I ask you to marry me? The whole thing's hopeless. Your father would never let you. I haven't a cent."

"What do I care? I love you."

He told her his plans. He had to earn money at once, and George Braunschmidt, an old friend of his family, had offered to take him into his own business. He was a South Sea merchant, and he had agencies in many of the islands of the Pacific. He had suggested that Edward should go to Tahiti for a year or two, where under the best of his managers he could learn the details of that varied trade, and at the end of that time he promised the young man a position in Chicago. It was a wonderful opportunity, and when he had finished his explanations Isabel was once more all smiles.

"You foolish boy, why have you been trying to make me miserable?"

His face lit up at her words and his eyes flashed.

"Isabel, you don't mean to say you'll wait for me?"

"Don't you think you're worth it?" she smiled.

"Ah, don't laugh at me now. I beseech you to be serious. It may be for two years."

"Have no fear. I love you, Edward. When you come back I will marry you."

Edward's employer was a man who did not like delay and he had told him that if he took the post he offered he must sail that day week from San Francisco. Edward spent his last evening with Isabel. It was after dinner that Mr Longstaffe, saying he wanted a word with Edward, took him into the smoking-room. Mr Longstaffe had accepted good-naturedly the arrangement which his daughter had told him of and Edward could not imagine what mysterious communication he had now to make. He was not a little perplexed to see that his host was embarrassed. He faltered. He talked of trivial things. At last he blurted it out.

"I guess you've heard of Arnold Jackson," he said, looking at Edward with a frown.

Edward hesitated. His natural truthfulness obliged him to admit a knowledge he would gladly have been able to deny.

"Yes, I have. But it's a long time ago. I guess I didn't pay very much attention."

"There are not many people in Chicago who haven't heard of Arnold Jackson," said Mr Longstaffe bitterly, "and if there are they'll have no difficulty in finding someone who'll be glad to tell them. Did you know he was Mrs Longstaffe's brother?"

"Yes, I knew that."

"Of course we've had no communication with him for many years. He left the country as soon as he was able to, and I guess the country wasn't sorry to see the last of him. We understand he lives in Tahiti. My advice to you is to give him a wide berth, but if you do hear anything about him Mrs Longstaffe and I would be very glad if you'd let us know."

"Sure."

"That was all I wanted to say to you. Now I daresay you'd like to join the ladies."

There are few families that have not among their members one whom, if their neighbours permitted, they would willingly forget, and they are fortunate when the lapse of a generation or two has invested his vagaries with a romantic glamour. But when he is actually alive, if his peculiarities are not of the kind that can be condoned by the phrase, "he is nobody's enemy but his own," a safe one when the culprit has no worse to answer for than alcoholism or wandering affections, the only possible course is silence. And it was this which the Longstaffes had adopted towards Arnold Jackson. They never talked of him. They would not even pass through the street in which he had lived. Too kind to make his wife and children suffer for his misdeeds, they had supported them for years, but on the understanding that they should live in Europe. They did everything they could to blot out all recollection of Arnold Jackson and yet were conscious that the story was as fresh in the public mind as when first the scandal burst upon a gaping world. Arnold Jackson was as black a sheep as any family could suffer from. A wealthy banker, prominent in his church, a philanthropist, a man respected by all, not only for his connections (in his veins ran the blue blood of Chicago), but also for his upright character, he was arrested one day on a charge of fraud; and the dishonesty which the trial brought to light was not of the sort which could be explained by a sudden temptation; it was deliberate and systematic. Arnold Jackson was a rogue. When he was sent to the penitentiary for seven years there were few who did not think he had escaped lightly.

When at the end of this last evening the lovers separated it was with many protestations of devotion. Isabel, all tears, was consoled a little by her certainty of Edward's passionate love. It was a strange feeling that she had. It made her wretched to part from him and yet she was happy because he adored her.

This was more than two years ago.

He had written to her by every mail since then, twenty-four letters in all, for the mail went but once a month, and his letters had been all that a lover's letters should be. They were intimate and charming, humorous sometimes, especially of late, and tender. At first they suggested that he was homesick, they were full of his desire to get back to Chicago and Isabel; and, a little anxiously, she wrote begging him to persevere. She was afraid that he might throw up his opportunity and come racing back. She did not want her lover to lack endurance and she quoted to him the lines:

> *"I could not love thee, dear, so much,*
> *Loved I not honour more."*

But presently he seemed to settle down and it made Isabel very happy to observe his growing enthusiasm to introduce American methods into that forgotten corner of the world. But she knew him, and at the end of the year, which was the shortest time he could possibly stay in Tahiti, she expected to have to use all her influence to dissuade him from coming home. It was much better that he should learn the business thoroughly, and if they had been able to wait a year there seemed no reason why they should not wait another. She talked it over with Bateman Hunter, always the most generous of friends (during those first few days after Edward went she did not know what she would have done without him), and they decided that Edward's future must stand before everything. It was with relief that she found as the time passed that he made no suggestion of returning.

"He's splendid, isn't he?" she exclaimed to Bateman.

"He's white, through and through."

"Reading between the lines of his letter I know he hates it over there, but he's sticking it out because . . ."

She blushed a little and Bateman, with the grave smile which was so attractive in him, finished the sentence for her.

"Because he loves you."

"It makes me feel so humble," she said.

"You're wonderful, Isabel, you're perfectly wonderful."

But the second year passed and every month Isabel continued to receive a letter from Edward, and presently it began to seem a little strange that he did not speak of coming back. He wrote as though he were settled definitely in Tahiti, and what was more, comfortably settled. She was surprised. Then she read his letters again, all of them, several times; and now, reading between the lines indeed, she was puzzled to notice a change which had escaped her. The later letters were as tender and as delightful as the first, but the tone was different. She was vaguely suspicious of their humour, she had the instinctive mistrust of her sex for that unaccountable quality, and she discerned in them now a flippancy which perplexed her. She was not quite certain that the Edward who wrote to her now was the same Edward that she had known. One afternoon, the day after a mail had arrived from Tahiti, when she was driving with Bateman he said to her:

"Did Edward tell you when he was sailing?"

"No, he didn't mention it. I thought he might have said something to you about it."

"Not a word."

"You know what Edward is," she laughed in reply, "he has no sense of time. If it occurs to you next time you write you might ask him when he's thinking of coming."

Her manner was so unconcerned that only Bateman's acute sensitiveness could have discerned in her request a very urgent desire. He laughed lightly.

"Yes. I'll ask him. I can't imagine what he's thinking about."

A few days later, meeting him again, she noticed that something troubled him. They had been much together since Edward left Chicago; they were both devoted to him and each in his desire to talk of the absent one found a willing listener; the consequence was that Isabel knew every expression of Bateman's face, and his denials now were useless against her keen instinct. Something told her that his harassed look had to do with Edward and she did not rest till she had made him confess.

"The fact is," he said at last, "I heard in a roundabout way that Edward was no longer working for Braunschmidt and Co., and yesterday I took the opportunity to ask Mr Braunschmidt himself."

"Well?"

"Edward left his employment with them nearly a year ago."

"How strange he should have said nothing about it!"

Bateman hesitated, but he had gone so far now that he was obliged to tell the rest. It made him feel dreadfully embarrassed.

"He was fired."

"In heaven's name what for?"

"It appears they warned him once or twice, and at last they told him to get out. They say he was lazy and incompetent."

"Edward?"

They were silent for a while, and then he saw that Isabel was crying. Instinctively he seized her hand.

"Oh, my dear, don't, don't," he said. "I can't bear to see it."

She was so unstrung that she let her hand rest in his. He tried to console her.

"It's incomprehensible, isn't it? It's so unlike Edward. I can't help feeling there must be some mistake."

She did not say anything for a while, and when she spoke it was hesitatingly.

"Has it struck you that there was anything queer in his letters lately?" she asked, looking away, her eyes all bright with tears.

He did not quite know how to answer.

"I have noticed a change in them," he admitted. "He seems to have lost that high seriousness which I admired so much in him. One would almost think that the things that matter—well, don't matter."

Isabel did not reply. She was vaguely uneasy.

"Perhaps in his answer to your letter he'll say when he's coming home. All we can do is to wait for that."

Another letter came from Edward for each of them, and still he made no mention of his return; but when he wrote he could not have received Bateman's enquiry. The next mail would bring them an answer to that. The next mail came, and Bateman brought Isabel the letter he had just received; but the first glance of his face was enough to tell her that he was disconcerted. She read it through carefully and then, with slightly tightened lips, read it again.

"It's a very strange letter," she said. "I don't quite understand it."

"One might almost think that he was joshing me," said Bateman, flushing.

"It reads like that, but it must be unintentional. That's so unlike Edward."

"He says nothing about coming back."

"If I weren't so confident of his love I should think ... I hardly know what I should think."

It was then that Bateman had broached the scheme which during the afternoon had formed itself in his brain. The firm, founded by his father, in which he was now a partner, a firm which manufactured all manner of motor vehicles, was about to establish agencies in Honolulu, Sidney, and Wellington; and Bateman proposed that himself should go instead of the manager who had been suggested. He could return by Tahiti; in fact, travelling from Wellington, it was inevitable to do so; and he could see Edward.

"There's some mystery and I'm going to clear it up. That's the only way to do it."

"Oh, Bateman, how can you be so good and kind?" she exclaimed.

"You know there's nothing in the world I want more than your happiness, Isabel."

She looked at him and she gave him her hands.

"You're wonderful, Bateman. I didn't know there was anyone in the world like you. How can I ever thank you?"

"I don't want your thanks. I only want to be allowed to help you."

She dropped her eyes and flushed a little. She was so used to him that she had forgotten how handsome he was. He was as tall as Edward and as well made, but he was dark and pale of face, while Edward was ruddy. Of course she knew he loved her. It touched her. She felt very tenderly towards him.

It was from this journey that Bateman Hunter was now returned.

The business part of it took him somewhat longer than he expected and he had much time to think of his two friends. He had come to the conclusion that it could be nothing serious that prevented Edward from coming home, a pride, perhaps, which made him determined to make good before he claimed the bride he adored; but it was a pride that must be reasoned with. Isabel was unhappy. Edward must come back to Chicago with him and marry her at once. A position could be found for him in the works of the Hunter Motor Traction and Automobile Company. Bateman, with a bleeding heart, exulted at the prospect of giving happiness to the two persons he loved best in the world at the cost of his own. He would never marry. He would be godfather to the children of Edward and Isabel, and many years later when they were both dead he would tell Isabel's daughter how long, long ago he had loved her mother. Bateman's eyes were veiled with tears when he pictured this scene to himself.

Meaning to take Edward by surprise he had not cabled to announce his arrival, and when at last he landed at Tahiti he allowed a youth, who said he was the son of the house, to lead him to the Hotel de la Fleur. He chuckled when he thought of his friend's amazement on seeing him, the most unexpected of visitors, walk into his office.

"By the way," he asked, as they went along, "can you tell me where I shall find Mr. Edward Barnard?"

"Barnard?" said the youth. "I seem to know the name."

"He's an American. A tall fellow with light brown hair and blue eyes. He's been here over two years."

"Of course. Now I know who you mean. You mean Mr Jackson's nephew."

"Whose nephew?"

"Mr Arnold Jackson."

"I don't think we're speaking of the same person," answered Bateman, frigidly.

He was startled. It was queer that Arnold Jackson, known apparently to all and sundry, should live here under the disgraceful name in which he had been convicted. But Bateman could not imagine whom it was that he passed off as his nephew. Mrs Longstaffe was his only sister and he had never had a brother. The young man by his side talked volubly in an English that had something in it of the intonation of a foreign tongue, and Bateman, with a sidelong glance, saw, what he had not noticed before, that there was in him a good deal of native blood. A touch of hauteur involuntarily entered into his manner. They reached the hotel. When he had arranged about his room Bateman asked to be directed to the premises of Braunschmidt & Co. They were on the front, facing the lagoon, and, glad to feel the solid earth under his feet after eight days at sea, he sauntered down the sunny road to the water's edge. Having found the place he sought, Bateman sent in his card to the manager and was led through a lofty barn-like room, half store and half warehouse, to an office in which sat a stout, spectacled, bald-headed man.

"Can you tell me where I shall find Mr Edward Barnard? I understand he was in this office for some time."

"That is so. I don't know just where he is."

"But I thought he came here with a particular recommendation from Mr Braunschmidt. I know Mr Braunschmidt very well."

The fat man looked at Bateman with shrewd, suspicious eyes. He called to one of the boys in the warehouse.

"Say, Henry, where's Barnard now, d'you know?"

"He's working at Cameron's, I think," came the answer from someone who did not trouble to move.

The fat man nodded.

"If you turn to your left when you get out of here you'll come to Cameron's in about three minutes."

Bateman hesitated.

"I think I should tell you that Edward Barnard is my greatest friend. I was very much surprised when I heard he'd left Braunschmidt & Co."

The fat man's eyes contracted till they seemed like pin-points, and their scrutiny made Bateman so uncomfortable that he felt himself blushing.

"I guess Braunschmidt & Co. and Edward Barnard didn't see eye to eye on certain matters," he replied.

Bateman did not quite like the fellow's manner, so he got up, not without dignity, and with an apology for troubling him bade him good-day. He left the place with a singular feeling that the man he had just interviewed had much to tell him, but no intention of telling it. He walked in the direction indicated and soon found himself at Cameron's. It was a trader's store, such as he had passed half a dozen of on his way, and when he entered the first person he saw, in his shirt sleeves, measuring out a length of trade cotton, was Edward. It gave him a start to see him engaged in so humble an occupation. But he had scarcely appeared when Edward, looking up, caught sight of him, and gave a joyful cry of surprise.

"Bateman! Who ever thought of seeing you here?"

He stretched his arm across the counter and wrung Bateman's hand. There was no self-consciousness in his manner and the embarrassment was all on Bateman's side.

"Just wait till I've wrapped this package."

With perfect assurance he ran his scissors across the stuff, folded it, made it into a parcel, and handed it to the dark-skinned customer.

"Pay at the desk, please."

Then, smiling, with bright eyes, he turned to Bateman.

"How did you show up here? Gee, I am delighted to see you. Sit down, old man. Make yourself at home."

"We can't talk here. Come along to my hotel. I suppose you can get away?"

This he added with some apprehension.

"Of course I can get away. We're not so businesslike as all that in Tahiti." He called out to a Chinese who was standing behind the opposite counter. "Ah-Ling, when the boss comes tell him a friend of mine's just arrived from America and I've gone out to have a drain with him."

"All-light," said the Chinese, with a grin.

Edward slipped on a coat and, putting on his hat, accompanied Bateman out of the store. Bateman attempted to put the matter facetiously.

"I didn't expect to find you selling three and a half yards of rotten cotton to a greasy nigger," he laughed.

"Braunschmidt fired me, you know, and I thought that would do as well as anything else."

Edward's candour seemed to Bateman very surprising, but he thought it indiscreet to pursue the subject.

"I guess you won't make a fortune where you are," he answered, somewhat dryly.

"I guess not. But I earn enough to keep body and soul together, and I'm quite satisfied with that."

"You wouldn't have been two years ago."

"We grow wiser as we grow older," retorted Edward, gaily.

Bateman took a glance at him. Edward was dressed in a suit of shabby white ducks, none too clean, and a large straw hat of native make. He was thinner than he had been, deeply burned by the sun, and he was certainly better looking than ever. But there was something in his appearance that disconcerted Bateman. He walked with a new jauntiness; there was a carelessness in his demeanour, a gaiety about nothing in particular, which Bateman could not precisely blame, but which exceedingly puzzled him.

"I'm blest if I can see what he's got to be so darned cheerful about," he said to himself.

They arrived at the hotel and sat on the terrace. A Chinese boy brought them cocktails. Edward was most anxious to hear all the news of Chicago and bombarded his friend with eager questions. His interest was natural and sincere. But the odd thing was that it seemed equally divided among a multitude of subjects. He was as eager to know how Bateman's father was as what Isabel was doing. He talked of her without a shade of embarrassment, but she might just as well have been his sister as his promised wife; and before Bateman had done analysing the exact meaning of Edward's remarks he found that the conversation had drifted to his own work and the buildings his father had lately erected. He was determined to bring the conversation back to Isabel and was looking for the occasion when he saw Edward wave his hand cordially. A man was advancing towards them on the terrace, but Bateman's back was turned to him and he could not see him.

"Come and sit down," said Edward gaily.

The new-comer approached. He was a very tall, thin man, in white ducks, with a fine head of curly white hair. His face was thin too, long, with a large, hooked nose and a beautiful, expressive mouth.

"This is my old friend Bateman Hunter. I've told you about him," said Edward, his constant smile breaking on his lips.

"I'm pleased to meet you, Mr Hunter. I used to know your father."

The stranger held out his hand and took the young man's in a strong, friendly grasp. It was not till then that Edward mentioned the other's name.

"Mr Arnold Jackson."

Bateman turned white and he felt his hands grow cold. This was the forger, the convict, this was Isabel's uncle. He did not know what to say. He tried to conceal his confusion. Arnold Jackson looked at him with twinkling eyes.

"I daresay my name is familiar to you."

Bateman did not know whether to say yes or no, and what made it more awkward was that both Jackson and Edward seemed to be amused. It was bad enough to have forced on him the acquaintance of the one man on the island he would rather have avoided, but worse to discern that he was being made a fool of. Perhaps, however, he had reached this conclusion too quickly, for Jackson, without a pause, added:

"I understand you're very friendly with the Longstaffes. Mary Longstaffe is my sister."

Now Bateman asked himself if Arnold Jackson could think him ignorant of the most terrible scandal that Chicago had ever known. But Jackson put his hand on Edward's shoulder.

"I can't sit down, Teddie," he said. "I'm busy. But you two boys had better come up and dine tonight."

"That'll be fine," said Edward.

"It's very kind of you, Mr Jackson," said Bateman, frigidly, "but I'm here for so short a time; my boat sails to-morrow, you know; I think if you'll forgive me, I won't come."

"Oh, nonsense. I'll give you a native dinner. My wife's a wonderful cook. Teddie will show you the way. Come early so as to see the sunset. I can give you both a shake-down if you like."

"Of course we'll come," said Edward. "There's always the devil of a row in the hotel on the night a boat arrives and we can have a good yarn up at the bungalow."

"I can't let you off, Mr Hunter," Jackson continued with the utmost cordiality. "I want to hear all about Chicago and Mary."

He nodded and walked away before Bateman could say another word.

"We don't take refusals in Tahiti," laughed Edward. "Besides, you'll get the best dinner on the island."

"What did he mean by saying his wife was a good cook? I happen to know his wife's in Geneva."

"That's a long way off for a wife, isn't it?" said Edward. "And it's a long time since he saw her. I guess it's another wife he's talking about."

For some time Bateman was silent. His face was set in grave lines. But looking up he caught the amused look in Edward's eyes, and he flushed darkly.

"Arnold Jackson is a despicable rogue," he said.

"I greatly fear he is," answered Edward, smiling.

"I don't see how any decent man can have anything to do with him."

"Perhaps I'm not a decent man."

"Do you see much of him, Edward?"

"Yes, quite a lot. He's adopted me as his nephew."

Bateman leaned forward and fixed Edward with his searching eyes.

"Do you like him?"

"Very much."

"But don't you know, doesn't everyone here know, that he's a forger and that he's been a convict? He ought to be hounded out of civilised society."

Edward watched a ring of smoke that floated from his cigar into the still, scented air.

"I suppose he is a pretty unmitigated rascal," he said at last. "And I can't flatter myself that any repentance for his misdeeds offers one an excuse for condoning them. He was a swindler and a hypocrite. You can't get away from it. I never met a more agreeable companion. He's taught me everything I know."

"What has he taught you?" cried Bateman in amazement.

"How to live."

Bateman broke into ironical laughter.

"A fine master. Is it owing to his lessons that you lost the chance of making a fortune and earn your living now by serving behind a counter in a ten cent store?"

"He has a wonderful personality," said Edward, smiling good-naturedly. "Perhaps you'll see what I mean to-night."

"I'm not going to dine with him if that's what you mean. Nothing would induce me to set foot within that man's house."

"Come to oblige me, Bateman. We've been friends for so many years, you won't refuse me a favour when I ask it."

Edward's tone had in it a quality new to Bateman. Its gentleness was singularly persuasive.

"If you put it like that, Edward, I'm bound to come," he smiled.

Bateman reflected, moreover, that it would be as well to learn what he could about Arnold Jackson. It was plain that he had a great ascendency over Edward, and if it was to be combated it was necessary to discover in what exactly it consisted. The more he talked with Edward the more conscious he became that a change had taken place in him. He had an instinct that it behooved him to walk warily, and he made up his mind not to broach the real purport of his visit till he saw his way more clearly. He began to talk of one thing and another, of his journey and what he had achieved by it, of politics in Chicago, of this common friend and that, of their days together at college.

At last Edward said he must get back to his work and proposed that he should fetch Bateman at five so that they could drive out together to Arnold Jackson's house.

"By the way, I rather thought you'd be living at this hotel," said Bateman, as he strolled out of the garden with Edward. "I understand it's the only decent one here."

"Not I," laughed Edward. "It's a deal too grand for me. I rent a room just outside the town. It's cheap and clean."

"If I remember right those weren't the points that seemed most important to you when you lived in Chicago."

"Chicago!"

"I don't know what you mean by that, Edward. It's the greatest city in the world."

"I know," said Edward.

Bateman glanced at him quickly, but his face was inscrutable.

"When are you coming back to it?"

"I often wonder," smiled Edward.

This answer, and the manner of it, staggered Bateman, but before he could ask for an explanation Edward waved to a half-caste who was driving a passing motor.

"Give us a ride down, Charlie," he said.

He nodded to Bateman, and ran after the machine that had pulled up a few yards in front. Bateman was left to piece together a mass of perplexing impressions.

Edward called for him in a rickety trap drawn by an old mare, and they drove along a road that ran by the sea. On each side of it were plantations, coconut and vanilla; and now and then they saw a great mango, its fruit yellow and red and purple among the massy green of the leaves; now and then they had a glimpse of the lagoon, smooth and blue, with here and there a tiny islet graceful with tall palms. Arnold Jackson's house stood on a little hill and only a path led to it, so they unharnessed the mare and tied her to a tree, leaving the trap by the side of the road. To Bateman it seemed a happy-go-lucky way of doing things. But when they went up to the house they were met by a tall, handsome native woman, no longer young, with whom Edward cordially shook hands. He introduced Bateman to her.

"This is my friend Mr Hunter. We're going to dine with you, Lavina."

"All right," she said, with a quick smile. "Arnold ain't back yet."

"We'll go down and bathe. Let us have a couple of *pareos*."

The woman nodded and went into the house.

"Who is that?" asked Bateman.

"Oh, that's Lavina. She's Arnold's wife."

Bateman tightened his lips, but said nothing. In a moment the woman returned with a bundle, which she gave to Edward; and the two men, scrambling down a steep path, made their way to a grove of coconut trees on the beach. They undressed and Edward showed his friend how to make the strip of red trade cotton which is called a *pareo* into a very neat pair of bathing-drawers. Soon they were splashing in the warm, shallow water. Edward was in great spirits. He laughed and shouted and sang. He might have been fifteen. Bateman had never seen him so gay, and afterwards when they lay on the beach, smoking cigarettes, in the limpid air, there was such an irresistible light-heartedness in him that Bateman was taken aback.

"You seem to find life mighty pleasant," said he.

"I do."

They heard a soft movement and looking round saw that Arnold Jackson was coming towards them.

"I thought I'd come down and fetch you two boys back," he said. "Did you enjoy your bath, Mr Hunter?"

"Very much," said Bateman.

Arnold Jackson, no longer in spruce ducks, wore nothing but a *pareo* round his loins and walked barefoot. His body was deeply browned by the sun. With his long, curling white hair and his ascetic face he made a fantastic figure in the native dress, but he bore himself without a trace of self-consciousness.

"If you're ready we'll go right up," said Jackson.

"I'll just put on my clothes," said Bateman.

"Why, Teddie, didn't you bring a *pareo* for your friend?"

"I guess he'd rather wear clothes," smiled Edward

"I certainly would," answered Bateman, grimly, as he saw Edward gird himself in the loincloth and stand ready to start before he himself had got his shirt on.

"Won't you find it rough walking without your shoes?" he asked Edward. "It struck me the path was a trifle rocky."

"Oh, I'm used to it."

"It's a comfort to get into a *pareo* when one gets back from town," said Jackson. "If you were going to stay here I should strongly recommend you to adopt it. It's one of the most sensible costumes I have ever come across. It's cool, convenient, and inexpensive."

They walked up to the house, and Jackson took them into a large room with white-washed walls and an open ceiling in which a table was laid for dinner. Bateman noticed that it was set for five.

"Eva, come and show yourself to Teddie's friend, and then shake us a cocktail," called Jackson.

Then he led Bateman to a long low window.

"Look at that," he said, with a dramatic gesture. "Look well."

Below them coconut trees tumbled down steeply to the lagoon, and the lagoon in the evening light had the colour, tender and varied, of a dove's breast. On a creek, at a little distance, were the clustered huts of a native village, and towards the reef was a canoe, sharply silhouetted, in which were a couple of natives fishing. Then, beyond, you saw the vast calmness of the Pacific and twenty miles away, airy and unsubstantial like the fabric of a poet's fancy, the unimaginable beauty of the island which is called Murea. It was all so lovely that Bateman stood abashed.

"I've never seen anything like it," he said at last.

Arnold Jackson stood staring in front of him, and in his eyes was a dreamy softness. His thin, thoughtful face was very grave. Bateman, glancing at it, was once more conscious of its intense spirituality.

"Beauty," murmured Arnold Jackson. "You seldom see beauty face to face. Look at it well, Mr Hunter, for what you see now you will never see again, since the moment is transitory, but it will be an imperishable memory in your heart. You touch eternity."

His voice was deep and resonant. He seemed to breathe forth the purest idealism, and Bateman had to urge himself to remember that the man who spoke was a criminal and a cruel cheat. But Edward, as though he heard a sound, turned round quickly.

"Here is my daughter, Mr Hunter."

Bateman shook hands with her. She had dark, splendid eyes and a red mouth tremulous with laughter; but her skin was brown, and her curling hair, rippling down her shoulders, was coal black. She wore but one garment, a Mother Hubbard of pink cotton, her feet were bare, and she was crowned with a wreath of white scented flowers. She was a lovely creature. She was like a goddess of the Polynesian spring.

She was a little shy, but not more shy than Bateman, to whom the whole situation was highly embarrassing, and it did not put him at his ease to see this sylph-like thing take a shaker and with a practised hand mix three cocktails.

"Let us have a kick in them, child," said Jackson.

She poured them out and smiling delightfully handed one to each of the men. Bateman flattered himself on his skill in the subtle art of shaking cocktails and he was not a little astonished, on tasting this one, to find that it was excellent. Jackson laughed proudly when he saw his guest's involuntary look of appreciation.

"Not bad, is it? I taught the child myself, and in the old days in Chicago I considered that there wasn't a bar-tender in the city that could hold a candle to me. When I had nothing better to do in the penitentiary I used to amuse myself by thinking out new cocktails, but when you come down to brass-tacks there's nothing to beat a dry Martini."

Bateman felt as though someone had given him a violent blow on the funny-bone and he was conscious that he turned red and then white. But before he could think of anything to say a native boy brought in a great bowl of soup and the whole party sat down to dinner. Arnold Jackson's remark seemed to have aroused in him a train of recollections, for he began to talk of his prison days. He talked quite naturally, without malice, as though he were relating his experiences at a foreign university. He addressed himself to Bateman and Bateman was confused and then confounded. He saw Edward's eyes fixed on him and there was in them a flicker of amusement. He blushed scarlet, for it struck him that Jackson was making a fool of him, and then because he felt absurd—and knew there was no reason why he should—he grew angry. Arnold Jackson was impudent—there was no other word for it—and his callousness, whether assumed or not, was outrageous. The dinner proceeded. Bateman was asked to eat sundry messes, raw fish and he knew not what, which only his civility induced him to swallow, but which he was amazed to find very good eating. Then an incident happened which to Bateman was the most mortifying experience of the evening. There was a little circlet of flowers in front of him, and for the sake of conversation he hazarded a remark about it.

"It's a wreath that Eva made for you," said Jackson, "but I guess she was too shy to give it you."

Bateman took it up in his hand and made a polite little speech of thanks to the girl.

"You must put it on," she said, with a smile and a blush.

"I? I don't think I'll do that."

"It's the charming custom of the country," said Arnold Jackson.

There was one in front of him and he placed it on his hair. Edward did the same.

"I guess I'm not dressed for the part," said Bateman, uneasily.

"Would you like a *pareo*?" said Eva quickly. "I'll get you one in a minute."

"No, thank you. I'm quite comfortable as I am."

"Show him how to put it on, Eva," said Edward.

At that moment Bateman hated his greatest friend. Eva got up from the table and with much laughter placed the wreath on his black hair.

"It suits you very well," said Mrs Jackson. "Don't it suit him, Arnold?"

"Of course it does."

Bateman sweated at every pore.

"Isn't it a pity it's dark?" said Eva. "We could photograph you all three together."

Bateman thanked his stars it was. He felt that he must look prodigiously foolish in his blue serge suit and high collar—very neat and gentlemanly— with that ridiculous wreath of flowers on his head. He was seething with indignation, and he had never in his life exercised more self-control than now when he presented an affable exterior. He was furious with that old man, sitting at the head of the table, half-naked, with his saintly face and the flowers on his handsome white locks. The whole position was monstrous.

Then dinner came to an end, and Eva and her mother remained to clear away while the three men sat on the verandah. It was very warm and the air was scented with the white flowers of the night. The full moon, sailing across an unclouded sky, made a pathway on the broad sea that led to the boundless realms of Forever. Arnold Jackson began to talk. His voice was rich and musical. He talked now of the natives and of the old legends of the country. He told strange stories of the past, stories of hazardous expeditions into the unknown, of love and death, of hatred and revenge. He told of the adventurers who had discovered those distant islands, of the sailors who, settling in them, had married the daughters of great chieftains, and of the beach-combers who had led their varied lives on those silvery shores. Bateman, mortified and exasperated, at first listened sullenly, but presently some magic in the words possessed him and he sat entranced. The mirage of romance obscured the light of common day. Had he forgotten that Arnold Jackson had a tongue of silver, a tongue by which he had charmed vast sums out of the credulous public, a tongue which very nearly enabled him to escape the penalty of his crimes? No one had a sweeter eloquence, and no one had a more acute sense of climax. Suddenly he rose.

"Well, you two boys haven't seen one another for a long time. I shall leave you to have a yarn. Teddie will show you your quarters when you want to go to bed."

"Oh, but I wasn't thinking of spending the night, Mr Jackson," said Bateman.

"You'll find it more comfortable. We'll see that you're called in good time."

Then with a courteous shake of the hand, stately as though he were a bishop in canonicals, Arnold Jackson took leave of his guest.

"Of course I'll drive you back to Papeete if you like," said Edward, "but I advise you to stay. It's bully driving in the early morning."

For a few minutes neither of them spoke. Bateman wondered how he should begin on the conversation which all the events of the day made him think more urgent.

"When are you coming back to Chicago?" he asked, suddenly.

For a moment Edward did not answer. Then he turned rather lazily to look at his friend and smiled.

"I don't know. Perhaps never."

"What in heaven's name do you mean?" cried Bateman.

"I'm very happy here. Wouldn't it be folly to make a change?"

"Man alive, you can't live here all your life. This is no life for a man. It's a living death. Oh, Edward, come away at once, before it's too late. I've felt that something was wrong. You're infatuated with the place, you've succumbed to evil influences, but it only requires a wrench, and when you're free from these surroundings you'll thank all the gods there be. You'll be like a dope-fiend when he's broken from his drug. You'll see then that for two years you've been breathing poisoned air. You can't imagine what a relief it will be when you fill your lungs once more with the fresh, pure air of your native country."

He spoke quickly, the words tumbling over one another in his excitement, and there was in his voice sincere and affectionate emotion. Edward was touched.

"It is good of you to care so much, old friend."

"Come with me to-morrow, Edward. It was a mistake that you ever came to this place. This is no life for you."

"You talk of this sort of life and that. How do you think a man gets the best out of life?"

"Why, I should have thought there could be no two answers to that. By doing his duty, by hard work, by meeting all the obligations of his state and station."

"And what is his reward?"

"His reward is the consciousness of having achieved what he set out to do."

"It all sounds a little portentous to me," said Edward, and in the lightness of the night Bateman could see that he was smiling. "I'm afraid you'll think I've degenerated sadly. There are several things I think now which I daresay would have seemed outrageous to me three years ago."

"Have you learnt them from Arnold Jackson?" asked Bateman, scornfully.

"You don't like him? Perhaps you couldn't be expected to. I didn't when I first came. I had just the same prejudice as you. He's a very extraordinary man. You saw for yourself that he makes no secret of the fact that he was in a penitentiary. I do not know that he regrets it or the crimes that led him there. The only complaint he ever made in my hearing was that when he came out his health was impaired. I think he does not know what remorse is. He is completely unmoral. He accepts everything and he accepts himself as well. He's generous and kind."

"He always was," interrupted Bateman, "on other people's money."

"I've found him a very good friend. Is it unnatural that I should take a man as I find him?"

"The result is that you lose the distinction between right and wrong."

"No, they remain just as clearly divided in my mind as before, but what has become a little confused in me is the distinction between the bad man and the good one. Is Arnold Jackson a bad man who does good things or a good man who does bad things? It's a difficult question to answer. Perhaps we make too much of the difference between one man and another. Perhaps even the best of us are sinners and the worst of us are saints. Who knows?"

"You will never persuade me that white is black and that black is white," said Bateman.

"I'm sure I shan't, Bateman."

Bateman could not understand why the flicker of a smile crossed Edward's lips when he thus agreed with him. Edward was silent for a minute.

"When I saw you this morning, Bateman," he said then, "I seemed to see myself as I was two years ago. The same collar, and the same shoes, the same blue suit, the same energy. The same determination. By God, I was energetic. The sleepy methods of this place made my blood tingle. I went about and everywhere I saw possibilities for development and enterprise. There were fortunes to be made here. It seemed to me absurd that the copra should be taken away from here in sacks and the oil extracted in America. It would be far more economical to do all that on the spot, with cheap labour, and save freight, and I saw already the vast factories springing up on the island. Then the way they extracted it from the coconut seemed to me hopelessly inadequate, and I invented a machine which divided the nut and scooped out the meat at the rate of two hundred and forty an hour. The harbour was not large enough. I made plans to enlarge it, then to form a syndicate to buy land, put up two or three large hotels, and bungalows for occasional residents; I had a scheme for improving the steamer service in order to attract visitors from California. In twenty years, instead of this half French, lazy little town of Papeete I saw a great American city with ten-story buildings and street-cars, a theatre and an opera house, a stock exchange and a mayor."

"But go ahead, Edward," cried Bateman, springing up from the chair in excitement. "You've got the ideas and the capacity. Why, you'll become the richest man between Australia and the States."

Edward chuckled softly.

"But I don't want to," he said.

"Do you mean to say you don't want money, big money, money running into millions ? Do you know what you can do with it? Do you know the power it brings? And if you don't care about it for yourself think what you can do, opening new channels for human enterprise, giving occupation to thousands. My brain reels at the visions your words have conjured up."

"Sit down, then, my dear Bateman," laughed Edward. "My machine for cutting the coconuts will always remain unused, and so far as I'm concerned street-cars shall never run in the idle streets of Papeete."

Bateman sank heavily into his chair.

"I don't understand you," he said.

"It came upon me little by little. I came to like the life here, with its ease and its leisure, and the people, with their good-nature and their happy smiling faces. I began to think. I'd never had time to do that before. I began to read."

"You always read."

"I read for examinations. I read in order to be able to hold my own in conversation. I read for instruction. Here I learned to read for pleasure. I learned to talk. Do you know that conversation is one of the greatest pleasures in life? But it wants leisure. I'd always been too busy before. And gradually all the life that had seemed so important to me began to seem rather trivial and vulgar. What is the use of all this hustle and this constant striving? I think of Chicago now and I see a dark, grey city, all stone—it is like a prison—and a ceaseless turmoil. And what does all that activity amount to? Does one get there the best out of life? Is that what we come into the world for, to hurry to an office, and work hour after hour till night, then hurry home and dine and go to a theatre? Is that how I must spend my youth ? Youth lasts so short a time, Bateman. And when I am old, what have I to look forward to? To hurry from my home in the morning to my office and work hour after hour till night, and then hurry home again, and dine and go to a theatre? That may be worth while if you make a fortune; I don't know, it depends on your nature; but if you don't, is it worth while then? I want to make more out of my life than that, Bateman."

"What do you value in life then?"

"I'm afraid you'll laugh at me. Beauty, truth, and goodness."

"Don't you think you can have those in Chicago?"

"Some men can, perhaps, but not I." Edward sprang up now. "I tell you when I think of the life I led in the old days I am filled with horror," he cried violently. "I tremble with fear when I think of the danger I have escaped. I never knew I had a soul till I found it here. If I had remained a rich man I might have lost it for good and all."

"I don't know how you can say that," cried Bateman indignantly. "We often used to have discussions about it."

"Yes, I know. They were about as effectual as the discussions of deaf mutes about harmony. I shall never come back to Chicago, Bateman."

"And what about Isabel?"

Edward walked to the edge of the verandah and leaning over looked intently at the blue magic of the night. There was a slight smile on his face when he turned back to Bateman.

"Isabel is infinitely too good for me. I admire her more than any woman I have ever known. She has a wonderful brain and she's as good as she's beautiful. I respect her energy and her ambition. She was born to make a success of life. I am entirely unworthy of her."

"She doesn't think so."

"But you must tell her so, Bateman."

"I?" cried Bateman. "I'm the last person who could ever do that."

Edward had his back to the vivid light of the moon and his face could not be seen. Is it possible that he smiled again?

"It's no good your trying to conceal anything from her, Bateman. With her quick intelligence she'll turn you inside out in five minutes. You'd better make a clean breast of it right away."

"I don't know what you mean. Of course I shall tell her I've seen you." Bateman spoke in some agitation. "Honestly I don't know what to say to her."

"Tell her that I haven't made good. Tell her that I'm not only poor, but that I'm content to be poor. Tell her I was fired from my job because I was idle and inattentive. Tell her all you've seen tonight and all I've told you."

The idea which on a sudden flashed through Bateman's brain brought him to his feet and in uncontrollable perturbation he faced Edward.

"Man alive, don't you want to marry her?"

Edward looked at him gravely.

"I can never ask her to release me. If she wishes to hold me to my word I will do my best to make her a good and loving husband."

"Do you wish me to give her that message, Edward? Oh, I can't. It's terrible. It's never dawned on her for a moment that you don't want to marry her. She loves you. How can I inflict such a mortification on her?"

Edward smiled again.

"Why don't you marry her yourself, Bateman? You've been in love with her for ages. You're perfectly suited to one another. You'll make her very happy."

"Don't talk to me like that. I can't bear it."

"I resign in your favour, Bateman. You are the better man."

There was something in Edward's tone that made Bateman look up quickly, but Edward's eyes were grave and unsmiling. Bateman did not know what to say. He was disconcerted. He wondered whether Edward could possibly suspect that he had come to Tahiti on a special errand. And though he knew it was horrible he could not prevent the exultation in his heart.

"What will you do if Isabel writes and puts an end to her engagement with you?" he said, slowly.

"Survive," said Edward.

Bateman was so agitated that he did not hear the answer.

"I wish you had ordinary clothes on," he said, somewhat irritably. "It's such a tremendously serious decision you're taking. That fantastic costume of yours makes it seem terribly casual."

"I assure you, I can be just as solemn in a *pareo* and a wreath of roses, as in a high hat and a cutaway coat."

Then another thought struck Bateman.

"Edward, it's not for my sake you're doing this? I don't know, but perhaps this is going to make a tremendous difference to my future. You're not sacrificing yourself for me? I couldn't stand for that, you know."

"No, Bateman, I have learnt not to be silly and sentimental here. I should like you and Isabel to be happy, but I have not the least wish to be unhappy myself."

The answer somewhat chilled Bateman. It seemed to him a little cynical. He would not have been sorry to act a noble part.

"Do you mean to say you're content to waste your life here? It's nothing less than suicide. When I think of the great hopes you had when we left college it seems terrible that you should be content to be no more than a salesman in a cheap-John store."

"Oh, I'm only doing that for the present, and I'm gaining a great deal of valuable experience. I have another plan in my head. Arnold Jackson has a small island in the Paumotas, about a thousand miles from here, a ring of land round a lagoon. He's planted coconut there. He's offered to give it me."

"Why should he do that?" asked Bateman.

"Because if Isabel releases me I shall marry his daughter."

"You?" Bateman was thunderstruck. "You can't marry a half-caste. You wouldn't be so crazy as that."

"She's a good girl, and she has a sweet and gentle nature. I think she would make me very happy."

"Are you in love with her?"

"I don't know," answered Edward reflectively. "I'm not in love with her as I was in love with Isabel. I worshipped Isabel. I thought she was the most wonderful creature I had ever seen. I was not half good enough for her. I don't feel like that with Eva. She's like a beautiful exotic flower that must be sheltered from bitter winds. I want to protect her. No one ever thought of protecting Isabel. I think she loves me for myself and not for what I may become. Whatever happens to me I shall never disappoint her. She suits me."

Bateman was silent.

"We must turn out early in the morning," said Edward at last. "It's really about time we went to bed."

Then Bateman spoke and his voice had in it a genuine distress.

"I'm so bewildered, I don't know what to say. I came here because I thought something was wrong. I thought you hadn't suc-ceeded in what you set out to do and were ashamed to come back when you'd failed. I never guessed I should be faced with this. I'm so desperately sorry, Edward. I'm so disappointed. I hoped you would do great things. It's almost more than I can bear to think of you wasting your talents and your youth and your chance in this lamentable way."

"Don't be grieved, old friend," said Edward. "I haven't failed. I've succeeded. You can't think with what zest I look forward to life, how full it seems to me and how significant. Sometimes, when you are married to Isabel, you will think of me. I shall build myself a house on my coral island and I shall live there, looking after my trees—getting the fruit out of the nuts in the same old way that they have done for unnumbered years—I shall grow all sorts of things in my garden, and I shall fish. There will be enough work to keep me busy and not enough to make me dull. I shall have my books and Eva, children, I hope, and above all, the infinite variety of the sea and the sky, the freshness of the dawn and the beauty of the sunset, and the rich magnificence of the night. I shall make a garden out of what so short a while ago was a wilderness. I shall have created something. The years will pass insensibly, and when I am an old man I hope that I shall be able to look back on a happy, simple, peaceful life. In my small way I too shall have lived in beauty. Do you think it is so little to have enjoyed contentment? We know that it will profit a man little if he gain the whole world and lose his soul. I think I have won mine."

Edward led him to a room in which there were two beds and he threw himself on one of them. In ten minutes Bateman knew by his regular breathing, peaceful as a child's, that Edward was asleep. But for his part he had no rest, he was disturbed in mind, and it was not till the dawn crept into the room, ghostlike and silent, that he fell asleep.

Bateman finished telling Isabel his long story. He had hidden nothing from her except what he thought would wound her or what made himself ridiculous. He did not tell her that he had been forced to sit at dinner with a wreath of flowers round his head and he did not tell her that Edward was prepared to marry her uncle's half-caste daughter the moment she set him free. But perhaps Isabel had keener intuitions than he knew, for as he went on with his tale her eyes grew colder and her lips closed upon one another more tightly. Now and then she looked at him closely, and if he had been less intent on his narrative he might have wondered at her expression.

"What was this girl like?" she asked when he finished. "Uncle Arnold's daughter. Would you say there was any resemblance between her and me?"

Bateman was surprised at the question.

"It never struck me. You know I've never had eyes for anyone but you and I could never think that anyone was like you. Who could resemble you?"

"Was she pretty?" said Isabel, smiling slightly at his words.

"I suppose so. I daresay some men would say she was very beautiful."

"Well, it's of no consequence. I don't think we need give her any more of our attention."

"What are you going to do, Isabel?" he asked then.

Isabel looked down at the hand which still bore the ring Edward had given her on their betrothal.

"I wouldn't let Edward break our engagement because I thought it would be an incentive to him. I wanted to be an inspiration to him. I thought if anything could enable him to achieve success it was the thought that I loved him. I have done all I could. It's hopeless. It would only be weakness on my part not to recognise the facts. Poor Edward, he's nobody's enemy but his own. He was a dear, nice fellow, but there was something lacking in him, I suppose it was backbone. I hope he'll be happy."

She slipped the ring off her finger and placed it on the table. Bateman watched her with a heart beating so rapidly that he could hardly breathe.

"You're wonderful, Isabel, you're simply wonderful."

She smiled, and, standing up, held out her hand to him.

"How can I ever thank you for what you've done for me?" she said. "You've done me a great service. I knew I could trust you."

He took her hand and held it. She had never looked more beautiful.

"Oh, Isabel, I would do so much more for you than that. You know that I only ask to be allowed to love and serve you."

"You're so strong, Bateman," she sighed. "It gives me such a delicious feeling of confidence."

"Isabel, I adore you."

He hardly knew how the inspiration had come to him, but suddenly he clasped her in his arms, and she, all unresisting, smiled into his eyes.

"Isabel, you know I wanted to marry you the very first day I saw you," he cried passionately.

"Then why on earth didn't you ask me?" she replied.

She loved him. He could hardly believe it was true. She gave him her lovely lips to kiss. And as he held her in his arms he had a vision of the works of the Hunter Motor Traction and Automobile Company growing in size and importance till they covered a hundred acres, and of the millions of motors they would turn out, and of the great collection of pictures he would form which should beat anything they had in New York. He would wear horn spectacles. And she, with the delicious pressure of his arms about her, sighed with happiness, for she thought of the exquisite house she would have, full of antique furniture, and of the concerts she would give, and of the *thés dansants,* and the dinners to which only the most cultured people would come. Bateman should wear horn spectacles.

"Poor Edward," she sighed.

A SPIDER PHAETON (1924)

William John Pickard

My Dear Mr. Eliot:

It would give us pleasure to have you with us over the next week end. There are not to be many guests, but among them are some that you know, and others, I hope, that you will enjoy meeting.

I trust that you will pardon the tardiness of this note. I wrote to you a week ago. To my dismay I have just discovered that through the carelessness of my secretary the letter was never mailed.

I hope that nothing will prevent your coming and that we may expect you in time for tea Friday afternoon.

Cordially yours,
Charlotte Chesterfield Kingsley

May twenty-first,
Nineteen twenty-three.

The white, silky linen with unravelled edges was engraved in miniature script:

The Kingsley Manor
Lake Forest, Illinois.

JOSEPH ELIOT HELD the stationery to the light. A soft transparency and a weave of many fine lines greeted his eyes. On the last sheet was a dim watermark of kissing doves and stars enclosed with a border of right angles and half circles. There was not the slightest suggestion of perfume, just the refreshing scent of elegant, finely woven linen.

He read the note again. His eyes blinked. He whipped out his glasses and read it for the third time. He blew on his glasses, wiped them with his cotton handkerchief, and read it the fourth time.

"There must be some mistake," he said to himself. Mrs. John Chesterfield Kingsley he had never met. Heard of her, yes, frequently. Who hadn't? All New York, Washington, Chicago, and parts more distant, that had a part in Society or worshipped its activities from afar—and such was the case with Joseph Eliot—had heard of Lady Kingsley. The society columns were crowded with her numerous yet not too numerous entertainments, and nearly as frequently illustrated with her pictures. "Among those present at the Opera at the Auditorium last night were Mr. and Mrs. John Chesterfield Kingsley. In their box with them were Lord and Lady Mount-Savage, Mr. and Mrs. Fifield Jones, and the John Henry Hendersons." As a social leader she had no peer, and her influence in the world of art, philanthropy, and politics had few bounds. It was whispered, as such things are, that she had made members of more than one President's Cabinet. To be invited to one of her week ends at her Lake Forest Estate automatically made our Joseph Eliot the envy of high diplomacy; counts, earls, dukes; the presidents of far flung corporations; others of lesser titles but no less distinction.

There certainly was a mistake. Although it was Joseph Eliot's address that appeared on the envelope, the invitation must have been meant for another person with the same name. No one was conscious of this error more than Joseph Eliot, himself. Furthermore, his was the quandary; he it was who had to decide whether or not to attend. There must be many famous Joseph Eliots in many honorable and noteworthy professions. Right at the moment he could not specifically remember reading about any, but the odds were all in favor of their existence.

However, adventure comes seldom, even to Evening American reporters, as Eliot well knew from his two years' work with that Chicago paper.

If he had been on the staff of the Social Column, perhaps the invitation would not have held such an unusual appeal. Its glamor to him was that of a flame to a moth. Why should he send it back to be re-addressed to the right Eliot. Here was his chance to attend an affair the like of which he had never seen before; and, moreover, never would see unless he grasped the present opportunity.

He read the invitation for the fifth time . . . "There are not to be many guests . . ." He smiled wisely; he knew what that meant— not more than a hundred. Mrs. John Chesterfield Kingsley's conception of a limited number was comparative.

There would be tennis, riding, golf, polo; accomplished ladies, beautiful debutantes. Yet, on the other hand, the humiliation of being an unwelcome guest, and the probability of encountering the right Mr. Eliot, was acutely deterring. Then, a real obstacle, he had no clothes. In the bank were his savings of two years; the money with which he planned to marry in the fall. Ah well, he might meet a wealthy debutante who would take a fancy to him. He was sorry for that thought, its injustice to his lovely fiancée. Nevertheless, he would plunge the money in clothes—Who was it that said "appearance is the best investment?" Oh yes, the House of Kuppenheimer in the Saturday Evening Post. But, to Eliot, Marcus Aurelius could have been no more convincing. It is easy for any slogan that phrases our desire to carry conviction. At that he probably would not have enough to include a riding suit and polo outfit. Oh well, he could not ride anyway. Although a good driver behind a buck-board or a plow, having been brought up on a farm, his knowledge astride a horse was limited. At the time he read of that great polo match between the Lake Forest Blues and the Detroit Free Lancers at the Onwentsia Club with "sons of prominent families as participants" he decided to take up polo. Astride a gymnasium horse of the nearest Y. M. C. A. he had swung heroically with a wooden mallet. Although not very satisfactory, this went on after hours for several nights until the janitor got wind of it and spilled him and his lusty steed.

Well, he would have to forego the riding; he could plead chronic appendicitis. Realizing that there was no time to spare, he went at once to an establishment on Michigan Boulevard, whose advertisements he had long devoured, that of a fashionable tailor, who finally agreed for an unethical consideration to rush the clothes through in time for him to depart Friday morning for Mrs. Chesterfield Kingsley's Manor.

That evening, walking down the row of poplar trees to the home of Louisa Neonardo, the thought came to him, though not bitterly, that if he had refrained from buying her a ring the month before, he could have included hurried riding lessons and the polo outfit. Joseph Eliot turned the corner; so did the poplar trees. They led right to her house and then stopped, as if to say that they knew where all good things dwelt. Her father, though an ignorant Italian, reaching this country long before selective immigration, had, with his vulgarity, an embracing love of nature and all that is beautiful. It was not by chance that he built his house at the end of the poplar row. Louisa was on the porch, rocking in a wobbly wicker chair; the season was early. Eliot stopped to smile at her before mounting the steps. He ended by gasping. He always did. Every evening her entrancing Latin beauty arrested him, threw him into breathlessness, before he could regain sufficient control of himself to speak the pleasantries of the day. She had that exquisite bewitching charm that sometimes comes from the marriage of an American girl to a man from one of the warm sunny countries that border the Mediterranean. Her hair, jet black, parted just to the left of center, flowed loosely down well over each ear before circling back to form a rather old fashioned knot at the nape of her neck. At times, retaining the part in the center, she drew it tight against her scalp, setting it off with a jade rhinestone comb, and then it was that she reminded Eliot of the portraits of Italian ladies in the Art Institute. He had not been far afield. Comb or no comb, brass earrings, at least two inches in diameter, hung at all times below the black hair. Her skin was olive, though not as dark an olive as would have been the case if straight Italian blood had run in her veins. Predominantly a true daughter of the Latins, her dress was at all times colorful. Now it was blending as best it could borders and figures of red and blue and black on a surface of pale yellow.

Mr. Neonardo was busy striking out at the June bugs that swished and sizzled about, swearing silently the while with a mixture of rolling "Yankee" oaths and a sharp staccato rendering of the blasphemy of his own land. Occasionally he spat with gusto over the railing onto the sidewalk. Mr. Neonardo had little more respect for sidewalks than for handkerchiefs. He could have managed very well without either.

The slight breeze which had commenced to stir the poplar trees was melody to his soul. He expatiated upon it.

"Father, dear, won't you please go in the house? Joseph and I have something we want to talk over together privately." Neonardo, loath to leave the breeze, and even feeling more kindly toward the June bugs, such is the influence of a contrary suggestion, sauntered in slowly. He had become Americanized to the extent of giving his daughter her way.

Joseph drew the kitchen chair, vacated by Mr. Neonardo, close to the rocker, and dove his hand into an inside coat pocket. "Louisa, dear, I must show you the letter that came for me in the afternoon mail." He gave her Mrs. John Chesterfield Kingsley's invitation with a flourishing, proud gesture. She read it slowly, her lips moving. "I wish you were going, Louisa." A smile stole from the corners of her red mouth; she dropped her eye lashes. So heavy were they that it seemed as if a black shadow rested on her cheeks. Her head came closer to Joseph.

Down Halsted Street, a few blocks away, the streetcars were clanging.

"You are going then?"

"Why yes, certainly. It will be a great opportunity for me to meet interesting and worth while people. Just think, Louisa. Counts, and dukes and earls, and financial leaders, and maybe kings will be there. A wonderful chance for me, even considering my work alone. Perhaps I will meet William Randolph Hearst, himself. And then Mrs. John Chesterfield Kingsley! Surely you have heard of her, Louisa."

"Oh, yes. Yes, I have. But how do you think she came to ask you, Joseph? Do you know her?"

"Well, no. That is, not well. But probably she has heard of the work, the writing, I have been doing on the American and wants to meet me. That could be, you know."

"Perhaps you will fall in love with one of the young ladies of—of high society." There was seriousness and a slight trembling in her voice.

"Oh, you mean a debutante: Oh no."

But Louisa was not certain; Joseph Eliot did not speak. He looked over the porch-rail, whistled, speculated. He did not mention the vast sums he was spending for clothes. A boy on a bicycle, the wick of the lamp turned far down to prevent smoking, went by, shoving hard, his short legs scarcely long enough to reach the pedals. A Ford horn sounded. Joseph Eliot jumped up. He couldn't stay any longer; had a lot to do in order to be ready for the week end. Of course he would see Louisa again before he left. He lit a cigarette quickly, blew smoke at Louisa, wheeled to run down the stairs, paused, snapped his fingers; spun back on his heels to kiss her. He went down the street, puffing more and more rapidly on his cigarette, the smoke stack of a locomotive. He had forgotten to write his acceptance to Mrs. John Chesterfield Kingsley. Very bad form to postpone that. He took the street car south on Halsted, transferred, reached the loop, got off at Seventh and walked into the Blackstone. The letter finished, he left the Blackstone for one of Thompson's restaurants, two blocks west. He slept going home on the bumpy cars. In his room, undressing, he lost his composure. The suits were ordered, the letter of acceptance was written on Blackstone stationery, but his courage was going. It was well to speak to Louisa of his hidden fame having reached Mrs. Chester-field Kingsley; but he knew otherwise. That night he dreamed of the right Mr. Eliot, a tall, ornate gentleman, faultlessly clad, who looked at him indifferently through a monocle, and then chased him to the top of the kitchen stove with a broom. He was falling down from the stove. Down, down, down—he woke up on the floor—crawled trembling to the light, and punched it on quickly, as if to get the jump on an adversary—but neither the tall ornate gentleman nor his broom were under the bed.

The matter of transportation was yet to be settled. How was he going to the Kingsley Manor? The "Rent a New Ford Company" could not be entrusted with solving the difficulty. There would be too many of the tall, the polished, the cool, passing in Packards, Cadillacs, and Rolls Royces—liveried footmen, Russian wolf hounds—while he chugged along with the aid of even a new Ford. Never ! He would have to hit upon something more auspicious. He wished to arrive in some sort of a distinguished vehicle of his own. Then there was the question of a valet. Should he bring one, or were they provided? Knowing of no one who would do for such an exacting task, for certainly Mr. Neonardo with his hawking and guttural Italian would be a misfit, he finally decided there would be one present. For the benefit of this gentleman he bought a silk dressing gown, and, also for his benefit, had it liberally mono-gramed on the upper left hand pocket and the cuffs of the sleeves. No chewed and charred dollar briar in the presence of a valet; he purchased a Dunhill. "How shall I dra-aw your bauth, sir, luke warm, hot?"

"No. Always cold, very cold, Gaston."

"Very good, Sir."

But there returned the pressing need of conveyance. The inspira-tion for determining it did not arrive until late Thursday afternoon. The grocery wagon drew up at the front door. Joseph Eliot was looking out the window. He jerked up his chin. He whipped out his glasses and pressed his forehead against the glass. There, to his mind, was a horse; as graceful and stylish a Hackney mare as he had ever seen at the shows. She was a glossy chestnut, heavy in proportion to her height, neck arched, tail bobbed, chest deep, and with the much desired white stockings. How well that mare would look, with blinders and appropriate harness, drawing a suitable rig. What was she doing hitched to a grocery wagon? In this day of cars, the fine horses were either relegated to the country, or else hitched to grocery wagons. It was a crime, he thought, as he went down the stairs three at a time. He rode back to the store with the boy.

The proprietor, a sputtering German, was dubious. "What do you want of my horse? She I prize big. Very valuable horse. My father once sent her to me from the farm. You run a grocery?"

"Oh no, Lord no!" Mr. Eliot replied. "I'm going to drive to Lake Forest." Lake Forest didn't seem to clarify matters for the Halsted Street Grocer. "I merely want to hire her for the week end."

"I know, I know, but mine Gott, what am I doing for deliveries?"

"Send a boy around; hire a Ford. I might be able to pay for it in addition to renting your mare." They finally agreed.

At a nearby livery stable all that could be found in the way of a conveyance was a tall enclosed carriage with coachman's seat aloft. The veteran liveryman assured Mr. Eliot that it had been the first carriage in all important Chicago weddings and funerals thirty years before, and, although it hadn't been on the streets since, that it could easily be dusted and set to rolling. But Mr. Eliot was not convinced. A further half day's search made him fear that he would have to go back to the grocery wagon. Finally he was rewarded; he discovered a very presentable Spider Phaeton. The seat for two in front was constructed on iron loops, which also aided in supporting the flimsy groom's seat in rear. The dark blue plush of the front seat and the large old fashioned lamps at the side stirred him with their forgotten elegance; and a thorough greasing banished the squeak from the small front and large rear wheels.

Mr. Neonardo was to have his day—if he wanted it. He was not certain that he wanted it. He saw a "different light." "Me, coachman? No Sir. Nota me." Not until the grandeur and pomp of a long coat with brass buttons, and a tall silk hat, was vividly painted did he consent.

The tailor had promised the clothes for early Friday morning. He did better than that. They were out Thursday night: one tweed sport, one blue serge suiting, a broadcloth dinner jacket and full dress, two pair of white flannel trousers, a tennis shirt, and sports blazer. Eliot took them out of the box and hung them up, well satisfied with their appearance. His satisfaction was short. They looked uncompromisingly new. Something would have to be done about that. He jumbled them back into the box, and rolled it around on the floor. Then, in turn, he put each on to go through calisthenics; brisk, severe exercising, feet over head for the suits. Simple flexing of the arms and legs had to suffice for the sport wear and sundries; he was getting tired. At that it was two o'clock before he was in bed. He arose that morning rather lame. This, however, did not prevent an early start. Lake Forest is a long way to go with a Hackney and a Spider Phaeton. Neonardo was on deck, anxious to be off in a display of his stylish raiment. He was a person of moods, was Neonardo, not to be handled with thick gloves.

The Hackney pranced. The blue ribbon winners of the gentle-man at whose restaurants Eliot ate most of his meals could scarcely have surpassed her for style. She responded to the days of yore. Her knees went higher and higher, as the dignity and ease of a Phaeton over that of a grocery wagon was impressed upon her. Eliot wished that she would save her style for Sheridan Road. He was erect, a gentleman, chamois driving gloves, his long yellow whip held diagonally in fair accordance with a picture he had noted in the equestrian number of the National Geographic. Back of him sat the camouflaged Neonardo, his silk hat a trifle too far back on his round head, the brass buttons shining with the early morning sun. It gave promise of being a very hot day.

Neonardo was somewhat of a worry to Eliot; the openness of the Phaeton encouraged his spitting, and the lack of an absorbing task left him free to stretch and twist his neck in every direction. Yet he was not a total failure as a groom; he was capable of abundant pomp and swagger. By the time, stepping east, that they reached Sheridan Road, Eliot was master of the reins. They swung onto the new outside drive, carefully keeping to the curb next to the lake. Cars whizzed by. Neonardo looked out over the calm water, sparkling with the sun. The sky was bluer above his Italy, yet he was content. There was also beauty here.

Many people thought they were a float for the opening of a new boulevard or the like. A few, that they were an advertisement for the Chauve Souris (for the Hackney was already commencing to tire.) But Eliot was not uncomfortable. On the faces of more than one he caught looks of approval and even envy. Perhaps his example might be the means of bringing back fashionable carriages to the streets of Chicago. There were many advantages. Even going through Rogers Park, they were not in danger of being "pinched." A Rolls Royce drew alongside, slowed down—a liveried chauffeur and footman, a Russian Wolf hound on the running board— undoubtedly bound for the Chesterfield Kingsley's. An assemblage of the exclusive, the elegant, the cool, leaned out. Mr. Joseph Eliot was sufficiently exclusive and elegant, but he was not cool. Neither was Neonardo. The sun was beating down on the open Spider with the intensity of an August noon. The mare was sweating; Neonardo was sweating; moreover he did not intend to put up with it. He had come prepared for such an emergency. The brims of silk hats are not broad enough. From beneath his long groom's coat he whipped a large red Italian umbrella, which, after opening to fully the circumference of the mammoth rear wheels, he hoisted over his head. The effect was colorful. Too colorful. Eliot protested vehemently, but Neonardo was obdurate. "What you thinka I do, seet and boil like lobster?" The fellow was evidently no more qualified to be a coachman than a valet. He had made a mistake. Finally they compromised by moving north on side streets, Neonardo retaining his red shade; for all the world like a farmer coming into market. Even on these obscure avenues, Eliot felt that they were watched by a thousand eyes. However, when they stopped in a deserted spot to lunch on Neonardo's sandwiches, he was glad to crawl under the umbrella. The mare munched in a feed bag, which Neonardo had strung over her neck—at least the fellow forgot nothing—blowing and snorting in it from time to time to disperse the dust and chaff. The more she ate the more particular she became, and the harder and oftener she blew. Neonardo, with a full stomach, stretched out for a nap. The mare nodded her approval. Eliot was in the minority. He paced back and forth. There was no hurrying an Italian. Eliot had washed out four pairs of socks and a shirt the night before. A night's hanging on the mirror had failed to dry them. They were jammed inside his new, monogramed Gladstone bag in a rubber covering. Thinking he might as well make use of the delay in some way, he cut off part of the rope with which the mare was tied, retied her, and strung the extra piece between the Spider's rear guards, which jutted out beyond the groom's seat. Thus there was an acceptable clothes line over which to hang in the sunlight his four pairs of socks and his shirt. Fortunately, the flies were bad.

Neonardo did not sleep long. On they went, the red umbrella a beacon to the front, the socks and shirt a signal to the rear. Eliot had forgotten them.

Caesar with all his array was never better equipped for a triumphal entry. As the afternoon cooled, entreaties succeeded in lowering the umbrella.

"And you socka." Eliot blushed. He pulled in the line. They returned to Sheridan Road.

As they approached the Chesterfield Kingsley estate, Eliot grew more and more excited, while even Neonardo, subconsciously scenting a great impending event, fidgeted on his seat. Eliot whipped up the horse, and that animal in a last valiant splurge dashed between the posts of the colossal stone gate, throwing her mane and champing the bit. Neonardo sat straight, motionless, riveted. A true Italian, there was never a time when he did not rise to a dramatic situation. Eliot, alone, quivered. Not, it is true, for the Spider, for that they would be envied, but because of the right Mr. Eliot. Sweat stood out on his forehead in contemplation of the cool reception he was bound to receive from Mrs. Chesterfield Kingsley for usurping the place of another. What would he say to her? What could he say to her? Now that he was here, he marvelled at his courage; he should never have come.

They were fashionably late. The guests were gathered on the lawn at tea. Eliot yanked the mare to a halt. Eyes were on him. He descended. An attendant, like his mistress, equal to any occasion, directed Neonardo and the charger to the stables. Eliot felt that his last support was gone. A tall stately lady approached smiling, Mrs. Chesterfield Kingsley. To Eliot she was a picture of supreme grace and charm. "I am Mr. Eliot," he said defiantly, an attempt at bravado to cover his shivering, "Mr. Joseph Eliot."

"Yes, of course. So nice of you to come at all." It was so sweet of him to arrive in a carriage. He was doing that which many of them had long wished the courage to accomplish. It was so lovely when carriages were in vogue. She hoped that his distinguished example would go a long way toward bringing them back. Would he join them now to have some tea, or go first to his room? He would find his bags there. He would first have tea? That was so nice of him. Would he have lemon or sugar in his tea. "Neither," he answered, though he was very fond of sugar. People looked at him.

He was afraid that his trousers might be too baggy. Several glances reassured him on this. In fact, it was apparent that he should have exercised longer in his. To the right he saw a distinguished looking gentleman, slender, combed, a monocle, in his button hole a white gardenia. He felt certain that he was *the* Mr. Eliot. He corresponded identically to the man with a broom, in his dream. Dodging his glance, he, like a criminal, trembling, about to make a confession, leaned toward Mrs. Chesterfield Kingsley, and asked her if she would mind telling him the name of the gentleman with the white gardenia. It was difficult for Mrs. Chesterfield Kingsley to tell whom he meant; there was more than one gentleman wearing a gardenia. She said Mr. Hawkinson—perhaps she had the wrong man in view. She asked if he would like to meet him. Eliot was emphatically negative in his answer. Mrs. Chesterfield Kingsley was a little surprised. After introducing him to an elaborate old dowager, she turned her conversation to others. The dowager asked if he belonged to the Virginia Eliots. He said he didn't think so. "Or the New England Eliots?" He thought it wasn't likely. His father was James Eliot, he ventured hesitantly. She looked blank, but replied that she had heard of him. Society is quite often polite. The dowager moved off, unquestionably to find a representative of the Virginia Eliots. Left alone, Joseph stood on one foot, then the other. There were people to whom he had been introduced chatting near him. Would it be all right to take part in their conversation? Certainly. He decided, however, to consider such a step for several minutes before taking it. The several minutes up, he came to the conclusion that it was then too late; that, having permitted them to talk among themselves for such a length of time, his entry would be conspicuous. He continued to balance from one foot to the other. Finally, one of the important editors of his newspaper, whose presence was among the blurred impressions of his arrival, came over to shake his hand.

"I didn't know that you were going to be here, Eliot. This is a pleasure. Come around to see me Monday. Have you known Mrs. Chesterfield Kingsley long?"

"No, not long. And listen, Mr. Parker, if anyone should try to tell you I was not invited, it is not so, I was. You can understand that, can't you?" Mr. Parker didn't know whether he could or not. Eliot escaped to his room. He wasn't unnerved, he assured himself, merely wanted time to dress leisurely for dinner. The valet was perfect. Everything was laid out. After steaming in a hot bath, he felt better. He puffed at his pipe while leisurely dressing, picturing beautiful debutantes in the smoke. Refreshed, he went down to dinner with courage and an appetite. In the living room, a cocktail buoyed his spirits to the ceiling. He felt in fine fettle. He should have feared the bursting of the bubble. Seated for dinner neither the appetite nor courage lasted a moment. The Eliot fellow was there, minus his gardenia, but nevertheless there, stealthily watching him from the other end of the table. He could not shake his eye, try as hard as he was able. He squirmed. After staring a long while in the other direction, Joseph stole a glance back at Eliot. It was no use. That fellow's eye was still riveted upon him. Dinner was agony. He boiled. To all purposes he was in the water of his bath again, now scalding, his head under, stewing. His hostess was remarkable in that she did not call him the impostor that he was. Perhaps it was fear of a scene which caused her to extend him courtesy that he did not deserve. Anyway, he could no longer continue the pretense. He felt that everyone knew his secret. Directly dinner was over, he would have to make a clean breast of it all to Mrs. Chesterfield Kingsley. He and Neonardo and the Hackney would go back from whence they had come.

"The right Mr. Eliot?" Mrs. Chesterfield Kingsley replied, dumbfounded. "You are he. There is no other Mr. Eliot here."

"The invitation was meant for me!"

"Why, certainly. Didn't Louisa Neonardo tell you?"

"Louisa! Louisa! You know Louisa?"

"She gives me all my marcelles. She is coming tomorrow morning. I wonder why she didn't tell you?"

"Tomorrow — tomorrow morning — for — for marcelles?"

"No, no, socially for the week-end. When I invited her she asked me sweetly if you might be included, which I was very glad to do. Louisa and you are engaged?"

"Yes."

"She is a very lovely girl." Then it was that Eliot remembered reading that Mrs. Chesterfield Kingsley was noted for frequently inviting beautiful young girls of a totally different station in life from that of the other guests to her affairs. She encouraged the unusual, and her position was strong enough to carry her way. Wasn't it most natural that a lady who had made and unmade cabinets should be successful in setting aside some of the trivial conventions of entertaining, particularly when it was greatly to the pleasure of her guests to do so, Eliot thought. Mrs. Chesterfield Kingsley had walked away. But Mr. Joseph Eliot was no longer embarrassed. The world to him had a new light. His invitation was bona fide, he was where he belonged, in the midst of luxury, elegance, and distinction, and because of Louisa. (He did not forget that.) From then on he mingled freely with the distinguished, and many thought him a charming young man. He took special delight in chatting with that slender gentleman, the Joseph Eliot of his nightmare.

Later Mr. Parker came up to him again. "I am glad that you are here, Eliot, and I am glad that you came the way you did. For what I was going to say before, Eliot, is this. I want you to write up your arrival with horse and gig. It will make the best interest story of the week. I will run it on the front page. Can you imagine the effect: 'Mr. Joseph Eliot' (give them my address as yours), 'a young man of one of our best families' (you can always put that in, you know), 'arrives at Mrs. Chesterfield Kingsley's in a Spider drawn by a blue blood chestnut Hackney. Mr. Eliot's example is of only slightly less importance among high social circles in this country than is that of the Prince of Wales in England,' et cetera, et cetera. Put it on thick. You know how. It will be a tremendous play for our paper. Mrs. Chesterfield Kingsley's name is a byword."

"I know it, that's just the trouble."

"What do you mean?"

"I mean, I am very sorry, Mr. Parker, but I am afraid I can't do it. I am a guest of Mrs. Kingsley's."

"Trust my thirty years of newspaper experience, Eliot. It will not get you in wrong with Mrs. Kingsley. Quite the contrary. She will thank you for it. Her name all over the front page. She is not dumb. How can she take offense. It is in connection with no scandal. Why, she will welcome the publicity, and well she may. Spearmint with all its advertising will never be able to achieve such a spread. Believe me, Eliot. Of course, don't write the story in the first person. Tell about yourself all you desire. The more the better, but write it as if it were being composed by someone else. But then it is not necessary for me to caution you in regard to that."

"No sir."

Eliot saw very little of the debutantes. Louisa, as was promised, arrived the next morning. They were inseparable. She was ravishing. He thought he had bought clothes, but he had not been thinking in the quantities of a girl's wardrobe.

Saturday evening was slightly cloudy. Lake Michigan's waves could be heard splashing on the wet sand. Sheridan Road curved in the distance. Sitting on the big stone to the right of the garage door, Neonardo sighed, and breathed deeply, as if he would inhale past escaping the beauty of the night.

Neonardo's daughter and Eliot walked away from the lake up the long gravel path, but Neonardo was not watching them. His nose was pointed to the moon, like that of a hound that barks at its mystery. They stopped at the arbor, vine covered, through whose crevices they watched Mrs. Chesterfield Kingsley's guests, between dances, pouring out onto the lawn.

"Louisa, dear, why didn't you tell me that it was through you that I was invited here? Of course, I remember that you have told me many times of giving marcelles, but I had no suspicion that Mrs. Chesterfield Kingsley was included in your work."

"She hasn't been long, just a couple of weeks."

"But why—"

"Well, I was going to. But that night you came over to see me, you were so proud of the invitation, and of Mrs. Chesterfield Kingsley having heard of you, that I didn't have the heart to spoil it all for you by telling that she hadn't heard of you at all, and that I had arranged it. So I decided to wait."

"It's a wonder your father didn't let the cat out of the bag."

"He's not as stupid as you think, Joseph."

"I don't think he's stupid."

"Yes you do, sometimes. But I love you just the same."

They drove back together in the Spider Sunday night, with Mr. Neonardo on his seat of vantage in the rear, a combination chaperone and groom. There wasn't much however, that he objected to in either capacity. He was in excellent spirits. Never in his life had he been dined, wined, and feted as he had been in the servants' quarters of the Chesterfield Kingsley Lake Forest mansion. "You go back once, taka me. Be sure, taka me."

Mr. Parker was right. The front page story immensely pleased Mrs. John Chesterfield Kingsley, and one Joseph Eliot (with Mr. Parker's address) found himself the recipient of many invitations to spend week ends at the various country homes and estates of lesser lights. And at the bottom were postscripts that generally read: "And do come as you did to Mrs. Chesterfield Kingsley's, with your carriage." But Joseph Eliot could not accept any of these. The long journey to Lake Forest and back was the last minuet of the Spider Phaeton. Its weary wheels had crumpled.

A BOTTLE OF MILK FOR MOTHER (1941)

Nelson Algren

I feel I am of them—
I belong to those convicts and prostitutes myself,
And henceforth I will not deny them—
For how can I deny myself?

Whitman

TWO MONTHS AFTER the Polish Warriors S.A.C. had had their heads shaved, Bruno Lefty Bicek got into his final difficulty with the Racine Street police. The arresting officers and a reporter from the *Dziennik Chicagoski* were grouped about the captain's desk when the boy was urged forward into the room by Sergeant Adamovitch, with two fingers wrapped about the boy's broad belt: a full-bodied boy wearing a worn and sleeveless blue work shirt grown too tight across the shoulders; and the shoulders themselves with a loose swing to them. His skull and face were shining from a recent scrubbing, so that the little bridgeless nose glistened between the protective points of the cheekbones. Behind the desk sat Kozak, eleven years on the force and brother to an alderman. The reporter stuck a cigarette behind one ear like a pencil.

"We spotted him followin' the drunk down Chicago——" Sergeant Comiskey began.

Captain Kozak interrupted. "Let the jackroller tell us how he done it hisself."

"I ain't no jackroller."

"What you doin' here, then?"

Bicek folded his naked arms.

"Answer me. If you ain't here for jackrollin' it must be for strong-arm robb'ry—'r you one of them Chicago Av'noo moll-buzzers?"

"I ain't that neither."

"C'mon, c'mon, I seen you in here before—what were you up to, followin' that poor old man?"

"I ain't been in here before."

Neither Sergeant Milano, Comiskey, nor old Adamovitch moved an inch; yet the boy felt the semicircle about him drawing closer. Out of the corner of his eye he watched the reporter undoing the top button of his mangy raccoon coat, as though the barren little query room were already growing too warm for him.

"What were you doin' on Chicago Av'noo in the first place when you live up around Division? Ain't your own ward big enough you have to come down here to get in trouble? What do you *think* you're here for?"

"Well, I was just walkin' down Chicago like I said, to get a bottle of milk for Mother, when the officers jumped me. I didn't even see 'em drive up, they wouldn't let me say a word, I got no idea what I'm here for. I was just doin' a errand for Mother 'n——"

"All right, son, you want us to book you as a pickup 'n hold you overnight, is that it?"

"Yes sir."

"What about this, then?"

Kozak flipped a spring-blade knife with a five-inch blade onto the police blotter; the boy resisted an impulse to lean forward and take it. His own double-edged double-jointed spring-blade cuts-all genuine Filipino twisty-handled all-American gut-ripper.

"Is it yours or ain't it?"

"Never seen it before, Captain."

Kozak pulled a billy out of his belt, spread the blade across the bend of the blotter before him, and with one blow clubbed the blade off two inches from the handle. The boy winced as though he himself had received the blow. Kozak threw the broken blade into a basket and the knife into a drawer.

"Know why I did that, son?"

"Yes sir."

"Tell me."

"'Cause it's three inches to the heart."

"No. 'Cause it's against the law to carry more than three inches of knife. C'mon, Lefty, tell us about it. 'N it better be good."

The boy began slowly, secretly gratified that Kozak appeared to know he was the Warriors' first-string left-hander: maybe he'd been out at that game against the Knothole Wonders the Sunday he'd finished his own game and then had relieved Dropkick Kodadek in the sixth in the second. Why hadn't anyone called him "Iron-Man Bicek" or "Fireball Bruno" for that one?

"Everythin' you say can be used against you," Kozak warned him earnestly. "Don't talk unless you want to." His lips formed each syllable precisely.

Then he added absently, as though talking to someone unseen. "We'll just hold you on an open charge till you do."

And his lips hadn't moved at all.

The boy licked his own lips, feeling a dryness coming into his throat and a tightening in his stomach. "We seen this boo-batch with his collar turned inside out cash'n his check by Konstanty Stachula's Tonsorial Palace of Art on Division. So I followed him a way, that was all. Just break'n the old monotony was all. Just a notion, you might say, that come over me. I'm just a neighborhood kid, Captain."

He stopped as though he had finished the story. Kozak glanced over the boy's shoulder at the arresting officers and Lefty began again hurriedly.

"Ever' once in a while he'd pull a little single-shot of scotch out of his pocket, stop a second t' toss it down, 'n toss the bottle at the car tracks. I picked up a bottle that didn't bust but there wasn't a spider left in 'er, the boobatch'd drunk her dry. 'N do you know, he had his pockets *full* of them little bottles? 'Stead of buyin' hisself a fifth in the first place. Can't understand a man who'll buy liquor that way. Right before the corner of Walton 'n Noble he popped into a hallway. That was Chiney-Eye-the-Princinct-Captain's hallway, so I popped right in after him. Me'n Chiney-Eye 'r just like that." The boy crossed two fingers of his left hand and asked innocently, "Has the alderman been in to straighten this out, Captain?"

"What time was all this, Lefty?"

"Well, some of the street lamps was lit awready 'n I didn't see nobody either way down Noble. It'd just started spitt'n a little snow 'n I couldn't see clear down Walton account of Wojciechowski's Tavern bein' in the way. He was a old guy, a dino you. He couldn't speak a word of English. But he started in cryin' about how every time he gets a little drunk the same old thing happens to him 'n he's gettin' fed up, he lost his last three checks in the very same hallway 'n it's gettin' so his family don't believe him no more . . ."

Lefty paused, realizing that his tongue was going faster than his brain. He unfolded his arms and shoved them down his pants pockets; the pants were turned up at the cuffs and the cuffs were frayed. He drew a colorless cap off his hip pocket and stood clutching it in his left hand.

"I didn't take him them other times, Captain," he anticipated Kozak.

"Who did?"

Silence.

"What's Benkowski doin' for a living these days, Lefty?"

"Just nutsin' around."

"What's Nowogrodski up to?"

"Goes wolfin' on roller skates by Riverview. The rink's open all year round."

"Does he have much luck?"

"Never turns up a hair. They go by too fast."

"What's that evil-eye up to?"

Silence.

"You know who I mean. Idzikowski."

"The Finger?"

"You know who I mean. Don't stall."

"He's hexin' fights, I heard."

"Seen Kodadek lately?"

"I guess. A week 'r two 'r a month ago."

"What was *he* up to?"

"Sir?"

"What was Kodadek doin' the last time you seen him?"

"You mean Dropkick? He was nutsin' around."

"Does he nuts around drunks in hallways?"

Somewhere in the room a small clock or wrist watch began ticking distinctly.

"Nutsin' around ain't jackrollin'."

"You mean Dropkick ain't a jackroller but you are."

The boy's blond lashes shuttered his eyes.

"All right, get ahead with your lyin' a little faster."

Kozak's head came down almost neckless onto his shoulders, and his face was molded like a flatiron, the temples narrow and the jaws rounded. Between the jaws and the open collar, against the graying hair of the chest, hung a tiny crucifix, slender and golden, a shade lighter than his tunic's golden buttons.

"I told him I wasn't gonna take his check, I just needed a little change, I'd pay it back someday. But maybe he didn't understand. He kept hollerin' how he lost his last check, please to let him keep this one. 'Why you drink'n it all up, then,' I put it to him, 'if you're that anxious to hold onto it? He gimme a foxy grin then 'n pulls out four of them little bottles from four different pockets, 'n each one was a different kind of liquor. I could have one, he tells me in Polish, which do I want, 'n I slapped all four out of his hands. All four. I don't like to see no full-grown man drinkin' that way. A Polak hillbilly he was, 'n certain'y no citizen.

"'Now let me have that change,' I asked him, 'n that wasn't so much t' ask. I don't go around just lookin' fer trouble, Captain. 'N my feet was slop-full of water 'n snow. I'm just a neighborhood fella. But he acted like I was gonna kill him 'r somethin'. I got one hand over his mouth 'n a half nelson behind him 'n talked polite-like in Polish in his ear, 'n he begun sweatin' 'n tryin' t' wrench away on me. 'Take it easy,' I asked him. 'Be reas'nable, we're both in this up to our necks now.' 'N he wasn't drunk no more then, 'n he was plenty t' hold onto. You wouldn't think a old boobatch like that'd have so much stren'th left in him, boozin' down Division night after night, year after year, like he didn't have no home to go to. He pulled my hand off his mouth 'n started hollerin', '*Mlody bandyla! Mlody bandyla!*' 'n I could feel him slippin'. He was just too strong fer a kid like me to hold———"

"Because you were reach'n for his wallet with the other hand?"

"Oh no. The reason I couldn't hold him was my right hand had the nelson 'n I'm not so strong there like in my left 'n even my left ain't what it was before I thrun it out pitchin' that double-header."

"So you kept the rod in your left hand?"

The boy hesitated. Then: "Yes sir." And felt a single drop of sweat slide down his side from under his armpit. Stop and slide again down to the belt.

"What did you get off him?"

"I tell you, I had my hands too full to get *anythin'*—that's just what I been tryin' to tell you. I didn't get so much as one of them little single-shots for all my trouble."

"How many slugs did you fire?"

"Just one, Captain. That was all there was in 'er. I didn't really fire, though. Just at his feet. T' scare him so's he wouldn't jump me. I fired in self-defense. I just wanted to get out of there." He glanced helplessly around at Comiskey and Adamovitch. "You do crazy things sometimes, fellas—well, that's all I was doin'.."

The boy caught his tongue and stood mute. In the silence of the query room there was only the scraping of the reporter's pencil and the unseen wrist watch. "I'll ask Chiney-Eye if it's legal, a reporter takin' down a confession, that's my out," the boy thought desperately, and added aloud, before he could stop himself: "'N beside I had to show him——"

"Show him what, son?"

Silence.

"Show him what, Left-hander?"

"That I wasn't just another greenhorn sprout like he thought."

"Did he say you were just a sprout?"

"No. But I c'd tell. Lots of people think I'm just a green kid. I show 'em. I guess I showed 'em now all right." He felt he should be apologizing for something and couldn't tell whether it was for strong-arming a man or for failing to strong-arm him.

"I'm just a neighborhood kid. I belonged to the Keep-Our-City-Clean Club at St. John Cant'us. I told him polite-like, like a Polish-American citizen, this was Chiney-Eye-a-Friend-of-Mine's hallway. 'No more after this one,' I told him. 'This is your last time gettin' rolled, old man. After this I'm pertectin' you, I'm seein' to it nobody touches you—but the people who live here don't like this sort of thing goin' on any more'n you 'r I do. There's gotta be a stop to it, old man—'n we all gotta live, don't we?' That's what I told him in Polish."

Kozak exchanged glances with the prim-faced reporter from the *Chicagoski*, who began cleaning his black tortoise-shell spectacles hurriedly yet delicately, with the fringed tip of his cravat. They depended from a black ribbon; he snapped them back onto his beak.

"You shot him in the groin, Lefty. He's dead."

The reporter leaned slightly forward, but perceived no special reaction and so relaxed. A pretty comfy old chair for a dirty old police station, he thought lifelessly. Kozak shaded his eyes with his gloved hand and looked down at his charge sheet. The night lamp on the desk was still lit, as though he had been working all night;

as the morning grew lighter behind him lines came out below his eyes, black as though packed with soot, and a curious droop came to the St Bernard mouth.

"You shot him through the groin—zip." Kozak's voice came, flat and unemphatic, reading from the charge sheet as though without understanding. "Five children. Stella, Mary, Grosha, Wanda, Vincent. Thirteen, ten, six, six, and one two months. Mother invalided since last birth, name of Rose. WPA fifty-five dollars. You told the truth about *that,* at least."

Lefty's voice came in a shout: "You know *what?* That bullet must of bounced, that's what!"

"Who was along?"

"I was singlin'. Lone-wolf stuff." His voice possessed the first faint touch of fear.

"You said, 'We seen the man.' Was he a big man? How big a man was he?"

"I'd judge two hunerd twenty pounds," Gomiskey offered, "at least. Fifty pounds heavier 'n this boy, just about. 'N half a head taller."

"Who's 'we,' Left-hander?"

"Captain, I said, 'We seen.' Lots of people, fellas, seen him is all I meant, cashin' his check by Stachula's when the place was crowded. Konstanty cashes checks if he knows you. Say, I even know the project that old man was on, far as that goes, because my old lady wanted we should give up the store so's I c'd get on it. But it was just me done it, Captain."

The raccoon coat readjusted his glasses. He would say something under a by-line like "This correspondent has never seen a colder gray than that in the eye of the wanton killer who arrogantly styles himself *the lone wolf of Potomac Street.*" He shifted uncomfortably, wanting to get farther from the wall radiator but disliking to rise and push the heavy chair.

"Where was that bald-headed pal of yours all this time?"

"Don't know the fella, Captain. Nobody got hair any more around the neighborhood, it seems. The whole damn Triangle went 'n got army haircuts by Stachula's."

"Just you 'n Benkowski, I mean. Don't be afraid, son—we're not tryin' to ring in anythin' you done afore this. Just this one you were out cowboyin' with Benkowski on; were you help'n him 'r was he help'n you? Did you 'r him have the rod?"

Lefty heard a Ford V-8 pull into the rear of the station, and a moment later the splash of the gas as the officers refueled. Behind him he could hear Milano's heavy breathing. He looked down at his shoes, carefully buttoned all the way up and tied with a double bowknot. He'd have to have new laces mighty soon or else start tying them with a single bow.

"That Benkowski's sort of a toothless monkey used to go on at the City Garden at around a hundred an' eighteen pounds, ain't he?"

"Don't know the fella well enough t' say."

"Just from seein' him fight once 'r twice is all. 'N he wore a mouthpiece, I couldn't tell about his teeth. Seems to me he came in about one thirty-three, if he's the same fella you're thinkin' of, Captain."

"I guess you fought at the City Garden once 'r twice yourself, ain't you?"

"Oh, once 'r twice."

"How'd you make out, Left'?"

"Won 'em both on K.O.s. Stopped both fights in the first. One was against that boogie from the Savoy. If he woulda got up I woulda killed him fer life. Fer Christ I would. I didn't know I could hit like I can."

"With Benkowski in your corner both times?"

"Oh no, sir."

"That's a bloodsuck'n lie. I seen him in your corner with my own eyes the time you won off Cooney from the C.Y.O. He's your manager, jackroller."

"I didn't say he wasn't."

"You said he wasn't secondin' you."

"He don't."

"Who does?"

"The Finger."

"You told me the Finger was your hex-man. Make up your mind."

"He does both, Captain. He handles the bucket 'n sponge 'n in between he fingers the guy I'm fightin', 'n if it's close he fingers the ref 'n judges. Finger, he never losed a fight. He waited for the boogie outside the dressing room 'n pointed him clear to the ring. He win that one for me awright." The boy spun the frayed greenish cap in his hand in a concentric circle about his index finger, remembering a time when the cap was new and had earlaps. The bright checks were all faded now, to the color of worn pavement, and the earlaps were tatters.

"What possessed your mob to get their heads shaved, Lefty?"

"I strong-armed him myself, I'm rugged as a bull." The boy began to swell his chest imperceptibly; when his lungs were quite full he shut his eyes, like swimming under water at the Oak Street beach, and let his breath out slowly, ounce by ounce.

"I didn't ask you that. I asked you what happened to your hair."

Lefty's capricious mind returned abruptly to the word "possessed" that Kozak had employed. That had a randy ring, sort of: "What possessed you boys?"

"I forgot what you just asked me."

"I asked you why you didn't realize it'd be easier for us to catch up with your mob when all of you had your heads shaved."

"I guess we figured there'd be so many guys with heads shaved it'd be harder to catch a finger than if we all had hair. But that was some accident all the same. A fella was gonna lend Ma a barber chair 'n go fifty-fifty with her shavin' all the Polaks on P'tom'c Street right back of the store, for relief tickets. So she started on me, just to show the fellas, but the hair made her sicker 'n ever 'n back of the store's the only place she got to lie down 'n I hadda finish the job myself.

"The fellas begun giv'n me a Christ-awful razzin' then, ever' day. God oh God, wherever I went around the Triangle, all the neighborhood fellas 'n little niducks 'n old-time hoods by the Broken Knuckle, whenever they seen me they was pointin' 'n laughin' 'n sayin', 'Hi, Baldy Bicek!' So I went home 'n got the clippers 'n the first guy I seen was Bibleback Watrobinski, you wouldn't know him. I jumps him 'n pushes the clip right through the middle of his hair—he ain't had a haircut since the alderman got indicted you— 'n then he took one look at what I done in the drugstore window 'n we both bust out laughin' 'n laughin', 'n fin'lly Bible says I better finish what I started. So he set down on the curb 'n I finished him. When I got all I could off that way I took him back to the store 'n heated water 'n shaved him close 'n Ma couldn't see the point at all.

"Me 'n Bible prowled around a couple days 'n here come Catfoot Nowogrodski from Fry Street you, out of Stachula's with a spanty-new sideburner haircut 'n a green tie. I grabbed his arms 'n let Bible run it through the middle just like I done him. Then it was Catfoot's turn, 'n we caught Chester Chekhovka fer *him,* 'n fer Chester we got Cowboy Okulanis from by the Nort'western Viaduct you, 'n fer him we got Mustang, 'n fer Mustang we got John from the Joint, 'n fer John we got Snake Baranowski, 'n we kep' right on goin' that way till we was doin' guys we never seen before even, Wallios 'n Greeks 'n a Flip from Clark Street he musta been, walkin' with a white girl we done it to. 'N fin'lly all the sprouts in the Triangle start comin' around with their heads shaved, they want to join up with the Baldheads A.C, they called it. They thought it was a club you.

"It got so a kid with his head shaved could beat up on a bigger kid because the big one'd be a-scared to fight back hard, he thought the Baldheads'd get him. So that's why we changed our name then, that's why we're not the Warriors any more, we're the Baldhead True American Social 'n Athletic Club.

"I played first for the Warriors when I wasn't on the mound," he added cautiously, "'n I'm enterin' the Gold'n Gloves next year 'less I go to collitch instead. I went to St. John Cant'us all the way through. Eight' grade, that is. If I keep on gainin' weight I'll be a hunerd ninety-eight this time next year 'n be five-foot-ten—I'm a fair-size light-heavy right this minute. That's what in England they call a cruiser weight you."

He shuffled a step and made as though to unbutton his shirt to show his proportions. But Adamovitch put one hand on his shoulders and slapped the boy's hand down. He didn't like this kid. This was a low-class Polak. He himself was a high-class Polak because his name was Adamovitch and not Adamowski. This sort of kid kept spoiling things for the high-class Polaks by always showing off instead of just being good citizens like the Irish. That was why the Irish ran the City Hall and Police Department and the Board of Education and the Post Office while the Polaks stayed on relief and got drunk and never got anywhere and had everybody down on them. All they could do like the Irish, old Adamovitch reflected bitterly, was to fight under Irish names to get their ears knocked off at the City Garden.

"That's why I want to get out of this jam," this one was saying beside him. "So's it don't ruin my career in the rope' arena. I'm goin' straight. This has sure been one good lesson fer me. Now I'll go to a big-ten collitch 'n make good you."

Now, if the college-coat asked him, "What big-ten college?" he'd answer something screwy like "The Boozological Stoodent-Collitch." That ought to set Kozak back awhile, they might even send him to a bug doc. He'd have to be careful— not *too* screwy. Just screwy enough to get by without involving Benkowski.

He scuffed his shoes and there was no sound in the close little room save his uneasy scuffling; square-toed boy's shoes, laced with a buttonhook. He wanted to look more closely at the reporter but every time he caught the glint of the fellow's glasses he felt awed and would have to drop his eyes; he'd never seen glasses on a string like that before and would have given a great deal to wear them a moment. He took to looking steadily out of the barred window behind Kozak's head, where the January sun was glowing sullenly, like a flame held steadily in a fog. Heard an empty truck clattering east on Chicago, sounding like either a '38 Chevvie or a '37 Ford dragging its safety chain against the car tracks; closed his eyes and imagined sparks flashing from the tracks as the iron struck, bounced, and struck again. The bullet had bounced too. Wow.

"What do you think we ought to do with a man like you, Bicek?"

The boy heard the change from the familiar "Lefty" to "Bicek" with a pang; and the dryness began in his throat again.

"One to fourteen is all I can catch fer manslaughter." He appraised Kozak as coolly as he could.

"You like farm work the next fourteen years? Is that okay with you?"

"I said that's all I could get, at the most. This is a first offense 'n self-defense too. I'll plead the unwritten law."

"Who give you *that* idea?"

"Thought of it myself. Just now. You ain't got a chance to send me over the road 'n you know it."

"We can send you to St. Charles, Bicek. 'N transfer you when you come of age. Unless we can make it first-degree murder."

The boy ignored the latter possibility.

"Why, a few years on a farm'd true me up fine. I planned t' cut out cigarettes 'n whisky anyhow before I turn pro—a farm'd be just the place to do that."

"By the time you're released you'll be thirty-two, Bicek—too late to turn pro then, ain't it?"

"I wouldn't wait that long. Hungry Piontek-from-by-the-Ware-house you, he lammed twice from that St. Charles farm. 'N Hungry don't have all his marbles even. He ain't even a citizen."

"Then let's talk about somethin' you couldn't lam out of so fast 'n easy. Like the chair. Did you know that Bogatski from Noble Street, Bicek? The boy that burned last summer, I mean."

A plain-clothes man stuck his head in the door and called confidently: 'That's the man, Captain. That's the man.'

Bicek forced himself to grin good-naturedly. He was getting pretty good, these last couple days, at grinning under pressure. When a fellow got sore he couldn't think straight, he reflected anxiously. And so he yawned in Kozak's face with deliberateness, stretching himself as effortlessly as a cat.

"Captain, I ain't been in serious trouble like this before..." he acknowledged, and paused dramatically. He'd let them have it straight from the shoulder now: "So I'm mighty glad to be so close to the alderman. Even if he is indicted."

There. Now they knew. He'd told them.

"You talkin' about my brother, Bicek?"

The boy nodded solemnly. Now they knew who they had hold of at last.

The reporter took the cigarette off his ear and hung it on his lower lip. And Adamovitch guffawed.

The boy jerked toward the officer: Adamovitch was laughing openly at him. Then they were all laughing openly at him. He heard their derision, and a red rain danced one moment before his eyes; when the red rain was past, Kozak was sitting back easily, regarding him with the expression of a man who has just been swung at and missed and plans to use the provocation without undue haste. The captain didn't look like the sort who'd swing back wildly or hurriedly. He didn't look like the sort who missed. His complacency for a moment was as unbearable to the boy as Adamovitch's guffaw had been. He heard his tongue going, trying to regain his lost composure by provoking them all.

"Hey, Stingywhiskers!" He turned on the reporter. "Get your Eversharp goin' there, write down I plugged the old rum-pot, write down Bicek carries a rod night 'n day 'n don't care where he points it. You, I go around slappin' the crap out of whoever I feel like——"

But they all remained mild, calm, and unmoved: for a moment he feared Adamovitch was going to pat him on the head and say something fatherly in Polish.

"Take it easy, lad," Adamovitch suggested. "You're in the query room. We're here to help you, boy. We want to see you through this thing so's you can get back to pugging. You just ain't letting us help you, son."

Kozak blew his nose as though that were an achievement in itself, and spoke with the false friendliness of the insurance man urging a fleeced customer toward the door.

"Want to tell us where you got that rod now, Lefty?"

"I don't want to tell you anything." His mind was setting hard now, against them all. Against them all in here and all like them outside. And the harder it set, the more things seemed to be all right with Kozak: he dropped his eyes to his charge sheet now and everything was all right with everybody. The reporter shoved his notebook into his pocket and buttoned the top button of his coat as though the questioning were over.

It was all too easy. They weren't going to ask him anything more, and he stood wanting them to. He stood wishing them to threaten, to shake their heads ominously, wheedle and cajole and promise him mercy if he'd just talk about the rod.

"I ain't mad, Captain. I don't blame you men either. It's your job, it's your bread 'n butter to talk tough to us neighborhood fellas—ever'body got to have a racket, 'n yours is talkin' tough." He directed this last at the captain, for Comiskey and Milano had left quietly. But Kozak was studying the charge sheet as though Bruno Lefty Bicek were no longer in the room. Nor anywhere at all.

"I'm still here," the boy said wryly, his lip twisting into a dry and bitter grin.

Kozak looked up, his big, wind-beaten, impassive face looking suddenly to the boy like an autographed pitcher's mitt he had once owned. His glance went past the boy and no light of recognition came into his eyes. Lefty Bicek felt a panic rising in him: a desperate fear that they weren't going to press him about the rod, about the old man, about his feelings. "Don't look at me like I ain't nowheres," he asked. And his voice was struck flat by fear.

Something else! The time he and Dropkick had broken into a slot machine! The time he and Casey had played the attention racket and made four dollars! Something! Anything else!

The reporter lit his cigarette.

"Your case is well disposed of," Kozak said, and his eyes dropped to the charge sheet forever.

"I'm born in this country, I'm educated here——"

But no one was listening to Bruno Lefty Bicek any more.

He watched the reporter leaving with regret—at least the guy could have offered him a drag—and stood waiting for someone to tell him to go somewhere now, shifting uneasily from one foot to the other. Then he started slowly, backward, toward the door: he'd make Kozak tell Adamovitch to grab him. Halfway to the door he turned his back on Kozak.

There was no voice behind him. Was this what "well disposed of" meant? He turned the knob and stepped confidently into the corridor; at the end of the corridor he saw the door that opened into the courtroom, and his heart began shaking his whole body with the impulse to make a run for it. He glanced back and Adamovitch was five yards behind, coming up catfooted like only an old man who has been a citizen-dress man can come up cat-footed, just far enough behind and just casual enough to make it appear unimportant whether the boy made a run for it or not.

The Lone Wolf of Potomac Street waited miserably, in the long unlovely corridor, for the sergeant to thrust two fingers through the back of his belt. Didn't they realize that he might have Dropkick and Catfoot and Benkowski with a sub-machine gun in a streamlined cream-colored roadster right down front, that he'd zigzag through the courtroom onto the courtroom fire escape and—swish—down off the courtroom roof three stories with the chopper still under his arm and through the car's roof and into the driver's seat? Like that George Raft did that time he was innocent at the Chopin, and cops like Adamovitch had better start ducking when Lefty Bicek began making a run for it. He felt the fingers thrust overfamiliarly between his shirt and his belt.

A cold draft came down the corridor when the door at the far end opened; with the opening of the door came the smell of disinfectant from the basement cells. Outside, far overhead, the bells of St. John Cantius were beginning. The boy felt the winding steel of the staircase to the basement beneath his feet and heard the whining screech of a Chicago Avenue streetcar as it paused on Ogden for the traffic lights and then screeched on again, as though a cat were caught beneath its back wheels. Would it be snowing out there still? he wondered, seeing the whitewashed basement walls.

"Feel all right, son?" Adamovitch asked in his most fatherly voice, closing the cell door while thinking to himself: "The kid don't *feel* guilty is the whole trouble. You got to make them *feel* guilty or they'll never go to church at all. A man who goes to church without feeling guilty for *something* is wasting his time, I say." Inside the cell he saw the boy pause and go down on his knees in the cell's gray light. The boy's head turned slowly toward him, a pious oval in the dimness. Old Adamovitch took off his hat.

"This place'll rot down 'n mold over before Lefty Bicek starts prayin', boobatch. Prays, squeals, 'r bawls. So run along 'n I'll see you in hell with yer back broke. I'm lookin' for my cap I dropped is all."

Adamovitch watched him crawling forward on all fours, groping for the pavement-colored cap; when he saw Bicek find it he put his own hat back on and left feeling vaguely dissatisfied.

He did not stay to see the boy, still on his knees, put his hands across his mouth and stare at the shadowed wall.

Shadows were there within shadows.

"I knew I'd never get to be twenty-one anyhow," Lefty told himself softly at last.

LUNCH HOUR: 1923 (1945)

James T. Farrell

My sweetie went away, but she didn't say where,
  she didn't say when, didn't say why,
    Or bid me good-by . . .

TOM FINNEGAN AND Al Bates rushed into the song shop on West Monroe Street. It was a large store. The floor was of tile, and silver dollars were embedded in it in a regular pattern. On the right of the entrance there were counters, and on the left-hand side, directly down from the doorway, there was a glass case. In the back, there were several glassed-in booths with victrolas and chairs inside them.

"Rain'n', all right," Al Bates said.

Tom nodded.

The female song plugger, a blonde with a slightly bloated face, sang to the crowd in a cracked falsetto.

I know she loves another, but she didn't say who, she didn't say which, she didn't say what her papa has got—that took my sweetie from me.

"Keen, all right," Al said.

Tom nodded. He looked around at the crowd of youths like himself, and at the girls, cake-eaters and flappers who came here almost every lunch hour to listen to the new songs. They were all about the store, singly and in groups, and some of them swayed and kept time to the songs by swinging their shoulders or tapping their feet in fast rhythms.

"I'd like to have all of them on the floor," Al said, pointing at one of the silver dollars.

I know that I'll die—Why don't she hurry back home . . .

Al mumbled the first lines of the song, *My Sweetie Went Away,*
and then he said:

"Keen."

Tom, medium-sized, blond, good-looking, gazed around to see
if he might spot anyone he knew, or else try and catch the eye of
a girl.

"Nice mamas come here," Al said.

"Uh yeah," Tom answered. "If I had dough, though, I wouldn't
be coming here."

"That's why I said I wish I had the dollars in the floor, and more
of the same," Al said.

The proprietor sang in a broken-voiced tenor.

> *You're the kind of a girl that men forget,*
> *Just a toy to enjoy for a while . . .*

"Sad song," Al said.

His eyes roved here and there and fastened on a thin blonde girl
in a raccoon coat. She stood by herself, her face betraying a sentimental absorption in the singer.

"You'd get a lot of mamas if you owned a shop like this," Al said.

> *And you'll soon realize you're not so wise . . .*

"I like the blonde mama in the raccoon coat," Al said.

"Me, too," Tom said.

> *When they play Here Comes the Bride, you'll stand outside*
> *Just a girl that men forget . . .*

Young people came and left continually, and there was a constant
noise of shuffling feet. Three cake-eaters lounged by the glass case
a foot or so away from Tom and Al and surveyed the scene with an
air of sophisticated superiority. Al and Tom looked at them. They
were better dressed than Al and Tom, taller, and better built.

"Those cakes are dressed collegiate. Keen. Hot," Al said.

"Uh huh!" Tom exclaimed.

They wore long, loose, beltless coats, and their black hats slanted
devilishly over their foreheads. Their shirts looked brand new, and
they had on colorful ties. They wore new tan brogans, also.

Tom looked outside. He was not so well dressed. It was raining
out, and his clothes were damp and had lost their press. He looked
back a bit enviously at the three cakes.

No, no, Nora, nobody but you, dear . . .

Many in the crowd shuffled their feet. Patent-leather toes wiggled, slid on the floor. Bell bottoms flounced, and hips and shoulders swung and swayed.

And would I trade you for kisses?

"Ah, boy. Keen," Al said.

A blond youth began moving and dancing back and forth in a radius of about two square feet, doing what seemed like a combination of the 'frisco and a cake walk, sticking out plump buttocks now and then, shaking and wiggling them, holding his chest erect, his face clouding with an expression of intense absorption in himself and his movements. He snapped his fingers, bent, squatted, rose, swayed, and toe-danced, while others clapped and cheered, and swayed their shoulders in rhythm with him.

"Ummm," exclaimed Al.

No, no, Nora, no, no!

Then there was a bustle of conversation in the store. A girl's giggle rose above the talk. Al and Tom looked outside. It was still raining.

A lad of about seventeen with full, round, red cheeks was flirting with the girl who had giggled. He wore a blue herringbone suit with wide bell bottoms, a belted overcoat, and a brown felt hat with its crown squared. The girl who had giggled was talking with him and smiled. He noticed Al and Tom.

"Hi!" he exclaimed.

"Hi!" exclaimed Al.

"Hi!" exclaimed Tom.

"Like it?" he asked.

"Nice," Al said.

"Yeh," Tom said.

"Nice mamas here," he said.

"I'll say they are!" Al said.

"The cat's," Tom said.

Tom watched a baby-doll blonde with avid eyes.

"Like her?" asked Al.

"Yeh."

"I'd like to make her on the back porch," Al said.

"I'd like to make her any place, back porch, front porch, park, on a raft, any place."

"Nice," Al said.

> *Yes, we have no bananas . . .*

Al looked around greedily. Tom rubbed his hand over the down on his upper lip. He gazed down at the frayed cuff on his bell-bottom trousers.

"I know that one," he said, nodding in the direction of a brunette.

"Yeh?"

"Her name is Peggy," Tom said.

"Nice. Peg of my heart," Al said.

"I'd let her be the peg of my heart," Tom said.

> *Monday night, I sat alone,*
> *Tuesday night, you didn't phone,*
> *Wednesday night, you didn't call . . .*

A tall lad, of athletic build, wearing a yellow slicker, was talking to the girl named Peggy. Tom frowned at him. The lad took off his gray fedora and held it ostentatiously, exposing his blond, wavy hair.

"Handsome brute," Al said.

"Vain. He gets his hair curled," Tom said.

"Maybe she's the peg of his heart?" Al said.

"He looks like a bum halfback to me," Tom said.

"More like a parlor athlete to me," Al said.

> *But you brought three girls for companee . . .*

Al swung into the rhythm of the song, snapped his fingers, twirled his feet, shook his shoulders. Others did likewise, and soon the store was full of shuffling, swaying, dancing, 'friscoing boys and girls, while an infant-faced songplugger sang with a whine in her voice, and the piano jingled. Eyes met eyes, and smiles were exchanged. With ecstasy and desire shining in his eyes and on his face, Al tapped on the floor and shook. Tom was caught up in the rhythm, and he imitated Al. As he did so, his eyes met those of the girl named Peggy. She smiled at him. He smiled back.

The music stopped. Peggy left the lad in the slicker and came toward Tom and Al. She smiled.

"You don't remember me," she said.

"Peggy, of course I do."

"Do you come here often?" she asked.

"No, I came today because of the rain."

"So did I."

"Yes, it's rainin' out," Al said.

"Say, I'm glad I saw you. How about a date on Saturday night? Saves me the nickel for phoning," Tom said.

"Use a slug," Al said.

"Why, all right, I'm not doing anything," she said.

"Suppose I call at eight-thirty?"

"Okay."

"Oh, excuse me. Peggy Shanahan, this is Al Bates. He works in my office."

"How do you do," she said.

"I do do do doodle de do," Al said.

"I have to dash, but I'll see you Saturday night then, Tom?"

"Be ready 'bout half-past eight," Al sing-songed.

"All right. We'll go dancing," Tom said.

"I'd like that. And I'm glad to have met you, Mr. Bates," she said, and she walked out.

They looked after her, eyeing her slender, young figure.

"Keen. A neat mama you copped off."

"Yes, she'll pass in a crowd."

"Ever take her out before?"

"No, but I've been thinking of trying to date her. She's a decent girl, but a good dancer, and she's good fun."

"Neat, neat and a hot mama."

"She's pretty," Tom said.

"Yeh. Keen."

"She graduated last June from Saint Paul's," Tom bragged.

"Does she rate?"

"Yes, she rates. That's why I dated her."

"So, she rates?" asked Al.

"Yes, she rates," Tom said proudly.

A look of weariness came over the round face of a girl near them, and she exclaimed to another girl:

"If I dance tonight, I'll die-e."

"But, dearie, Jack and Pete are going to be at the Gardens tonight, and you know they're simply divine."

"So are we," Al said.

"What?"

"Divine," Al said.

"What an old line you got," the first girl said.

"Da-dad-dad-da-da deedee da da . . ." Al sang at the girl.

"You sing worse," the second girl said.

"But you don't know what I can do," Al said.

"I don't want to," the first girl said, turning her back on him.

"Tramps," Al said.

"Polacks," Tom said.

"Smarties," Al said.

"You know, Peggy, now—she's different," Tom said.

They heard thunder outside, and some of the lads and girls hurried in, laughing.

"I'm going dancing tonight. Keen. Come along," Al said.

"No, I'll have to save my pennies for Saturday night's date. She rates. I'll have to take her in cabs," Tom said.

"Too bad. It's going to be keen," Al said.

"I'll get enough dancing Saturday night," Tom said boastfully.

"Is that all?"

"She's decent and rates."

"Can't she kiss?"

"Well, I'm not sayin'," Tom said.

"Let's go in and play some records," Al suggested.

They went into an empty booth. Al put a hot jazz piece on the victrola. Tom sat on the couch. His face was thoughtful.

"Thinking of Peggy?" asked Al.

"I'm not sayin'," Tom said.

"She looks worth thinkin' about," Al said.

The music was very fast, and they tapped their feet on the floor.

"Makes you wish you had a piece on the back porch," Al said.

"Or any place," Tom said.

"Hot," Al exclaimed enthusiastically, as a cornet wah-wahed.

Al got up and danced, shaking his abdomen and making eyes at the glass.

"Daddadada," he sing-songed.

He paused, looked at Tom, and said:

"Whoops, Finnegan, where's your pep?"

"I'll save it for Peggy."

"I think you're gone on her already," Al said.

"She rates," Tom said.

Al danced, shook his buttocks, and mumbled to the wild, burning jazz.

"Ummmmmm," he exclaimed as the cornet again wah-wahed.

He stuck his tongue out, slobbered it across his lower lip, and made slobbering noises with his tongue by forcing saliva against the membranes of his mouth. Tom swayed his shoulders and tapped his feet to the music.

The record ended.

"Say, we got to dash or we'll be late," Al said.

"Yeh," Tom said.

They left the booth. The store was still crowded.

My wonderful one . . .

"She's singing about your Peggy," Al said.

"I wish she was mine," Tom said, moodily.

"Maybe she will be. Don't give up the ship," Al said.

"I wish it was Saturday night," Tom said.

"We'll have to run," Al said.

"The damned rain, too," Tom said.

They lit out east on Monroe Street, running in and out among people with umbrellas.

Winded, they entered the building where they worked.

"Well, you achieved something on your lunch hour," Al said.

My wonderful one, whenever I'm dreaming love's love-light,
I'm dreaming of you.

"Yes, you're singing about her already," Al said.

"You'd sing, too, if you had a date with her. She rates," Tom said.

They entered the elevator and were whisked up to their office.

THE MAN WHO WENT TO CHICAGO (1961)

Richard Wright

WHEN I ROSE in the morning the temperature had dropped below zero. The house was as cold to me as the Southern streets had been in winter. I dressed, doubling my clothing. I ate in a restaurant, caught a streetcar, and rode south, rode until I could see no more black faces on the sidewalks. I had now crossed the boundary line of the Black Belt and had entered the territory where jobs were perhaps to be had from white folks. I walked the streets and looked into shop windows until I saw a sign in a delicatessen: PORTER WANTED.

I went in and a stout white woman came to me.

"Vat do you vant?" she asked.

The voice jarred me. She's Jewish, I thought, remembering with shame the obscenities I used to shout at Jewish storekeepers in Arkansas.

"I thought maybe you needed a porter," I said.

"Meester 'Offman, he eesn't here yet," she said. "Vill you vait?"

"Yes, ma'am."

"Seet down."

"No, ma'am, I'll wait outside."

"But eet's cold out zhere," she said.

"That's all right," I said.

She shrugged. I went to the sidewalk. I waited for half an hour in the bitter cold, regretting that I had not remained in the warm store, but unable to go back inside. A bald, stoutish white man went into the store and pulled off his coat. Yes, he was the boss man . . .

"Zo you vant a job?" he asked.

176

"Yes, sir," I answered, guessing at the meaning of his words.

"Vhere you vork before?"

"In Memphis, Tennessee."

"My brudder-in-law vorked in Tennessee vonce," he said.

I was hired. The work was easy, but I found to my dismay that I could not understand a third of what was said to me. My slow Southern ears were baffled by their clouded, thick accents. One morning Mrs. Hoffman asked me to go to a neighboring store—it was owned by a cousin of hers—and get a can of chicken à la king. I had never heard the phrase before and I asked her to repeat it.

"Don't you know nosing?" she demanded of me.

"If you would write it down for me, I'd know what to get," I ventured timidly.

"I can't vite!" she shouted in a sudden fury. "Vat kinda boy iss you?"

I memorized the separate sounds that she had uttered and went to the neighboring store.

"Mrs. Hoffman wants a can Cheek Keeng Awr Lar Keeng," I said slowly, hoping he would not think I was being offensive.

"All vite," he said, after staring at me a moment.

He put a can into a paper bag and gave it to me; outside in the street I opened the bag and read the label: Chicken à la King. I cursed, disgusted with myself. I knew those words. It had been her thick accent that had thrown me off. Yet I was not angry with her for speaking broken English; my English, too, was broken. But why could she not have taken more patience? Only one answer came to my mind. I was black and she did not care. Or so I thought . . . I was persisting in reading my present environment in the light of my old one. I reasoned thus: though English was my native tongue and America my native land, she, an alien, could operate a store and earn a living in a neighborhood where I could not even live. I reasoned further that she was aware of this and was trying to protect her position against me.

It was not until I had left the delicatessen job that I saw how grossly I had misread the motives and attitudes of Mr. Hoffman and his wife. I had not yet learned anything that would have helped me to thread my way through these perplexing racial relations. Accepting my environment at its face value, trapped by my own emotions, I kept asking myself what had black people done to bring this crazy world upon them?

The fact of the separation of white and black was clear to me; it was its effect upon the personalities of people that stumped and dismayed me. I did not feel that I was a threat to anybody; yet, as soon as I had grown old enough to think, I had learned that my entire personality, my aspirations, had long ago been discounted; that, in a measure, the very meaning of the words I spoke could not be fully understood.

And when I contemplated the area of No Man's Land into which the Negro mind in America had been shunted I wondered if there had ever been in all human history a more corroding and devastating attack upon the personalities of men than the idea of racial discrimination. In order to escape the racial attack that went to the roots of my life, I would have gladly accepted any way of life but the one in which I found myself. I would have agreed to live under a system of feudal oppression, not because I preferred feudalism but because I felt that feudalism made use of a limited part of a man, defined man, his rank, his function in society. I would have consented to live under the most rigid type of dictatorship, for I felt that dictatorships, too, defined the use of men, however degrading that use might be.

While working as a porter in Memphis I had often stood aghast as a friend of mine had offered himself to be kicked by the white men; but now, while working in Chicago, I was learning that perhaps even a kick was better than uncertainty ... I had elected, in my fevered search for honorable adjustment to the American scene, not to submit and in doing so I had embraced the daily horror of anxiety, of tension, of eternal disquiet. I could now sympathize with—though I could never bring myself to approve—those tortured blacks who had given up and had gone to their white tormentors and had said: "Kick me, if that's all there is for me; kick me and let me feel at home, let me have peace!"

Color-hate defined the place of black life as below that of white life; and the black man, responding to the same dreams as the white man, strove to bury within his heart his awareness of this difference because it made him lonely and afraid. Hated by whites and being an organic part of the culture that hated him, the black man grew in turn to hate in himself that which others hated in him. But pride would make him hate his self-hate, for he would not want whites to know that he was so thoroughly conquered by them that his total life was conditioned by their attitude; but in the act of hiding his self-hate, he could not help but hate those who evoked his self-hate in him. So each part of his day would be consumed in a war with himself, a good part of his energy would be spent in keeping control of his unruly emotions, emotions which he had not wished to have, but could not help having. Held at bay by the hate of others, preoccupied with his own feelings, he was continuously at war with reality. He became inefficient, less able to see and judge the objective world. And when he reached that state, the white people looked at him and laughed and said:

"Look, didn't I tell you niggers were that way?"

To solve this tangle of balked emotion, I loaded the empty part of the ship of my personality with fantasies of ambition to keep it from toppling over into the sea of senselessness. Like any other American, I dreamed of going into business and making money; I dreamed of working for a firm that would allow me to advance until I reached an important position; I even dreamed of organizing secret groups of blacks to fight all whites . . . And if the blacks would not agree to organize, then they would have to be fought. I would end up again with self-hate, but it was now a self-hate that was projected outward upon other blacks. Yet I knew—with that part of my mind that the whites had given me—that none of my dreams were possible. Then I would hate myself for allowing my mind to dwell upon the unattainable. Thus the circle would complete itself.

Slowly I began to forge in the depths of my mind a mechanism that repressed all the dreams and desires that the Chicago streets, the newspapers, the movies were evoking in me. I was going through a second childhood; a new sense of the limit of the possible was being born in me. What could I dream of that had the barest possibility of coming true? I could think of nothing. And, slowly, it was upon exactly that nothingness that my mind began to dwell, that constant sense of wanting without having, of being hated without reason. A dim notion of what life meant to a Negro in America was coming to consciousness in me, not in terms of external events, lynchings, Jim Crowism, and the endless brutalities, but in terms of crossed-up feeling, of emotional tension. I sensed that Negro life was a sprawling land of unconscious suffering, and there were but few Negroes who knew the meaning of their lives, who could tell their story.

Word reached me that an examination for postal clerk was impending and at once I filed an application and waited. As the date for the examination drew near, I was faced with another problem. How could I get a free day without losing my job? In the South it would have been an unwise policy for a Negro to have gone to his white boss and asked for time to take an examination for another job. It would have implied that the Negro did not like to work for the white boss, that he felt he was not receiving just consideration and, inasmuch as most jobs that Negroes held in the South involved a personal, paternalistic relationship, he would have been risking an argument that might have led to violence.

I now began to speculate about what kind of man Mr. Hoffman was, and I found that I did not know him; that is, I did not know his basic attitude toward Negroes. If I asked him, would he be sympathetic enough to allow me time off with pay? I needed the money. Perhaps he would say: "Go home and stay home if you don't like this job!" I was not sure of him. I decided, therefore, that I had better not risk it. I would forfeit the money and stay away without telling him.

The examination was scheduled to take place on a Monday; I had been working steadily and I would be too tired to do my best if I took the examination without benefit of rest. I decided to stay away from the shop Saturday, Sunday, and Monday. But what could I tell Mr. Hoffman? Yes, I would tell him that I had been ill. No, that was too thin. I would tell him that my mother had died in Memphis and that I had gone down to bury her. That lie might work.

I took the examination and when I came to the store on Tuesday, Mr. Hoffman was astonished, of course.

"I didn't sink you vould ever come back," he said.

"I'm awfully sorry, Mr. Hoffman."

"Vat happened?"

"My mother died in Memphis and I had to go down and bury her," I lied.

He looked at me, then shook his head.

"Rich, you lie," he said.

"I'm not lying," I lied stoutly.

"You vanted to do somesink, zo you zayed ervay," he said, shrugging.

"No, sir. I'm telling you the truth," I piled another lie upon the first one.

"No. You lie. You disappoint me," he said.

"Well, all I can do is tell you the truth," I lied indignantly.

"Vy didn't you use the phone?"

"I didn't think of it," I told a fresh lie.

"Rich, if your mudder die, you vould tell me," he said.

"I didn't have time. Had to catch the train," I lied yet again.

"Vhere did you get the money?"

"My aunt gave it to me," I said, disgusted that I had to lie and lie again.

"I don't vant a boy vat tells lies," he said.

"I don't lie," I lied passionately to protect my lies.

Mrs. Hoffman joined in and both of them hammered at me.

"Ve know. You come from ze Zouth. You feel you can't tell us ze truth. But ve don't bother you. Ve don't feel like people in ze Zouth. Ve treat you nice, don't ve?" they asked.

"Yes, ma'am," I mumbled.

"Zen vy lie?"

"I'm not lying," I lied with all my strength.

I became angry because I knew that they knew that I was lying. I had lied to protect myself, and then I had to lie to protect my lie. I had met so many white faces that would have violently disapproved of my taking the examination that I could not have risked telling Mr. Hoffman the truth. But how could I tell him that I had lied because I was so unsure of myself? Lying was bad, but revealing my own sense of insecurity would have been worse. It would have been shameful, and I did not like to feel ashamed.

Their attitudes had proved utterly amazing. They were taking time out from their duties in the store to talk to me, and I had never encountered anything like that from whites before. A Southern white man would have said: "Get to hell out of here!" or "All right, nigger. Get to work." But no white people had ever stood their ground and probed at me, questioned me at such length. It dawned upon me that they were trying to treat me as an equal, which made it even more impossible for me ever to tell them that I had lied, why I had lied. I felt that if I confessed I would be giving them a moral advantage over me that would have been unbearable.

"All vight, zay and vork," Mr. Hoffman said. "I know you're lying, but I don't care, Rich."

I wanted to quit. He had insulted me. But I liked him in spite of myself. Yes, I had done wrong; but how on earth could I have known the kind of people I was working for? Perhaps Mr. Hoffman would have gladly consented for me to take the examination; but my hopes had been far weaker than my powerful fears.

Working with them from day to day and knowing that they knew I had lied from fear crushed me. I knew that they pitied me and pitied the fear in me. I resolved to quit and risk hunger rather than stay with them. I left the job that following Saturday, not telling them that I would not be back, not possessing the heart to say good-by. I just wanted to go quickly and have them forget that I had ever worked for them.

After an idle week, I got a job as a dishwasher in a North Side café that had just opened My boss, a white woman, directed me in unpacking barrels of dishes, setting up new tables, painting, and so on. I had charge of serving breakfast; in the late afternoon I carted trays of food to patrons in the hotel who did not want to come down to eat. My wages were fifteen dollars a week; the hours were long, but I ate my meals on the job.

The cook was an elderly Finnish woman with a sharp, bony face. There were several white waitresses. I was the only Negro in the café. The waitresses were a hard, brisk lot, and I was keenly aware of how their attitudes contrasted with those of Southern white girls. They had not been taught to keep a gulf between me and themselves; they were relatively free of the heritage of racial hate.

One morning as I was making coffee, Cora came forward with a tray loaded with food and squeezed against me to draw a cup of coffee.

"Pardon me, Richard," she said.

"Oh, that's all right," I said in an even tone.

But I was aware that she was a white girl and that her body was pressed closely against mine, an incident that had never happened to me before in my life, an incident charged with the memory of dread. But she was not conscious of my blackness or of what her actions would have meant in the South. And had I not been born in the South, her trivial act would have been as unnoticed by me as it was by her. As she stood close to me, I could not help thinking that if a Southern white girl had wanted to draw a cup of coffee, she would have commanded me to step aside so that she might not come in contact with me. The work of the hot and busy kitchen would have had to cease for the moment so that I could have taken my tainted body far enough away to allow the Southern white girl a chance to get a cup of coffee. There lay a deep, emotional safety in knowing that the white girl who was now leaning carelessly against me was not thinking of me, had no deep, vague, irrational fright that made her feel that I was a creature to be avoided at all costs.

One summer morning a white girl came late to work and rushed into the pantry where I was busy. She went into the women's room and changed her clothes; I heard the door open and a second later I was surprised to hear her voice:

"Richard, quick! Tie my apron!"

She was standing with her back to me and the strings of her apron dangled loose. There was a moment of indecision on my part, then I took the two loose strings and carried them around her body and brought them again to her back and tied them in a clumsy knot.

"Thanks a million," she said, grasping my hand for a split second, and was gone.

I continued my work, filled with all the possible meanings that that tiny, simple, human event could have meant to any Negro in the South where I had spent most of my hungry days.

I did not feel any admiration or any hate for the girls. My attitude was one of abiding and friendly wonder. For the most part I was silent with them, though I knew that I had a firmer grasp of life than most of them. As I worked I listened to their talk and perceived its puzzled, wandering, superficial fumbling with the problems and facts of life. There were many things they wondered about that I could have explained to them, but I never dared.

During my lunch hour, which I spent on a bench in a near-by park, the waitresses would come and sit beside me, talking at random, laughing, joking, smoking cigarettes. I learned about their tawdry dreams, their simple hopes, their home lives, their fear of feeling anything deeply, their sex problems, their husbands. They were an eager, restless, talkative, ignorant bunch, but casually kind and impersonal for all that. They knew nothing of hate and fear, and strove instinctively to avoid all passion.

I often wondered what they were trying to get out of life, but I never stumbled upon a clue, and I doubt if they themselves had any notion. They lived on the surface of their days; their smiles were surface smiles, and their tears were surface tears. Negroes lived a truer and deeper life than they, but I wished that Negroes, too, could live as thoughtlessly, serenely, as they. The girls never talked of their feelings; none of them possessed the insight or the emotional equipment to understand themselves or others. How far apart in culture we stood! All my life I had done nothing but feel and cultivate my feelings; all their lives they had done nothing but strive for petty goals, the trivial material prizes of American life. We shared a common tongue, but my language was a different language from theirs.

It was in the psychological distance that separated the races that the deepest meaning of the problem of the Negro lay for me. For these poor, ignorant white girls to have understood my life would have meant nothing short of a vast revolution in theirs. And I was convinced that what they needed to make them complete and grown-up in their living was the inclusion in their personalities of a knowledge of lives such as I lived and suffered containedly.

As I, in memory, think back now upon those girls and their lives I feel that for white America to understand the significance of the problem of the Negro will take a bigger and tougher America than any we have yet known. I feel that America's past is too shallow, her national character too superficially optimistic, her very morality too suffused with color hate for her to accomplish so vast and complex a task. Culturally the Negro represents a paradox: Though he is an organic part of the nation, he is excluded by the entire tide and direction of American culture. Frankly, it is felt to be right to exclude him, and it is felt to be wrong to admit him freely. Therefore if, within the confines of its present culture, the nation ever seeks to purge itself of its color hate, it will find itself at war with itself, convulsed by a spasm of emotional and moral confusion. If the nation ever finds itself examining its real relation to the Negro, it will find itself doing infinitely more than that; for the anti-Negro attitude of whites represents but a tiny part—though a symbolically significant one—of the moral attitude of the nation. Our too-young and too-new America, lusty because it is lonely, aggressive because it is afraid, insists upon seeing the world in terms of good and bad, the holy and the evil, the high and the low, the white and the black; our America is frightened by fact, by history, by processes, by necessity. It hugs the easy way of damning those whom it cannot understand, of excluding those who look different; and it salves its conscience with a self-draped cloak of righteousness. Am I damning my native land? No; for I, too, share these faults of character! And I really do not think that America, adolescent and cocksure, a stranger to suffering and travail, an enemy of passion and sacrifice, is ready to probe into its most fundamental beliefs.

I knew that not race alone, not color alone, but the daily values that gave meaning to life stood between me and those white girls with whom I worked. Their constant outward-looking, their mania for radios, cars, and a thousand other trinkets, made them dream and fix their eyes upon the trash of life, made it impossible for them to learn a language that could have taught them to speak of what was in theirs or others' hearts. The words of their souls were the syllables of popular songs.

The essence of the irony of the plight of the Negro in America, to me, is that he is doomed to live in isolation, while those who condemn him seek the basest goals of any people on the face of the earth. Perhaps it would be possible for the Negro to become reconciled to his plight if he could be made to believe that his sufferings were for some remote, high, sacrificial end; but sharing the culture that condemns him, and seeing that a lust for trash is what blinds the nation to his claims, is what sets storms to rolling in his soul.

Though I had fled the pressure of the South, my outward conduct had not changed. I had been schooled to present an unalteringly smiling face and I continued to do so despite the fact that my environment allowed more open expression. I hid my feelings and avoided all relationships with whites that might cause me to reveal them.

Tillie, the Finnish cook, was a tall, ageless, red-faced, raw-boned woman with long snow-white hair, which she balled in a knot at the nape of her neck. She cooked expertly and was superbly efficient. One morning as I passed the sizzling stove, I thought I heard Tillie cough and spit, but I saw nothing; her face, obscured by steam, was bent over a big pot. My senses told me that Tillie had coughed and spat into that pot, but my heart told me that no human being could possibly be so filthy. I decided to watch her. An hour or so later I heard Tillie clear her throat with a grunt, saw her cough and spit into the boiling soup. I held my breath; I did not want to believe what I had seen.

Should I tell the boss lady? Would she believe me? I watched Tillie for another day to make sure that she was spitting into the food. She was; there was no doubt of it. But who would believe me if I told them what was happening? I was the only black person in the café. Perhaps they would think that I hated the cook. I stopped eating my meals there and bided my time.

The business of the café was growing rapidly and a Negro girl was hired to make salads. I went to her at once.

"Look, can I trust you?" I asked.

"What are you talking about?" she asked.

"I want you to say nothing, but watch that cook."

"For what?"

"Now, don't get scared. Just watch the cook."

She looked at me as though she thought I was crazy; and, frankly, I felt that perhaps I ought not to say anything to anybody.

"What do you mean?" she demanded.

"All right," I said. "I'll tell you. That cook spits in the food."

"What are you saying?" she asked aloud.

"Keep quiet," I said.

"Spitting?" she asked me in a whisper. "Why would she do that?"

"I don't know. But watch her."

She walked away from me with a funny look in her eyes. But half an hour later she came rushing to me, looking ill, sinking into a chair.

"Oh, God, I feel awful!"

"Did you see it?"

"She *is* spitting in the food!"

"What ought we do?" I asked.

"Tell the lady," she said.

"She wouldn't believe me," I said.

She widened her eyes as she understood. We were black and the cook was white.

"But I can't work here if she's going to do that," she said.

"Then you tell her," I said.

"She wouldn't believe me either," she said.

She rose and ran to the women's room. When she returned she stared at me. We were two Negroes and we were silently asking ourselves if the white boss lady would believe us if we told her that her expert white cook was spitting in the food all day long as it cooked on the stove.

"I don't know," she wailed, in a whisper, and walked away.

I thought of telling the waitresses about the cook, but I could not get up enough nerve. Many of the girls were friendly with Tillie. Yet I could not let the cook spit in the food all day. That was wrong by any human standard of conduct. I washed dishes, thinking, wondering; I served breakfast, thinking, wondering; I served meals in the apartments of patrons upstairs, thinking, wondering. Each time I picked up a tray of food I felt like retching. Finally the Negro salad girl came to me and handed me her purse and hat.

"I'm going to tell her and quit, goddamn," she said.

"I'll quit too, if she doesn't fire her," I said.

"Oh, she won't believe me," she wailed, in agony.

"You tell her. You're a woman. She might believe you."

Her eyes welled with tears and she sat for a long time; then she rose and went abruptly into the dining room. I went to the door and peered. Yes, she was at the desk, talking to the boss lady. She returned to the kitchen and went into the pantry; I followed her.

"Did you tell her?" I asked.

"Yes."

"What did she say?"

"She said I was crazy."

"Oh, God!" I said.

"She just looked at me with those gray eyes of hers," the girl said. "Why would Tillie do that?"

"I don't know," I said.

The boss lady came to the door and called the girl; both of them went into the dining room. Tillie came over to me; a hard cold look was in her eyes.

"What's happening here?" she asked.

"I don't know," I said, wanting to slap her across the mouth.

She muttered something and went back to the stove, coughed, and spat into a bubbling pot. I left the kitchen and went into the back areaway to breathe. The boss lady came out.

"Richard," she said.

Her face was pale. I was smoking a cigarette and I did not look at her.

"Is this true?"

"Yes, ma'am."

"It couldn't be. Do you know what you're saying?"

"Just watch her," I said.

"I don't know," she moaned.

She looked crushed. She went back into the dining room, but I saw her watching the cook through the doors. I watched both of them, the boss lady and the cook, praying that the cook would spit again. She did. The boss lady came into the kitchen and stared at Tillie, but she did not utter a word. She burst into tears and ran back into the dining room.

"What's happening here?" Tillie demanded.

No one answered. The boss lady came out and tossed Tillie her hat, coat, and money.

"Now, get out of here, you dirty dog!" she said.

Tillie stared, then slowly picked up her hat, coat, and the money; she stood a moment, wiped sweat from her forehead with her hand, then spat—this time on the floor. She left.

Nobody was ever able to fathom why Tillie liked to spit into the food.

Brooding over Tillie, I recalled the time when the boss man in Mississippi had come to me and had tossed my wages to me and said:

"Get out, nigger! I don't like your looks."

And I wondered if a Negro who did not smile and grin was as morally loathsome to whites as a cook who spat into the food.

The following summer I was called for temporary duty in the post office, and the work lasted into the winter. Aunt Cleo succumbed to a severe cardiac condition and, hard on the heels of her illness, my brother developed stomach ulcers. To rush my worries to a climax, my mother also became ill. I felt that I was maintaining a private hospital. Finally, the post-office work ceased altogether and I haunted the city for jobs. But when I went into the streets in the morning I saw sights that killed my hope for the rest of the day. Unemployed men loitered in doorways with blank looks in their eyes, sat dejectedly on front steps in shabby clothing, congregated in sullen groups on street corners, and filled all the empty benches in the parks of Chicago's South Side.

Luck of a sort came when a distant cousin of mine, who was a superintendent for a Negro burial society, offered me a position on his staff as an agent. The thought of selling insurance policies to ignorant Negroes disgusted me.

"Well, if you don't sell them, somebody else will," my cousin told me. "You've got to eat, haven't you?"

During that year I worked for several burial and insurance societies that operated among Negroes, and I received a new kind of education. I found that the burial societies, with some exceptions, were mostly "rackets." Some of them conducted their business legitimately, but there were many that exploited the ignorance of their black customers.

I was paid under a system that netted me fifteen dollars for every dollar's worth of new premiums that I placed upon the company's books, and for every dollar's worth of old premiums that lapsed I was penalized fifteen dollars. In addition, I was paid a commission of ten per cent on total premiums collected, but during the Depression it was extremely difficult to persuade a black family to buy a policy carrying even a dime premium. I considered myself lucky if, after subtracting lapses from new business, there remained fifteen dollars that I could call my own.

This "gambling" method of remuneration was practiced by some of the burial companies because of the tremendous "turnover" in policyholders, and the companies had to have a constant stream of new business to keep afloat. Whenever a black family moved or suffered a slight reverse in fortune, it usually let its policy lapse and later bought another policy from some other company.

Each day now I saw how the Negro in Chicago lived, for I visited hundreds of dingy flats filled with rickety furniture and ill-clad children. Most of the policyholders were illiterate and did not know that their policies carried clauses severely restricting their benefit payments, and, as an insurance agent, it was not my duty to tell them.

After tramping the streets and pounding on doors to collect premiums, I was dry, strained, too tired to read or write. I hungered for relief and, as a salesman of insurance to many young black girls, I found it. There were many comely black housewives who, trying desperately to keep up their insurance payments, were willing to make bargains to escape paying a ten-cent premium. I had a long, tortured affair with one girl by paying her ten-cent premium each week. She was an illiterate black child with a baby whose father she did not know. During the entire period of my relationship with her, she had but one demand to make of me: she wanted me to take her to a circus. Just what significance circuses had for her, I was never able to learn.

After I had been with her one morning—in exchange for the dime premium—I sat on the sofa in the front room and began to read a book I had with me. She came over shyly.

"Lemme see that," she said.

"What?" I asked.

"That book," she said.

I gave her the book; she looked at it intently. I saw that she was holding it upside down.

"What's in here you keep reading?" she asked.

"Can't you really read?" I asked.

"Naw," she giggled. "You know I can't read."

"You can read *some,*" I said.

"Naw," she said.

I stared at her and wondered just what a life like hers meant in the scheme of things, and I came to the conclusion that it meant absolutely nothing. And neither did my life mean anything.

"How come you looking at me that way for?"

"Nothing."

"You don't talk much."

"There isn't much to say."

"I wished Jim was here," she sighed.

"Who's Jim?" I asked, jealous. I knew that she had other men, but I resented her mentioning them in my presence.

"Just a friend," she said.

I hated her then, then hated myself for coming to her.

"Do you like Jim better than you like me?" I asked.

"Naw. Jim just likes to talk."

"Then why do you be with me, if you like Jim better?" I asked, trying to make an issue and feeling a wave of disgust because I wanted to.

"You all right," she said, giggling. "I like you."

"I could kill you," I said.

"What?" she exclaimed.

"Nothing," I said, ashamed.

"Kill me, you said? You crazy, man," she said.

"Maybe I am," I muttered, angry that I was sitting beside a human being to whom I could not talk, angry with myself for coming to her, hating my wild and restless loneliness.

"You oughta go home and sleep," she said. "You tired."

"What do you ever think about?" I demanded harshly.

"Lotta things."

"What, for example?"

"You," she said, smiling.

"You know I mean just one dime to you each week," I said.

"Naw, I thinka lotta you."

"Then what do you think?"

"'Bout how you talk when you talk. I wished I could talk like you," she said seriously.

"Why?" I taunted her.

"When you gonna take me to a circus?" she demanded suddenly.

"You ought to be in a circus," I said.

"I'd like it," she said, her eyes shining.

I wanted to laugh, but her words sounded so sincere that I could not.

"There's no circus in town," I said.

"I bet there is and you won't tell me 'cause you don't wanna take me," she said, pouting.

"But there's no circus in town, I tell you!"

"When will one come?"

"I don't know."

"Can't you read it in the papers?" she asked.

"There's nothing in the papers about a circus."

"There is," she said. "If I could read, I'd find it."

I laughed, and she was hurt.

"There *is* a circus in town," she said stoutly.

"There's no circus in town," I said. "But if you want to learn to read, then I'll teach you."

She nestled at my side, giggling.

"See that word?" I said, pointing.

"Yeah."

That's an 'and,'" I said.

She doubled, giggling.

"What's the matter?" I asked.

She rolled on the floor, giggling.

"What's so funny?" I demanded.

"You," she giggled. "You so funny."

I rose.

"The hell with you," I said.

"Don't you go and cuss me now," she said. "I don't cuss you."

"I'm sorry," I said.

I got my hat and went to the door.

"I'll see you next week?" she asked.

"Maybe," I said.

When I was on the sidewalk, she called to me from a window.

"You promised to take me to a circus, remember?"

"Yes." I walked close to the window. "What is it you like about a circus?"

"The animals," she said simply.

I felt that there was a hidden meaning, perhaps, in what she had said, but I could not find it. She laughed and slammed the window shut.

Each time I left her I resolved not to visit her again. I could not talk to her; I merely listened to her passionate desire to see a circus. She was not calculating; if she liked a man, she just liked him. Sex relations were the only relations she had ever had; no others were possible with her, so limited was her intelligence.

Most of the other agents also had their bought girls and they were extremely anxious to keep other agents from tampering with them. One day a new section of the South Side was given to me as a part of my collection area, and the agent from whom the territory had been taken suddenly became very friendly with me.

"Say, Wright," he asked, "did you collect from Ewing on Champlain Avenue yet?"

"Yes," I answered, after consulting my book.

"How did you like her?" he asked, staring at me.

"She's a good-looking number," I said.

"You had anything to do with her yet?" he asked.

"No, but I'd like to," I said laughing.

"Look," he said. "I'm a friend of yours."

"Since when?" I countered.

"No, I'm really a friend," he said.

"What's on your mind?"

"Listen, that gal's sick," he said seriously.

"What do you mean?"

"She's got the clap," he said. "Keep away from her. She'll lay with anybody."

"Gee, I'm glad you told me," I said.

"You had your eye on her, didn't you?" he asked.

"Yes, I did," I said.

"Leave her alone," he said. "She'll get you down."

That night I told my cousin what the agent had said about Miss Ewing. My cousin laughed.

"That gal's all right," he said. "That agent's been fooling around with her. He told you she had a disease so that you'd be scared to bother her. He was protecting her from you."

That was the way the black women were regarded by the black agents. Some of the agents were vicious; if they had claims to pay to a sick black woman and if the woman was able to have sex relations with them, they would insist upon it, using the claims money as a bribe. If the woman refused, they would report to the office that the woman was a malingerer. The average black woman would submit because she needed the money badly.

As an insurance agent, it was necessary for me to take part in one swindle. It appears that the burial society had originally issued a policy that was—from their point of view—too liberal in its provisions, and the officials decided to exchange the policies then in the hands of their clients for other policies carrying stricter clauses. Of course, this had to be done in a manner that would not allow the policyholder to know that his policy was being switched—that he was being swindled. I did not like it, but there was only one thing I could do to keep from being a party to it: I could quit and starve. But I did not feel that being honest was worth the price of starvation.

The swindle worked in this way. In my visits to the homes of the policyholders to collect premiums, I was accompanied by the superintendent who claimed to the policyholder that he was making a routine inspection. The policyholder, usually an illiterate black woman, would dig up her policy from the bottom of a trunk or chest and hand it to the superintendent. Meanwhile I would be marking the woman's premium book, an act which would distract her from what the superintendent was doing. The superintendent would exchange the old policy for a new one which was identical in color, serial number, and beneficiary, but which carried smaller payments. It was dirty work and I wondered how I could stop it. And when I could think of no safe way I would curse myself and the victims and forget about it. (The black owners of the burial societies were leaders in the Negro communities and were respected by whites.)

When I reached the relief station, I felt that I was making a public confession of my hunger. I sat waiting for hours, resentful of the mass of hungry people about me. My turn finally came and I was questioned by a middle-class Negro woman who asked me for a short history of my life. As I waited, I became aware of something happening in the room. The black men and women were mumbling quietly among themselves; they had not known one another before they had come here, but now their timidity and shame were wearing off and they were exchanging experiences. Before this they had lived as individuals, each somewhat afraid of the other, each seeking his own pleasure, each stanch in that degree of Americanism that had been allowed him. But now life had tossed them together, and they were learning to know the sentiments of their neighbors for the first time; their talking was enabling them to sense the collectivity of their lives, and some of their fear was passing.

Did the relief officials realize what was happening? No. If they had, they would have stopped it. But they saw their "clients" through the eyes of their profession, saw only what their "science" allowed them to see. As I listened to the talk, I could see black minds shedding many illusions. These people now knew that the past had betrayed them, had cast them out; but they did not know what the future would be like, did not know what they wanted. Yes, some of the things that the Communists said were true; they maintained that there came times in history when a ruling class could no longer rule. And now I sat looking at the beginnings of anarchy. To permit the birth of this new consciousness in these people was proof that those who ruled did not quite know what they were doing, assuming that they were trying to save themselves and their class. Had they understood what was happening, they would never have allowed millions of perplexed and defeated people to sit together for long hours and talk, for out of their talk was rising a new realization of life. And once this new conception of themselves had formed, no power on earth could alter it.

I left the relief station with the promise that food would be sent to me, but I also left with a knowledge that the relief officials had not wanted to give to me. I had felt the possibility of creating a new understanding of life in the minds of people rejected by the society in which they lived, people to whom the Chicago *Tribune* referred contemptuously as the "idle" ones, as though these people had deliberately sought their present state of helplessness.

Who would give these people a meaningful way of life? Communist theory defined these people as the molders of the future of mankind, but the Communist speeches I had heard in the park had mocked that definition. These people, of course, were not ready for a revolution; they had not abandoned their past lives by choice, but because they simply could not live the old way any longer. Now, what new faith would they embrace? The day I begged bread from the city officials was the day that showed me I was not alone in my loneliness; society had cast millions of others with me. But how could I be with them? How many understood what was happening? My mind swam with questions that I could not answer.

I was slowly beginning to comprehend the meaning of my environment; a sense of direction was beginning to emerge from the conditions of my life. I began to feel something more powerful than I could express. My speech and manner changed. My cynicism slid from me. I grew open and questioning. I wanted to know.

If I were a member of the class that rules, I would post men in all the neighborhoods of the nation, not to spy upon or club rebellious workers, not to break strikes or disrupt unions, but to ferret out those who no longer respond to the system under which they live. I would make it known that the real danger does not stem from those who seek to grab their share of wealth through force, or from those who try to defend their property through violence, for both of these groups, by their affirmative acts, support the values of the system under which they live. The millions that I would fear are those who do not dream of the prizes that the nation holds forth, for it is in them, though they may not know it, that a revolution has taken place and is biding its time to translate itself into a new and strange way of life.

I feel that the Negroes' relation to America is symbolically peculiar, and from the Negroes' ultimate reactions to their trapped state a lesson can be learned about America's future. Negroes are told in a language they cannot possibly misunderstand that their native land is not their own; and when, acting upon impulses which they share with whites, they try to assert a claim to their birthright, whites retaliate with terror, never pausing to consider the consequences should the Negroes give up completely. The whites never dream that they would face a situation far more terrifying if they were confronted by Negroes who made no claims at all than by those who are buoyed up by social aggressiveness. My knowledge of how

Negroes react to their plight makes me declare that no man can possibly be individually guilty of treason, that an insurgent act is but a man's desperate answer to those who twist his environment so that he cannot fully share the spirit of his native land. Treason is a crime of the State.

Christmas came and I was once more called to the post office for temporary work. This time I met many young white men and we discussed world happenings, the vast armies of unemployed, the rising tide of radical action. I now detected a change in the attitudes of the whites I met; their privations were making them regard Negroes with new eyes, and, for the first time, I was invited to their homes.

When the work in the post office ended, I was assigned by the relief system as an orderly to a medical research institute in one of the largest and wealthiest hospitals in Chicago. I cleaned operating rooms, dog, rat, mice, cat, and rabbit pans, and fed guinea pigs. Four of us Negroes worked there and we occupied an underworld position, remembering that we must restrict ourselves—when not engaged upon some task—to the basement corridors, so that we would not mingle with white nurses, doctors, or visitors.

The sharp line of racial division drawn by the hospital authorities came to me the first morning when I walked along an underground corridor and saw two long lines of women coming toward me. A line of white girls marched past, clad in starched uniforms that gleamed white; their faces were alert, their step quick, their bodies lean and shapely, their shoulders erect, their faces lit with the light of purpose. And after them came a line of black girls, old, fat, dressed in ragged gingham, walking loosely, carrying tin cans of soap powder, rags, mops, brooms ... I wondered what law of the universe kept them from being mixed? The sun would not have stopped shining had there been a few black girls in the first line, and the earth would not have stopped whirling on its axis had there been a few white girls in the second line. But the two lines I saw graded social status in purely racial terms.

Of the three Negroes who worked with me, one was a boy about my own age, Bill, who was either sleepy or drunk most of the time. Bill straightened his hair and I suspected that he kept a bottle hidden somewhere in the piles of hay which we fed to the guinea pigs. He did not like me and I did not like him, though I tried harder than he to conceal my dislike. We had nothing in common except that we were both black and lost. While I contained my frustration, he drank to drown his. Often I tried to talk to him, tried in simple words to convey to him some of my ideas, and he would listen in sullen silence. Then one day he came to me with an angry look on his face.

"I got it," he said.

"You've got what?" I asked.

"This old race problem you keep talking about," he said.

"What about it?"

"Well, it's this way," he explained seriously. "Let the government give every man a gun and five bullets, then let us all start over again. Make it just like it was in the beginning. The ones who come out on top, white or black, let them rule."

His simplicity terrified me. I had never met a Negro who was so irredeemably brutalized. I stopped pumping my ideas into Bill's brain for fear that the fumes of alcohol might send him reeling toward some fantastic fate.

The two other Negroes were elderly and had been employed in the institute for fifteen years or more. One was Brand, a short, black, morose bachelor; the other was Cooke, a tall, yellow, spectacled fellow who spent his spare time keeping track of world events through the Chicago *Tribune*. Brand and Cooke hated each other for a reason that I was never able to determine, and they spent a good part of each day quarreling.

When I began working at the institute, I recalled my adolescent dream of wanting to be a medical research worker. Daily I saw young Jewish boys and girls receiving instruction in chemistry and medicine that the average black boy or girl could never receive. When I was alone, I wandered and poked my fingers into strange chemicals, watched intricate machines trace red and black lines on ruled paper. At times I paused and stared at the walls of the rooms, at the floors, at the wide desks at which the white doctors sat, and I realized—with a feeling that I could never quite get used to—that I was looking at the world of another race.

My interest in what was happening in the institute amused the three other Negroes with whom I worked. They had no curiosity about "white folks' things," while I wanted to know if the dogs being treated for diabetes were getting well; if the rats and mice in which cancer had been induced showed any signs of responding to treatment. I wanted to know the principle that lay behind the Aschheim-Zondek tests that were made with rabbits, the Wassermann tests that were made with guinea pigs. But when I asked a timid question I found that even Jewish doctors had learned to imitate the sadistic method of humbling a Negro that the others had cultivated.

"If you know too much, boy, your brains might explode," a doctor said one day.

Each Saturday morning I assisted a young Jewish doctor in slitting the vocal cords of a fresh batch of dogs from the city pound. The object was to devocalize the dogs so that their howls would not disturb the patients in the other parts of the hospital. I held each dog as the doctor injected Nembutal into its veins to make it unconscious; then I held the dog's jaws open as the doctor inserted the scalpel and severed the vocal cords. Later, when the dogs came to, they would lift their heads to the ceiling and gape in a soundless wail. The sight became lodged in my imagination as a symbol of silent suffering.

To me Nembutal was a powerful and mysterious liquid, but when I asked questions about its properties I could not obtain a single intelligent answer. The doctor simply ignored me with:

"Come on. Bring me the next dog. I haven't got all day."

One Saturday morning, after I had held the dogs for their vocal cords to be slit, the doctor left the Nembutal on a bench. I picked it up, uncorked it, and smelled it. It was odorless. Suddenly Brand ran to me with a stricken face.

"What're you doing?" he asked.

"I was smelling this stuff to see if it had any odor," I said.

"Did you really smell it?" he asked me.

"Yes."

"Oh, God!" he exclaimed.

"What's the matter?" I asked.

"You shouldn't've done that!" he shouted.

"Why?"

He grabbed my arm and jerked me across the room.

"Come on!" he yelled, snatching open the door.

"What's the matter?" I asked.

"I gotta get you to a doctor 'fore it's too late," he gasped.

Had my foolish curiosity made me inhale something dangerous?

"But—Is it poisonous?"

"Run, boy!" he said, pulling me. "You'll fall dead."

Filled with fear, with Brand pulling my arm, I rushed out of the room, raced across a rear areaway, into another room, then down a long corridor. I wanted to ask Brand what symptoms I must expect, but we were running too fast. Brand finally stopped, gasping for breath. My heart beat wildly and my blood pounded in my head. Brand then dropped to the concrete floor, stretched out on his back, and yelled with laughter, shaking all over. He beat his fists against the concrete; he moaned, giggled, he kicked.

I tried to master my outrage, wondering if some of the white doctors had told him to play the joke. He rose and wiped tears from his eyes, still laughing. I walked away from him. He knew that I was angry and he followed me.

"Don't get mad," he gasped through his laughter.

"Go to hell," I said.

"I couldn't help it," he giggled. "You looked at me like you'd believe anything I said. Man, you was scared."

He leaned against the wall, laughing again, stomping his feet. I was angry, for I felt that he would spread the story. I knew that Bill and Cooke never ventured beyond the safe bounds of Negro living, and they would never blunder into anything like this. And if they heard about this, they would laugh for months.

"Brand, if you mention this, I'll kill you," I swore.

"You ain't mad?" he asked, laughing, staring at me through tears.

Sniffing, Brand walked ahead of me. I followed him back into the room that housed the dogs. All day, while at some task, he would pause and giggle, then smother the giggling with his hand, looking at me out of the corner of his eyes, shaking his head. He laughed at me for a week. I kept my temper and let him amuse himself. I finally found out the properties of Nembutal by consulting medical books; but I never told Brand.

One summer morning, just as I began work, a young Jewish boy came to me with a stop watch in his hand.

"Dr.——— wants me to time you when you clean a room," he said. "We're trying to make the institute more efficient."

"I'm doing my work, and getting through on time," I said.

"This is the boss's order," he said.

"Why don't you work for a change?" I blurted, angry.

"Now, look," he said. "*This* is my work. Now *you* work."

I got a mop and pail, sprayed a room with disinfectant, and scrubbed at coagulated blood and hardened dog, rat, and rabbit feces. The normal temperature of a room was ninety, but, as the sun beat down upon the skylights, the temperature rose above a hundred. Stripped to my waist, I slung the mop, moving steadily like a machine, hearing the boy press the button on the stop watch as I finished cleaning a room.

"Well, how is it?" I asked.

"It took you seventeen minutes to clean that last room," he said. "That ought to be the time for each room."

"But that room was not very dirty," I said.

"You have seventeen rooms to clean," he went on as though I had not spoken. "Seventeen times seventeen make four hours and forty-nine minutes." He wrote upon a little pad. "After lunch, clean the five lights of stone stairs. I timed a boy who scrubbed one step and multiplied that time by the number of steps. You ought to be through by six."

"Suppose I want relief?" I asked.

"You'll manage," he said and left.

Never had I felt so much the slave as when I scoured those stone steps each afternoon. Working against time, I would wet five steps, sprinkle soap powder, and then a white doctor or a nurse would come along and, instead of avoiding the soapy steps, would walk on them and track the dirty water onto the steps that I had already cleaned. To obviate this, I cleaned but two steps at a time, a distance over which a ten-year-old child could step. But it did no good. The white people still plopped their feet down into the dirty water and muddied the other clean steps. If I ever really hotly hated unthinking whites, it was then. Not once during my entire stay at the institute did a single white person show enough courtesy to avoid a wet step. I would be on my knees, scrubbing, sweating, pouring out what limited energy my body could wring from my meager diet, and I would hear feet approaching. I would pause and curse with tense lips:

"These sonofabitches are going to dirty these steps again, god-damn their souls to hell!"

Sometimes a sadistically observant white man would notice that he had tracked dirty water up the steps, and he would look back down at me and smile and say:

"Boy, we sure keep you busy, don't we?"

And I would not be able to answer.

The feud that went on between Brand and Cooke continued. Although they were working daily in a building where scientific history was being made, the light of curiosity was never in their eyes. They were conditioned to their racial "place," had learned to see only a part of the whites and the white world; and the whites, too, had learned to see only a part of the lives of the blacks and their world.

Perhaps Brand and Cooke, lacking interests that could absorb them, fuming like children over trifles, simply invented their hate of each other in order to have something to feel deeply about. Or perhaps there was in them a vague tension stemming from their chronically frustrating way of life, a pain whose cause they did not know; and, like those devocalized dogs, they would whirl and snap at the air when their old pain struck them. Anyway, they argued about the weather, sports, sex, war, race, politics, and religion; neither of them knew much about the subjects they debated, but it seemed that the less they knew the better they could argue.

The tug of war between the two elderly men reached a climax one winter day at noon. It was incredibly cold and an icy gale swept up and down the Chicago streets with blizzard force. The door of the animal-filled room was locked, for we always insisted that we be allowed one hour in which to eat and rest. Bill and I were sitting on wooden boxes, eating our lunches out of paper bags. Brand was washing his hands at the sink. Cooke was sitting on a rickety stool, munching an apple and reading the Chicago *Tribune*.

Now and then a devocalized dog lifted his nose to the ceiling and howled soundlessly. The room was filled with many rows of high steel tiers. Perched upon each of these tiers were layers of steel cages containing the dogs, rats, mice, rabbits, and guinea pigs. Each cage was labeled in some indecipherable scientific jargon. Along the walls of the room were long charts with zigzagging red and black lines that traced the success or failure of some experiment. The lonely piping of guinea pigs floated unheeded about us. Hay rustled as a rabbit leaped restlessly about in its pen. A rat scampered around in its steel prison. Cooke tapped the newspaper for attention.

"It says here," Cooke mumbled through a mouthful of apple, "that this is the coldest day since 1888."

Bill and I sat unconcerned. Brand chuckled softly.

"What in hell you laughing about?" Cooke demanded of Brand.

"You can't believe what that damn *Tribune* says," Brand said.

"How come I can't?" Cooke demanded. "It's the world's greatest newspaper."

Brand did not reply; he shook his head pityingly and chuckled again.

"Stop that damn laughing at me!" Cooke said angrily.

"I laugh as much as I wanna," Brand said. "You don't know what you talking about. The *Herald-Examiner* says it's the coldest day since 1873."

"But the *Trib* oughta know," Cooke countered. "It's older'n that *Examiner*."

"That damn *Trib* don't know nothing!" Brand drowned out Cooke's voice.

"How in hell you know?" Cooke asked with rising anger.

The argument waxed until Cooke shouted that if Brand did not shut up he was going to "cut his black throat."

Brand whirled from the sink, his hands dripping soapy water, his eyes blazing.

"Take that back," Brand said.

"I take nothing back! What you wanna do about it?" Cooke taunted.

The two elderly Negroes glared at each other. I wondered if the quarrel was really serious, or if it would turn out harmlessly as so many others had done.

Suddenly Cooke dropped the Chicago *Tribune* and pulled a long knife from his pocket; his thumb pressed a button and a gleaming steel blade leaped out. Brand stepped back quickly and seized an ice pick that was stuck in a wooden board above the sink.

"Put that knife down," Brand said.

"Stay 'way from me, or I'll cut your throat," Cooke warned.

Brand lunged with the ice pick. Cooke dodged out of range. They circled each other like fighters in a prize ring. The cancerous and tubercular rats and mice leaped about in their cages. The guinea pigs whistled in fright. The diabetic dogs bared their teeth and barked soundlessly in our direction. The Aschheim-Zondek rabbits flopped their ears and tried to hide in the corners of their pens. Cooke now crouched and sprang forward with the knife. Bill and I jumped to our feet, speechless with surprise. Brand retreated. The eyes of both men were hard and unblinking; they were breathing deeply.

"Say, cut it out!" I called in alarm.

"Them damn fools is really fighting," Bill said in amazement.

Slashing at each other, Brand and Cooke surged up and down the aisles of steel tiers. Suddenly Brand uttered a bellow and charged into Cooke and swept him violently backward. Cooke grasped Brand's hand to keep the ice pick from sinking into his chest. Brand broke free and charged Cooke again, sweeping him into an animal-filled steel tier. The tier balanced itself on its edge for an indecisive moment, then toppled.

Like kingpins, one steel tier lammed into another, then they all crashed to the floor with a sound as of the roof falling. The whole aspect of the room altered quicker than the eye could follow. Brand and Cooke stood stock-still, their eyes fastened upon each other, their pointed weapons raised; but they were dimly aware of the havoc that churned about them.

The steel tiers lay jumbled; the doors of the cages swung open. Rats and mice and dogs and rabbits moved over the floor in wild panic. The Wassermann guinea pigs were squealing as though judgment day had come. Here and there an animal had been crushed beneath a cage.

All four of us looked at one another. We knew what this meant. We might lose our jobs. We were already regarded as black dunces; and if the doctors saw this mess they would take it as final proof. Bill rushed to the door to make sure that it was locked. I glanced at the clock and saw that it was 12:30. We had one half-hour of grace.

"Come on," Bill said uneasily. "We got to get this place cleaned."

Brand and Cooke stared at each other, both doubting.

"Give me your knife, Cooke," I said.

"Naw! Take Brand's ice pick *first*," Cooke said.

"The hell you say!" Brand said. "Take his knife *first!*"

A knock sounded at the door.

"Sssssh," Bill said.

We waited. We heard footsteps going away. We'll all lose our jobs, I thought.

Persuading the fighters to surrender their weapons was a difficult task, but at last it was done and we could begin to set things right. Slowly Brand stooped and tugged at one end of a steel tier. Cooke stooped to help him. Both men seemed to be acting in a dream. Soon, however, all four of us were working frantically, watching the clock.

As we labored we conspired to keep the fight a secret; we agreed to tell the doctors—if any should ask—that we had not been in the room during our lunch hour; we felt that that lie would explain why no one had unlocked the door when the knock had come.

We righted the tiers and replaced the cages; then we were faced with the impossible task of sorting the cancerous rats and mice, the diabetic dogs, the Aschheim-Zondek rabbits, and the Wassermann guinea pigs. Whether we kept our jobs or not depended upon how shrewdly we could cover up all evidence of the fight. It was pure guesswork, but we had to try to put the animals back into the correct cages. We knew that certain rats or mice went into certain cages, but we did not know *what* rat or mouse went into *what* cage. We did not know a tubercular mouse from a cancerous mouse— the white doctors had made sure that we would not know. They had never taken time to answer a single question; though we worked in the institute, we were as remote from the meaning of the experiments as if we lived in the moon. The doctors had laughed at what they felt was our childlike interest in the fate of the animals.

First we sorted the dogs; that was fairly easy, for we could remember the size and color of most of them. But the rats and mice and guinea pigs baffled us completely.

We put our heads together and pondered, down in the under-world of the great scientific institute. It was a strange scientific conference; the fate of the entire medical research institute rested in our ignorant, black hands.

We remembered the number of rats, mice, or guinea pigs—we had to handle them several times a day—that went into a given cage, and we supplied the number helter-skelter from those animals that we could catch running loose on the floor. We discovered that many rats, mice, and guinea pigs were missing—they had been killed in the scuffle. We solved that problem by taking healthy stock from other cages and putting them into cages with sick animals. We repeated this process until we were certain that, numerically at least, all the animals with which the doctors were experimenting were accounted for.

The rabbits came last. We broke the rabbits down into two general groups; those that had fur on their bellies and those that did not. We knew that all those rabbits that had shaven bellies—our scientific knowledge adequately covered this point because it was our job to shave the rabbits—were undergoing the Aschheim-Zondek tests. But in what pen did a given rabbit belong? We did not know. I solved the problem very simply. I counted the shaven rabbits; they numbered seventeen. I counted the pens labeled "Aschheim-Zondek," then proceeded to drop a shaven rabbit into each pen at random. And again we were numerically successful. At least white America had taught us how to count . . .

Lastly we carefully wrapped all the dead animals in newspapers and hid their bodies in a garbage can.

At a few minutes to one the room was in order; that is, the kind of order that we four Negroes could figure out. I unlocked the door and we sat waiting, whispering, vowing secrecy, wondering what the reaction of the doctors would be.

Finally a doctor came, gray-haired, white-coated, spectacled, efficient, serious, taciturn, bearing a tray upon which sat a bottle of mysterious fluid and a hypodermic needle.

"My rats, please."

Cooke shuffled forward to serve him. We held our breath. Cooke got the cage which he knew the doctor always called for at that hour and brought it forward. One by one, Cooke took out the rats and held them as the doctor solemnly injected the mysterious fluid under their skins.

"Thank you, Cooke," the doctor murmured.

"Not at all, sir," Cooke mumbled with a suppressed gasp.

When the doctor had gone we looked at one another, hardly daring to believe that our secret would be kept. We were so anxious that we did not know whether to curse or laugh. Another doctor came.

"Give me A-Z rabbit number 14."

"Yes, sir," I said.

I brought him the rabbit and he took it upstairs to the operating room. We waited for repercussions. None came.

All that afternoon the doctors came and went. I would run into the room—stealing a few seconds from my step-scrubbing—and ask what progress was being made and would learn that the doctors had detected nothing. At quitting time we felt triumphant.

"They won't ever know," Cooke boasted in a whisper.

I saw Brand stiffen. I knew that he was aching to dispute Cooke's optimism, but the memory of the fight he had just had was so fresh in his mind that he could not speak.

Another day went by and nothing happened. Then another day. The doctors examined the animals and wrote in their little black books, in their big black books, and continued to trace red and black lines upon the charts.

A week passed and we felt out of danger. Not one question had been asked.

Of course, we four black men were much too modest to make our contribution known, but we often wondered what went on in the laboratories after that secret disaster. Was some scientific hypothesis, well on its way to validation and ultimate public use, discarded because of unexpected findings on that cold winter day? Was some tested principle given a new and strange refinement because of fresh, remarkable evidence? Did some brooding research worker—those who held stop watches and slopped their feet carelessly in the water of the steps I tried so hard to keep clean—get a wild, if brief, glimpse of a new scientific truth? Well, we never heard ...

I brooded upon whether I should have gone to the director's office and told him what had happened, but each time I thought of it I remembered that the director had been the man who had ordered the boy to stand over me while I was working and time my movements with a stop watch. He did not regard me as a human being. I did not share his world. I earned thirteen dollars a week and I had to support four people with it, and should I risk that thirteen dollars by acting idealistically? Brand and Cooke would have hated me and would have eventually driven me from the job had I "told" on them. The hospital kept us four Negroes as though we were close kin to the animals we tended, huddled together down in the underworld corridors of the hospital, separated by a vast psychological distance from the significant processes of the rest of the hospital—just as America had kept us locked in the dark underworld of American life for three hundred years—and we had made our own code of ethics, values, loyalty.

LOOKING FOR
MR. GREEN (1968)

Saul Bellow

Whatsoever thy hand findeth to do,
do it with thy might....

HARD WORK? NO, it wasn't really so hard. He wasn't used to walking and stair-climbing, but the physical difficulty of his new job was not what George Grebe felt most. He was delivering relief checks in the Negro district, and although he was a native Chicagoan this was not a part of the city he knew much about—it needed a depression to introduce him to it. No, it wasn't literally hard work, not as reckoned in foot-pounds, but yet he was beginning to feel the strain of it, to grow aware of its peculiar difficulty. He could find the streets and numbers, but the clients were not where they were supposed to be, and he felt like a hunter inexperienced in the camouflage of his game. It was an unfavorable day, too—fall, and cold, dark weather, windy. But, anyway, instead of shells in his deep trench-coat pocket he had the cardboard of checks, punctured for the spindles of the file, the holes reminding him of the holes in player-piano paper. And he didn't look much like a hunter, either; his was a city figure entirely, belted up in this Irish conspirator's coat. He was slender without being tall, stiff in the back, his legs looking shabby in a pair of old tweed pants gone through and fringy at the cuffs. With this stiffness, he kept his head forward, so that his face was red from the sharpness of the weather; and it was an indoors sort of face with gray eyes that persisted in some kind of thought and yet seemed to avoid definiteness of conclusion. He wore sideburns that surprised you somewhat by the tough curl of the blond hair and the effect of assertion in their length. He was not so mild as he looked, nor so youthful; and nevertheless there was no effort on his part to seem what he was not. He was an educated man; he was a bachelor; he was in some ways simple; without lushing, he liked a drink; his luck had not been good. Nothing was deliberately hidden.

He felt that his luck was better than usual today. When he had reported for work that morning he had expected to be shut up in the relief office at a clerk's job, for he had been hired downtown as a clerk, and he was glad to have, instead, the freedom of the streets and welcomed, at least at first, the vigor of the cold and even the blowing of the hard wind. But on the other hand he was not getting on with the distribution of the checks. It was true that it was a city job; nobody expected you to push too hard at a city job. His supervisor, that young Mr. Raynor, had practically told him that. Still, he wanted to do well at it. For one thing, when he knew how quickly he could deliver a batch of checks, he would know also how much time he could expect to clip for himself. And then, too, the clients would be waiting for their money. That was not the most important consideration, though it certainly mattered to him. No, but he wanted to do well, simply for doing-well's sake, to acquit himself decently of a job because he so rarely had a job to do that required just this sort of energy. Of this peculiar energy he now had a superabundance; once it had started to flow, it flowed all too heavily. And, for the time being anyway, he was balked. He could not find Mr. Green.

So he stood in his big-skirted trench coat with a large envelope in his hand and papers showing from his pocket, wondering why people should be so hard to locate who were too feeble or sick to come to the station to collect their own checks. But Raynor had told him that tracking them down was not easy at first and had offered him some advice on how to proceed. "If you can see the postman, he's your first man to ask, and your best bet. If you can't connect with him, try the stores and tradespeople around. Then the janitor and the neighbors. But you'll find the closer you come to your man the less people will tell you. They don't want to tell you anything."

"Because I'm a stranger."

"Because you're white. We ought to have a Negro doing this, but we don't at the moment, and of course you've got to eat, too, and this is public employment. Jobs have to be made. Oh, that holds for me too. Mind you, I'm not letting myself out. I've got three years of seniority on you, that's all. And a law degree. Otherwise, you might be back of the desk and I might be going out into the field this cold day. The same dough pays us both and for the same, exact, identical reason. What's my law degree got to do with it? But you have to pass out these checks, Mr. Grebe, and it'll help if you're stubborn, so I hope you are."

"Yes, I'm fairly stubborn."

Raynor sketched hard with an eraser in the old dirt of his desk, left-handed, and said, "Sure, what else can you answer to such a question. Anyhow, the trouble you're going to have is that they don't like to give information about anybody. They think you're a plainclothes dick or an installment collector, or summons-server or something like that. Till you've been seen around the neighborhood for a few months and people know you're only from the relief."

It was dark, ground-freezing, pre-Thanksgiving weather; the wind played hob with the smoke, rushing it down, and Grebe missed his gloves, which he had left in Raynor's office. And no one would admit knowing Green. It was past three o'clock and the postman had made his last delivery The nearest grocer, himself a Negro, had never heard the name Tulliver Green, or said he hadn't. Grebe was inclined to think that it was true, that he had in the end convinced the man that he wanted only to deliver a check. But he wasn't sure. He needed experience in interpreting looks and signs and, even more, the will not to be put off or denied and even the force to bully if need be. If the grocer did know, he had got rid of him easily. But since most of his trade was with reliefers, why should he prevent the delivery of a check? Maybe Green, or Mrs. Green, if there was a Mrs. Green, patronized another grocer. And was there a Mrs. Green? It was one of Grebe's great handicaps that he hadn't looked at any of the case records. Raynor should have let him read files for a few hours. But he apparently saw no need for that, probably considering the job unimportant. Why prepare systematically to deliver a few checks?

But now it was time to look for the janitor. Grebe took in the building in the wind and gloom of the late November day—trampled, frost-hardened lots on one side; on the other, an automobile junk yard and then the infinite work of Elevated frames, weak-looking, gaping with rubbish fires; two sets of leaning brick porches three stories high and a flight of cement stairs to the cellar. Descending, he entered the underground passage, where he tried the doors until one opened and he found himself in the furnace room. There someone rose toward him and approached, scraping on the coal grit and bending under the canvas-jacketed pipes.

"Are you the janitor?"

"What do you want?"

"I'm looking for a man who's supposed to be living here. Green."

"What Green?"

"Oh, you maybe have more than one Green?" said Grebe with new, pleasant hope. "This is Tulliver Green."

"I don't think I c'n help you, mister. I don't know any."

"A crippled man."

The janitor stood bent before him. Could it be that he was crippled? Oh, God! what if he was. Grebes gray eyes sought with excited difficulty to see. But no, he was only very short and stooped. A head awakened from meditation, a strong-haired beard, low, wide shoulders. A staleness of sweat and coal rose from his black shirt and the burlap sack he wore as an apron.

"Crippled how?"

Grebe thought and then answered with the light voice of unmixed candor, "I don't know. I've never seen him." This was damaging, but his only other choice was to make a lying guess, and he was not up to it. "I'm delivering checks for the relief to shut-in cases. If he weren't crippled he'd come to collect himself. That's why I said crippled. Bedridden, chair-ridden—is there anybody like that?"

This sort of frankness was one of Grebe's oldest talents, going back to childhood. But it gained him nothing here.

"No suh. I've got four buildin's same as this that I take care of. I don' know all the tenants, leave alone the tenants' tenants. The rooms turn over so fast, people movin' in and out every day. I can't tell you."

The janitor opened his grimy lips, but Grebe did not hear him in the piping of the valves and the consuming pull of air to flame in the body of the furnace. He knew, however, what he had said.

"Well, all the same, thanks. Sorry I bothered you. I'll prowl around upstairs again and see if I can turn up someone who knows him."

Once more in the cold air and early darkness he made the short circle from the cellarway to the entrance crowded between the brickwork pillars and began to climb to the third floor. Pieces of plaster ground under his feet; strips of brass tape from which the carpeting had been torn away marked old boundaries at the sides. In the passage, the cold reached him worse than in the street; it touched him to the bone. The hall toilets ran like springs. He thought grimly as he heard the wind burning around the building with a sound like that of the furnace, that this was a great piece of constructed shelter. Then he struck a match in the gloom and searched for names and numbers among the writings and scribbles on the walls. He saw WHOODY-DOODY GO TO JESUS, and zigzags, caricatures, sexual scrawls, and curses. So the sealed rooms of pyramids were also decorated, and the caves of human dawn.

The information on his card was, TULLIVER GREEN—APT 3D. There were no names, however, and no numbers. His shoulders drawn up, tears of cold in his eyes, breathing vapor, he went the length of the corridor and told himself that if he had been lucky enough to have the temperament for it he would bang on one of the doors and bawl out "Tulliver Green!" until he got results. But it wasn't in him to make an uproar and he continued to burn matches, passing the light over the walls. At the rear, in a corner off the hall, he discovered a door he had not seen before and he thought it best to investigate. It sounded empty when he knocked, but a young Negress answered, hardly more than a girl. She opened only a bit, to guard the warmth of the room.

"Yes suh?"

"I'm from the district relief station on Prairie Avenue. I'm looking for a man named Tulliver Green to give him his check. Do you know him?"

No, she didn't; but he thought she had not understood anything of what he had said. She had a dream-bound, dream-blind face, very soft and black, shut off. She wore a man's jacket and pulled the ends together at her throat. Her hair was parted in three directions, at the sides and transversely, standing up at the front in a dull puff.

"Is there somebody around here who might know?"

"I jus' taken this room las' week."

He observed that she shivered, but even her shiver was somnambulistic and there was no sharp consciousness of cold in the big smooth eyes of her handsome face.

"All right, miss, thank you. Thanks," he said, and went to try another place.

Here he was admitted. He was grateful, for the room was warm. It was full of people, and they were silent as he entered—ten people, or a dozen, perhaps more, sitting on benches like a parliament. There was no light, properly speaking, but a tempered darkness that the window gave, and everyone seemed to him enormous, the men padded out in heavy work clothes and winter coats, and the women huge, too, in their sweaters, hats, and old furs. And, besides, bed and bedding, a black cooking range, a piano piled towering to the ceiling with papers, a dining-room table of the old style of prosperous Chicago. Among these people Grebe, with his cold-heightened fresh color and his smaller stature, entered like a schoolboy. Even though he was met with smiles and goodwill, he knew, before a single word was spoken, that all the currents ran against him and that he would make no headway. Nevertheless he began. "Does anybody here know how I can deliver a check to Mr. Tulliver Green?"

"Green?" It was the man that had let him in who answered. He was in short sleeves, in a checkered shirt, and had a queer, high head, profusely overgrown and long as a shako; the veins entered it strongly from his forehead. "I never heard mention of him. Is this where he live?"

"This is the address they gave me at the station. He's a sick man, and he'll need his check. Can't anybody tell me where to find him?"

He stood his ground and waited for a reply, his crimson wool scarf wound about his neck and drooping outside his trench coat, pockets weighted with the block of checks and official forms. They must have realized that he was not a college boy employed afternoons by a bill collector, trying foxily to pass for a relief clerk, recognized that he was an older man who knew himself what need was, who had had more than an average seasoning in hardship. It was evident enough if you looked at the marks under his eyes and at the sides of his mouth.

"Anybody know this sick man?"

"No suh." On all sides he saw heads shaken and smiles of denial. No one knew. And maybe it was true, he considered, standing silent in the earthen, musky human gloom of the place as the rumble continued. But he could never really be sure.

"What's the matter with this man?" said shako-head.

"I've never seen him. All I can tell you is that he can't come in person for his money. It's my first day in this district."

"Maybe they given you the wrong number?"

"I don't believe so. But where else can I ask about him?" He felt that this persistence amused them deeply, and in a way he shared their amusement that he should stand up so tenaciously to them. Though smaller, though slight, he was his own man, he retracted nothing about himself, and he looked back at them, gray-eyed, with amusement and also with a sort of courage. On the bench some man spoke in his throat, the words impossible to catch, and a woman answered with a wild, shrieking laugh, which was quickly cut off.

"Well, so nobody will tell me?"

"Ain't nobody who knows."

"At least, if he lives here, he pays rent to someone. Who manages the building?"

"Greatham Company. That's on Thirty-ninth Street."

Grebe wrote it in his pad. But, in the street again, a sheet of wind-driven paper clinging to his leg while he deliberated what direction to take next, it seemed a feeble lead to follow. Probably this Green didn't rent a flat, but a room. Sometimes there were as many as twenty people in an apartment; the real-estate agent would know only the lessee. And not even the agent could tell you who the renters were. In some places the beds were even used in shifts, watchmen or jitney drivers or short-order cooks in night joints turning out after a day's sleep and surrendering their beds to a sister, a nephew, or perhaps a stranger, just off the bus. There were large numbers of newcomers in this terrific, blight-bitten portion of the city between Cottage Grove and Ashland, wandering from house to house and room to room. When you saw them, how could you know them? They didn't carry bundles on their backs or look picturesque. You only saw a man, a Negro, walking in the street or riding in the car, like everyone else, with his thumb closed on a transfer. And therefore how were you supposed to tell? Grebe thought the Greatham agent would only laugh at his question.

But how much it would have simplified the job to be able to say that Green was old, or blind, or consumptive. An hour in the files, taking a few notes, and he needn't have been at such a disadvantage. When Raynor gave him the block of checks Grebe asked, "How much should I know about these people?" Then Raynor had looked as though Grebe were preparing to accuse him of trying to make the job more important than it was. Grebe smiled, because by then they were on fine terms, but nevertheless he had been getting ready to say something like that when the confusion began in the station over Staika and her children.

Grebe had waited a long time for this job. It came to him through the pull of an old schoolmate in the Corporation Counsel's office, never a close friend, but suddenly sympathetic and interested—pleased to show, moreover, how well he had done, how strongly he was coming on even in these miserable times. Well, he was coming through strongly, along with the Democratic administration itself. Grebe had gone to see him in City Hall, and they had had a counter lunch or beers at least once a month for a year, and finally it had been possible to swing the job. He didn't mind being assigned the lowest clerical grade, nor even being a messenger, though Raynor thought he did.

This Raynor was an original sort of guy and Grebe had taken to him immediately. As was proper on the first day, Grebe had come early, but he waited long, for Raynor was late. At last he darted into his cubicle of an office as though he had just jumped from one of those hurtling huge red Indian Avenue cars. His thin, rough face was wind-stung and he was grinning and saying something breathlessly to himself. In his hat, a small fedora, and his coat, the velvet collar a neat fit about his neck, and his silk muffler that set off the nervous twist of his chin, he swayed and turned himself in his swivel chair, feet leaving the ground, so that he pranced a little as he sat. Meanwhile he took Grebe's measure out of his eyes, eyes of an unusual vertical length and slightly sardonic. So the two men sat for a while, saying nothing, while the supervisor raised his hat from his miscombed hair and put it in his lap. His cold-darkened hands were not clean. A steel beam passed through the little makeshift room, from which machine belts once had hung. The building was an old factory.

"I'm younger than you; I hope you won't find it hard taking orders from me," said Raynor. "But I don't make them up, either. You're how old, about?"

"Thirty-five."

"And you thought you'd be inside doing paperwork. But it so happens I have to send you out."

"I don't mind."

"And it's mostly a Negro load we have in this district."

"So I thought it would be."

"Fine. You'll get along. *C'est un bon boulot.* Do you know French?"

"Some."

"I thought you'd be a university man."

"Have you been in France?" said Grebe.

"No, that's the French of the Berlitz School. I've been at it for more than a year, just as I'm sure people have been, all over the world, office boys in China and braves in Tanganyika. In fact, I damn well know it. Such is the attractive power of civilization. It's overrated, but what do you want? *Que voulez-vous?* I get *Le Rire* and all the spicy papers, just like in Tanganyika. It must be mystifying, out there. But my reason is that I'm aiming at the diplomatic service. I have a cousin who's a courier, and the way he describes it is awfully attractive. He rides in the *wagon-lits* and reads books. While we—What did you do before?"

"I sold."

"Where?"

"Canned meat at Stop and Shop. In the basement."

"And before that?"

"Window shades, at Goldblatt's."

"Steady work?"

"No, Thursdays and Saturdays. I also sold shoes."

"You've been a shoe-dog too. Well. And prior to that? Here it is in your folder." He opened the record. "Saint Olaf's College, instructor in classical languages. Fellow, University of Chicago, 1926–27. I've had Latin, too. Let's trade quotations—'*Dum spiro spero.*'"

"'*De dextram misero.*'"

"'*Alea jacta est.*'"

"'*Excelsior.*'"

Raynor shouted with laughter, and other workers came to look at him over the partition. Grebe also laughed, feeling pleased and easy. The luxury of fun on a nervous morning.

When they were done and no one was watching or listening, Raynor said rather seriously, "What made you study Latin in the first place? Was it for the priesthood?"

"No."

"Just for the hell of it? For the culture? Oh, the things people think they can pull!" He made his cry hilarious and tragic. "I ran my pants off so I could study for the bar, and I've passed the bar, so I get twelve dollars a week more than you as a bonus for having seen life straight and whole. I'll tell you, as a man of culture, that even though nothing looks to be real, and everything stands for something else, and that thing for another thing, and that thing for a still further one—there ain't any comparison between twenty-five and thirty-seven dollars a week, regardless of the last reality. Don't you think that was clear to your Greeks? They were a thoughtful people, but they didn't part with their slaves."

This was a great deal more than Grebe had looked for in his first interview with his supervisor. He was too shy to show all the astonishment he felt. He laughed a little, aroused, and brushed at the sunbeam that covered his head with its dust. "Do you think my mistake was so terrible?"

"Damn right it was terrible, and you know it now that you've had the whip of hard times laid on your back. You should have been preparing yourself for trouble. Your people must have been well-off to send you to the university. Stop me, if I'm stepping on your toes. Did your mother pamper you? Did your father give in to you? Were you brought up tenderly, with permission to go and find out what were the last things that everything else stands for while everybody else labored in the fallen world of appearances?"

"Well, no, it wasn't exactly like that." Grebe smiled. *The fallen world of appearances!* no less. But now it was his turn to deliver a surprise. "We weren't rich. My father was the last genuine English butler in Chicago—"

"Are you kidding?"

"Why should I be?"

"In a livery?"

"In livery. Up on the Gold Coast."

"And he wanted you to be educated like a gentleman?"

"He did not. He sent me to the Armour Institute to study chemical engineering. But when he died I changed schools."

He stopped himself, and considered how quickly Raynor had reached him. In no time he had your valise on the table and all your stuff unpacked. And afterward, in the streets, he was still reviewing how far he might have gone, and how much he might have been led to tell if they had not been interrupted by Mrs. Staika's great noise.

But just then a young woman, one of Raynor's workers, ran into the cubicle exclaiming, "Haven't you heard all the fuss?"

"We haven't heard anything."

"It's Staika, giving out with all her might. The reporters are coming. She said she phoned the papers, and you know she did."

"But what is she up to?" said Raynor.

"She brought her wash and she's ironing it here, with our current, because the relief won't pay her electric bill. She has her ironing board set up by the admitting desk, and her kids are with her, all six. They never are in school more than once a week. She's always dragging them around with her because of her reputation."

"I don't want to miss any of this," said Raynor, jumping up. Grebe, as he followed with the secretary, said, "Who is this Staika?"

"They call her the 'Blood Mother of Federal Street.' She's a professional donor at the hospitals. I think they pay ten dollars a pint. Of course it's no joke, but she makes a very big thing out of it and she and the kids are in the papers all the time."

A small crowd, staff and clients divided by a plywood barrier, stood in the narrow space of the entrance, and Staika was shouting in a gruff, mannish voice, plunging the iron on the board and slamming it on the metal rest.

"My father and mother came in a steerage, and I was born in our house, Robey by Huron. I'm no dirty immigrant. I'm a U.S. citizen. My husband is a gassed veteran from France with lungs weaker'n paper, that hardly can he go to the toilet by himself. These six children of mine, I have to buy the shoes for their feet with my own blood. Even a lousy little white Communion necktie, that's a couple of drops of blood; a little piece of mosquito veil for my Vadja so she won't be ashamed in church for the other girls, they take my blood for it by Goldblatt. That's how I keep goin'. A fine thing if I had to depend on the relief. And there's plenty of people on the rolls—fakes! There's nothin' *they* can't get, that can go and wrap bacon at Swift and Armour anytime. They're lookin' for them by the Yards. They never have to be out of work. Only they rather lay in their lousy beds and eat the public's money." She was not afraid, in a predominantly Negro station, to shout this way about Negroes.

Grebe and Raynor worked themselves forward to get a closer view of the woman. She was flaming with anger and with pleasure at herself, broad and huge, a golden-headed woman who wore a cotton cap laced with pink ribbon. She was barelegged and had on black gym shoes, her Hoover apron was open and her great breasts, not much restrained by a man's undershirt, hampered her arms as she worked at the kid's dress on the ironing board. And the children, silent and white, with a kind of locked obstinacy, in sheepskins and lumber-jackets, stood behind her. She had captured the station, and the pleasure this gave her was enormous. Yet her grievances were true grievances. She was telling the truth. But she behaved like a liar. The look of her small eyes was hidden, and while she raged she also seemed to be spinning and planning.

"They send me out college caseworkers in silk pants to talk me out of what I got comin'. Are they better'n me? Who told them? Fire them. Let 'em go and get married, and then you won't have to cut electric from people's budget."

The chief supervisor, Mr. Ewing, couldn't silence her and he stood with folded arms at the head of his staff, bald—bald-headed, saying to his subordinates like the ex-school principal he was, "Pretty soon she'll be tired and go."

"No she won't," said Raynor to Grebe. "She'll get what she wants. She knows more about the relief even than Ewing. She's been on the rolls for years, and she always gets what she wants because she puts on a noisy show. Ewing knows it. He'll give in soon. He's only saving face. If he gets bad publicity, the commissioner'll have him on the carpet, downtown. She's got him submerged; she'll submerge everybody in time, and that includes nations and governments."

Grebe replied with his characteristic smile, disagreeing completely. Who would take Staika's orders, and what changes could her yelling ever bring about?

No, what Grebe saw in her, the power that made people listen, was that her cry expressed the war of flesh and blood, perhaps turned a little crazy and certainly ugly, on this place and this condition. And at first, when he went out, the spirit of Staika somehow presided over the whole district for him, and it took color from her; he saw her color, in the spotty curb fires, and the fires under the El, the straight alley of flamey gloom. Later, too, when he went into a tavern for a shot of rye, the sweat of beer, association with West Side Polish streets, made him think of her again.

He wiped the corners of his mouth with his muffler, his handkerchief being inconvenient to reach for, and went out again to get on with the delivery of his checks. The air bit cold and hard and a few flakes of snow formed near him. A train struck by and left a quiver in the frames and a bristling icy hiss over the rails.

Crossing the street, he descended a flight of board steps into a basement grocery, setting off a little bell. It was a dark, long store and it caught you with its stinks of smoked meat, soap, dried peaches, and fish. There was a fire wrinkling and flapping in the little stove, and the proprietor was waiting, an Italian with a long, hollow face and stubborn bristles. He kept his hands warm under his apron.

No, he didn't know Green. You knew people but not names. The same man might not have the same name twice. The police didn't know, either, and mostly didn't care. When somebody was shot or knifed they took the body away and didn't look for the murderer. In the first place, nobody would tell them anything. So they made up a name for the coroner and called it quits. And in the second place, they didn't give a goddamn anyhow. But they couldn't get to the bottom of a thing even if they wanted to. Nobody would get to know even a tenth of what went on among these people. They stabbed and stole, they did every crime and abomination you ever heard of, men and men, women and women, parents and children, worse than the animals. They carried on their own way, and the horrors passed off like a smoke. There was never anything like it in the history of the whole world.

It was a long speech, deepening with every word in its fantasy and passion and becoming increasingly senseless and terrible: a swarm amassed by suggestion and invention, a huge, hugging, despairing knot, a human wheel of heads, legs, bellies, arms, rolling through his shop.

Grebe felt that he must interrupt him. He said sharply, "What are you talking about! All I asked was whether you knew this man."

"That isn't even the half of it. I been here six years. You probably don't want to believe this. But suppose it's true?"

"All the same," said Grebe, "there must be a way to find a person."

The Italian's close-spaced eyes had been queerly concentrated, as were his muscles, while he leaned across the counter trying to convince Grebe. Now he gave up the effort and sat down on his stool. "Oh—I suppose. Once in a while. But I been telling you, even the cops don't get anywhere."

"They're always after somebody. It's not the same thing."

"Well, keep trying if you want. I can't help you."

But he didn't keep trying. He had no more time to spend on Green. He slipped Green's check to the back of the block. The next name on the list was FIELD, WINSTON.

He found the backyard bungalow without the least trouble; it shared a lot with another house, a few feet of yard between. Grebe knew these two-shack arrangements. They had been built in vast numbers in the days before the swamps were filled and the streets raised, and they were all the same—a boardwalk along the fence, well under street level, three or four ball-headed posts for clothes-lines, greening wood, dead shingles, and a long, long flight of stairs to the rear door.

A twelve-year-old boy let him into the kitchen, and there the old man was, sitting by the table in a wheelchair.

"Oh, it's d' Government man," he said to the boy when Grebe drew out his checks. "Go bring me my box of papers." He cleared a space on the table.

"Oh, you don't have to go to all that trouble," said Grebe. But Field laid out his papers: Social Security card, relief certification, letters from the state hospital in Manteno, and a naval discharge dated San Diego, 1920.

"That's plenty," Grebe said. "Just sign."

"You got to know who I am," the old man said. "You're from the Government. It's not your check, it's a Government check and you got no business to hand it over till everything is proved."

He loved the ceremony of it, and Grebe made no more objections. Field emptied his box and finished out the circle of cards and letters.

"There's everything I done and been. Just the death certificate and they can close book on me." He said this with a certain happy pride and magnificence. Still he did not sign; he merely held the little pen upright on the golden-green corduroy of his thigh. Grebe did not hurry him. He felt the old man's hunger for conversation.

"I got to get better coal," he said. "I send my little gran'son to the yard with my order and they fill his wagon with screening. The stove ain't made for it. It fall through the grate. The order says Franklin County egg-size coal."

"I'll report it and see what can be done."

"Nothing can be done, I expect. You know and I know. There ain't no little ways to make things better, and the only big thing is money. That's the only sunbeams, money. Nothing is black where it shines, and the only place you see black is where it ain't shining. What we colored have to have is our own rich. There ain't no other way."

Grebe sat, his reddened forehead bridged levelly by his close-cut hair and his cheeks lowered in the wings of his collar—the caked fire shone hard within the isinglass-and-iron frames but the room was not comfortable—sat and listened while the old man unfolded his scheme. This was to create one Negro millionaire a month by subscription. One clever, good-hearted young fellow elected every month would sign a contract to use the money to start a business employing Negroes. This would be advertised by chain letters and word of mouth, and every Negro wage earner would contribute a dollar a month. Within five years there would be sixty millionaires.

"That'll fetch respect," he said with a throat-stopped sound that came out like a foreign syllable. "You got to take and organize all the money that gets thrown away on the policy wheel and horse race. As long as they can take it away from you, they got no respect for you. Money, that's d' sun of humankind!" Field was a Negro of mixed blood, perhaps Cherokee, or Natchez; his skin was reddish. And he sounded, speaking about a golden sun in this dark room, and looked—shaggy and slab-headed—with the mingled blood of his face and broad lips, and with the little pen still upright in his hand, like one of the underground kings of mythology, old judge Minos himself.

And now he accepted the check and signed. Not to soil the slip, he held it down with his knuckles. The table budged and creaked, the center of the gloomy, heathen midden of the kitchen covered with bread, meat, and cans, and the scramble of papers.

"Don't you think my scheme'd work?"

"It's worth thinking about. Something ought to be done, I agree."

"It'll work if people will do it. That's all. That's the only thing, anytime. When they understand it in the same way, all of them."

"That's true," said Grebe, rising. His glance met the old man's.

"I know you got to go," he said. "Well, God bless you, boy, you ain't been sly with me. I can tell it in a minute."

He went back through the buried yard. Someone nursed a candle in a shed, where a man unloaded kindling wood from a sprawl-wheeled baby buggy and two voices carried on a high conversation. As he came up the sheltered passage he heard the hard boost of the wind in the branches and against the house fronts, and then, reaching the sidewalk, he saw the needle-eye red of cable

towers in the open icy height hundreds of feet above the river and
the factories—those keen points. From here, his view was
obstructed all the way to the South Branch and its timber banks,
and the cranes beside the water. Rebuilt after the Great Fire, this
part of the city was, not fifty years later, in ruins again, factories
boarded up, buildings deserted or fallen, gaps of prairie between.
But it wasn't desolation that this made you feel, but rather a falter-
ing of organization that set free a huge energy, an escaped, unat-
tached, unregulated power from the giant raw place. Not only must
people feel it but, it seemed to Grebe, they were compelled to
match it. In their very bodies. He no less than others, he realized.
Say that his parents had been servants in their time, whereas he was
supposed not to be one. He thought that they had never done any
service like this, which no one visible asked for, and probably flesh
and blood could not even perform. Nor could anyone show why
it should be performed; or see where the performance would lead.
That did not mean that he wanted to be released from it, he realized with a grimly pensive face. On the contrary. He had something to do. To be compelled to feel this energy and yet have no
task to do—that was horrible; that was suffering; he knew what that
was. It was now quitting time. Six o'clock. He could go home if
he liked, to his room, that is, to wash in hot water, to pour a drink,
lie down on his quilt, read the paper, eat some liver paste on crackers before going out to dinner. But to think of this actually made
him feel a little sick, as though he had swallowed hard air. He had
six checks left, and he was determined to deliver at least one of
these: Mr. Green's check.

So he started again. He had four or five dark blocks to go, past
open lots, condemned houses, old foundations, closed schools,
black churches, mounds, and he reflected that there must be many
people alive who had once seen the neighborhood rebuilt and new.
Now there was a second layer of ruins; centuries of history accomplished through human massing. Numbers had given the place
forced growth; enormous numbers had also broken it down.
Objects once so new, so concrete that it could never have occurred
to anyone they stood for other things, had crumbled. Therefore,
reflected Grebe, the secret of them was out. It was that they stood
for themselves by agreement, and were natural and not unnatural
by agreement, and when the things themselves collapsed the agreement became visible. What was it, otherwise, that kept cities from

looking peculiar? Rome, that was almost permanent, did not give rise to thoughts like these. And was it abidingly real? But in Chicago, where the cycles were so fast and the familiar died out, and again rose changed, and died again in thirty years, you saw the common agreement or covenant, and you were forced to think about appearances and realities. (He remembered Raynor and he smiled. Raynor was a clever boy.) Once you had grasped this, a great many things became intelligible. For instance, why Mr. Field should conceive such a scheme. Of course, if people were to agree to create a millionaire, a real millionaire would come into existence. And if you wanted to know how Mr. Field was inspired to think of this, why, he had within sight of his kitchen window the chart, the very bones of a successful scheme—the El with its blue and green confetti of signals. People consented to pay dimes and ride the crash-box cars, and so it was a success. Yet how absurd it looked; how little reality there was to start with. And yet Yerkes, the great financier who built it, had known that he could get people to agree to do it. Viewed as itself, what a scheme of a scheme it seemed, how close to an appearance. Then why wonder at Mr. Field's idea? He had grasped a principle. And then Grebe remembered, too, that Mr. Yerkes had established the Yerkes Observatory and endowed it with millions. Now how did the notion come to him in his New York museum of a palace or his Aegean-bound yacht to give money to astronomers? Was he awed by the success of his bizarre enterprise and therefore ready to spend money to find out where in the universe being and seeming were identical? Yes, he wanted to know what abides; and whether flesh is Bible grass; and he offered money to be burned in the fire of suns. Okay then, Grebe thought further, these things exist because people consent to exist with them—we have got so far—and also there is a reality which doesn't depend on consent but within which consent is a game. But what about need, the need that keeps so many vast thousands in position? You tell me that, you *private* little gentleman and *decent* soul—he used these words against himself scornfully. Why is the consent given to misery? And why so painfully ugly? Because there is *something* that is dismal and permanently ugly? Here he sighed and gave it up, and thought it was enough for the present moment that he had a real check in his pocket for a Mr. Green who must be real beyond question. If only his neighbors didn't think they had to conceal him.

This time he stopped at the second floor. He struck a match and found a door. Presently a man answered his knock and Grebe had the check ready and showed it even before he began. "Does Tulliver Green live here? I'm from the relief."

The man narrowed the opening and spoke to someone at his back.

"Does he live here?"

"Uh-uh. No."

"Or anywhere in this building? He's a sick man and he can't come for his dough." He exhibited the check in the light, which was smoky—the air smelled of charred lard—and the man held off the brim of his cap to study it.

"Uh-uh. Never seen the name."

"There's nobody around here that uses crutches?"

He seemed to think, but it was Grebe's impression that he was simply waiting for a decent interval to pass.

"No, suh. Nobody I ever see."

"I've been looking for this man all afternoon"—Grebe spoke out with sudden force—"and I'm going to have to carry this check back to the station. It seems strange not to be able to find a person to *give* him something when you're looking for him for a good reason. I suppose if I had bad news for him I'd find him quick enough."

There was a responsive motion in the other man's face. "That's right, I reckon."

"It almost doesn't do any good to have a name if you can't be found by it. It doesn't stand for anything. He might as well not have any," he went on, smiling. It was as much of a concession as he could make to his desire to laugh.

"Well, now, there's a little old knot-back man I see once in a while. He might be the one you lookin' for. Downstairs."

"Where? Right side or left? Which door?"

"I don't know which. Thin-face little knot-back with a stick."

But no one answered at any of the doors on the first floor. He went to the end of the corridor, searching by matchlight, and found only a stairless exit to the yard, a drop of about six feet. But there was a bungalow near the alley, an old house like Mr. Field's. To jump was unsafe. He ran from the front door, through the underground passage and into the yard. The place was occupied. There was a light through the curtains, upstairs. The name on the ticket under the broken, scoop-shaped mailbox was Green! He exultantly rang the bell and pressed against the locked door. Then the lock clicked faintly and a long staircase opened before him. Someone was slowly coming down—a woman. He had the impression in the weak light that she was shaping her hair as she came, making herself presentable, for he saw her arms raised. But it was for support that they were raised; she was feeling her way downward, down the wall, stumbling. Next he wondered about the pressure of her feet on the treads; she did not seem to be wearing shoes. And it was a freezing stairway. His ring had got her out of bed, perhaps, and she had forgotten to put them on. And then he saw that she was not only shoeless but naked; she was entirely naked, climbing down while she talked to herself, a heavy woman, naked and drunk. She blundered into him. The contact of her breasts, though they touched only his coat, made him go back against the door with a blind shock. See what he had tracked down, in his hunting game!

The woman was saying to herself, furious with insult, "So I cain't fuck, huh? I'll show that son of a bitch kin I, cain't I."

What should he do now? Grebe asked himself. Why, he should go. He should turn away and go. He couldn't talk to this woman. He couldn't keep her standing naked in the cold. But when he tried he found himself unable to turn away.

He said, "Is this where Mr. Green lives?"

But she was still talking to herself and did not hear him.

"Is this Mr. Green's house?"

At last she turned her furious drunken glance on him. "What do you want?"

Again her eyes wandered from him; there was a dot of blood in their enraged brilliance. He wondered why she didn't feel the cold.

"I'm from the relief."

"Awright, what?"

"I've got a check for Tulliver Green."

This time she heard him and put out her hand.

"No, no, for *Mr.* Green. He's got to sign," he said. How was he going to get Green's signature tonight!

"I'll take it. He cain't."

He desperately shook his head, thinking of Mr. Field's precautions about identification. "I can't let you have it. It's for him. Are you Mrs. Green?"

"Maybe I is, and maybe I ain't. Who want to know?"

"Is he upstairs?"

"Awright. Take it up yourself, you goddamn fool."

Sure, he was a goddamn fool. Of course he could not go up because Green would probably be drunk and naked, too. And perhaps he would appear on the landing soon. He looked eagerly upward. Under the light was a high narrow brown wall. Empty! It remained empty!

"Hell with you, then!" he heard her cry. To deliver a check for coal and clothes, he was keeping her in the cold. She did not feel it, but his face was burning with frost and self-ridicule. He backed away from her.

"I'll come tomorrow, tell him."

"Ah, hell with you. Don't never come. What you doin' here in the nighttime? Don' come back." She yelled so that he saw the breadth of her tongue. She stood astride in the long cold box of the hall and held on to the banister and the wall. The bungalow itself was shaped something like a box, a clumsy, high box pointing into the freezing air with its sharp, wintry lights.

"If you are Mrs. Green, I'll give you the check," he said, changing his mind.

"Give here, then." She took it, took the pen offered with it in her left hand, and tried to sign the receipt on the wall. He looked around, almost as though to see whether his madness was being observed, and came near to believing that someone was standing on a mountain of used tires in the auto-junking shop next door.

"But are you Mrs. Green?" he now thought to ask. But she was already climbing the stairs with the check, and it was too late, if he had made an error, if he was now in trouble, to undo the thing. But he wasn't going to worry about it. Though she might not be Mrs. Green, he was convinced that Mr. Green was upstairs. Whoever she was, the woman stood for Green, whom he was not to see this time. Well, you silly bastard, he said to himself, so you think you found him. So what? Maybe you really did find him—what of it? But it was important that there was a real Mr. Green whom they could not keep him from reaching because he seemed to come as an emissary from hostile appearances. And though the self-ridicule was slow to diminish, and his face still blazed with it, he had, nevertheless, a feeling of elation, too. "For after all," he said, "he *could* be found!"

CHOPIN IN WINTER (1990)

Stuart Dybek

THE WINTER DZIA-DZIA came to live with us in Mrs. Kubiac's building on Eighteenth Street was the winter that Mrs. Kubiac's daughter, Marcy, came home pregnant from college in New York. Marcy had gone there on a music scholarship, the first person in Mrs. Kubiac's family to go to high school, let alone college.

Since she had come home I had seen her only once. I was playing on the landing before our door, and as she came up the stairs we both nodded hi. She didn't look pregnant. She was thin, dressed in a black coat, its silvery fur collar pulled up around her face, her long blonde hair tucked into the collar. I could see the snowflakes on the fur turning to beads of water under the hall light bulb. Her face was pale and her eyes the same startled blue as Mrs. Kubiac's.

She passed me almost without noticing and continued up the next flight of stairs, then paused and, leaning over the banister, asked, "Are you the same little boy I used to hear crying at night?"

Her voice was gentle, yet kidding.

"I don't know," I said.

"If your name is Michael and if your bedroom window is on the fourth floor right below mine, then you are," she said. "When you were little sometimes I'd hear you crying your heart out at night. I guess I heard what your mother couldn't. The sound traveled up."

"I really woke you up?"

"Don't worry about that. I'm a very light sleeper. Snow falling wakes me up. I used to wish I could help you as long as we were both up together in the middle of the night with everyone else snoring."

"I don't remember crying," I said.

"Most people don't once they're happy again. It looks like you're happy enough now. Stay that way, kiddo." She smiled. It was a lovely smile. Her eyes seemed surprised by it. "Too–da–loo." She waved her fingers.

"Too–da–loo." I waved at her. A minute after she was gone I began to miss her.

Our landlady, Mrs. Kubiac, would come downstairs for tea in the afternoons and cry while telling my mother about Marcy. Marcy, Mrs. Kubiac said, wouldn't tell her who the child's father was. She wouldn't tell the priest. She wouldn't go to church. She wouldn't go anywhere. Even the doctor had to come to the house, and the only doctor that Marcy would allow was Dr. Shtulek, her child-hood doctor.

"I tell her, 'Marcy, darling, you have to do something,'" Mrs. Kubiac said. "What about all the sacrifices, the practice, the lessons, teachers, awards? Look at rich people—they don't let anything interfere with what they want.'"

Mrs. Kubiac told my mother these things in strictest confidence, her voice at first a secretive whisper, but growing louder as she recited her litany of troubles. The louder she talked the more broken her English became, as if her worry and suffering were straining the lan-guage past its limits. Finally, her feelings overpowered her; she began to weep and lapsed into Bohemian, which I couldn't understand.

I would sit out of sight beneath the dining-room table, my plastic cowboys galloping through a forest of chair legs, while I listened to Mrs. Kubiac talk about Marcy. I wanted to hear everything about her, and the more I heard the more precious the smile she had given me on the stairs became. It was like a secret bond between us. Once I became convinced of that, listening to Mrs. Kubiac seemed like spying. I was Marcy's friend and conspirator. She had spoken to me as if I was someone apart from the world she was shunning. Whatever her reasons for the way she was acting, what-ever her secrets, I was on her side. In daydreams I proved my loy-alty over and over.

At night we could hear her playing the piano—a muffled rum-bling of scales that sounded vaguely familiar. Perhaps I actually remembered hearing Marcy practicing years earlier, before she had gone on to New York. The notes resonated through the kitchen ceiling while I wiped the supper dishes and Dzia-Dzia sat soaking his feet. Dzia–Dzia soaked his feet every night in a bucket of steaming water into which he dropped a tablet that fizzed, immediately turning the water to bright pink. Between the steaming water and pink dye, his feet and legs, up to the knees where his trousers were rolled, looked permanently scalded.

Dzia–Dzia's feet seemed to be turning into hooves. His heels and soles were swollen nearly shapeless and cased in scaly calluses. Nails, yellow as a horse's teeth, grew gnarled from knobbed toes. Dzia–Dzia's feet had been frozen when as a young man he walked most of the way from Krakow to Gdansk in the dead of winter escaping service in the Prussian army. And later he had frozen them again mining for gold in Alaska. Most of what I knew of Dzia–Dzia's past had mainly to do with the history of his feet.

Sometimes my uncles would say something about him. It sounded as if he had spent his whole life on the move—selling dogs to the Igorot in the Philippines after the Spanish-American War; mining coal in Johnstown, Pennsylvania; working barges on the Great Lakes; riding the rails out West. No one in the family wanted much to do with him. He had deserted them so often, my uncle Roman said, that it was worse than growing up without a father.

My grandma had referred to him as *Pan Djabel*, "Mr. Devil," though the way she said it sounded as if he amused her. He called her a *gorel*, a hillbilly, and claimed that he came from a wealthy, educated family that had been stripped of their land by the Prussians.

"Landowners, all right!" Uncle Roman once said to my mother. "Besides acting like a bastard, according to Ma, he actually *was* one in the literal sense."

"Romey, shhh, what good's bitter?" my mother said.

"Who's bitter, Ev? It's just that he couldn't even show up to bury her. I'll never forgive that."

Dzia–Dzia hadn't been at Grandma's funeral. He had disappeared again, and no one had known where to find him. For years Dzia–Dzia would simply vanish without telling anyone, then suddenly show up out of nowhere to hang around for a while, ragged and smelling of liquor, wearing his two suits one over the other, only to disappear yet again.

"Want to find him? Go ask the bums on skid row," Uncle Roman would say.

My uncles said he lived in boxcars, basements, and abandoned buildings. And when, from the window of a bus, I'd see old men standing around trash fires behind billboards, I'd wonder if he was among them.

Now that he was very old and failing he sat in our kitchen, his feet aching and numb as if he had been out walking down Eighteenth Street barefoot in the snow.

It was my aunts and uncles who talked about Dzia-Dzia "failing." The word always made me nervous. I was failing, too—failing spelling, English, history, geography, almost everything except arithmetic, and that only because it used numbers instead of letters. Mainly, I was failing penmanship. The nuns complained that my writing was totally illegible, that I spelled like a DP, and threatened that if I didn't improve they might have to hold me back.

Mother kept my failures confidential. It was Dzia-Dzia's they discussed during Sunday visits in voices pitched just below the level of an old man's hearing. Dzia-Dzia stared fiercely but didn't deny what they were saying about him. He hadn't spoken since he had reappeared, and no one knew whether his muteness was caused by senility of stubbornness, or if he'd gone deaf. His ears had been frozen as well as his feet. Wiry white tufts of hair that matched his horned eyebrows sprouted from his ears. I wondered if he would hear better if they were trimmed.

Though Dzia-Dzia and I spent the evenings alone together in the kitchen, he didn't talk any more than he did on Sundays. Mother stayed in the parlor, immersed in her correspondence courses in bookkeeping. The piano rumbled above us through the ceiling. I could feel it more than hear it, especially the bass notes. Sometimes a chord would be struck that made the silverware clash in the drawer and the glasses hum.

Marcy had looked very thin climbing the stairs, delicate, incapable of such force. But her piano was massive and powerful-looking. I remembered going upstairs once with my mother to visit Mrs. Kubiac. Marcy was away at school then. The piano stood unused—top lowered, lid down over the keys—dominating the apartment. In the afternoon light it gleamed deeply, as if its dark wood were a kind of glass. Its pedals were polished bronze and looked to me more like pedals I imagined motormen stamping to operate streetcars.

"Isn't it beautiful, Michael?" my mother asked.

I nodded hard, hoping that Mrs. Kubiac would offer to let me play it, but she didn't.

"How did it get up here?" I asked. It seemed impossible that it could fit through a doorway.

"Wasn't easy," Mrs. Kubiac said, surprised. "Gave Mr. Kubiac a rupture. It come all the way on the boat from Europe. Some old German, a great musician, brang it over to give concerts, then got sick and left it. Went back to Germany. God knows what happened to him—I think he was a Jew. They auctioned it off to pay his hotel bill. That's life, huh? Otherwise who could afford it? We're not rich people."

"It must have been very expensive anyway," my mother said.

"Only cost me a marriage," Mrs. Kubiac said, then laughed, but it was forced. "That's life too, huh?" she asked. "Maybe a woman's better off without a husband?" And then, for just an instant, I saw her glance at my mother, then look away. It was a glance I had come to recognize from people when they caught themselves saying something that might remind my mother or me that my father had been killed in the war.

The silverware would clash and the glasses hum. I could feel it in my teeth and bones as the deep notes rumbled through the ceiling and walls like distant thunder. It wasn't like listening to music, yet more and more often I would notice Dzia-Dzia close his eyes, a look of concentration pinching his face as his body swayed slightly. I wondered what he was hearing. Mother had said once that he'd played the fiddle when she was a little girl, but the only music I'd ever seen him show any interest in before was the "Frankie Yankovitch Polka Hour," which he turned up loud and listened to with his ear almost pressed to the radio. Whatever Marcy was playing, it didn't sound like Frankie Yankovitch.

Then one evening, after weeks of silence between us, punctuated only by grunts, Dzia-Dzia said, "That's boogie-woogie music."

"What, Dzia-Dzia?" I asked, startled.

"Music the boogies play."

"You mean from upstairs? That's Marcy."

"She's in love with a colored man."

"What are you telling him, Pa?" Mother demanded. She had just happened to enter the kitchen while Dzia-Dzia was speaking.

"About boogie-woogie." Dzia-Dzia's legs jiggled in the bucket so that the pink water sloshed over onto the linoleum.

"We don't need that kind of talk in the house."

"What talk, Evusha?"

"He doesn't have to hear that prejudice in the house," Mom said. "He'll pick up enough on the street."

"I just told him boogie-woogie."

"I think you better soak your feet in the parlor by the heater," Mom said. "We can spread newspaper."

Dzia-Dzia sat, squinting as if he didn't hear.

"You heard me, Pa, I said soak your feet in the parlor," Mom repeated on the verge of shouting.

"What, Evusha?"

"I'll yell as loud as I have to, Pa."

"Boogie-woogie, boogie-woogie, boogie-woogie," the old man muttered as he left the kitchen, slopping barefoot across the linoleum.

"Go soak your head while you're at it," Mom muttered behind him, too quietly for him to hear.

Mom had always insisted on polite language in the house. Someone who failed to say "please" or "thank you" was as offensive to her ears as someone who cursed.

"The word is 'yes,' not 'yeah,'" she would correct. Or "If you want 'hey,' go to a stable." She considered "ain't" a form of laziness, like not picking up your dirty socks.

Even when they got a little drunk at the family parties that took place at our flat on Sundays, my uncles tried not to swear—and they had all been in the army and the marines. Nor were they allowed to refer to the Germans as Krauts, or the Japanese as Nips. As far as Mom was concerned, of all the misuses of language, racial slurs were the most ignorant, and so the most foul.

My uncles didn't discuss the war much anyway, though whenever they got together there was a certain feeling in the room as if beneath the loud talk and joking they shared a deeper, sadder mood. Mom had replaced the photo of my father in his uniform with an earlier photo of him sitting on the running board of the car they'd owned before the war. He was grinning and petting the neighbor's Scottie. That one and their wedding picture were the only photos that Mom kept out. She knew I didn't remember my father, and she seldom talked about him. But there were a few times when she would read aloud parts of his letters. There was one passage in particular that she read at least once a year. It had been written while he was under bombardment, shortly before he was killed.

When it continues like this without letup you learn what it is to really hate. You begin to hate them as a people and want to punish them all—civilians, women, children, old people—it makes no difference, they're all the same, none of them innocent, and for a while your hate and anger keep you from going crazy with fear. But if you let yourself hate and believe in hate, then no matter what else happens, you've lost. Eve, I love our life together and want to come home to you and Michael, as much as I can, the same man who left.

I wanted to hear more but didn't ask. Perhaps because everyone seemed to be trying to forget. Perhaps because I was afraid. When the tears would start in Mom's eyes I caught myself wanting to glance away as Mrs. Kubiac had.

There was something more besides Mom's usual standards for the kind of language allowed in the house that caused her to lose her temper and kick Dzia-Dzia out of his spot in the kitchen. She had become even more sensitive, especially where Dzia-Dzia was concerned, because of what had happened with Shirley Popel's mother.

Shirley's mother had died recently. Mom and Shirley had been best friends since grade school, and after the funeral, Shirley came back to our house and poured out the story.

Her mother had broken a hip falling off a curb while sweeping the sidewalk in front of her house. She was a constantly smiling woman without any teeth who, everyone said, looked like a peasant. After forty years in America she could barely speak English, and even in the hospital refused to remove her babushka.

Everyone called her Babushka, Babush for short, which meant "granny," even the nuns at the hospital. On top of her broken hip, Babush caught pneumonia, and one night Shirley got a call from the doctor saying Babush had taken a sudden turn for the worse. Shirley pushed right over, taking her thirteen-year-old son, Rudy. Rudy was Babushka's favorite, and Shirley hoped that seeing him would instill the will to live in her mother. It was Saturday night and Rudy was dressed to play at his first dance. He wanted to be a musician and was wearing clothes he had bought with money saved from his paper route. He'd bought them at Smoky Joe's on Maxwell Street—blue suede loafers, electric-blue socks, a lemon-yellow one-button roll-lapel suit with padded shoulders and pegged trousers, and a parrot-green satin shirt. Shirley thought he looked cute.

When they got to the hospital they found Babush connected to tubes and breathing oxygen.

"Ma," Shirley said, "Rudy's here."

Babush raised her head, took one look at Rudy, and smacked her gray tongue.

"Rudish," Babush said, "you dress like nigger." Then suddenly her eyes rolled; she fell back, gasped, and died.

"And those were her last words to any of us, Ev," Shirley wept, "words we'll carry for the rest of our lives, but especially poor little Rudy—*you dress like nigger.*"

For weeks after Shirley's visit, no matter who called, Mom would tell them Shirley's story over the phone.

"Those aren't the kind of famous last words we're going to hear in this family if I can help it," she promised more than once, as if it were a real possibility. "Of course," she'd sometimes add, "Shirley always has let Rudy get away with too much. I don't see anything cute about a boy going to visit his grandmother dressed like a hood."

Any last words Dzia-Dzia had he kept to himself. His silence, however, had already been broken. Perhaps in his own mind that was a defeat that carried him from failing to totally failed. He returned to the kitchen like a ghost haunting his old chair, one that appeared when I sat alone working on penmanship.

No one else seemed to notice a change, but it was clear from the way he no longer soaked his feet. He still kept up the pretense of sitting there with them in the bucket. The bucket went with him the way ghosts drag chains. But he no longer went through the ritual of boiling water: boiling it until the kettle screeched for mercy, pouring so the linoleum puddled and steam clouded around him, and finally dropping in the tablet that fizzed furiously pink, releasing a faintly metallic smell like a broken thermometer.

Without his bucket steaming, the fogged windows cleared. Mrs. Kubiac's building towered a story higher than any other on the block. From our fourth-story window I could look out at an even level with the roofs and see the snow gathering on them before it reached the street.

I sat at one end of the kitchen table copying down the words that would be on the spelling test the next day. Dzia-Dzia sat at the other, mumbling incessantly, as if finally free to talk about the jumble of the past he'd never mentioned—wars, revolutions, strikes, journeys to strange places, all run together, and music, especially Chopin. "Chopin," he'd whisper hoarsely, pointing to the ceiling with the reverence of nuns pointing to heaven. Then he'd close his eyes and his nostrils would widen as if he were inhaling the fragrance of sound.

It sounded no different to me, the same muffled thumping and rumbling we'd been hearing ever since Marcy had returned home. I could hear the intensity in the crescendos that made the silverware clash, but it never occurred to me to care what she was playing. What mattered was that I could hear her play each night, could feel her playing just a floor above, almost as if she were in our apartment. She seemed that close.

"Each night Chopin—it's all she thinks about, isn't it?"

I shrugged.

"You don't know?" Dzia-Dzia whispered, as if I were lying and he was humoring me.

"How should I know?"

"And I suppose how should you know the 'Grande Valse brillante' when you hear it either? How should you know Chopin was twenty-one when he composed it?—about the same age as the girl upstairs. He composed it in Vienna, before he went to Paris. Don't they teach you that in school? What are you studying?"

"Spelling."

"Can you spell *dummkopf*?"

The waves of the keyboard would pulse through the warm kitchen and I would become immersed in my spelling words, and after that in penmanship. I was in remedial penmanship. Nightly penmanship was like undergoing physical therapy. While I concentrated on the proper slant of my letters my left hand smeared graphite across the loose-leaf paper.

Dzia-Dzia, now that he was talking, no longer seemed content to sit and listen in silence. He would continually interrupt.

"Hey, Lefty, stop writing with your nose. Listen how she plays."

"Don't shake the table, Dzia-Dzia."

"You know this one? No? 'Valse brillante.'"

"I thought that was the other one."

"What other one? The E-flat? That's 'Grande Valse brillante.' This one's A-flat. Then there's another A-flat—Opus 42—called 'Grande Valse.' Understand?"

He rambled on like that about A- and E-flat and sharps and opuses and I went back to compressing my capital M's. My homework was to write five hundred of them. I was failing penmanship yet again, my left hand, as usual, taking the blame it didn't deserve. The problem with *M* wasn't my hand. It was that I had never been convinced that the letters could all be the same widths. When I wrote, *M* automatically came out twice as broad as *N, H,* double the width of I.

"This was Paderewski's favorite waltz. She plays it like an angel."

I nodded, staring in despair at my homework. I had made the mistake of interconnecting the *M's* into long strands. They hummed in my head, drowning out the music, and I wondered if I had been humming aloud. "Who's Paderewski?" I asked, thinking it might be one of Dzia-Dzia's old friends, maybe from Alaska.

"Do you know who's George Washington, who's Joe DiMaggio, who's Walt Disney?"

"Sure."

"I thought so. Paderewski was like them, except he played Chopin. Understand? See, deep down inside, Lefty, you know more than you think."

Instead of going into the parlor to read comics or play with my cowboys while Mom pored over her correspondence courses, I began spending more time at the kitchen table, lingering over my homework as an excuse. My spelling began to improve, then took a turn toward perfection; the slant of my handwriting reversed toward the right; I began to hear melodies in what had sounded like muffled scales.

Each night Dzia-Dzia would tell me more about Chopin, describing the preludes or ballades or mazurkas, so that even if I hadn't heard them I could imagine them, especially Dzia-Dzia's favorites, the nocturnes, shimmering like black pools.

"She's playing her way through the waltzes," Dzia-Dzia told me, speaking as usual in his low, raspy voice as if we were having a confidential discussion. "She's young but already knows Chopin's secret—a waltz can tell more about the soul than a hymn."

By my bedtime the kitchen table would be shaking so much that it was impossible to practice penmanship any longer. Across from me, Dzia-Dzia, his hair, eyebrows, and ear tufts wild and white, swayed in his chair, with his eyes squeezed closed and a look of rapture on his face as his fingers pummeled the tabletop. He played the entire width of the table, his body leaning and twisting as his fingers swept the keyboard, left hand pounding at those chords that jangled silverware, while his right raced through runs across tacky oilcloth. His feet pumped the empty bucket. If I watched him, then closed my eyes, it sounded as if two pianos were playing.

One night Dzia-Dzia and Marcy played so that I expected at any moment the table would break and the ceiling collapse. The bulbs began to flicker in the overhead fixture, then went out. The entire flat went dark.

"Are the lights out in there, too?" Mom yelled from the parlor. "Don't worry, it must be a fuse."

The kitchen windows glowed with the light of snow. I looked out. All the buildings down Eighteenth Street were dark and the streetlights were out. Spraying wings of snow, a snow-removal machine, its yellow lights revolving, disappeared down Eighteenth like the last blinks of electricity. There wasn't any traffic. The block looked deserted, as if the entire city was deserted. Snow was filling the emptiness, big flakes floating steadily and softly between the darkened buildings, coating the fire escapes, while on the roofs a blizzard swirled up into the clouds.

Marcy and Dzia-Dzia never stopped playing.

"Michael, come in here by the heater, or if you're going to stay in there put the burners on," Mom called.

I lit the burners on the stove. They hovered in the dark like blue crowns of flame, flickering Dzia-Dzia's shadow across the walls. His head pitched, his arms flew up as he struck the notes. The walls and windowpanes shook with gusts of wind and music. I imagined plaster dust wafting down, coating the kitchen, a fine network of cracks spreading through the dishes.

"Michael?" Mother called.

"I'm sharpening my pencil." I stood by the sharpener grinding it as hard as I could, then sat back down and went on writing. The table rocked under my point, but the letters formed perfectly. I spelled new words, words I'd never heard before, yet as soon as I wrote them their meanings were clear, as if they were in another language, one in which words were understood by their sounds, like music. After the lights came back on I couldn't remember what they meant and threw them away.

Dzia-Dzia slumped back in his chair. He was flushed and mopped his forehead with a paper napkin.

"So, you like that one," he said. "Which one was it?" he asked.
He always asked me that, and little by little I had begun recognizing
their melodies.

"The polonaise," I guessed. "In A-flat major."

"Ahhh," he shook his head in disappointment. "You think
everything with a little spirit is the polonaise."

"The 'Revolutionary' etude!"

"It was a waltz," Dzia-Dzia said.

"How could that be a waltz?"

"A posthumous waltz. You know what 'posthumous' means?"

"What?"

"It means music from after a person's dead. The kind of waltz
that has to carry back from the other side. Chopin wrote it to a
young woman he loved. He kept his feelings for her secret but
never forgot her. Sooner or later feelings come bursting out. The
dead are as sentimental as anyone else. You know what happened
when Chopin died?"

"No."

"They rang the bells all over Europe. It was winter. The Prussians
heard them. They jumped on their horses. They had cavalry then,
no tanks, just horses. They rode until they came to the house where
Chopin lay on a bed next to a grand piano. His arms were crossed
over his chest, and there was plaster drying on his hands and face.
The Prussians rode right up the stairs and barged into the room,
slashing with their sabers, their horses stamping and kicking up their
front hooves. They hacked the piano and stabbed the music, then
wadded up the music into the piano, spilled on kerosene from the
lamps, and set it on fire. Then they rolled Chopin's piano to the
window—it was those French windows, the kind that open out and
there's a tiny balcony. The piano wouldn't fit, so they rammed it
through, taking out part of the wall. It crashed three stories into the
street, and when it hit it made a sound that shook the city. The
piano lay there smoking, and the Prussians galloped over it and left.
Later, some of Chopin's friends snuck back and removed his heart
and sent it in a little jeweled box to be buried in Warsaw."

Dzia-Dzia stopped and listened. Marcy had begun to play again
very faintly. If he had asked me to guess what she was playing I
would have said a prelude, the one called "The Raindrop."

★ ★ ★

I heard the preludes on Saturday nights, sunk up to my ears in bath-water. The music traveled from upstairs through the plumbing, and resonated as clearly underwater as if I had been wearing earphones.

There were other places I discovered where Marcy's playing car-ried. Polonaises sometimes reverberated down an old trash chute that had been papered over in the dining room. Even in the parlor, provided no one else was listening to the radio or flipping pages of a newspaper, it was possible to hear the faintest hint of mazurkas around the sealed wall where the stovepipe from the space heater disappeared into what had once been a fireplace. And when I went out to play on the landing, bundled up as if I was going out to climb on the drifts piled along Eighteenth Street, I could hear the piano echoing down the hallways. I began to creep higher up the stairs to the top floor, until finally I was listening at Mrs. Kubiac's door, ready to jump away if it should suddenly open, hoping I would be able to think of some excuse for being there, and at the same time almost wishing they would catch me.

I didn't mention climbing the stairs in the hallway, nor any of the other places I'd discovered, to Dzia-Dzia. He never seemed interested in anyplace other than the kitchen table. It was as if he were attached to the chair, rooted in his bucket.

"Going so early? Where are you rushing off to?" he'd ask at the end of each evening, no matter how late, when I'd put my pencil down and begun buckling my books into my satchel.

I'd leave him sitting there, with his feet in his empty bucket, and his fingers, tufted with the same white hair as his ears, still tracing arpeggios across the tabletop, though Marcy had already stopped playing. I didn't tell him how from my room, a few times lately after everyone was asleep, I could hear her playing as clearly as if I were sitting at her feet.

Marcy played less and less, especially in the evenings after supper, which had been her regular time.

Dzia-Dzia continued to shake the table nightly, eyes closed, hair flying, fingers thumping, but the thump of his fingers against the oilcloth was the only sound other than his breathing—rhythmic and labored as if he were having a dream or climbing a flight of stairs.

I didn't notice at first, but Dzia-Dzia's solos were the start of his return to silence.

"What's she playing, Lefty?" he demanded more insistently than ever, as if still testing whether I knew.

Usually now, I did. But after a while I realized he was no longer testing me. He was asking because the sounds were becoming increasingly muddled to him. He seemed able to feel the pulse of the music but could no longer distinguish the melodies. By asking me, he hoped perhaps that if he knew what Marcy was playing he would hear it clearly himself.

Then he began to ask what she was playing when she wasn't playing at all.

I would make up answers. 'The polonaise ... in A–flat major."

"The polonaise! You always say that. Listen harder. Are you sure it's not a waltz?"

"You're right, Dzia–Dzia. It's the 'Grande Valse'."

"The 'Grande Valse'. . . . which one is that?"

"A–flat, Opus 42. Paderewski's favorite, remember? Chopin wrote it when he was twenty-one, in Vienna."

"In Vienna?" Dzia–Dzia asked, then pounded the table with his fist. "Don't tell me numbers and letters! A-flat, Z-sharp, Opus 0, Opus 1,000! Who cares? You make it sound like a bingo game instead of Chopin."

I was never sure if he couldn't hear because he couldn't remember, or couldn't remember because he couldn't hear. His hearing itself still seemed sharp enough.

"Stop scratching with that pencil all the time, Lefty, and I wouldn't have to ask you what she's playing," he'd complain.

"You'd hear better, Dzia–Dzia, if you'd take the kettle off the stove."

He was slipping back into his ritual of boiling water. The kettle screeched like a siren. The windows fogged. Roofs and weather vanished behind a slick of steam. Vapor ringed the overhead light bulbs. The vaguely metallic smell of the fizzing pink tablets hung at the end of every breath.

Marcy played hardly at all by then. What little she played was muffled, far off as if filtering through the same fog. Sometimes, staring at the steamed windows, I imagined Eighteenth Street looked that way, with rings of vapor around the streetlights and headlights, clouds billowing from exhaust pipes and manhole covers, breaths hanging, snow swirling like white smoke.

Each night water hissed from the kettle's spout as from a blown valve, rumbling as it filled the bucket, brimming until it slopped

over onto the warped linoleum. Dzia-Dzia sat, bony calves half
submerged, trousers rolled to his knees. He was wearing two suits
again, one over the other, always a sure sign he was getting ready
to travel, to disappear without saying good-bye. The fingers of his
left hand still drummed unconsciously along the tabletop as his feet
soaked. Steam curled up the arteries of his scalded legs, hovered
over his lap, smoldered up the buttons of his two vests, traced his
mustache and white tufts of hair until it enveloped him. He sat in
a cloud, eyes glazed, fading.

I began to go to bed early. I would leave my homework unfinished,
kiss Mother good night, and go to my room.

My room was small, hardly space for more than the bed and
bureau. Not so small, though, that Dzia-Dzia couldn't have fit.
Perhaps, had I told him that Marcy played almost every night now
after everyone was sleeping, he wouldn't have gone back to filling
the kitchen with steam. I felt guilty, but it was too late, and I shut
the door quickly before steam could enter and fog my window.

It was a single window. I could touch it from the foot of the bed.
It opened onto a recessed, three-sided air shaft and faced the roof
of the building next door. Years ago a kid my age named Freddy
had lived next door and we still called it Freddy's roof.

Marcy's window was above mine. The music traveled down as
clearly as Marcy said my crying had traveled up. When I closed
my eyes I could imagine sitting on the Oriental carpet beside her
huge piano. The air shaft actually amplified the music just as it had
once amplified the arguments between Mr. and Mrs. Kubiac,
especially the shouting on those nights after Mr. Kubiac had
moved out, when he would return drunk and try to move back
in. They'd argued mostly in Bohemian, but when Mr. Kubiac
started beating her, Mrs. Kubiac would yell out in English, "Help
me, police, somebody, he's killing me!" After a while the police
would usually come and haul Mr. Kubiac away. I think sometimes
Mom called them. One night Mr. Kubiac tried to fight off the
police, and they gave him a terrible beating. "You're killing him
in front of my eyes!" Mrs. Kubiac began to scream. Mr. Kubiac
broke away and, with the police chasing him, ran down the hallways pounding on doors, pleading for people to open up. He
pounded on our door. Nobody in the building let him in. That
was their last argument.

The room was always cold. I'd slip, still wearing my clothes, under the goose-feather-stuffed *piersyna* to change into my pajamas. It would have been warmer with the door open even a crack, but I kept it closed because of the steam. A steamed bedroom window reminded me too much of the winter I'd had pneumonia. It was one of the earliest things I could remember: the gurgling hiss of the vaporizer and smell of benzoin while I lay sunk in my pillows watching steam condense to frost on the pane until daylight blurred. I could remember trying to scratch through the frost with the key to a windup mouse so that I could see how much snow had fallen, and Mother catching me. She was furious that I had climbed out from under the warmth of my covers and asked me if I wanted to get well or to get sicker and die. Later, when I asked Dr. Shtulek if I was dying, he put his stethoscope to my nose and listened. "Not yet." He smiled. Dr. Shtulek visited often to check my breathing. His stethoscope was cold like all the instruments in his bag, but I liked him, especially for unplugging the vaporizer. "We don't need this anymore," he confided. Night seemed very still without its steady exhaling. The jingle of snow chains and the scraping of shovels carried from Eighteenth Street. Maybe that was when I first heard Marcy practicing scales. By then I had grown used to napping during the day and lying awake at night. I began to tunnel under my *piersyna* to the window and scrape at the layered frost. I scraped for nights, always afraid I would get sick again for disobeying. Finally, I was able to see the snow on Freddy's roof. Something had changed while I'd been sick—they had put a wind hood on the tall chimney that sometimes blew smoke into our flat. In the dark it looked as if someone was standing on the roof in an old-fashioned helmet. I imagined it was a German soldier. I'd heard Freddy's landlord was German. The soldier stood at attention, but his head slowly turned back and forth and hooted with each gust of wind. Snow drove sideways across the roof, and he stood banked by drifts, smoking a cigar. Sparks flew from its tip. When he turned completely around to stare in my direction with his faceless face, I'd duck and tunnel back under my *piersyna* to my pillows and pretend to sleep. I believed a person asleep would be shown more mercy than a person awake. I'd lie still, afraid he was marching across the roof to peer in at me through the holes I'd scraped. It was a night like that when I heard Mother crying. She was walking from room to room crying like I'd never heard anyone cry before. I must have called out because she came into my room and tucked the covers around me. "Everything will be all right," she whispered; "go back to sleep." She sat on my bed, toward the foot where she could look out the window, crying softly until her shoulders began to shake. I lay pretending to sleep. She cried like that for nights after my father was killed. It was my mother, not I, whom Marcy had heard.

It was only after Marcy began playing late at night that I remembered my mother crying. In my room, with the door shut against the steam, it seemed she was playing for me alone. I would wake already listening and gradually realize that the music had been going on while I slept, and that I had been shaping my dreams to it. She played only nocturnes those last weeks of winter. Sometimes they seemed to carry over the roofs, but mostly she played so softly that only the air shaft made it possible to hear. I would sit huddled in my covers beside the window listening, looking out at the white dunes on Freddy's roof. The soldier was long gone, his helmet rusted off. Smoke blew unhooded; black flakes with sparking edges wafted out like burning snow. Soot and music and white gusts off the crests buffeted the pane. Even when the icicles began to leak and the streets to turn to brown rivers of slush, the blizzard in the air shaft continued.

Marcy disappeared during the first break in the weather. She left a note that read: "Ma, don't worry."

"That's all," Mrs. Kubiac said, unfolding it for my mother to see. "Not even 'love,' not even her name signed. The whole time I kept telling her 'do something,' she sits playing the piano, and now she does something, when it's too late, unless she goes to some butcher. Ev, what should I do?"

My mother helped Mrs. Kubiac call the hospitals. Each day they called the morgue. After a week, Mrs. Kubiac called the police, and when they couldn't find Marcy, any more than they had been able to find Dzia-Dzia, Mrs. Kubiac began to call people in New York— teachers, old roommates, landlords. She used our phone. "Take it off the rent," she said. Finally, Mrs. Kubiac went to New York herself to search.

When she came back from New York she seemed changed, as if she'd grown too tired to be frantic. Her hair was a different shade of gray so that now you'd never know it had once been blonde. There was a stoop to her shoulders as she descended the stairs on the way to novenas. She no longer came downstairs for tea and long talks. She spent much of her time in church, indistinguishable among the other women from the old country, regulars at the morning requiem mass, wearing babushkas and dressed in black like a sodality of widows, droning endless mournful litanies before the side altar of the Black Virgin of Czestochowa.

By the time a letter from Marcy finally came, explaining that the entire time she had been living on the South Side in a Negro neighborhood near the university, and that she had a son whom she'd named Tatum Kubiac—"Tatum" after a famous jazz pianist— it seemed to make little difference. Mrs. Kubiac visited once but didn't go back. People had already learned to glance away from her when certain subjects were mentioned—daughters, grandchildren, music. She had learned to glance away from herself. After she visited Marcy she tried to sell the piano, but the movers couldn't figure how to get it downstairs, nor how anyone had ever managed to move it in.

It took time for the music to fade. I kept catching wisps of it in the air shaft, behind walls and ceilings, under bathwater. Echoes traveled the pipes and wallpapered chutes, the bricked-up flues and dark hallways. Mrs. Kubiac's building seemed riddled with its secret passageways. And, when the music finally disappeared, its channels remained, conveying silence. Not an ordinary silence of absence and emptiness, but a pure silence beyond daydream and memory, as intense as the music it replaced, which, like music, had the power to change whoever listened. It hushed the close-quartered racket of the old building. It had always been there behind the creaks and drafts and slamming doors, behind the staticky radios, and the flushing and footsteps and crackling fat, behind the wails of vacuums and kettles and babies, and the voices with their scraps of conversation and arguments and laughter floating out of flats where people locked themselves in with all that was private. Even after I no longer missed her, I could still hear the silence left behind.